DEAD LETTERS

Episodes of Epistolary Horror

Edited by Jacob Steven Mohr

Let the world know:
#IGotMyCLPBook!

Crystal Lake Publishing
www.CrystalLakePub.com

WELCOME
TO ANOTHER

CRYSTAL LAKE PUBLISHING
CREATION

Join today at www.crystallakepub.com & www.patreon.com/CLP

Table of Contents

The Parthas UFO Incident

T.T. Madden

The following materials were included among the mass declassification of Pentagon documents in 2020. They were compiled by the Bureau of Special Services and concern the Sept. 1994 Parthas, Nevada UFO Incident.

****

Transcript of a 911 call placed from an emergency roadside telephone booth near Nevada State Route 375 mile marker 52 on August 15, 1994, at 3:33 AM.

Operator: "911, what is—"

Unknown Caller: "Please please please, God, you have to help me! Send somebody!"

Operator: "What is your location? What's the nature of your emergency?"

Unknown Caller: "He's following me."

Operator: "Who's been following you?"

Unknown Caller: "The double man!"

Operator: "Is there a man trying to harm you?"

T. T. Madden

Unknown Caller: " . . . oh, God . . . "

[A momentary pause before the caller screams. Indecipherable shouting and crashing, glass shattering, followed by a pause of about ten seconds. Soft breathing can be heard now. The breaths are spaced too far apart, like the person must consciously order their lungs to inflate.]

New Voice: "Hello . . . ?"

Operator: "Who is this? Identify yourself."

[The new voice chuckles. It sounds like multiple voices, two people laughing quietly into the receiver. The line goes dead.]

A responding Nevada Highway Patrol car discovered the telephone booth about an hour later, shattered to bits and strewn across the highway. The highway itself had been scorched black, and the sand in the surrounding desert superheated to glass.

***

Letter written to the Shikashi Observatory outside Parthas, Nevada.

Dear scientists,

I am not the kind of woman prone to flights of fancy, and it is because of that I hesitated to write this letter. Hesitated for too long, I fear. But I have exhausted every other avenue. The police, as usual, are of no help. They don't believe our stories, no matter how many of us tell them the same thing. Even after what so many of us saw the weekend of July Fourth. I believe you, who spend so much time looking up into the stars, are the only ones who can help us. Or you will at least be able to get those who can listen to reason.

For the past several months, Parthas has been haunted by a presence. At first we thought it to be nothing more than a prank. Children from around town would mention something in the sky, a dark shape moving through the night. There have been strange things out in the desert, and even so, we thought little of it.

The Parthas UFO Incident

And then they started mentioning the men. Some people may think we're hicks, living out here in the desert, but there's no place in the world where parents won't pay attention when their children say a strange man tried to talk to them.

The paper has pictures of all of them, what they arrived in and the men themselves. It looks like a pyramid hovering in the sky. Like an invisible hand lifting one of those Ancient Egyptian structures, except this one is all black. Black as the night.

The pictures of the men are different. There's always two of them, and they're always together. People say they see them out in the desert think they're lost hikers, a duo who always disappear when people get close. At first, some of us were starting to think a new urban legend was happening right before our eyes. Like the ghost girl who leaves her sweater in your car.

But then something turned.

For the past several weeks, this presence around Parthas has menaced us. I do not know what caused their attitudes to change. Perhaps it was the fireworks. Perhaps they interpreted them as an attack. Since the Fourth of July, the number of car crashes and abandoned vehicles on the highway has gone up exponentially. People driving along the highway say the shapes in the sky follow them. Not engaging, just following. Watching. They say they pass the two men over and over again, standing on the shoulder, eternal hitchhikers begging for a ride that's never coming.

I know what you must think, that I'm just repeating stories I've heard. That people out here in the middle of the desert have nothing better to do than spin tales. No. I've seen these things myself, the pyramids and the men, lurking in the sky, in the desert, just outside the trailer park. Always at night. Like they're waiting for something. Some signal for them to finally come in.

This is the Nevada desert. There is so, so much open sky. There's no place they can't see us.

T. T. Madden

Please. Please send someone.

Gretchen Danik
Armadillo Trailer Park, Parthas, Nevada
Sept. 1, 1994

***

Description of the photograph mentioned in the Gretchen Danik letter, first published by the Parthas Chronicle, on Saturday, July 2, 1994. Original negatives have been confiscated and are currently in the possession of the BSS.

[A crowd gathers on a small-town street at sunset. They are all wearing red, white, and blue, many of them holding drinks and American flags. None notice a picture is being taken; they are too busy celebrating.

In the corner of the picture, in the sky above the town, there is a strange shape that appears neither bird, nor plane, nor stray balloon.

The paper has enhanced the photo, blown it up and provided a zoomed image in the corner of the larger photograph. It reveals a single black pyramid of indeterminable size hovering above the crowd in the twilit sky, the revelers ignorant to its presence.]

***

Transcript of the cassette-recorded field notes of Bureau Agent Morgan Ian Bartholomew. Recovered at the scene.

It is Sept 5, 1994, and I've been dispatched to the town of Parthas, Nevada to investigate the case of several missing persons alongside repeated sightings of unidentified aerial phenomena accompanied by an unidentified terrestrial visitor. Over the past several months, multiple individuals have gone missing along this stretch of Nevada State Route 375, often accompanying strange objects sighted in the desert and appearances of a mysterious man.

The Parthas UFO Incident

The Bureau has not officially ruled out anomalous phenomena nor ordinary human malfeasance.

I've reviewed all evidence so far and have, at the moment, no firm opinion on the events. There simply isn't enough information as of yet. Yes, the Bureau deals with bizarre cases every day. However, Parthas is also located several miles east of Homey Airport, more commonly known to civilians as Area 51. Perhaps close proximity to such a site is fueling the town's imaginations?

Without talking to them, it's impossible to say.

★★★

Transcript of the cassette-recorded interview between Bureau Agent Morgan Ian Bartholomew and Gretchen Danik. Discovered at the scene.

MB: "Okay, Mrs. Danik. Speak slowly and clearly. The microphone on the cassette recorder will be able to pick you up. It is September 5, 1994, my name is Special Agent Morgan Ian Bartholomew, and I am speaking with Mrs. Gretchen Danik of the Armadillo Trailer Park."

GD: "Hello."

MB: "Mrs. Danik, could you tell me, as clearly as possible, the meaning of a letter you sent to the Shikashi Observatory a few days ago?"

GD: "About the double man."

MB: "Who is that?"

GD: "He comes with the pyramid. Or should we call him *they?* I mean, there's two of him."

MB: "Tell me about him. And about the pyramid."

GD: "People have seen them ever since the Fourth of July. My nephew drew a picture of him."

[Light rustling, the sound of footsteps shuffling on carpet, and then paper being unfolded.]

GD: "Here."

MB: "I see. Do you mind if I keep this? As evidence?"

GD: "Please. I'd like it out of my house. Away from my nephew."

MB: "So, tell me about the Fourth of July."

GD: "Yes, yes. So, there wasn't anything out of the ordinary. We set up our fireworks as usual. Even that night itself no one saw anything strange. But the night after was the first time anyone saw the double man. I don't know who it was, but a bunch of kids were out in the desert, probably drinking, said they saw a man stumble out of the night. But said he was 'all blurry.' Their words. Like I said, we thought they'd just had a few too many. Or were trying to start up some scares. But then more and more people started the double man over the next couple weeks. Started seeing the pyramid in the sky. I've thought about it since the letter, and I truly think it was the fireworks. I think the pyramid thought we were attacking it."

MB: "This double man and this pyramid, what do they do when people see them?"

GD: "At first they just lingered, you know? Watched from a distance. Always at a distance where it was impossible to make out any details. Just far enough away to see there was something wrong about him—or them. The pyramid, it's only ever come at night. We can see it moving between us and the stars."

MB: "And has anyone ever been hurt as a result of these sightings?"

GD: "They've been *killed*. Do you know how many abandoned cars have been found along this stretch of highway recently?"

The Parthas UFO Incident

MB: "Why do you think this man or men do something like that?"

GD: "I don't know. All I know is I don't go outside at night anymore."

****

Description of what is assumed to be the drawing mentioned in the Gretchen Danik interview recorded in Agent Bartholomew's field notes. Discovered at the scene.

The drawing is on thick, unlined paper, and appears to be torn from a spiralbound notebook (which was not recovered). It is largely rendered in black crayon, with hard, aggressive strokes. Thick lines portray a humanoid figure, what appears to be a man in a suit. But there is another identical man drawn atop the first, only about half an inch to the right, done in a dark gray. The effect the drawing creates brings to mind a double exposure photograph.

There is a strange amorphous shape surrounding the double-figure, also in black. Possibly mist, fog, or perhaps meant to indicate night, considering the stars and the crescent moon drawn in white above. The entire figure is colored black, except for the eyes, which are thick yellow circles. Desert brown appears as a flat horizontal plane beneath its feet. It possesses no facial features other than its yellow eyes.

Hovering in the sky above the figure there is a large pyramid, its tip pointing upward. Several more are lurking among the stars, drawn smaller as if to indicate distance.

The artist has captioned the picture "The double man."

****

Visual description and audio transcript of footage taken from a handheld camera recovered at the scene. Timestamp indicates this footage was taken on Sept. 6, 1994, at 1:55 AM.

[Footage opens on an extreme close-up of an unidentified young man. Caucasian, teens, brown hair. The angle quickly pulls back to reveal desert and starlit night sky behind him.]

Voice (O.S): "I got it, I got it."

Young Man: "Okay, then get it, look, look!"

[The camera whips around, pointing up into the sky. At first nothing shows. But after a moment's adjustment, something enormous appears, suspended in the air above, blocking the stars. A three-pointed slab of darkness. It moves slowly in absolute silence, like a shark through the water. A sheet of black passing between the camera and the stars, hiding them from view.]

Young Man: "Are you getting it?"

[The sheet of darkness stops. It remains motionless in the sky. Then slowly it begins to turn.]

Voice (O.S): "Oh, shit, it's coming!"

[Video cuts.]

★★★

The following is the transcript of a 911 call, placed on September 6, 1994, at 1:57 AM from Armadillo Trailer Park.

Operator: "911, what is your emergency?"

Female Caller (whispering): "Oh, God, he's back."

Operator: "Ma'am, what's your location?"

Female Caller: "I'm at the Armadillo Trailer Park. The man is outside my house again."

Operator: "Again? Ma'am, is this man threatening you? Do you know him?"

The Parthas UFO Incident

Female Caller: "He's been here before. He's going to try to get in. He's going to try to . . . *take* me. He's taken people before. The missing people along the highway. They're because of him. He's coming right towards my house."

Operator: "Ma'am, I'm sending a unit to your location. Please stay on the line. Tell me, do you know this man?"

Female Caller: "The double man. It's the double man. He takes people and takes them to the pyramid. Oh, God, he's coming to the window!"

Operator: "Ma'am, get away from the window. Get somewhere safe, somewhere you can hide."

Female Caller(whispering): "He's right outside my window. He's looking at me! Please, don't let him take me. Not there, anywhere but there!"

[A scream. Sound of breaking glass. Something heavy moves or falls.]

Operator: "Ma'am?"

[The sounds of a scuffle. Muffled grunting. Something hard and heavy hitting something soft.]

Operator: "Ma'am . . . ?"

[No response. Shuffling movement on the other end of the line.]

Operator: "Ma'am? Are you there?"

[Breathing.]

Operator: "Ma'am?"

[The line goes dead.]

***

T. T. Madden

Visual description and audio transcript of dashcam footage from a responding Nevada Highway Patrol car, dated Sept. 6, 1994, 2:13 AM.

[The patrol car roars down the highway towards a cluster of lights in the distance: a trailer park. Not a single star can be seen in the sky above, making the dark even more smothering. The car pulls off the highway, passing by a large, well-lit sign reading ARMADILLO TRAILER PARK.]

Officer: "NHP-52, arriving at the Armadillo Trailer Park . . . There supposed to be a storm or something? It's dark as hell out here."

Dispatch: "Negative, NHP-52. Clear skies tonight."

[The car lurches to a stop suddenly when a dark figure comes into view, the camera jerking forward before snapping back into place. The figure is tall and undefined in the darkness. The video footage glitches and distorts making there appear to be two men, like a double exposure.]

Officer: "What . . . I can't see . . . "

[The figure(s) turn and face the patrol car. Two hot-yellow points glows in its(their) face(s), like embers. Sound of a car door opening.]

Officer (O.S.): "Freeze!"

[The figure(s) ignores the command, running away around a corner. Before the officer can pursue, a man in a suit runs into the frame with his hands raised. When he moves closer to frame, he can be identified as Bureau of Special Services Agent Morgan Ian Bartholomew. After a moment of indistinct conversation with the officer, he reaches for his identification. The officer appears satisfied, then draws his sidearm.

The officer follows Agent Bartholomew out of frame, in pursuit of the strange figure.]

The Parthas UFO Incident

****

Closed-circuit television footage taken from the single camera available outside the Armadillo Trailer Park leasing office. No sound is available, no timestamp appears. No other cameras are known to exist.

[Bureau Agent Bartholomew and the Highway Patrol Officer round the corner together, immediately lifting their firearms and leveling them at something offscreen. Both of them are seen shouting. They pause, then shout again.

They discharge their weapons, flares lighting up the night.

Their faces sink at whatever they see just out of frame.

The men lower their weapons and begin taking slow, tentative steps back.

The entire image brightens, like the contrast is being turned up. It gets brighter and brighter and brighter, forcing the men to shield their faces.

A shape enters the frame, visible only for a brief glimpse of something impossibly tall, striding on stilt-like legs. Long, spindly arms reach for the men before the footage cuts to static.]

****

The following is the visual description and audio transcript of footage taken from the cockpit of an AT-301 experimental aircraft deployed from Homey Airport after Agent Bartholomew missed his third scheduled check-in.

[The camera is from the POV of a low-flying high-speed aircraft. Desert whips by underneath it, open night sky and stars above.]

Pilot: "On approach."

[A small highway comes quickly into view. Centered in the frame is a small cluster of shapes that the feed itself announces as ARMADILLO TRAILER PARK with a circle and an arrow. There is an unidentified object hovering above the trailer park—a large, black pyramid as wide as the park itself. Its surface is dusted brown, like a car that's spent too much time in the desert.]

Pilot: "What the [expletive deleted] is that?"

[The object shifts when the pilot speaks, one of its faces turning in the direction of the aircraft.]

Pilot: "It didn't just hear me . . . "

[The surface of the object ripples with a gasoline-puddle sheen. Suddenly the object is night-black, shedding the dust across its surface. It takes off. There are no signs of propulsion anywhere on the craft. No heat shimmers of engines. It moves without sound, as if a giant, invisible hand pulled it through the sky. The pilot pursues, he's outmatched, outflown. He can only keep up for about ten seconds, following it in an arc around a thunderhead. The clouds clear. The pilot decelerates when he sees what's on the other side.

Another pyramid, this one enormous, far bigger than the first.]

Pilot: "Control? Can you see . . . ?"

[The first pyramid flies silently towards the second, disappearing somewhere within its seemingly infinite black mass. No portholes or docking bays open up, the larger simply swallows the smaller. The second pyramid tilts itself ever-so-slightly in the direction of the pilot's plane, and a ripple sweeps across its surface. Something saying *I dare you.*]

[The enormous pyramid tilts back to its former position, turns away from the pilot, then simply vanishes between frames. The clouds surrounding it are sucked into the space the pyramid once occupied, filling the vacuum, but otherwise it is as if the craft was never there at all.]

"..."

Patrick Barb

[MESSAGES: UNKNOWN NUMBER]

Dude. I think someone messed with my phone at the party
Saturday night.

My contacts are super weird.

(frowning emoji)

I couldn't even find your number.

Hello?

Earth to Julian. Anyone home?

I'm looking right at you in the cafeteria.

I'm waving. Your waving back.

You're*

Now you've got your phone out.

Goddamn you're a slow texter.

WTF? We're the hell's my text?

Patrick Barb

How did you get this number? Where did you get that phone?

Ha ha. Real funny J.

Is this Eric?

Look OK I know it must be tough. Everything that happened with Bryan and all.

Wait. Hold up. What the duck are you talking about?

*duck

*DUCK

Whoever this is, you better keep my bro's name out of your texts.

I dunno what kinda telephone wizardry you pulled to copy my friend's number.

But he'd know better.

Who is this?

Bryan.

No.

Uh yeah.

No it's not.

Can't be.

Uh last time I checked YEAH.

Don't text this number again you sick fuck.

I'll call the cops.

14

"*. . .*"

We haven't even buried him yet.

Dude. What the hell?

Hello?

Did you block me?

★★★

[MESSAGES: ERIC]

Hey Bry. I know you can't answer. Not for real.

But Father Donnelly suggested trying this.

God you'd give me so much crap if you knew I was following our priest's advice.

I can picture you throwing up the horns.

But whatever. You're gone and your big bros gonna get as soppy as I want.

Everybody misses you.

I wanted to let you know how much we all miss you.

Mom hasn't stopped crying. And Dad

Well it's Dad ya know?

He's been hanging out with Uncle Mitch a lot.

He and Dad skipped your wake to go to the gun range.

Can you believe it?

Dad came back smelling like oil and burnt knuckle hair.

Patrick Barb

Mom made him take off his clothes on the back deck.

I don't understand what's happening here.

Or what kinda prank you're trying to pull whoever you are.

But how dare

u.

Oh.

Its u. You're the one Julian was yelling about outside the chapel.

How'd u get my brothers phone or number or whatever?

OK is this Julian on someone else's phone or what?

I'm on my phone.

Thought it fell into that Cassie Wilbur girl's pool

Must have taken it out before I hit my cannonball from her garage roof.

Things have been messed up ever since though.

That's what I told you in AP Bio Julian.

Remember?

Probably considering the Google eyes you were making at Cassie.

*googly

This is Eric. Bryan's brother.

Yeah I saw the name in the contacts.

But Eric died in an accident years ago.

"..."

If this is Julian or someone else supposed to be my friend they'd know that.

No.

I didn't.

Bryan came to my graduation last year.

He was supposed to visit my dorm the weekend after the Wilbur girl's party.

Ha.

FU whoever this is.

Next you'll tell me "Bryan's" dead.

Yes.

God are you that stupid of a scammer?

My little brother died. He didn't cannonball off a roof. He fell.

Hard

From the top of a garage with a bunch of drunk ass high schoolers.

I take it back. he didn't fall.

He got pushed.

Nobody will say it.

None of the kids from the party. But I know some of them know who did it.

Code of silence BS.

Someone pushed him hard.

He missed the pool entirely.

Mom and Dad told me not to look but some jerk put the police photos online.

Do you wanna see what happened to my bro's head when it hit the concrete?

[IMG1.JPG]

Jesus.

***

[MESSAGES: ERIC]

Eric?

What. ?

Oh ty.

Thank you.

OK.

I don't know what's happening. I don't know where these texts come from.

Or where mine are going.

I talked to Julian about them again though. Told him what u said.

He got weird. But like

I GET THAT. IT's weird as hell right?

"..."

He wanted to see the phone. But I wouldn't

Couldn't show him.

When I told him about the picture I didn't like how he reacted.

I didn't like it.

I thought he'd try and grab the phone away from me.

Then he left. Said he had to go hang out with Cassie.

Which is weird cuz like that party was the only time we hung out with her.

He did say something about parallel realities before he left though.

maybe he was ducking with me

*DUCKING

NM

I've been thinking about it over the last couple of days

About this.

Told Mom. Kinda.

I mentioned you. Asked her if she could imagine a world where Eric was alive.

She broke down crying.

Dad yelled. No surprise there.

"Get the hail out!"

"Why'd you have to bringt hat up?"

19

Patrick Barb

Heard em turn on Family Feud after I left.

I'm here in my room looking at the London Calling poster on my closet door.

Sitting on my bed that has that stack of Playboys under it.

The ones Julian gave me.

Ones he stole from his Grandpa.

And I can hear Steve Harvey from the living room.

Of course my brother wouldn't know about any of that.

He's been dead too long.

So u checked out Bryan's stuff. What'd you do crib this from his social media?

Well congrats.

Remember when we burnt down Mom's fairy garden in the backyard?

hhjfgty@ma!

?

Bryan?

The one and only.

Though not huh?

Remember we were doing sacrifices of our GI Joes.

Used a little too much gasoline near the peonies.

"..."

Whoosh.

Damn right whoosh.

big whoosh

Julian was there too.

It was like right after he'd moved here.

Oh yeah.

He took the blame for it too. Dad was pissed.

God.

I'd like just met the dude.

Dad was threatening to press charges but Mom talked him down.

So weird to think of him doing something like that for u.

Said he did because he knew I'd pay him back when the time came.

Huh.

What's going on here?

I don't know.

Parallel realities? But for real?

Wonder if your Bryan has my phone over there.

But I'm dead over there, so I guess it doesn't matter.

Well not you but

You know what I mean Eric.

And I'm dead there?

Yeah

I died at Cassie Wilbur's party?

Really?

Your girlfriend.

Who?

Cassie.

WHAT???

No.

No way.

Explains some things about the phone though.

Like why she's in my contacts on this phone but I barely talk to
her over here.

Over here in the real world Julian was the one who insisted we
had to go.

This IS the real world.Bry.

I wake up every morning soaked in sweat. Hoarse too.

My roommate said I scream in my sleep.

I figured he was about a week away from requesting a room
reassignment.

School called Mom and Dad and told em I should take a semester
off.

"..."

I'm home.

Guess I'm not taking the YOU I knew being gone well as I thought huh?

I mean I'm losing my mind

"Texting" my dead little brother. Dreaming up a world where I'm the one who died

I don't have to take psych classes to see the issues here.

LOL

god this is U. this is exactly what you'd be like grown-up.

(smiling emoji)

I need time.

Please.

Yeah. Ok.

Ok.

***

[MESSAGES: CASSIE <3]

Hey. Had fun in study hall.

What the fuck?

Shit. Wrong Cassie. I mean

Wrong phone.

***

[MESSAGES: ERIC]

Dude. Did you text Cassie?

Aw crap. How'd you hear about that?

Julian.

Makes sense. He's always talking about her here too.

You can't text other people from this world or whatever like that.

It's not right.

Whatever you say Mom.

Ass.

This is nice.

What is?

Talking with you.

No response?

Eric?

Hello?

BRYAN?

BRYAN?

Yes?

BRYAN. OHMYGOD. my sweet boy.

SWEET BUNNY BOY.

"..."

mommy?

Oh Mom.

I gotta go. I can't.

Sorry she snuck up on me. Had to tell her these were old texts.

From before.

***

[MESSAGES: JULIAN]

Don't mind me.

Seeing if you blocked me.

Guess so.

You were so pissed at me yesterday.

Not you-you.

The you I know. From this world.

I told you about Cassie coming over.

For our make-up project in AP Bio

We were supposed to do it a month ago

Before the party.

Do you know the one with the pool and the roof?

Where I guess I died in your world.

I told you I kissed her and I've never seen you so angry.

25

Patrick Barb

But like quiet angry.

Now the other you won't talk to me.

So I'm stuck texting you.

A stranger but also my friend.

And I don't even know if your there.

I'm not your friend Bryan.

I think you are.

And that's why I'm worried.

Because I finally worked up the nerve to check this phone's
Camera Roll.

The last photo's blurry and hard to see. But I can kinda see your
face. And your hands.

Arm stretched out like

Like you're pushing something out of the way.

Or someone.

****

[MESSAGES: ERIC]

Did the other me ever say anything about Julian before he died?

Hey bro. Great to hear from you.

I'm good. And you?

Okay okay I get it.

"..."

Point made.

I'm just trying to figure out some things. Where our worlds overlap and where they diverge.

Like when did I start dating Cassie?

I dunno. Few months before you died?

She mentioned an AP Bio project at the funeral. Said that's where you hit it off.

Guess that happened a bit later over here.

And Julian?

he's weird. UR right about that.

Not fun weird?

No. Definitely not.

He came by the house. Said he also went to Uncle Mitch's. Looking for me.

What? Why?

Says he has something of yours to show me.

Hmm.

He say what?

No.

Hm.

Can u get Mom?

Dude.

Cmon.

Please.

I need this.

I

HELLO

WHOSE THIS

BRYAN IT SAYS ITS ERIC

OH THE PHONE WRITES DOWN WHAT I SAY

OKAY I THINK I CAT

CAT

CAT

GET IT!

Happy?

She's gone?

I didn't get to write anything back.

Dude. Go talk to your own mom.

Yeah. OK.

You know you say dude as much as he did. My Bryan.

"..."

Our Bryan.

****

[MESSAGES: INVALID NUMBER]

Eric?

ERROR. INVALID NUMBER.

Eric??

ERROR. INVALID NUMBER.

ERIC!

ERROR. INVALID NUMBER.

What was it you said? What was it?

ERROR. INVALID NUMBER.

(frowning emoji)

ERROR. INVALID NUMBER.

Julian wanted to see you. Show you something?

ERROR. INVALID NUMBER.

Julian's avoiding me here.

ERROR. INVALID NUMBER.

Snuck a peek into his locker. Never looked in there before. Never
had reason to.

ERROR. INVALID NUMBER.

I mean why would I?

ERROR. INVALID NUMBER.

> He had these pictures of Cassie in there.

ERROR. INVALID NUMBER.

> But not school pics. Not

ERROR. INVALID NUMBER.

> He shouldn't have those pictures of her.

ERROR. INVALID NUMBER.

> Duck.

ERROR. INVALID NUMBER.

> Not again. I can't lose you again.

ERROR. INVALID NUMBER.

***

[MESSAGES: CASSIE <3]

> Cassie.

> I'm sorry.

Julian?

> No it's

I swear to God I didn't see whatever it is you think I saw up on my garage that night.

I was drunk. I was so drunk. And what I said to you at school

I was mad. I AM mad. But about what happened.

"..."

I miss him so much.

I'm crazy though. Please don't listen to me.

Please.

This ISN'T Julian.

Who is this?

I'm someone who cares.

This is weird.

Are you a bot?

What'd you do clone Bryan's number?

Do you even know who he is?

Was?

I

Sure. Yeah.

I'm a bot.

I know it's you Julian.

It's not m

God are you pulling up? What were you texting and driving here?

Oh no

Oh my God.

You're not Julian. are you?

Cassie?

What's wrong?

He said

He said he got the

What's happening? What can I do?

GUN

Bryan's dad. he got the gun from Bryan

's dad

Oh God ohJesus

Gotta call 911

Be careful.

Please.

★★★

[MESSAGES: MOM]

Mom?

Mommy?

Mom

You there?

★★★

[MESSAGES: DAD]

"..."

Dad.

Dammit dad what did you do?

You knew better about Uncle Mitch over here.

Learned your lesson.

All Eric wanted to do was impress you with a trick shot from the
pistol you should've locked up.

You don't let us talk about him.

Not me or Mom

Not anyone.

How dare you.

Guess you never learned over there.

***

[MESSAGES: CASSIE <3]

Sorry. Sorry it took so long. I texted a bunch of random numbers.

Hoping someone took me seriously and sent help.

Cassie?

Did you call 911?

Are you safe?

No. Yes. No.

Julian?

Dammit. I swear if you

What do you care?

You're already dead.

This isn't your world.

So why don't you leave us alone here? Like I wanted.

***

[MESSAGES: JULIAN]

Julian?

C'mon I know you're there.

What can I do to you?

I'm dead over there anyway

No one will believe me. Over here or over there.

I just wanted to say this is gonna be the last time I contact you.

Or anyone else on this phone.

I'm gonna throw it away after you answer my question.

I won't ask why or how could you

Nothing like that.

I think I know

Or I know enough.

What do you want Bryan?

“ . . . ”

There you are.

Pinky swear you’re not my guilty conscience.

I don’t think you have one.

Heh.

I wanna ask you something

About yourself

I mean about the you that’s over here.

Look I know I know. you’re not the same

Not exactly

But you’re close enough

Yeah.

Julian

My Julian

I showed him everything.

The texts

Yours.

Eric’s

Mom’s

Cassie’s

We’re best friends.

Patrick Barb

What else was I supposed to do?

He hasn't been around much since me and Cassie started

Well you already lived through that part.

He came by a few minutes ago

He's waiting for me now in his old Toyota

Is that what you drive there?

Honda

Sure OK.

My Julian says he found something cool in the park. Deep in
there. Off one of those paths.

Do you know the dirt ones where you can wander and get lost?

I think I know why he wants me there.

I mean I've got all the texts on this phone. The picture.

But he's still my friend.

He hasn't done ANYTHING here

Not yet.

I feel like.

I dunno maybe there's a chance

to stop this

Turn it around or whatever.

I can get in the car. Or I can stay.

36

"..."

So I wanna ask

Should I get in the car with you?

With him?

Cmon. One last answer for old time's sake?

I can wait.

. . .

***

The transcripts provided above were recovered from a phone left in the bedroom of Bryan Bell following his disappearance, and that of classmate Julian Watson. In checking the registration and data from the phone, police found no record of Bryan or anyone in his family ever owning said phone, in spite of the shocking and baffling message content contained on the device's chat logs. The final pending message of Bryan's final exchange remains in apparent limbo.

Authorities and surviving members of the Bell family await the day when those three dots will disappear, replaced by answers at last.

37

Next of Kin

Sandra Henriques

January 20—Edith Fortunato's social media post

It is with great sadness that I confirm the passing of author Madeleine Jones. She died peacefully in her sleep, in the company of her loved ones. MJ was a dear friend and a fiercely creative woman who hardly took no for an answer, especially when it came from me, her editor. Madeleine will be truly missed but will live on through her work and her loyal readers.

We ask you for privacy at this time of grief. A public ceremony to honor her legacy will be held soon. Please check the link in my bio for more details.

****

February 11—Email from Edith Fortunato to Madeleine Jones' daughters, Regan and Rosemary

From: Edith Fortunato <edith.fortunato@ef-publishing.com>
To: Rosemary Jones <rose.jones@gmail.com>; Regan Jones-Anderson <regan.jones.anderson@icloud.com>
Subject: MJ's Journal

Dear Rose and Rey,

I hope you are well. Although we haven't spoken in a while, I'm hopeful we can put grievances aside to discuss pressing issues regarding your mother's death.

Next of Kin

I noticed neither of you came to the funeral or the public ceremony in her honor after that, and I can't say I blame you. Madeleine was not the easy-breezy person people believed her to be, although she was pretty good at faking it for her fans. She loved the spotlight, and I'm sorry she could not or would not be the mother you deserved. Robert did a wonderful job raising you two.

But let's not dwell in the past. It's too late to amend her wrongdoings, so I'll cut to the chase. I know that a few months ago you renounced your right to inherit Madeleine's work and book royalties, her apartment downtown, and any money she'd have left in her bank account (there wasn't much, I can tell you that), but among her belongings was a journal that I believe shouldn't be made public or become the property of EF Publishing. I didn't disclose this finding to my business partners, and I ask (I hope) you will do the same. The notebook's contents are personal, as far as I could tell from briefly leafing through it. Some parts of it contain erratic scribbles, definitely written by Madeleine because I recognize her handwriting, but they don't make sense to me. Maybe seclusion was finally getting to her. Even though she insisted that living alone was the dream for any writer, I sincerely believe she felt lonelier than she'd like to admit.

Please let me know if you'd like me to send you the notebook. If you don't want it, rest assured that I won't keep it or make it public.

I hope to hear back from you soon. Text me or give me a call. I'd love to catch up.

All my love,

Aunt Edith

***

February 13—Email from Rosemary Jones to Edith Fortunato

From: Rosemary Jones <rose.jones@gmail.com>
To: Edith Fortunato <edith.fortunato@ef-publishing.com>

CC: Regan Jones-Anderson <regan.jones.anderson@icloud.com>
Subject: RE: MJ's Notebook

Hello, Edith.

Thank you for your email.

After careful consideration, Regan and I decided to accept your offer. Please have the journal delivered to my office at your earliest convenience.

Best regards,

Rosemary Jones & Regan Jones-Anderson

★★★

February 14—text messages between Rosemary and Regan

Rey: Did you read it yet?

Rose: No. Not sure if I want to.

Rey: We decided we wanted closure. This is closure, Rose.

Rose: Yeah, but she didn't want us around, so why should we bother to read her crap? Everything about her is a lie. Did you read Edith's post? She died in the company of her loved ones? WTF?

Rey: PR crap. You know that. Do you think she knew?

Rose: What?

Rey: Like that she was dying? When she tried calling us?

Rose: She probably choked on her vomit, drunk as shit. IDGAF Rey.

Rey: Sigh. I kinda know you do give a fuck, so stop the act.

Rose: Fine. Wanna come over and read it together? Open a bottle of wine? Or do shots every time we read "me" or "I."

Rey: LOL It's a journal! She probably wrote "me" and "I" a lot. How do you think I write in mine?

Rose: Dear Diary? I don't know! Humor me, please!

Rey. OK. I'll see you later.

★★★

From the journal of Madeleine Jones

May 7

Had brunch with Regan today. I always have to treat her with extra care, order the blueberry pancakes and pretend to like them just because one day, when she was 5, I told her they were my very favorite. She hadn't eaten properly for days, and I was worried sick. Rosemary didn't bother showing up or calling with an excuse. She was practically self-raised, that one, like a premixed cake that you throw in the oven after tossing all the ingredients together. I can't say I'm proud of my parenting style; neither turned out like I expected. Robert told me once I couldn't pretend my children were one of the characters in my books, manipulate them, and make them do the dirty work for me. By dirty work, he meant parenting.

Regan is always odd, but she was uneasy today, poking the blueberries with her fork, picking on the scrambled eggs, and complaining they were too runny. "No clue" was Rosemary's answer to the text I sent her once I got home. At least she had the courtesy of texting me back.

Edith pestered me again about the book. *When, when, when*; that's all they care about. It's never how or why. Edith the Editor, I wish she was fictional; it's an excellent name for a villain.

May 17

Sent a draft of the first chapter to Edith. Told her it needs more research to tie some loose ends, but these first pages should give her an idea about the tone. She'll say it's different from what Madeleine Jones usually writes, whatever that means. She always says that whenever I try something different. What writer does she expect me to be? This is what I want to write.

May 18

I woke up to Edith's one-line email, "We need to talk." I called her immediately, only to be scolded over the phone for 10 minutes. Felt like a little girl who just ripped her Sunday dress before church.

"This is not going to work, Madeleine. If this is the novel you want to write, find another publisher or use a pen name. I won't be able to have your back. This isn't worthy of a Madeleine Jones book. And your loyal readers are eager for a new MJ book next spring. It's been five years, so you better get to work fast, before the March 19th deadline."

What the fuck does she know about Madeleine Jones books, anyway. I printed the first chapter so I could rip it into pieces and flush them down the toilet.

Emptying the trash bin on my desktop is not satisfying enough.

May 18

To add to the new this-is-a-madeleine-jones-book:

I opened the bedroom window to let in the summer breeze. The humidity clung to my bare skin like a thin veil of mist and rose perfume. My hands smelled of his coconut oil. "Come back to bed," the soft voice whispered behind me, tapping the satin sheets gently. My eyes were bloodshot, the dark circles under them growing deeper every night. The night air weighed on my chest like a marble tombstone. "You told me not to breathe."

Next of Kin

May 31

I've patched things up with Edith. I can't do it any other way if I want to be able to pay my bills next year. I'll continue to work on both stories if I can muster the energy. It's so warm and humid here. I open all the apartment windows at night to let the cool air flow, and it doesn't help. Sometimes it smells of sweet summer flowers; other times, it stinks of a musty pile of clothes someone forgot in a closed attic. Both are nauseating.

June 2

Edith is thrilled with the three chapters I already sent her. "A sure bestseller," she told me on the phone, practically squealing like a small child at their birthday party. They want a Madeleine Jones book; I'll give them a Madeleine Jones book. It's several MJ books, actually. I'm copying portions of my previous novels and rearranging them in a new story. I wonder when (if?) Edith will tell.

June 8

A whiff of hydrangeas spread around the room as it swirled and swirled and swirled until it thrust itself on the floor with a loud thud. I sat motionless, the soft light on my bedside table casting deep shadows on the wall. When it rose from the ground, aching and wailing, I instinctively opened my arms for a cuddle. And both, together, fused, rocked back and forth to the sound of a childhood lullaby only we knew until exhaustion drove us to slumber.

July 27

Half the book is done. The other story, though, is coming in irregular outbursts. Like a gust of wind that whooshes through a house, knocking down vases, opening windows, and shutting doors with loud bangs. And then the dust settles, revealing nothing. Just everything as it was before. Sometimes I question whether there's a story there or merely a collection of odd notes.

It's peering from its hideaway on the wall. I don't know what to feed it or whether it needs feeding. Usually it asks for a snuggle, but tonight it recoils whenever I get closer.

July 30

I couldn't open the windows last night. I stretched my arms out the window to let the rain soothe my warm skin, and it punched me in the shin, pulled me by my hair back inside, and asked for cuddles. Again. I felt the burning vomit in the back of my throat. *Cuddles, cuddles, cuddles*, it wailed and wailed, and my head was spinning. I pretended to sleep until it disappeared through the hole in the wall. I didn't feed it, but it grew. I can tell the hideout is getting tighter.

July 31

It stared at me staring at the blank page this morning. Motionless, wheezing, scratching at its bald scalp. I could hear the nails peeling out flake after flake of dead, greasy, pustulent skin. I wiped my sweaty palms on my naked legs and called, "Come here." It wobbled on its belly, dragging the blackened feet behind it. Its toothless mouth, wide open, latched on to my salty thigh.

August 2

My cracked lips have begun to peel. I pick at them, slowly rolling the edges of dead skin and gently pulling them. Sometimes I manage to remove a large piece without it breaking. Translucent, I can see the patterns of cells and creases. Then I blow it away.

Is this what aging feels like? I'll peel myself away, piece by piece, until I'm just tissue on the floor? Is that what you are? A mass of dead tissue, slurping my remains between your two teeth?

August 3

I'm not being fair to Edith. What if she decides to publish the book? I called Rosemary, but she didn't pick up. I didn't want Regan to pick up, but of course she did. I hung up.

I'm emailing Edith to tell her I was messing with her.

August 7

Edith isn't replying to my emails or my calls. She's pissed.

August 8

Another sleepless night, staring at blank pages. "How dramatic of you, Madeleine," Edith would say. I miss Edith, but I don't think she'll ever forgive me. And I miss Rose and Rey.

It no longer melts away in the hole in the wall. It used to sit in the corner, wheezing, the viscous drool hanging from its lower lip and licking its tiny, sharp teeth with the tip of that charcoal-black tongue. Waiting for my signal.

Now it clings to me, unannounced, its chubby lifeless feet hanging by my ribs, rubbing its wet belly against my bare back while it feverishly sucks the beads of sweat from my neck. Soft but unsatiated gurgling sounds come out of its throat. And for the first time, it speaks, with a guttural, labored voice: "Skin."

I feed it a small patch I peel from my bloody lip; it rolls its eyes as the tissue melts in its mouth.

August 20

Edith is still pissed. I pondered calling Rosemary and Regan but didn't know what to say. That I'm old and sorry and want to make it up to them? That I'm suddenly afraid of the dark and I can't sleep? That the next book I'm writing, the one Aunt Edith doesn't want to publish, is about me and them and our struggle to tolerate each other?

The groceries delivery boy stared at me when I opened the door. My lips are sore and cracked and caked in dried blood. "Herpes— don't come near me," I warned. He stepped back, eager to get to the elevator down the hall. I grabbed the bags and closed the door.

I'm growing used to the dark and humid apartment. It always smells of flowers and perspiration.

I find it oddly exhilarating.

August 22

It drenched the bed in sweat and urine, kicking and screaming, hungry. "Skiiiiiiiinnnn," it wails. My lips are sore and running out of fresh, healed skin. It no longer fits under the desk, where it used to curl at my feet, grinding its teeth, sniffing my toes, trying to scrape my calves, and snarling.

No Edith, no Rosemary, no Regan. Just the company of this flesh-colored, hairless creature that once learned to crawl out from a hole in the wall. I think I should name it James.

August 30

James, little what. What should I say you are? All you do is eat, cry for food, or beg for cuddles. Like a defunct, abandoned boogeyman some child left behind when they outgrew the monsters under the bed.

I believe the delivery boy can't stand the sight of me after the fake herpes incident, so he just left the bags outside my door, knocked, and shouted, "Mrs. Jones, I'm leaving your groceries here." Or maybe he doesn't like the smell of piss and sweat and flowers when I open the door? Or do the long red gashes in my forearms make him uneasy? Well, James has to eat. Either I feed him or stay awake all night. But I don't sleep either way.

August 31

Edith emailed me a copy of my contract and a threat. I fired her as my publisher and editor. I told her I'd welcome her for friendly drinks anytime at my place, as long as we didn't talk about work. I don't think there's anything between us besides work anymore, so I don't think she'll show up at my doorstep anytime soon.

Next of Kin

September 14

I have lost track of time, although my phone shows me it's September 14. James stopped growing, which is a relief. Now it just sits in the corner of my bedroom like a dirty stuffed bear. Except stuffed animals have hair, of course. Unless I sit at my desk to write, then it crawls to its spot underneath, curling at my feet. That warm, damp mass weighing on my toes, oozing the viscous, nauseating sweet-smelling liquid from its every pore.

I'm trying a new technique to have an endless supply of dead skin. I'm going to feed James until it can no longer stand! Until it bursts! Little pieces of James' tissue exploding like confetti!

I think James is blind, although I can see its eyes glowing in the dark, orange, fixed on me. If I move, it blinks and pants as if getting ready for a hunt. Could I outrun it?

September 16

Today's burns produced large, juicy swathes of skin. I mashed them in a greasy little ball the size of a bead and stuffed it down James' throat. It panted and moaned and gurgled and choked. "Chew, James, chew," I said. And it chewed, the saliva dripping from the corners of its mouth down its neck, puddling on the top of the engorged belly.

I watched it eat and weep. "More skin," it said, under labored breaths.

September 20

James is sick. I'm sick. I stopped feeding it. We're both starving. It hardly moves now. I poked James with a letter opener, and my arm began to bleed.

September 27

I opened a window to breathe, and James hissed like a feral cat. I closed the blinds, but it never seemed bothered by the light. It's the fresh air on my skin that burns it inside, consuming it in a slow-burning fire. My stomach aches, too.

October 8

I lay on the kitchen floor for what felt like weeks, the cold and hard terracotta tiles pressing the sore skin against my bones. I fed James one last time. It's wheezing in the corner of the room; its eyes—now a pale yellow—don't glow in the dark anymore. I forgot to breathe, and it screeched until its screams pierced my brain, and I inhaled deeply, desperate.

I have to kill it.

★★★

February 20—Email from Rosemary Jones to Edith Fortunato

From: Rosemary Jones <rose.jones@gmail.com>
To: Edith Fortunato <edith.fortunato@ef-publishing.com>
CC: Regan Jones-Anderson <regan.jones.anderson@icloud.com>
Subject: RE: MJ's Notebook

Edith,

We finished reading the journal and agree this should never be made public. I've requested my lawyers draft us a non-disclosure agreement (attached) that we kindly ask you to read, sign, and return as soon as possible.

We understand you voided the contract with our mother on August 31. Is this date accurate? Please be aware we will be taking this matter to our legal team.

We wish you the best of luck in your future endeavors.

Regards,

Rosemary Jones & Regan Jones-Anderson

Next of Kin

***

February 20—Email from Edith Fortunato to Rosemary Jones and Regan-Jones Anderson

From: Edith Fortunato <edith.fortunato@ef-publishing.com>
To: Rosemary Jones <rose.jones@gmail.com>
CC: Regan Jones-Anderson <regan.jones.anderson@icloud.com>
Subject: RE: MJ's Notebook

I'm sorry, you're pursuing legal action against *me?* Are you kidding, Rose? Where were you and Rey in the last months of her life? I called her every day, emailed her, asked the building caretaker to check up on her, sent her groceries. Where the hell were you?

You better believe you'll hear from my lawyers immediately.

Take care,

Edith

***

February 21—text messages between Regan Jones-Anderson and Edith Fortunato

Regan: Hi, Edith. It's Regan. Rey. Can we talk?

Edith: . . .

Regan: I'm not with Rose. And you can ask your lawyers before texting me back.

Edith: It's OK. I can talk. How are you?

Regan: Fine. I need to ask you this, how did my mother die?

Edith: . . .

Regan: Edith, please. How did she die?

Edith: The coroner's report said she starved and tried eating her skin. She was bruised and scarred and emaciated when they found her. The person who delivered the groceries knocked and she didn't reply, so he called me, and I called the building caretaker, who called the police.

Regan: . . .

Edith: I'm truly sorry, Regan.

Regan: Thank you. And James?

Edith: Who?

Regan: James. She talks about him in her journal.

Edith: She was alone.

***

From the journal of Regan Jones-Anderson

February 21

I can tell the hideout is getting tighter.

I picked at my cracked lip, peeled a tiny piece of tissue, and placed it on the floor. It peered out of the hole in my bedroom wall warily and slurped it off the ground with the tip of its black tongue.

My mother called hers James; *what should I call you?*

Echo Chamber

Gemma Files

From: Creepgal1991@gmail.com
To: ross.puget@freihoeveninst.ca
Re: TRYING TO TRACK THIS DOWN, CAN YOU HELP

You don't know me and I don't know you but we have friends in common through the Freihoeven Institute, which is how I got this email (obviously). I have a podcast transcript but no podcast to go with it—the podcaster appears to have deleted the file and disappeared, so I can't get in touch with them. Everything else is still up on the website, except that episode. No one's answering the main contact email anymore, and the company hosting the podcast isn't responding either. It's not a big deal, but I'd like to be completist (again, obviously).

Not sure if you've ever heard of The Weal, but it started out as a sort of alternative to a shortwave "college" radio show done over at Mundiplex (scare-quotes around college, because Mundiplex is a straight-up diploma mill specializing in whatever lures Ontario HS grads to take out government educational loans—music production, CGI, SP/FX, etc.), but in podcast form, ostensibly because the team couldn't go into the studio anymore due to COVID. The host/deejay, Meander Denny, also has an ASMR YouTube channel; that's not updating either, now.

I started listening to her there as self-care when my anxiety was spiking, blah blah blah. So while I was binging through those she started cross-promoting The Weal, and I subscribed to that too.

Liked it a lot, especially since she seemed to program most of it out of her personal music collection, and I'd never heard most of the stuff she tended to fall back on (all this late 80s early 90s stuff, on vinyl and tape? Her producer must be some sort of old dead tech addict too. Or was).

I don't know much about Denny, aside from what's still available online. Not even if that was really her name. The whole website is super-rudimentary, like they just heard a bunch of Pacific Northwest Stories ads for squarespace.com and ran with them (check out that shit they set up for The Black Tapes, you'll see what I mean). And just like with TBT, the actual transcripts are done by somebody else on Reddit, probably the same person who moderates r/TheWeal. Which *also* hasn't been updated since they posted this, come to think, hidey hidey hoooooo.

Anyhow. I guess I just tend to get obsessive (that's why they call it OCD, ha ha), but if you could help me out with this quest of mine, I sure do need some. People speak highly of your Weird Crap Locating skillz, and I'm gonna shut up now; read the attached, tell me what you think, yes/no.

All best, stay safe, whatever.

Ulee Schaw (you can get me here or by DM on TwitterX, @Creepgal1991, that's me)

PS . . . Carra Devize says to say hey, so hey.

★★★

@rpuget hey, got your email. you want me to find a copy of the episode, that it?

@Creepgal1991 oh hey hi!!!! yeah that would be coool but if you can't then maybe just the song shes talking about???

@rpuget sorry, what song was that?

@Creepgal1991 dude seriously did you read the attached or what???

Echo Chamber

@rpuget you know you can use just one question mark, right?

@rpuget okay, sorry, bad night last night. i read the first couple of pages. tell me what song you're talking about, i'll look.

@Creepgal1991 millennial much? don't feel like you have to humour me.

@rpuget kid, c'mon.

@Creepgal1991 fine, okay. its called sheetshake by yseult haight. dont bother googling her discography, she never officially recorded it. its actually not even supposed to exist.

@rpuget okay, that's never good.

@Creepgal1991 :D :D :D i know, right?! seriously, go read what meander says about it. ill wait.

@rpuget don't doubt it.

***

TRANSCRIPT: "THE WEAL", EP. 73, *orig. broadcast 2/11/2021*

DENNY: Hi, kids. I'm Meander Denny, and this is The Weal.

As you all know, or should, I'm a huge fan of musical oddities, especially ones from female artists. And one of the oddest ladies to ever make music may have been Yseult Haight, former British child model and actress turned self-taught multi-instrumentalist, music producer and performance artist. Over the course of her surprisingly long and completely unsuccessful career, she and various collaborators recorded under a variety of band-names: Night Mouths, Blood Spire, Corpse Medicine, Arsenic Sword; Wolf-Whore and Glad of War and Prey for Worms; Sweat Trench and Plague Box; We Are All Made of Blood. As London rock critic Jo Gaiters once put it, back in 1999 (TERRIBLE COCKNEY ACCENT):

53

"That girl changes bands more often than she changes her underwear . . . and considering how rarely she performs wearing anything else but lingerie, that's sayin' something."

. . . sorry about that. (LAUGHTER)

All of Haight's projects read as some subset of goth; she was doom before doom, gloom before gloom, and consistently occult-referential. The one I want to talk about today was supposed to be included on her final album, *Memento Vivere*, the one that came out after her disappearance from public life; half the critics out there think it's her best work and the other half call it a spectacular public flameout. My own impulse is to say, "Both, both—both are good." Well, not *good* in this case, but true, anyway, because even if you don't remember the album, you just might have heard of this song—the song which isn't supposed to exist, the song the record execs pulled from the album before it came out, the song that *Rolling Stone* critic said was—hang on here, I wrote this down: "Based on the description alone, I'm confident it will prove the *ne plus ultra* of either sheer genius or pretentious bullshit."

(LAUGHS) It's called "Sheetshake".

Odd title, right? Haight said it derived most directly from a song called "The Shaking of the Sheets," possibly written sometime in the seventeenth century, and eventually recorded by classic British folk-rock band Steeleye Span. Themed after the mediaeval *danza macabra* or Dance of Death, it was a meditation on basic human existentialism through the lens of the Black Death, the Great Mortality—the bubonic plague, brought via flea-infested rats, which raged through Europe from 1347 to 1351 and killed either 75 or 200 million people, with no distinctions made between saints or sinners, aristocrats or peasants, old or young, hale or lame, beautiful or ugly. The sheets being shaken here are winding-sheets, grave cerements; the central image is an endless parade of corpses dancing in a huge circle, spinning round and round, but always willing to make room for one more.

"As you are now, so once was I; as I am now, so shall you be." Sound familiar?

Echo Chamber

Haight being Haight, though, there are loads more influences at work here—a lot more resonances, or perhaps assonances. During the Black Death, for example, penitents who believed the plague was an apocalyptic God's punishment for humankind's wickedness roamed from city to city in an ecstasy of self-harm; they'd whip themselves bloody and march until they died of shock, infection, exsanguination or starvation, tranced out and singing hymns to the very last—like a crowd of naked, bony, musical zombies, the literal Walking Dead.

And after that, you get another odd phenomenon: In July of 1518, a woman named Frau Troffea suddenly began "to dance fervently" in the middle of a Strasbourg street, in the heart of the Holy Roman Empire. Not only did she keep it up herself for weeks, others began to join in—over four hundred at final count, many collapsing, even dying from heart attack or stroke. Most psychologists believe this "Dancing Epidemic" was an incident of stress-related religious mass hysteria, though other people have since blamed things like demonic possession, epilepsy or convulsive ergotism—the same thing that *might* have caused the Salem Witch Trials. One way or the other, it seemed to start tapering off after sufferers made a pilgrimage to the shrine of Saint Vitus, which is why convulsions of any sort have sometimes been called St Vitus's Dance.

Here's the really weird thing, though. At the height of the Dancing Epidemic, not only were the main symptoms dancing—jigging in place and flailing a lot, at any rate—but the recommended cure was *also* supposed to be dancing. By September 1518, Strasbourg's government had set up a stage in the town square where musicians would continually perform to help the shuffling, bone-weary "infected" keep going without succumbing to fainting or seizures. And what was the music they played to make these people dance? No one knows, not for sure. Could it have been something like "Sheetshake"?

Or think about this: We all know the one about how that old familiar kindergarten rhyme "Ring Around the Rosies" is *really* about the Black Death—how the rosies are buboes, the pocket full of posies are herbs and flowers used to ward off either infection or the smell of rotting corpses, and "ashes, ashes, we all fall down" is about how bodies would be collected in carts, dumped into plague pits and then sprinkled with quicklime and ash before being buried. But what about the "ring around" or "ringa ringa" part? It almost sounds like a description of infected people dancing in a circle, so long and so intensely that they eventually fall over and die . . . and then what? The others just keep on dancing over them until *they* die, and so on, and so on? Until there's no one left?

***

r/lostmusic [PRIVATE] • 1 day ago
by **creepgal1991**
COMMUNICATION THREAD FOR YH SONG PROJECT

Hi, whoever gets the login information to post to this thread, I'm really looking forward to meeting you and getting started on the project!

mlhenderson • 19 hours ago
I'm assuming from the alias that this is Ulee Schaw? My name is Morgan Henderson, Ross Puget gave me your contact details and suggested I could be of use to you. Touchy stuff first: I charge £20/hr for my services, plus expenses, three-hour minimum, and if I need to go into risky areas of the dark net, I ask for a £2,000 deposit for emergency legal expenses up front (returned if not needed). Nowadays that should be roughly 2,500 USD.

creepgal1991 • 19 hours ago
Wow, okay, that's more of a commitment than I expected. Is the deposit necessary?

mlhenderson • 19 hours ago
No, but it may limit my ability to find what you're looking for, especially if the original file is extremely old and obscure, which Ross's description suggests it is. There are some servers it can be legally dangerous to find your login credentials on, even if you never touch a single file.

creepgal1991 • 19 hours ago
It's just a song. Where do you think it's going to turn up? On an ISIS web forum?

mlhenderson • 19 hours ago
It's data. It could be anywhere. You have to decide how much finding it's worth to you.

creepgal1991 • 19 hours ago
You get right to the point, don't you?

mlhenderson • 19 hours ago
I'm trying to save us both time. I've had people try to back out of paying before. For what it's worth, I'm more inclined to believe you *because* you're balking at the price. People who plan on cheating me from the beginning tend not to protest.

creepgal1991 • 19 hours ago
Well, you know what? Okay. It's more than I expected, but I'm serious about this, and Ross says you're really good, so it's an investment, right? Send me the e-transfer address.

mlhenderson • 19 hours ago
Will do

mlhenderson • 18 hours ago
If it's any reassurance, your request piqued my curiosity. Mostly my clients are ad companies who want me to find lost copies of 60s and 70s commercial jingles, so they can make sure they're not breaching copyright somewhere. You're an intriguing change.

creepgal1991 • 18 hours ago
Thanks, I think?

★★★

TRANSCRIPT: "THE WEAL", EP. 73 (*cont'd*)

DENNY: In woodcuts, murals or bas reliefs of the Dance of Death found in churches all over Europe, the skeletons are often depicted playing instruments as they lead freshly-dead humans through the *danza macabra:* Flutes, violins, drums, bagpipes, hurdy-gurdys. Interestingly, these are all instruments Yseult Haight could—and did—play, looping individual tracks through playback rigs and layering them around her vocals as she performed live. She was also fascinated by ancient musical traditions such as mouth music, vocal percussion and drones, as popularized by Real World Music artists like Sheila Chandra, Iarla Ó Lionáird and the Tsinandali Choir—and this is where we get another one of those weird, maybe-not-so-coincidental parallels. Because sadly, much like Sheila Chandra's, Haight's career would come to an abrupt, screeching end in 2011, when she suddenly announced she'd been diagnosed with "burning mouth" syndrome.

What BMS consists of is exactly what the name suggests, basically—a constant burning or scalding sensation in your mouth and throat. Sufferers report that it makes speaking above a whisper, let alone singing, unspeakably agonizing. However, it primarily affects postmenopausal women and is defined by its lack of identifiable medical cause, so strangely enough, it doesn't grab a lot of headlines or research attention—the word "psychosomatic" gets thrown around a lot. Why doctors think people like Chandra or Haight would give up their music if they didn't have to—or why they'd need to make up an excuse, if they decided they *wanted* to—is beyond me, but God forbid we take women at their word.

Anyway, after Haight announced she'd developed BMS during the recording sessions for *Memento Vivere*, and that it would be her last album, ticket sales for her last concert performance went through the roof . . . which doesn't sound good either, does it, in terms of "oh boy, THIS isn't some sort of scam."

Still: cynicism's easy, sincerity's hard. And nobody goes to the sort of effort Haight went to while putting "Sheetshake" together without being *very* sincere indeed about . . . something.

Maybe just about going out with a bang, if nothing else.

"Sheetshake" is one of what Haight's fans call her Ghost Tracks, the songs that she liked to perform by improvising around what she claimed were actual paranormal "ghost box" EVP recordings that she'd play as a backing track. For extra punch, she liked to do this in venues she and her groups claimed were haunted; I don't know if any of them *were*, but I can tell you there is a documented incident of Haight applying to play in the famous Winchester House and getting denied. *That* would have been a concert worth paying a couple thousand bucks for; fuck you, Taylor Swift. (LAUGHTER)

One early Ghost Track, for example, was layered over an EVP supposedly recording the last breaths of an Englishwoman who died giving birth to an equally dead baby in what had formerly been a tuberculosis hospital, during the post-World War I influenza pandemic. I'm amazed the entire audience didn't run out of there puking pea soup when she played *that* one, and I don't even *believe* in EVP.

Anyway, getting to the point: when Yseult Haight held her very last performance, ever, she held it in the French cave system called La Grotte des Chuchotement—the "Cave of Whispering", a series of caverns near Dordogne where French peasants went to hide from, guess what? That's right: the Black Death. Motifs coming full circle, here.

Even that isn't the end of it, though. See, some archaeologists think this may have also been a site for pagan ritual, going back all the way through Celtic France to prehistoric times. A sacred place where certain people sacrificed themselves to the spirit of whatever might be threatening their tribe—famine, plague, predators either human or inhuman—in order to save everyone else. Because deep inside the caves, you see, they've found full and partial skeletons laid out in painstakingly-excavated rock shelves: Young people, strong people, their bodies excarnated by hand and then re-encased in mud mixed with yellow ochre, surrounded by dried flowers.

Even stranger, each skeleton was apparently buried with a polished quartz stone inside their lower jawbone, where their tongue should have been. Proof that the tribesmen and women thus interred might have actually competed for this honour, maybe dancing in a round until "caught" as part of a choosing game, the way some people think "London Bridge is Falling Down" might have originally been used to pick which stoneworker became a human pillar inside the foundations of whatever they were building?

Well, whatever—I don't believe it, necessarily, but Yseult Haight might have. So from her POV, if there was ever a place you could listen to the dead, those caves would be it.

And this is where Haight played "Sheetshake" for the first and last time, a ballad she wrote based on—as she put it—"a long history of plague songs and poems," layered over an hour of ambient tone they took the night before. This, they assumed, couldn't fail to include various EVP. "Whatever we pick up, we'll use," Haight apparently told her fans, in what would become her final tweet. And the thing they hoped to pick up was a trail of plague stuff going back back back, possibly forever.

Okay, right now I can hear you all saying, "But Meander, if nobody ever *recorded* this song, how do you know she played it there?" Well, there *is* a recording, supposedly. Something claimed to be one at least. The story is, a fan had one of the very first smartphones with them, one with a good enough mike and camera to record live music, and snuck it into the Grotte, intent on capturing not so much the *song* as the moment—Haight's last performance. And the .mp3 that came out of that has been floating around odd corners of the Internet for nearly fifteen years, copied and recopied, remixed and resampled, until God knows whether anything from the original's left of it at all.

I keep saying "last," don't I? That's because while everyone who attended Haight's performance at La Grotte has clear memories of rocking out until they essentially fell into some sort of trance, waking up the next morning either still shuffling or at rest where they fell, none of them seem to have any idea what happened to Yseult Haight—not even her own musical cohort. I guess it's not hard to vanish off the grid if you're barely on it to begin with; whatever fame Haight's name comes attached to has always existed mainly in the minds of those obsessed with her, after all, like me. And yet: Here we are, left behind, with only a song to tell us where she might have gone. An impossible song.

Ever notice how when people say you can't have something, that's when you start to want it most? Or how just the fact that something's known to be lost makes you utterly *determined* to find it?

Well . . . I did, I think.

And in a moment or so, I'm going to play it for all of you.

***

From: Morgan Henderson mlhenderson233@yahoo.co.uk
To: Ulee Schaw Creepgal1991@gmail.com
Re: YH Song Project, Report #1

Dear Ms. Schaw,

I've attached the itemized report for the first week of my investigation—you'll see I've discounted the first three hours as a gesture of good faith, since I reassured you in previous emails that I expected to be done well before this. I still believe a telephone conversation would be useful to us both, but I understand the time zone difficulties.

You'll also note that I've attached a second file; this is a transcript of an interview I had with an historian at a London college, someone who specializes in mediaeval music and the communities who fetishize it. You may or may not find it relevant to deciding whether to continue.

Regards,
Morgan Henderson

***

TRANSCRIPT P 2/3
MH/DR L BRAZDA, NEWCOMB COLLEGE 5/9/2024

LB (CONT'D): must understand, it is misleading to think of a "song" as a specific performance or arrangement. It is more useful to see a piece in terms of its, let us say, its DNA—its position in a line of descent, like a set of mitochondrial markers, connecting different versions to each other throughout age after age. In terms of the particular piece of music your client is looking for, there are works sharing its heritage in nearly every era since the Black Death, or even before. In Elizabethan England it was a drinking song called "The Dancing Girls". In Germany, during the Thirty Years' War, it was a funeral lament called "Sie legte morgens ihren Kopf hin", which means roughly, "She lay down her head in the morning". Then there's a nineteenth-century ragtime tune, sometimes credited erroneously to Scott Joplin, called "Putting On the Devil's Shoes".

And the line goes on, through Tin Pan Alley, some blues tunes from the '50s just before Elvis Presley hit it big, even samples in some music from the '80s and afterwards. Like a taproot system, underlying and connecting all the trees of the forest. One never simply "listens to music", Miss Henderson. Every song carries history with it. More than most people can, or will, ever know.

MH: And the folklore around it is part of this . . . this root system? This DNA?

LB: Well, yes, if you believe in that sort of thing. Many of my friends in the historical recovery communities do; others do not. I wish to stay friends with both groups, so I take no position.

MH: But you'd no doubt agree that the number of deaths and disappearances reported around performances of these songs is . . . atypical, if true.

LB: What is "typical", Miss Henderson? Music was doubtless playing in proximity to nearly any death or disaster in history. "Amazing Grace" is played at thousands of funerals every year. Is it cursed?

MH: That isn't an answer, exactly.

LB: No. It isn't, is it?

Echo Chamber

***

TRANSCRIPT: "THE WEAL", EP. 73 (*cont'd*)

DENNY: Our special guest today is sound engineer Mike Purvis, who I've invited in to, in his words, "fuck around with this track and see what we end up with." Say hi to everyone, Mike.

PURVIS: Hi to everyone, Mike.

DENNY: (LAUGHTER) Dude, you promised.

PURVIS: Yeah, I promise a lot of things.

DENNY: So I've heard. (LAUGHTER) Okay, enough banter. Tell us about exactly what you're going to do here.

PURVIS: Well, the first step is basically to start the song playing, then run it through what we call a separation filter, which should give us the ability to pare the song back to its, um . . . formative layers? Remove the ambience, the crowd sound, remove the instrumentation and/or looping level by level, remove the vocals, until we disclose whatever's at the bottom of everything.

DENNY: The ghost track. The EVP.

PURVIS: Yep, that's the one. You down?

DENNY: Always.

***

FINAL INTERVIEW WITH YSEULT HAIGHT, *Palimpsest* Magazine, August 2010 (unpublished, due to magazine going out of business in June of that year):

HAIGHT: There's a line in a song I like—"Kala," by Bill Laswell, from his album *City of Light*. It's about watching bodies being reduced to ash on a ghat in Varanasi, about giving up your flesh and embracing impermanence: *Once the breath goes out, it's fit to burn*. And this is something I've come to accept, as a singer, as a musician—that breath is the centre of human existence, not just physically, but creatively. Breath can heal and breath can harm. It allows you to manipulate other people's emotions—to soothe them, to seduce them, to enrage them, to provoke fear and confusion. When people talk about psychic vampirism, I truly believe what they're often actually talking about is this sort of vocal work. They just don't realize it.

INTERVIEWER: Like a cat sucking a baby's breath while it's asleep? Or like SIDS?

HAIGHT: You may very well laugh, and yet.

INTERVIEWER: Miss Haight, I'm not laughing.

HAIGHT: Aren't you? (PAUSE) It's been proven there are certain tones the mind finds extremely difficult to deal with, and while they're hard to reproduce vocally, it's not impossible. Throat singers do it, for example, especially in unison. Shamanistic meditation employs it as well; breath is used to invoke and evoke, to create a numinous, ritual state in which the performer convinces those around them that they're entering an alternate dimension where spirits might appear. At any rate, breath keeps you going, and at the end, it's all you have left. One last, long exhalation. That's why live performance is so important—because you're all sharing a breath, together. The crowd responds to you, and you respond to them, and something is created that otherwise would never exist except at that moment.

INTERVIEWER: So a song played live becomes a different song, is that what you're saying?

HAIGHT: *Part* of what I'm saying, yes. It becomes something that can only be understood in that exact context. Something impossible to reproduce, under any circumstances.

INTERVIEWER: You're not a fan of live recordings.

Echo Chamber

HAIGHT: No more than I'm a fan of bad taxidermy.

INTERVIEWER: Tell me about "Sheetshake."

HAIGHT: Ah yes. "Sheetshake" will be played once and once only, by design. What it becomes in that moment will be *very* interesting. And the rest . . . will be silence.

★★★

@mlhenderson found it

@Creepgal1991 the ep????

@mlhenderson obviously, yes

@Creepgal1991 holy shit dude how????

@mlhenderson contacted mike purvis's partner, as it happens

@mlhenderson he himself is in hospital, but the other gentleman was very helpful indeed

@Creepgal1991 in hospital?? why??

@mlhenderson some sort of mental breakdown, I believe. and exhaustion

@mlhenderson they found him in the mundiplex studio, passed out, marching fractures to both feet

@mlhenderson his partner says there've been surgeries scheduled

@mlhenderson attaching the .mp3 to my bill

@mlhenderson do tell me what you think, after

@Creepgal1991 thanks, will do!!!

@Creepgal1991 did mike say what happened to meander????

@mlhenderson miss denny? I believe not

@mlhenderson his partner says he hasn't said anything about anything, thus far

@Creepgal1991 but it's been like a year?!?!?

@mlhenderson even so

@Creepgal1991 well okay

@Creepgal1991 thanks again!!!!!

@Creepgal1991 ps

@Creepgal1991 did you listen???

@mlhenderson absolutely not

***

From: Creepgal1991@gmail.com
To: ross.puget@freihoeveninst.ca
Re: FOUND IT AND NOW I'M GONNA LISTEN

Hey man, just wanted to dash this off to you first, because I'm so! Excited!!!! (Sorry not sorry, back on my Zlennial bullshit again;)) Morgan was a trip, cleaned me out for sure, but it's gonna be worth it. And it's all because of you, you grumpy M-word you (I don't mean motherfucker;))).

Oh shit, my texts are beeping. Is that you????

***

@rpuget hey Ulee, yes it's me, hold off a minute PLEASE

@Creepgal1991 wtf????

Echo Chamber

@rpuget listen, you know how I know carra, right? You know why?

@Creepgal1991 freihoeven inst creepy shit yeah yeah

@Creepgal1991 fckin SO?!?

@rpuget Morgan got hold of me, she's worried about you

@rpuget and she doesn't GET worried so that worries me

@Creepgal1991 sweet I guess???

@rpuget SHUT UP ULEE

@rpuget MPs bf sent her his emails theres this stuff he and MD talked about beforehand about how MDs mom died of covid, she had COPD lived in a building full of people who wouldn't mask, MD thought YH maybe wanted to use the performance to cure herself but if she did it wouldntve worked because you can only use that place la grotte to cure others by sacrificing yourself ANYHOW ARE YOU LISTENING

@rpuget MD told MP wouldnt it be great if everyone who heard this could be rendered immune to or cured of covid and he said but one of us would have to disappear/die and she said shed be fine w/that so even if it only makes you dance til you pass out that doesn't sound like anything you want to hear man

@rpuget ulee

@rpuget ulee

. . .

. . .

@Creepgal1991 already pressed play sorry

***

TRANSCRIPT: "THE WEAL", EP. 73 (*cont'd*)

(MUSIC)
(BEAT)
(BREATH)
(VOICE)

Hmmmmmm
Hmmmmmm
Hmmmmm
Hmmmmm

In and out and round and round
In and out and round and round
Take away the young man take away the old
Every one in his degree

When you hear the music everyone must dance
The shaking of the sheets with me
Low and high together everyone must dance
The shaking of the sheets with me

Hmmmmm
Hmmmmm
Hmmmmm
Hmmmmm

In and out and in and out and innnn
and out and in and out and innnn
and round and round and round and round
and round and round and round and round

Adieu, farewell, earth's bliss;
This world uncertain is;
Fond are life's lustful joys;
Death proves them all but toys;
Rich men, trust not in wealth,
Gold cannot buy you health;
Physic himself must fade.
All things to end are made,

Echo Chamber

Brightness falls from the air;
Queens have died young and fair;
Dust hath closed Helen's eye.
Mount we unto the sky.
I am sick, I must die.
Lord, have mercy on us!

Hmmmmm Hmmmmm Hmmmmm Hmmmmmmmmmm

and in and out and innnn and round and in and out and innnn and
rrrrrrrounnnddddddd

As. ye. ar. Nou.
So. onc. vas. Ay.
As. Ay. am.
So. Sal. Ye. be.
Remembre. Man.
That. Thou. Mist. dei.

Hmmmm Hmmmm Hmmmm Hmmmm Hmmmmmmmmmm
mmmmmmmmmmmmmmmmmmmm

MEANDER: (UP UNDER) plagues, there's plagues all through
history, and every time a plague happens someone redoes the
song—disease to flesh as distortion is to sound, something that
changes it, sets it against itself, breaks it open, breaks it down. And
La Grotte, the cave is an echo chamber, reverberating—if if you
bend a note it becomes something else, in and out and round and
round and in and out and round and round, Pied Piper plague
legend, opening a door through a mountain through sound

(MUSIC, BEAT, BREATH, VOICE, UP OVER, TOGETHER)
Young
Old
High
Low
Shake
Shake
Shake
Shake

The breath the life the breath the spark the breath makes life keeps
life alive the spark nurtured the air consumed breathe out breathe
in breathe in breathe out

In for fuel and out to heal
Out for song the sound that fuels
The fire that burns away the weal
The weal the weal the weal the weallllllllllllllllllllllll

and at the moment of death we release the sound that lives forever
that moves forwards backwards into the spaces between all things
the vibrating nothing that makes up everything pure potential the
universal pulse an overlay a retuning a returning a trance a seizure
a frequency no human ears designed to hear

It makes you a receiver
It makes you a speaker
It makes you an echo chamber
The skull the skull the skull the skull
Open your jaws and let it come through
Open your jaws and speak

Channeling
Channeling
Channeling

The note the beat the beat the note the cut throat's note the skin
drum's beat

And break the skin wide open break the skywide opennnnnn the
skin the sky the sky the skin the skin the sky the sky the skin

Dance
Dance
Dance
Dance
Dance
DANCE
DANCE
DANCE

The Night Nurses
of Verdun

Gregg Stewart

Dear Sir,

Thank you for agreeing to read the enclosed journal. As I said on the phone, I am hesitant to part with it. You'll learn why soon enough—but first, please allow an old fool a long-overdue preamble.

I must tell you: in my youth, my Great-uncle Joseph was my favorite member of the family. He and his wife, my Great-aunt Roseline, would visit every Christmas Eve—only on that one night—arriving after dark and bearing gifts, ready for a celebration. They were a charismatic couple; my sisters and I could watch them dance for hours. Uncle Joe had met Roseline while in France during the First World War. We were fascinated by her, and intimidated by her beauty, all raven hair and coal-black eyes. Her English carried a slight French accent, which we mimicked for days after they left.

Aunt Roseline was all of five-foot-nothing, and soon as she and Uncle Joseph arrived, she would have me and my sisters stand back-to-back with her to discover who had surpassed her in height that year. She then awarded a Walking Liberty silver half-dollar to anyone taller than her—quite the treasure in those days.

Afterward, Uncle Joseph would gather us around the fire and tell the most fantastic stories about Saint Nick, elves, reindeer, and the wild country to the north. Each year his tales would differ, but he always cast my sisters and me as heroes who overcame impossible odds to save Christmas.

When morning came, they'd be gone, leaving us feeling like the best Christmas gift had slipped through our fingers. We'd whine as we unwrapped our presents, asking why they had to leave so soon. We never received a straight answer. And no matter how often I asked to visit them at their farmhouse in Red Lake, the reply was always the dreaded, "We'll see." Of course, we never went.

A week after Pearl Harbor, news reached us of Joseph and Roseline's disappearance. I was distraught, beyond consolation. The police had discovered their car half-submerged in an icy lake but never recovered their bodies.

The pain of their loss (and my fond memories of those Christmas Eves) faded as the years passed. By the time I was in my twenties, I'm ashamed to say I seldom gave them much thought. So it came as a great surprise when, upon my fortieth birthday in 1970, I received a letter from the Minnesota law firm of Drille & Boan stating they had discovered the will of Mr. Joseph Scanlon.

In it, I was named the sole inheritor of the Red Lake farm.

Eager as I was to visit at long last, I regret it took me months before I could find the time to venture from my home in Chicago to meet with Mr. Drille. Once there, I was unsure what to do with it. To say it was a disappointment would be an understatement. The place was in utter disrepair. The roof seemed ready to cave, and vandals had painted every window black. Mr. Drille advised that I take a few days to remove any personal effects before selling the property. I agreed.

Over three days, I scrounged through what scarce items remained: mostly moth-eaten clothes, tarnished flatware, cracked dishes, and a varied selection of mildewed books. Perusing the bookshelf, I found a peculiar journal handwritten by my Great-uncle. The year was 1916, and the U.S. had yet to join the Great War, but young Joseph Scanlon believed he had a role to play in an Allied victory, so he went to fight alongside the French. He was nineteen.

Given this journal's strange contents, I've endeavored to keep it secret for over fifty years. However: last week, I came upon my old Walking Liberty silver half-dollar, and seeing it made me reconsider the price of keeping such a thing hidden. I turned ninety-four this past October. As I contemplate this final chapter, I realize there are circumstances where secrets help no one. The truth must come out in the end, for better or worse.

And so, what follows is either the ramblings of a young man trying to cope with death all around him or perhaps they are simply a fantasy he created to distract and entertain his comrades. He was my favorite storyteller, after all.

Or maybe they are something more sinister. I leave you to decide.

Whatever the case, please understand that the following pages contain my Great-uncle's words precisely as he wrote them. I cannot fathom how you may perceive them, but here they are, as I said—for better or worse.

Sheridan Scanlon, Christmas Eve, 2023

Tuesday, 26th of September 1916

I have traveled for five weeks across the French countryside, and in that time, I have learned a thing or two of war. It is brutal and tragic, and although I understood this before I arrived, the proof is in my bones now. Still, nothing could have prepared me for my first sighting of *Verdun-sur-Meuse*. It is, with all sincerity, a Hell no sane mind could conjure in a thousand nightmares.

I came to Paris to enlist and aid the French in their long struggle to rid themselves of German occupation. I fear I may have arrived too late.

Gregg Stewart

My Irish father thinks me insane to travel so far for a fight that is not mine, though deep down, I believe him proud to have raised a son who follows his convictions. My French mother tells me she respects my passion for defending my ancestral homeland, but I know the truth: she thinks me insane. I hope the U.S. enters this war soon, and that I am one of many Americans who will join the fight for peace. Only time will tell whether my hope bears fruit.

The battle here in Verdun began in late February and now rages for over two hundred days. Until I witnessed it, I could not imagine a single battle lasting so long, but the results are clear: Entire villages reduced to rubble, with no evidence that there had ever been standing structures, let alone inhabitants. To my eyes, it seems as if Death has wormed his way into every corner of the land. Seeing it repulses me as much as it hardens my resolve.

Upon my arrival at Verdun, I reported bleary-eyed to my duty officer, who promptly handed me as much ammunition as they could spare and sent me off to this ragged trench, which is little more than a muddy divot. I must lay flat to keep my head below the line of fire. Having grown up on a farm, I may speak plainly when I say there is a level of filth here no living person should witness, let alone live amongst. My French compatriots have taken to shoving garlic cloves up their noses to stave off the stench and combat 'other things.'

Those were their words, though I am unsure if I have the translation correct. I would be stuffing my nose with garlic too, were I not allergic to the stuff.

These brave Frenchmen and their Moroccan brothers-in-arms have been stationed here in three-week rotations for the past few months. They are ghosts, withered fractions of the vital young men they once were. And yet, their gazes pass through me as if *I* was the specter, not they.

Once I'd settled into my mud hole, it did not take long for curiosity to get the better of me. Peering over the ledge to survey the battlefield, I discovered a mile-long stretch of brown mud, blackened detritus, and pale dead bodies heaped in all manner of repose and decay. They say four-thousand men die at Verdun every day. The number was incomprehensible until I stared, mouth agape, at this battlefield. My reward for such fool's courage was a German bullet whizzing past, mere inches from my face. I ducked down, bile rising in my throat, and quickly learned these ghosts were at least capable of some emotion. They snickered at my idiocy.

"Ne refais plus ça," the soldier next to me murmured. My cheeks reddened, feeling every inch the neophyte I am. We are in accord, my friend. I won't be doing that again.

I lay here now, considering that dark sea of corpses. What kind of vermin does so much death attract? What will they do with all those bodies?

Worse, what if some still live out there? Who will help them?

On my way to Verdun, I learned that all this death rests at the feet of one man: the German General Erich von Falkenhayn. He is the architect of this onslaught, this war of attrition. He has commanded his troops to 'Bleed France White.' Though I can appreciate this phrase's multi-layered meaning—the bloodless bodies and the flag of surrender—I cannot comprehend how a man, any man, could view such an unfathomable death toll as anything but apocalyptic.

It is why we must be victorious. We *must* drive the Germans out and restore France to its dignity.

Truly, we are fighting the war to end all wars.

Dusk is settling, and I am losing the light. My eyesight grows weary, so I will set down my pen and step off my soapbox. I should rest. I am unclear if our fight commences again tonight or at daybreak. If this journal contains this first entry and nothing more, know that I endeavored to serve here with honor.

Thursday, 28th of September

The constant thrum of bullets has been ringing in my ears for two days straight. Shooting. Shooting. More shooting. This is my life now. At least I may count myself among the living.

I have no appetite for the slop they bring around, and though I know I should eat, I must instead write down the small piece of good fortune that blessed my weary soul earlier today while I still have enough light to write.

Will Carson is here. I am proud to say he's joined the American Field Service as an ambulance driver. At last, America is doing something! My eyes scarcely believed the sight of my former chemistry lab partner. I am pleased to have someone here who knows me from my old life. And yet, I am dismayed that anyone I care for might also be experiencing this Hell on earth.

Still, joy has won the day. When I saw Will, I set down my rifle and took him up in my arms, tears pricking the corners of my eyes. At first, I feared he did not recognize me—I've grown thin and worn as an old apron—but I held onto him until, at last, he whispered my name. I nodded into his shoulder, and he squeezed me with all his might. *Oh, to be held.* I will treasure this small kindness for all my days. When I released him, his cheeks were wet too, and we laughed.
I thought I might never laugh again, but if Verdun has taught me one thing, you grab the joy when you find it, even the tiniest speck. Grip it and hold tight.

Will showed me a letter he received last month from his brother, Bobby. In it, the boy spoke of milk cows, the new Appaloosa foal, Fourth of July fireworks, and a detailed account of every frog he caught that summer. It was an ordinary tale—mundane in every way. I read it aloud over and again as if reciting Holy Scripture. Will sat beside me, listening, and hiding more tears. By the third reading, we'd had all we could bear. I carefully folded the letter, placing my lips to the envelope before returning it.

Will Carson is a good man and a kind friend, and I am so grateful he is here.

I fear all this talk of tears makes us appear weaklings and

softhearted fools. We are not. It is merely the effects of this place, with Death's hand hovering over us day and night. It does something to a man. Your nerves are at their rawest edges; they scratch against your feelings until you cannot control your outbursts. It is why the soldiers who have spent any extended time here are all but ghosts. They've had to dull their senses to endure the sight of so much killing.

If I survive my time here, I expect to spend my remaining days remembering how to feel again.

Monday, 1st of October

It is late, with scant light to write by, so please forgive my poor penmanship. A few moments ago, there were sounds on the battlefield, something akin to a pack of wolves—snarling, biting, slurping sounds—and perhaps my ears deceived me, but I thought I heard stifled screams.

I had wondered about scavengers the bodies would attract. *Could it be wolves?* When I found the courage to peer over the edge of my mud hole, two women in white were carrying a soldier in a stretcher between them, silhouetted against the smoky grey and purple sky. No wolves. Just two of the bravest, most courageous women I had ever seen. There are rumors both the male and female French nurses are of strong mind and body, but I am in awe. The moment I saw them, it was as if I were gazing upon beauty itself amongst a vast sea of ugliness, and I knew at once I must mark this first sighting in my journal.

We live in a time when women must also witness the terrible aftermath of battle. I am not ashamed to say that within me lies a protective instinct, a belief that I may shield these women from so much destruction. I am a fool, I know. To find them enduring their roles with more strength and perseverance than us menfolk has left me humbled.

I want to meet these women. My French is still abysmal, but if I could tell them how much their compassion and courage meant and how it inspired me, it would provide a small solace. That these women would risk their lives in the dead of night to attempt to save any of us moves me to my core. On this night, I bow my head to the brave nurses of France, and I pray for their safety.

Friday, 6th of October

After a week of bloodshed, I am stunned to discover myself among the living. All around me, men have fought and died, and somehow, I remain to fight another day.

Am I blessed or cursed? I cannot say.

The strain caused me to do a fool thing last night—a stupid thing.

I'd heard the wolves again. And whether they were real or imagined, I cannot say, but when I scanned the battlefield, I spied those two nurses in white again. I'm unsure if it was exhaustion or insanity that drove me to it, but I climbed from my mud divot and strode toward them, unconscious of any danger, like a sleepwalker with his head in the icebox.

The women hesitated, their eyes wide with concern at my arrival, but they did not set down the empty stretcher. I waved, like an idiot, realizing as I did it that they couldn't wave back and did not wish to risk speaking. The taller one cocked her head in confusion, but the shorter one giggled at the sight of me waving. The taller woman shot her a disdainful look, and the petite nurse turned away, biting her lip to suppress more laughter.

I whispered the words the French soldiers had taught me: *"Tes beaux culs m'inspirent,"* and their eyes went even wider. I assumed my accent must be off, so I repeated the phrase in English:

"Parles tu anglais? I mean to say, your bravery inspires me."

At this, the short one burst with laughter, speaking in a flurry of French to the other. Now they were both snickering. I asked what I'd said.

"Ah, you Americans," she replied, her English near flawless. "Such a source of entertainment."

The Night Nurses of Verdun

I grinned like a schoolboy and tipped my helmet, unsure of what I'd done or said. The taller woman whispered something in French, and the shorter spoke in a low hush, telling me it was too dangerous for me to be there. "Please, you must return to the line. As much as we enjoy your company, we have much work this night."

I returned to my post feeling elated that she claimed to enjoy my company. She was being polite, of course, but I am nonetheless smitten. As I dipped into my mud hole, she whispered into the misty night, *"Bonne nuit, douce Americaine."*

I promised myself I would meet her again, whatever it took.

Monday, 9th of October

The fighting is relentless these past few days, so I must be brief. I saw Will Carson today. His father, Governor Carson, is pressuring him to come home, but he is resolved to not abandon the French. I applaud his courage. I mentioned the brave French nurses, and he agreed he'd also witnessed their daring. But, when I spoke of their beauty, he stopped me cold.

He tells me no female nurses are at Verdun. I tell him he is wrong. He shakes his head, unsure, and now I am skeptical. Was I hallucinating? Dreaming? With every inch we gain in this fight, have I lost an inch of my sanity along the way?

I must locate these nurses. I must confirm their existence before I go mad.

Sunday, 15th of October

Her name is Roseline Argonne, and she is most assuredly a female and a nurse. She was a resident of Douaumont, a village close to Verdun, until earlier this year. All memory of it is gone now. When German forces razed it to the ground, she and her sister, Vivienne, fled to the Argonne, living in the forest and 'scavenging for their sustenance,' as she calls it. Who knows what they were living on? Berries? Rats? I shudder at the thought.

Gregg Stewart

When French troops discovered the women, they tried to ship them to Paris, but Roseline and her sister chose to stay behind to enlist in the war effort.

I have learned these details over the past week. We have been meeting in short bursts under cover of night at the edge of the woods. She tells me of a tiny cabin in the forest where they keep themselves hidden from the Germans. At night, they scour the battlefield for any who still breathe, taking them to the ambulance drivers or, more often, to the field hospital, almost a full kilometer behind the front line. I marvel that she can carry a grown man such a distance, and she smiles and flexes her petite arm in reply.

I ask if she knows Will Carson, and she shakes her head. She says Vivienne does not like her speaking to the men, ever. I ask why she talks to me. Her reply is mysterious.

She pulls an American silver half-dollar from her pocket, a Walking Liberty coin. I do not know who gave it to her or where she found it. She says it's her most revered treasure, one of her last remaining items of value after the bombings.

She tells me I walked like the woman on the coin when I first approached. I laugh, then realize she is serious. I ask if she thinks I walk like a woman. She says I walk like a liberator.

"France desperately needs liberation," she tells me. "I know why you are here, Joe, and I feel sure I can trust you." She leans in, and her lips caress my cheek. A rush of warmth courses through my veins, and I close my eyes to keep from keeling over.

When I open them, she has vanished.

I cannot tell if it is insomnia, duress, or creeping madness, but I think I am falling in love. So much for my concerns about never feeling anything again.

Is it fair that I find love in such a place? Shouldn't I be more concerned with other things? Why does she consume my imagination and spark such strong emotions in me? Her smile, her laughter—did I mention she speaks *six languages?* I have never met another person like her. Whenever I am near her, I fight the urge to take her in my arms and never let go. Thus far, I have resisted humiliating myself with these boorish urges, but I am unsure how much longer I may hold out. The way she looks at me. Her dark, almost black eyes pierce my heart. The shape of her lips begs for kissing.

My God, this is folly! I must get ahold of myself. We have our duties to uphold. Roseline is here to save men while I drive off our shared enemy. I cannot spend my time at war waxing poetic about a French girl living in the forest. It is pure fantasy. And yet . . .

Oh, Roseline. You have given me the will to live through this nightmare. You are my rainbow at the end of this storm. When this war is over, if I am lucky enough to survive it, I will live in France and never return home if it means staying by your side.

Wednesday, 18th of October

It has been a bloody few days, leaving no time for writing or late-night rendezvous. My thoughts drift to Roseline whenever there is a break in the fighting. I scan the battlefield at night for signs but have yet to see her silhouette against the purple midnight sky. I pray for her and Vivienne's safety. I pray for myself and my comrades.

We may grow paler but not yet white with surrender. Never. We will fight on.

Thursday, 19th of October

It is early morning, and I am unsure I should write what I have seen this night. I fear it may be proof I have lost my senses. I have my duties and cannot allow madness to waylay me. Still, if I do not write it down, I fear I may convince myself I dreamt it all, and I am very much awake.

It began with those same unnerving wolf-sounds—biting, ripping, slurping—with stifled screams coming now and again. My heart raced. Was something feeding upon innocent men injured on the battlefield? I squinted into the darkness, raising my rifle to fire upon the first wild dog I encountered. My curiosity will be the death of me, I know, but I stepped out of the trench and into the foggy night, hoping to find the source of those gut-churning noises.

As I walked closer, the sounds abruptly stopped. Peering into the haze, I saw the silhouettes of two people entwined. So, not a wolf— yet I am aghast. The woman crouched over the man's prone body, her face buried in his neck. Were they . . . *copulating* on the battlefield? Had a soldier snuck some harlot out here for privacy among the dead? I had never considered such depravity, and I am not ashamed to admit the sight made me queasy.

Still, it was not my place to reprimand them for their indecency, so I retreated a step to leave them to it. That's when the harlot looked up to find me standing not twenty paces away. She was white as death. Blood covered her mouth and lips, dripping onto the man's prone body. She wiped her mouth with the back of her hand, leaving a crimson smear across her cheek as she bared white fangs. Acting on pure instinct, I raised my rifle—and shot the woman in the chest.

She reeled, falling on the muddy ground.

I ran.

The mere sight of this monster ignited such fear in me that I bolted like an alley cat until I was diving into my mud hole, covering my eyes like a child in the throes of a nightmare. It was then that the woman's face became clear.

Vivienne.

Roseline's sister.

The folktales of my youth flooded my mind. Soon after, memories of my meetings with Roseline pierced my fractured psyche.

The Night Nurses of Verdun

I have never seen her during daylight hours.

I have yet to witness her eat a bite of food.

She has unnatural strength.

She casts an allure upon me that I cannot explain.

She speaks six languages with fluency. How does a twenty-two-year-old from the remote countryside learn six languages?

She lives deep in the forest and once said she 'scavenged for sustenance.' Could she have meant blood? Men? I scan my writings, hunting for clues, and find my questions about 'the vermin such a battlefield might attract.' I consider the four thousand men who die here each day and the gallons upon gallons of warm blood spilling onto the ground. How far does the scent of it travel? Are Roseline and her so-called sister even *from* Douaumont? Telling people you are from a ghost village with no other survivors is a convenient story.

No matter how much I try to explain away tonight's encounter—it *wasn't* Vivienne, it *wasn't* blood, it was a mere trick of the fog, I didn't shoot her—my mind reaches the same conclusion.

I lay with my heart pounding in my ears, breathing like a fish yanked from the lake. A cold sweat runs along my spine, and my hands are too clammy to continue writing. Oh, dear God.

Roseline, my love, *what are you?*

Saturday, 21st of October

Last evening, as battle waned, I made my way into the forest. The moment I stepped through the thicket of trees, it became clear I was somewhere I shouldn't be. Still, I had to find Roseline. She had mentioned their cabin deep in the woods, and so I made my way on instinct alone, hoping I might stumble upon the place.

It was like searching for Ol' Snapper, the famed giant turtle of Red

Gregg Stewart

Lake. As a young boy, I hunted him every year. At the start of summer, some kid would claim to have seen him, and off we'd run to capture the famed beast and claim immortality.

We never found him. I often wonder if he even existed.

The feeling returns as I step through the woods, recalling Will Carson's firm belief that there are no female nurses at Verdun. Had Roseline and Vivienne been dressing in stolen nurses' outfits and carting men to their lair? My blood runs cold at the thought.

Had Vivienne survived the bullet wound? I grow colder still.

There are no birdcalls in this forest, only the echoes of mortar fire in the distance and the close crackle of dead leaves under my boots. I peer into the dense foliage and discover a dilapidated structure. I hesitate, reconsidering my plan. What if Roseline is in there? What will I do?

A snapping twig causes me to spin on my heel. A German soldier stands not thirty paces off. I leap to the ground as he raises his rifle and shoots, screaming the alarm to his comrades. With no chance of taking them all on, I jump up and dash for the cabin.

The door is locked, but I force it open, slamming it shut behind me. I peer into the darkness, hoping for something to crouch behind and better defend myself should these soldiers find my hiding spot. Inside, a macabre setting greets my tired eyes. Spider webs fill the dark corners, and debris covers the dirt floor. Two coffins sit in the far corner, and I shudder. One is open. I peer in to find it empty. As for the other coffin, I am too afraid to disturb the lid and look inside. Instead, I hunker down behind it, panting like a fox. The German hounds bark at one another outside the cabin in what sounds like an argument. I wait an eternity until their heavy footsteps march away.

By nightfall, I have crouched so long in my hiding place that exhaustion overtakes me. When I awaken, the lid of the second coffin is open. In the dim moonlight, my shaking hand reaches inside, and my fingertips brush the bottom of the empty casket.

The Night Nurses of Verdun

Bringing them to my nose, I breathe in Roseline's unmistakable scent and fall to my knees.

As I leave the forest under cover of starlight, I consider all I have discovered. My love, how do I reconcile this reality? I am enraged by your deception, repulsed by your truth, yet I remain in love with you beyond all reason.

How will I ever explain these feelings? What has become of me?

Sunday, 22nd of October

Dearest Roseline, you have taught me my greatest lesson: I came to liberate, but instead, I have learned I must submit. No matter what you are, I love you. I cannot pretend otherwise. And so, I raise my white flag to you. I surrender.

Monday, 23rd of October

I spoke with her tonight. At first, she was wary of my questions, but she confessed all when I reminded her that she trusted me and that I would never betray her.

First, she is *not* from Douaumont. She was born in Brittany. When she and Vivienne were first transformed, they lived in The Netherlands. At the time, the Dutch were fighting for their independence from Spain. The history books call it the Eighty Years War, which commenced in 1568, making Roseline and her sister three-and-a-half centuries old.

Fields of battle offer a convenient food source for her kind. When the war ended, the two women traveled to England for the Great Rebellion, and after that, to Belgium for the War of Devolution. On it went, and forgive me, but there have been too many wars to keep track of her whereabouts. The tragedies that haunt me in Verdun are nothing new to her. In truth, humans have been killing one another by the thousands for a long, long time. Throughout the ages, her kind has picked clean our atrocities in the dead of night.

She insists they have never murdered a soul, and I quote:

<h1 style="text-align:center">Gregg Stewart</h1>

"If anything, we have helped ease the suffering of dying men."

I believe her.

As she finishes her tale, Roseline breaks down, sharing that she cannot find Vivienne. She feels lost without her sister. They have been side-by-side for longer than any two alive today. Is alive even the right word?

My blood turns icy as I consider the lie I must tell her. It will not take Roseline long to realize my questions do not come out of thin air. She will surmise I discovered her true nature before confronting her. And since I did not learn it from her, she will conclude I heard it from Vivienne.

As my mind races, her dark eyes narrow. She asks if I've seen her sister. My mouth goes dry, and my mind goes blank. The only recurring thought is the certainty that she will hate me once she hears the truth, and I will lose her forever.

It takes all my resolve to open my journal and read the entry from the night I last saw Vivienne. Without a breath, the words pour from my mouth. I speak to her as if from the bottom of a deep well. Like a broken floodgate, I drown her world.

Before I finish, she is up and running. She moves like a panther, disappearing into the forest, and is gone before I can pursue. I consider heading for the cabin but fear I may lose my way again. No. I have lost her. I must accept it. I was a fool to believe I would survive this war.

Tomorrow we plan to retake Fort Douaumont. I must rest and be ready.

Tuesday, 24th of October

I am dying. Please tell her that I

The Night Nurses of Verdun

Monday, 13th of November

Today is the first time I have felt strong enough to write, and there is much to tell.

The doctors expect me to make a full recovery—provided there is no gangrene. I have suffered a bayonet and bullet wound—stabbed in my left shoulder and shot in my left thigh. I do not recommend getting shot or stabbed, but if you ever find yourself in that unfortunate situation, it is best when they miss the vital organs in your torso and head.

What I mean to say is: I am lucky.

I am also thankful the medical staff here removed the bullet and saved my leg, though they say it may be weeks before I stand and months before I walk without limping.

I have but three hazy memories between the battle to retake Fort Douaumont on October 24th and the evening of November 2nd, when I awoke to the cheers at retaking Fort Vaux and found myself in this field hospital.

First, I remember lying in pain, waiting to die, with no recollection of how my injuries occurred.

Second, the face of Will Carson came into view. He pulled me into the ambulance and assured me I would survive, though I could not be sure if it was him or a hallucination.

Third, and this is important—Roseline at my bedside, crying and whispering, "Please, please, I cannot lose you too."

Wednesday, 15th of November

She came to me again last night. Her joy at finding me awake and alive almost made up for the tragic news I had received earlier that day. There are not one but two catastrophic events I must endure. Either might have broken me, so I feel sure I cannot survive both.

Gregg Stewart

First, the French Army has decided to ship me home. They plan to award me a medal for my courage, but they do not have the funds or resources to rehabilitate an American expatriate here.

Second, I received news that Will Carson was shot and killed while carrying wounded soldiers off the battlefield. I never had the chance to thank him for saving my life.

With his father's political influence, they are shipping Will's body home for burial on U.S. soil at an exorbitant expense. Why do I return home, celebrated as a hero, while Will travels in a coffin? I cannot make sense of such injustice.

Roseline holds me close as I share the news. The idea of being separated from her by an ocean leaves me grief-stricken. I want to ask if I may rehabilitate in Paris. I'm sure it would be possible. I begged her to come to the city, promising to protect her from daylight and keep her safe. Once I recover, I will find work. We would be together.

As I share this folly, her eyes tell me Paris might as well be Minnesota. I am lost. But my fractured mind hatches an impossible plan—a way she may travel to Red Lake to be together.

She refuses outright, telling me I cannot give her what she needs. I ask if she means blood. She answers with a look, sending shivers through me. I will find a way. I swear it to her, then ask if it would pain her to watch me grow old.

She says I may not have to, and her dark eyes chill my soul.

I beg Roseline to do what I ask. I promise I will come for her.

When she leaves, I am unsure if she will do it.

Friday, 17th of November

I leave Verdun this afternoon. The fight is not over for France, but it is for me.

The Night Nurses of Verdun

I pray for the brave men and women I have met here. I also pray for the Germans. May they soon see reason and end this useless bloodshed. I am sorry I could not do more.

Roseline has yet to return. My heart is an empty, broken battlefield.

Monday, 22nd of November

I am on a ship in rough Atlantic seas. They tell me I will be home by Christmas. I look forward to being with my family. I do hope my father received my letter.

Wednesday, 4th of December

My body shakes with so much joy that I can barely write!

Upon arriving in New York, I discovered a note tucked into my jacket pocket. 'Promise you WILL come for me.' It is her writing.

She has done it! I know what this means and what I must do. Upon my return, I will promptly pay my respects to the Carson family.

Saturday, 23rd of December

The night was cold and moonless as I hobbled off the bus at the Oklee station. My family waited there for me, bursting with excitement, more alive than I may ever be again. My safe return has eased their anxiety, though my mother cried the whole drive home. My escapades have been torturous upon them. I will endeavor to stay put now that I've returned.

I am pleased to say my father received my letter, and with the small sum I've kept in savings, he has purchased a humble farmhouse near Red Lake Falls on my behalf.

Dr. Baldridge, head physician at the Shady Grove home for the elderly and infirmed, has agreed to hire me, honored to have a returning war hero on his staff. I don't consider myself a hero, but I'm grateful for the opportunity and relieved at what it means for Roseline.

Gregg Stewart

Sunday, 24th of December

Earlier today, I paid my respects at the Carson home. Bobby took me to his brother's grave where I wept tears of sorrow and joy.

Will Carson—thank you for saving my life, not once but twice. I hope your spirit forgives me for what I have done. I will miss you, friend.

Roseline, I am here. Tonight I return with a shovel and crowbar to bring you home.

Monday, 25th of December

It's Christmas morning and the first day of the rest of our lives. Roseline is beside me under heavy blankets in our basement, where no light may find us. I want to keep holding her, to stay here forever, just as we are. Roseline tells me how much she loves the farmhouse. I tell her how much I love that she's here with me.

My memories of last night are a hazy dream this morning. My body aches and my limbs burn after so much digging in the frost-covered ground. But all that pain is gone now. The moment I forced open the casket—with the yearning of a pirate unearthing buried treasure and the wonderment of a grinning boy on Christmas morning—I knew my life would never be the same.

I found her in the coffin, curled beside Will's decaying body. I admit, for a moment, seeing her body so close to his—and knowing her mouth was on his neck for weeks—sent pangs of jealousy through me. But the second she opened her eyes and looked upon me with so much love and longing, I swore I would be hers for all eternity.

My love, I will make a life for us. I swear it. Tomorrow, I begin my new job as the night clerk at Shady Grove, less than a mile down the road. I hope it will be enough to sustain us.

If not, we can always find another war.

Family Dirt

Justin Allec

Saturday, May 28, 2022, 09:27

To: Cons. Miriam Fortune, m.fortune@on.rcmp.ca
From: Flo Martinez, fmartinez@martinezfamilylaw.ca
Subject: Whitley family, others missing

Hello, Cons. Fortune,

I am writing to supply additional details and documentation to the missing person's reports for Samantha Halford (#0032589-12), Jack Whitley (#0032588-35), and Douglas Eustance (#0032544-25).

As has been established by your office with assistance from the Thunder Bay Police, the actions of Jack Whitley are believed to be directly responsible for the horrifying medical conditions of his ex-wife, Lana Halford, and her two children, as well the subsequent disappearance of Samantha Halford, Lana's sister.

In the supplied documents, you'll see the origins of this present situation began on Monday, April 11, 2022. This day marked the first recorded conflict between the ex-spouses as they exchanged custody of their children, Tracy (10) and Aron (8). The next significant date would be Wednesday, May 11, 2022, when Lana was found unconscious in the Cascades parking lot and Samantha was reported missing.

After Thunder Bay Police concluded their search on May 18, I contacted Mr. Eustance for assistance. As you are aware, Jack and Mr. Eustance, employees of Cobalt Mining, had attempted to survey the Cascades wilderness area during the spring and summer of 2021. I hired Mr. Eustance due to his knowledge of the area and familiarity with Jack; his last message to me was on May 24, 2022. Two days later, on May 26, 2022, suspecting Mr. Eustance was also missing, I decided to file another missing person's report.

I have included relevant documents to illustrate the movements of all involved family members and possibly provide some clues as to Jack's motivations or how his actions touched his ex-spouse, children, and Samantha. Most of these are transcripts from the MyFamilyTracker app, which Jack and Lana agreed to use as their primary mode of communication following their divorce proceedings in the fall of 2021, but they also include texts from Samantha forwarded to my office and all relevant emails.

Given the circumstances and the ongoing national attention, I fear the worst for Ms. Samantha Halford, Mr. Whitley, and Mr. Eustance, and hope that these materials may assist your team in the ongoing search of the Cascades.

I feel it is also worth conveying that the divorce, though initiated by Ms. Lana Halford in August of 2021, was fairly amicable in all areas, including the issues of child support and shared child custody. At no point during the divorce did Lana, the children, or Jack make any reference to any harmful practices or what could be considered abuse. The couple had cited 'irreconcilable differences as their reason for dissolution. In fact, I had mostly dismissed the case from my mind, the rare proceeding that left both parties satisfied, until I received a letter of concern from Lana on Tuesday, April 12.

I look forward to hearing from you.

Sincerely,
Flo Martinez, B.A. (Hons.), J.D.
Martinez Family Law

Family Dirt

Thursday, April 7, 2022, 19:22

Jack Whitley (807-415-3780) to Lana Halford (807-541-0236)

Jack: Checking that Aron is OK to read this Iron Man comic? I thought u didn't like those?

Lana: Its OK. I checked that 1. Not 2 much fighting but A is getting older. Its OK to see some violence sometimes. We talked context.

Jack: OK sounds good.

Lana: OK, see you Mon

Jack: OK

Friday, April 8, 2022, 08:30

Lana: FYI I'm going to Sam's camp Sat nite so I'll be out of reach. Just overnight.

Jack: OK have fun say hi

Lana: I'll grab the kids at 6 on Monday as usual. Are u taking the kids hiking this weekend?

Lana: Supposed to be cold. Still snow out there?

Lana: Oh—pls throw out those weird dental-floss toothpicks. Dr Early said theyre getting plaque bc they rn't flossing. YOU'll have to help them do it or just do it.

Jack: Can do about the floss. Yes to hiking—that trail N of Cascades is dry. We'll pack lots—make Tracy wear her toque. No camping b4 u ask—haha. Have a fire, lunch, maybe fish.

Jack: Hey wait.

Jack: Was dentist on my benefits? Ur supposed to let me KNOW if ur going to be filing claims. Your check ring a bell??

Lana: I paid for the dentist with THIER money and yes on your benefits bc theyre still covered. ~~DON'T tell me how to do the $$$ I know what I'm doing~~ (tone suggestions: thank you for reminding me / I had considered that / I wasn't going to bother you). Thank U for reminding me. Check the Expenses tab when u get home—you'll see what I did.

Monday, April 11, 2022, 09:15

Alphonse Chambers Elementary (807-665-6894) to Lana Halford (807-541-0236)

"Good day, this is an automated recording due to one or more children registered to this number being ABSENT for the day of Monday, April 11, 2022. Thank you for your time."

09:16

Lana: Jack the school called why r the kids absent today?

Lana: Is someone sick?

Lana: Jack?? Your voicemail is turned off.

Lana: Jack I tried calling where r you with the kids?

10:11

Lana: OK Jack just checking for you and the kids

Lana: Can you call me pls I'm worried

18:35

Lana: Where r u?

Lana: Its past 6

Lana: I'm here at your house

Family Dirt

Lana: Where r u?

Lana: JACK

Lana: WHERE ARE MY KIDS? WHERE ARE YOU???? (tone suggestions: I'm a bit concerned I haven't heard from you / could you tell me where you have been)

23:30

From: Lana Halford, lhalford807@gmail.com
To: Flo Martin, fmartinez@martinezfamilylaw.com
Subject: Agreement break? Already??

Flo, just wanting to check on something with the agreement, as I'm pretty sure it was covered but I'm not sure what to do about it.

Ok, so the long story is that I got a call from the school this morning saying that either Aron or Tracy were absent. I texted Jack right away but got no response. Tried calling but he wasn't picking up and his voicemail was turned off. I had to go to work so really only got a chance to try calling him at lunch, no answer again.

I went to pick the kids up on Monday evening. I reached Jack's place and they weren't home. I was there at six as per the agreement—I even took a video of myself checking to see if anyone was home. But the driveway was empty and no one answered the door. I messaged him right away to see what was happening. No reply.

We had texted Friday and had been a bit tense. I'm doing better at keeping my tone even to him (the tone suggestions help) though I still seem to need reminders when I see him in person. It's just that smug look on his face when the kids go to him. They're not excited to see him.
Anyway, closer to seven he finally pulled into the driveway. The kids were in the back, they were dirty, wet, and exhausted. Apparently, Jack had kept them out of school that day to take them hiking. For the third day in a row. They had been hiking every day

that weekend, spending all day on the trails north of the Cascades. He's taken them hiking before, but this sounded like some kind of marathon.

Also, nothing was packed up or ready for me to take. Their backpacks still had Friday's lunch. No homework done either. All the clothes were dirty.

We had a shouting match. I'm not proud to say that, but I'm worried that he made them miss school and that nothing was ready. We've barely got this agreement in place and he's already starting to break it. And I'm worried about what they were doing out there.

Please let me know,

Lana

Tuesday, April 12, 2022, 11:54

From: Flo Martin, fmartinez@martinezfamilylaw.com
To: Lana Halford, lhalford807@gmail.com
Re: Agreement break? Already??

Hi Lana, thanks for reaching out. I agree: that does sound like a cause for concern, and it does fall within the purview of your agreement with Jack. School is a very important part of the stability of Tracy and Aron's lives; we're trying to maintain that. As per sec.07, para.12:

- *HALFORD and WHITLEY shall ensure that Tracy WHITLEY and Aron WHITLEY attend every regularly scheduled school day. Exceptions for attending regularly scheduled school days shall be made through arrangements using the MyFamilyTracker at a minimum of two weeks (14 days) prior to the premeditated absence. As well, this absence shall only occur if both HALFORD and WHITLEY agree.*

So, pretty clear, Lana. He didn't ask you permission, certainly not two weeks prior, so yes, he's in violation of the agreement. There's additional language in sec.03, para. 1 to 7 that details the conditions Jack needs to meet and yes, clean laundry and homework relate to that section.

Remember: he signed the papers, which means that he supports the agreement, which means that he needs to hold up his end.

As for the hiking, it might be a concern if the kids were getting hurt. Tired, okay, but exercise and being outdoors aren't enough to raise an alarm. If they're similarly exhausted after his next weekend (April 23—24), please discuss some alternate activities with him for the kids. It's within your rights to make suggestions.

The fact that Jack decided to self-represent means I'm somewhat hands-off until the situation escalates, and I do have some vacation coming up. Unfortunately, there isn't much else we can do at this time except observe, record, and report. Keep all your texting to the MyFamilyTracker. Take photos of the kids when you exchange custody. We need to establish a pattern of Jack's new behaviours that will work in favour of you and the kids. Please keep me informed.

Sincerely,
Flo Martinez, B.A. (Hons.), J.D.
Martinez Family Law

Sunday, April 17, 2022, 14:23

Lana Halford (807-541-0236) to Jack Whitley (807-415-3780)

Lana: R u planning more hiking next weekend when u have the kids?

Jack: Depends on weather.

Lana: Right. I've set up a playdate 4 kids w/ Marigold kids for next Sun, 10am. Their house. U remember address from Toby M's birthday?

Jack: . . .

Lana: What is it?

Lana: Stan Marigold 807-897-5517, 246 Rydway Ave

Lana: They need 2 see their friends. They're at a social age. Don't want to hang our w/ mom and dad all the time. We can talk tomorrow when I drop them off.

Sunday, April 24, 2022, 06:23

Jack Whitley (807-415-3780) to Stan Marigold (807-897-5517)

"Um, good morning, hello, sorry about the hour, but, ah . . . this is Jack, Tracy and Aron's dad. FYI the kids won't be able to make it today—Tracy's been up all night. Sick. Just to be safe I'm going to keep them home. I guess you can make some arrangements with Lana to maybe reschedule next weekend? Sorry again, but I don't want to make anyone else sick. Goodbye."

Monday, April 25, 2022, 23:08

From: Lana Halford, lhalford807@gmail.com
To: Flo Martin, fmartinez@martinezfamilylaw.com
Re: Re: Agreement break? Already??

Hi Flo. Another weekend at Jack's, another weekend where something is off. I had a playdate set up for the kids on Sunday, but he canceled it at the last minute because he thought that Tracy was getting sick. I only found out when the father texted me about an hour ago to reschedule for next week. That was a lie from Jack because, you guessed it, they went hiking again.

I picked them up today after school like usual. Jack had at least made them go to school each day they were supposed to, but that was it. They were wearing the same clothes that I had dropped them off in; Tracy said that they had been wearing them all week. They stunk and were dirty. They smelt like campfire. They had their empty lunch containers, so he at least fed them today.

Family Dirt

I asked Jack why they looked like they hadn't had a bath in a week and he kind of shrugged it off, saying they had spent a lot of time outside. I got mad and said that they looked homeless, like they had been sleeping outside on the ground, and he said something like, "they should be so lucky" and then just kind of went back into his house.

Later, when I asked the kids about it, they said that he had never really given them a chance to change out of their clothes because they had been camping out every night. When he picked them up last Monday (the 18th) he headed straight out to the Cascades and marched them until dark when they finally reached a campsite. That was where they slept for the week. He woke them hours before the sun came up to hike back out and get to school on time. I guess he went to work during the days as well? They did that every day until the weekend.

Tracy said they didn't do much at the camp except sleep and eat and sit around. But he didn't even have a tent for them. They just unrolled their sleeping bags on the ground.

This whole camping/hiking thing is weird, and I'm scared. Is this enough evidence? That he's not keeping them clean? That they're exhausted from hiking hours through the woods every day?

What can I do??

Lana

23:09

From: Flo Martin, fmartinez@martinezfamilylaw.com
To: Lana Halford, lhalford807@gmail.com
Re: Re: Re: Agreement break? Already??

Hello; please note that I will be out of the office starting Friday, April 22, scheduled to return Monday, May 9. If you have any questions or concerns, please leave a message and my assistant, Mr. Grant, will reply shortly, as he is monitoring my accounts. If this is an urgent matter or an emergency, if you or someone you know is in danger or crisis, please contact Thunder Bay Crisis Centre at 807-998-9989 for assistance.

Sincerely,
Flo Martinez, B.A. (Hons.), J.D.
Martinez Family Law

23:25

Lana Halford (807-541-0236) to Samantha Halford (807-663-6542)

Lana: Hey big sis

Sam: Ugh I feel about a foot tall. Finally got Chris to bed. Fight night.

Lana: Oh no! Dinner again?

Sam: U know it. White diet strikes again. Should've known not to bother with any ground meat.

Lana: Aww but my kids love your meatballs—want to take them? Too bad Chris is still being tough that way. It's a phase.

Sam: LOL phase for life.

Sam: What up lil sis? U OK?

Sam: Jack the dick, Jack the deadbeat, Jack being his usual best dad ever

Lana: Kind of. Weirder. Past 2 weekends he's taken them hiking. Like, gone all day into the Cascades. First weekend he had them miss school on the Monday too. Last week they camped out every night. So I get them back dirty, in the same clothes. They're exhausted.

Sam: My poor dears!!!

Sam: Hiking?!? Jack camping? That IS weird. What's up at the Cascades?

Lana: Yes hiking. I don't get it either. Thought he had enough of that business.

Lana: I don't know what's up there. I've been up to see the falls obv and we used to party by Pitt's Bottomless but there's trails going north everywhere. They prop go deep into the bush. Cobalt had Jack try to do all that surveying up there last summer, not that it worked out.

Sam: Hmm what do the kids say? Are they OK with this?

Lana: They're tired tonight. Ate, TV, sleep. Didn't really get much else from Tracy other than they camped. I asked them if they wanted to go and they just shrugged. It was Jack's idea.

Lana: I mean I know they still love him, theyre mixed up about the divorce. Maybe think its their fault? But they still think he's same old dad. So if he makes it fun, adventure, special, of course they'll go along.

Sam: What do you think is going on? Have you talked to your lawyer? Is the agreement broken?

Lana: She's on fucking vacation.

Lana: I don't know what Jack's doing with my kids. I really don't want to send them next week.

Wednesday, April 27, 2022, 19:47

 MyFamilyTracker notice to Jack: Playdate scheduled for Sunday, May 8, 09:30, with Marigolds.

19:48

Jack Whitley (807-415-3780) to Lana Halford (807-541-0236)

Jack: Pls don't schedule my weekends with the kids.

Lana: Were you planning on going hiking again?

Monday, May 2, 15:54

Lana Halford (807-541-0236) to Jack Whitley (807-415-3780)

Lana: Before u get here pick up Tylenol for Aron. He's had a fever all day. He stayed home from school today.

Lana: NO HIKING NO CASCADES TONITE

Jack: Ok ok ok. Tylenol? The grape stuff?

Lana: ~~Don't forget to enter meds in Expenses~~. (tone suggestion: You can enter the meds in Expenses / It would help us both to document properly in Expenses) You can enter the meds in expenses. Can you cover childcare tomorrow if Aron has to stay home? Take a sick day?

Jack: . . .

Jack: I can if I need to.

Lana: I could keep both of them for an extra day or 2 until the fever is gone and they can go back to school?

Jack: No.

Jack: I said I would take a day if I needed to.

Tuesday, May 3, 2022, 09:16

Alphonse Chambers Elementary (807-665-6894) to Lana Halford (807-541-0236)

"Good day, this is an automated recording due to one or more children registered to this number being ABSENT for the day of Tuesday, May 3, 2022. Thank you for your time."

09:17

Lana Halford (807-541-0236) to Jack Whitley (807-415-3780)

Lana: Jack did Aron still have a fever today? Has it gone up?

Lana: How are they feeling? Did they sleep the night?

Lana: WHERE ARE YOU? (tone suggestions: Where have you been? What have you been up to? Where are you at?)

09:47

Lana: I called your work and they said you're on holidays for the next two weeks.

Lana: Where are you Jack?

Wednesday, May 4, 2022, 09:15

Alphonse Chambers Elementary (807-665-6894) to Lana Halford (807-541-0236)

"Good day, this is an automated recording due to one or more children registered to this number being ABSENT for the day of Wednesday, May 4, 2022. Thank you for your time."

09:17

Lana Halford (807-541-0236) to Jack Whitley (807-415-3780)

Lana: WHAT ARE YOU DOING WITH THEM?

Lana: I'm outside your fucking house and your fucking car isn't here so where the fuck are my kids (tone suggestion: options > turn off tone suggestions)

Lana: ARE YOU AT THE CASCADES

Lana: I'm going to find you.

10: 15

From: Lana Halford, lhalford807@gmail.com
To: Flo Martin, fmartinez@martinezfamilylaw.com
Re: Re: Re: Re: Agreement break? Already??

Flo, I need your help! I've tried calling your office but it always goes to voicemail. Your secretary isn't picking up.

Yesterday and today I got absent notices for my kids from the school.

I think Jack has taken my kids out to the Cascades again.

I know you're on vacation but I need help. I tried calling the police about it but they brushed me off. They thought since it was Jack's days, it was fine, even after I explained about our custody agreement and how he'd been taking the kids out hiking all day.

Lana

13:25

Titus Grant (807-476-3751) to Flo Martinez (807-714-9957)

Titus: Hey, Halford is going nuts. Called yesterday and today. Got an email. Says xhub has taken kids out of school. Can't reach him. Police won't do anything bc his days. Advise?

Flo: Ugh, that man. Figures police. OK, I'll get back to u.

Thursday, May 5, 2022, 09:36

Lana Halford (807-541-0236) to Jack Whitley (807-415-3780)

Lana: JACK WHERE THE FUCK ARE YOU??????

Jack: I'm at work. Where are you.

Lana: At home. Where are the kids?

Jack: At school.

Lana: What about Tues Weds??

Jack: Aron was still sick. They stayed home w/ me.

Lana: I got an absence msg.

Jack: OBV

Jack: U OK?

Lana: You didn't see my other texts?? I was worried.

Jack: OK.

Lana: ??? And . . .

Jack: I didn't see them.

10:18

Flo Martinez (807-714-9957) to Titus Grant (807-476-3751)

Flo: Any word?

Titus: From?

Flo: Halford, about the husband

Titus: No she's been quiet today

Titus: Other issues. Grandier is back w/ receipts. That new opposing counsel wants to talk arbitration.

Flo: Shit. Simmons! Ok. I didn't get anywhere with Halford's thing. No contacts picking up, diff time zones.

Flo: But nothing today from her?

Titus: Nope

Flo: Hm. Maybe she's OK

Friday, May 6, 2022, 09:15

Alphonse Chambers Elementary (807-665-6894) to Lana Halford (807-541-0236)

"Good day, this is an automated recording due to one or more children registered to this number being ABSENT for the day of Friday, May 6, 2022. Thank you for your time."

09:17

Lana Halford (807-541-0236) to Jack Whitley (807-415-3780)

Lana: JACK COME ON WHAT ARE YOU DOIN

Lana: Please have my babies call me

Lana: Why are you doing this??

09:25

Lana Halford (807-541-0236) to Samantha Halford (807-663-6542)

Lana: I don't know what to do. He has them, I know it. He's taken them back up there.

Sam: Isn't it his days?

Lana: It is but he's making them miss school. Almost all this week I've got absent calls.

Sam: Weird. Where is he going?

Lana: Hiking

Lana: Cascades

Sam: Fuck what's up there? Why?

Sam: Can you reach him?

Lana: He answered my texts yesterday but I think he was lying about where he was. I can't go by the house except in the evenings but he's not there. They aren't.

Sam: Lawyer? Cops?

Lana: Nothing doin

Sam: What about talking to Cobalt?

Lana: Maybe. I called there and they said he was on vacation. I don't know where Doug is working these days, last time Jack talked about him Doug was doing shut-downs in NE Que.

Sam: Yeah, that guy could help.

Lana: What do I do?

Sam: . . .

Sam: I think you're doing it. Unless you go start looking.

Saturday, May 7, 2022, 07:15

Lana Halford (807-541-0236) to Jack Whitley (807-415-3780)

Lana: Where u even home Thurs?

Lana: Cause ur not home now.

Lana: I went for a hike at the Cascades. I found a trail and followed it. I didn't find you.

Lana: But I will.

Sunday, May 8, 2022, 11:45

Lana Halford (807-541-0236) to Jack Whitley (807-415-3780)

Lana: I'm glad this is all being saved. If I get within arms reach of my kids you'll never touch them again. I spent all day looking again.

Monday, May 9, 2022, 16:02

Lana Halford (807-541-0236) to Jack Whitley (807-415-3780)

Lana: Jack

Jack: Hey

Lana: What is going with you? Where have you been?

Jack: What do you mean? Busy weekend. Aron felt better so we spent time outside.

Lana: At school today?

Jack: Yeah of course

Lana: Did you guys go to the Cascades?

Jack: Ask the kids about it.

Lana: OK

Lana: I'm on my way. Have them ready pls

Jack: OK c u

16:14

Lana Halford (807-541-0236) to Samantha Halford (807-663-6542)

Lana: Once again he's acting like its no big deal that he disappeared for a week.

Sam: He's at home? Kids?

Lana: Went to school today. I don't know, I'm going to get them.

23:14

Lana Halford (807-541-0236) to Jack Whitley (807-415-3780)

Lana: I just wanted to get all this on record. I need to write it down somewhere. So I'm not even texting you Jack I'm just writing all down here bc this is a court-monitored document. It's saved to the server. If your disgusting face sees these words, sure, that's fine.

Lana: You kept them out of school those days. But you didn't keep Aron home at all. You took them into the woods again. You camped out for almost a week. Even Thursday, the day we were texting. I don't know how you did that yet. But you were deep in the woods. For seven days.

Lana: I put the pictures of their haircuts in the PHOTOS section. Same with how filthy they looked when I picked them up. I think they've lost weight. You sent them to school like that. Tracy was humiliated. I want to show how you just hacked off their beautiful hair. The other stuff they said too. Fingernails. Eyebrow hairs, eyelashes. Jars for samples of their fluids? What the fuck Jack? Tracy said you got their tears—how did you make them cry? Blood? A jar of earwax? And why did you bag their poop, Jack? Why? What's going on?

Lana: They're exhausted. Aron is still sick. A week later and they're still sick because you haven't given them time to heal.

Tuesday, May 10, 2022, 08:15

Lana Halford (807-541-0236) to Jack Whitley (807-415-3780)

Lana: Jack the kids won't wake up

Lana: They won't wake up

Lana: DID YOU GIVE THEM SOMETHING

08:45

Lana Halford (807-541-0236) to Thunder Bay Emergency Response—911 Dispatch recording:

911: 911, please specify if you require ambulance, police, or fire—

Lana: Ambulance, oh god, please hurry, I'm at 67 Morse Street, my kids won't wake up!

911: To confirm, ma'am, sixty-seven-morse-street?

Lana: Yes! Yes, please hurry!

911: Ok, ma'am, please stay on the line, I've dispatched paramedics to that address. What can you tell me is happening?

Lana: My kids, my children, they won't wake up!

911: Ma'am, are your children breathing?

Lana: Yes, yes, they are. I checked that right away, they're breathing fine, they just won't wake up! I didn't know what to do, I picked them up from their dad's last night and now, now—

911: So it's like they're still asleep?

Lana: Yes. I've tried everything. Noise, lights are on, I tried shaking them . . .

911: Ok, ma'am, you said that you picked them up from their father's yesterday. Do they have any allergies? Any reactions to any food, chemicals, environmental elements?

Lana: Um, Aron used to have a milk-protein allergy, but that cleared up when he was five, and it just made him gassy . . .

911: Ok, so cause unknown—

Lana: How much longer until they're here?

13:34

Patient notes of Dr. Surit Angrawal, Pediatrician on call, Thunder Bay Regional Hospital.

"Patients are Tracy Whitley, age 10, and Aron Whitley, age 8, biological children of Lana Halford and Jack Whitley, parents divorced. Mother called paramedics when Tracy and Aron wouldn't wake up for school this morning. Paramedic notes detail that children were sleeping in their respective beds in Halford's residence and that they did not wake at any point during transport or any subsequent examinations. No allergies, all blood tests— CBC, UE, GFR, LFT—are all normal in range. Vitals are normal as well, though resting heart rate is on the lower side, 65 BMP. Slightly underweight considering their height. Children are still considered 'asleep'—electroencephalogram tracking shows normal brain activity for REM, but of course, REM shouldn't last twenty hours. Children have been put on fluids, catheters, and are being monitored through the EEP.

"Immediate thought is some kind of traumatic event that has triggered this advanced sleep state, though research suggests that the opposite reaction should be observed. Halford reports that Whitley was taking children for extended hikes and spending multiple nights out-of-doors in rustic camping conditions. Compounded physical exertion to the point of exhaustion would lead to deep sleep, but children should still be able to respond to stimuli. Further examination doesn't reveal anything of obvious concern: some small bruising, cuts, and scrapes to lowers legs and elbows consistent with reported activities. Nothing suspicious at this time, though they have some of the worst haircuts I've ever seen."

13:56

Lana Halford (807-541-0236) to Jack Whitley (807-415-3780)

Lana: I hope you're fucking happy

Lana: They're in the hospital

Lana: WHAT DID YOU DO TO THEM

Lana: They won't wake up

Lana: The doctors don't know what you did

Lana: I WILL FIND YOU

15:21

Partial transcript of Bethany Morrison, social worker for Thunder Bay Children's Aid Society, interview with Lana Halford.

Lana: Tracy said he kept hair clippings. Put them in a bag. He kept other bits of them as well.

Bethany: Go on.

Lana: Nails. Those went in a bottle. Hangnails went in a separate one. Then all their, um, fluids. He had bottles for each of their . . . mucus, ear wax, urine, tears, blood, poop . . .

Bethany: Blood? Tears? You think he got these fluids by force?

Lana: I don't know. The kids just kinda said that he did it, that after he cut their hair he just kept pulling bottles out of a backpack and putting their stuff in them. Aron had a scab on his knee that Jack pulled off with tweezers. They just kinda went along with it, somehow, Tracy said. He's their dad, after all.

Family Dirt

Bethany: [sighs] Filling a bottle with ear wax? How big were these bottles?

Lana: They said small. Maybe like a spice jar? Smaller?

Bethany: Did their stories match? Might this be fantasy?

Lana: What?

Bethany: Your children might be telling you stories about your ex. To play sides.

Lana: For god's sake, why? I mean—

Bethany: Did he ever exhibit any of this behavior when you were married? Hoard or collect bodily . . . items?

Lana: No? I don't know, he wasn't weird like this, or, I mean, he wasn't like this at first. Our relationship, it, it soured.

Bethany: Was that the reason for the divorce?

Lana: Maybe? I don't know. Marriage is hard, right? I mean, we did things pretty normally, weren't in huge debt, we enjoyed things together, even had a bit of a love life. Working for Cobalt took him out of town a lot, so he wasn't around as much as me. Jack made enough I could stay home with the kids. I did some books on the side for grocery money but it was mostly him.

Things dried up, I guess. We were so busy we were always running in opposite directions. Shared a bed but not a bedtime. As the kids got older he got more distant. Not indifferent, or cold, but just . . . flat. He was good with them, loved them, but never got them excited about anything. I haven't heard him laugh in years.

Then he did a pretty intense bit of work in the Cascades last year, just him and another guy for like a whole summer. On his off days he was distant, but I figured it was the work tiring him out. We talked and Jack said he wanted a desk job once he was done with the Cascades, he was tired of the field. He got the desk job but nothing changed.

Bethany: Do you blame his work for your divorce?

Lana: I don't know. All that time away in the forest just provided the right push, maybe. I mean, he's sticking with his desk job but every moment off he's back at the Cascades. Have you talked with Jack?

Bethany: [coughing] We're, ah, we're having trouble reaching him.

Lana: I see. Did you check the Cascades?

Bethany: No, um, I'm afraid I couldn't. I don't have those kinds of resources. Checked his workplace, that sort of thing.

Lana: Is it too early to get the police involved?

Bethany: [sigh] They are involved. I'm assuming he doesn't know what's happened to the kids?

Lana: [laugh] It's his fault. I've pretty much told him.

Bethany: We don't know that yet, Ms. Halford. The doctors can't say for certain.

Lana: That's bullshit. If he cared he'd be here. He put them to sleep, somehow. If the kids were in trouble, he'd be there for them. Not for me. But if he's not here, and I've told him, numerous times, what's happening, it's because he doesn't want to be here. He wants to be somewhere else. Tracy and Aron aren't his kids anymore.

Bethany: What do you mean by that?

Lana: Out with the old.

Family Dirt

15:21

Patient notes of Dr. Surit Angrawal, Pediatrician on call, Thunder Bay Regional Hospital.

"Additional development for Whitley children. Approximately one hour after I committed my notes both of them began exuding what appeared to be dirt from their pores. Duty nurses first noticed what appeared to be dust surrounding the children's outlines, so initiated efforts to clean bedding appeared to resolve the issue. However, subsequent rounds discovered even more dirt had began piling up around the children at a faster rate, filling creases between arms and torso, between legs, between buttocks, behind back of neck. Dirt also began spilling from ears, tear ducts, nostrils, urinary tract. Currently two nurses are tasked with each child to keep them clear . . . I fear at the rate the dirt is piling up, they would be buried in no time.

"Dirt samples have been submitted for spectrometer analysis. Vitals are consistent with previous charting. I've never heard of anything like this."

15:23

Lana Halford (807-541-0236) to Samantha Halford (807-663-6542)

Lana: I've been at the hospital all day.

Sam: WHAT

Lana: Something is wrong with the kids. They won't wake up.

Sam: WHAT

Sam: Whats going on

Lana: I think Jack did something. The doctors don't know what it is. Just that the kids won't wake up and now they're covered in dirt.

Sam: Slow, sis. They won't wake up? Like, coma?

Lana: Kind of.

Sam: And they're dirty?

Lana: No. The dirt is coming out of them. Like out of their skin.

Sam: Ok, that's—

Lana: It's a lot of dirt. It's trying to bury them.

Lana: I think it has something to do with the Cascades. Jack had them up there and he cut their hair. Took fingernail clippings, etc.

Sam: He did what? Sis that sounds crazy.

Lana: They can't find him. So I'm going to go back there. Walk the trails until I find him.

Sam: What, tonight? It's a fucking maze up there. You went before and didn't find anything. You don't know what you're looking for.

Lana: I have to do something.

Sam: Let me help! I can come. We can both go.

Lana: No. You got Chris to look after. I'm just going to take one trail. I'll text later.

16:22:

Jack Whitley (807-415-3780) to Lana Halford (807-541-0236)

Jack: Hey where are u

Lana: Where have you been

Jack: At home, Cascades

Lana: The kids are sick. They're in the hospital.

Jack: OK

Lana: That's it? OK? There's something weird happening with them.

Jack: Well, they're your kids, right?

Lana: What does that mean?

Jack: I mean they're yours. Custody.

Lana: So you'll care that they're in the hospital next week? When its your turn?

Jack: No. I'm not doing it this way anymore.

Lana: ???

Jack: I could show you.

Lana: Show me what?

Jack: Meet at the Cascades parking at 6

Lana: Ok

16:25:

Lana Halford (807-541-0236) to Samantha Halford (807-663-6542)

Lana: Hey, finally got a hold of Jack. He's being weird. But, I'm going with him up to the Cascades. I need to know. It could help the kids.

Sam: What no that's crazy

Sam : Send the police

Sam: Hey you didn't pick up

Sam: Are you gone already

22:10

Samantha Halford (807-663-6542) to Lana Halford (807-541-0236)

Sam: Hey

Sam: Where are you

Sam: Call me pls

Sam: I'm so scared

Wednesday, May 11, 2022, 09:46

Flo Martinez (807-714-9957) to Lana Halford (807-541-0236)

"Hi Lana, it's Flo, I'm finally back in the office. I'm sorry Mr. Grant wasn't able to help you at all, I had trouble accessing my resources from where I was staying. I hope everything is going okay with the kids. I'm guessing it is because this is your week and I didn't hear from you on Monday. Please keep me in the loop."

09:52

Samantha Halford (807-663-6542) to Lana Halford (807-541-0236)

Sam: You there? Pls call me

Sam: The hospital called. Kids still asleep. Dirt is getting worse.

14:25

Lana Halford (807-541-0236) to Samantha Halford (807-663-6542)

Lana: I'm here.

Lana: Jack introduced them to me. Out there.

Lana: I met Jack's kids.

Lana: He made new ones. They're beautiful.

16:47

Patient Notes of Dr. Anita Needem, Emergency Physician on Call, Thunder Bay Regional Hospital

"Attending notes for Lana Halford, age 36, brought into ER approx. 15:00 hrs by paramedics. Halford was found, unconscious in Cascades parking lot, by her sister, Samantha Halford, after text exchange. Apparently Halford had been hiking and camping in the area with her ex-husband since the previous afternoon. However, patient shows signs consistent with extreme, long-term exposure: severe dehydration, total sunburn, some rapid weight loss consistent with starvation diet, as well as an untold number of small contusions, burns, scrapes, bug bites, etc. Patient's hair was cut, but no other signs of abuse or violence. No known allergies.

"Patient's vitals are currently stable, administering fluids, catheter. Since being found she shows no sign of waking; brain wave patterns are consistent with REM sleep. Given Halford's condition, I've no doubt that the mysterious dirt which has plagued the children, Tracy and Aron Whitley, under the care of Dr. Angrawal, will soon begin affecting Lana. I'm advising round-the-clock observation until otherwise noted."

16:49

From: Samantha Halford, dizzychick14@hotmail.com
To: Flo Martin, fmartinez@martinezfamilylaw.com
Subject: Lana Halford

Hi Flo, this is Sam, Lana's sister. I'm not sure if you're aware but things are pretty bad for Lana.

She's in the hospital. I just got back from seeing her. Tracy and Aron have been there since Tuesday morning. The kids won't wake up and this weird dirt keeps leaking out of their skin. I think it'll start with Lana soon, too. She followed Jack into the Cascades sometime on Tuesday evening and didn't come out until this afternoon. She texted me and she's been asleep ever since.

I'm letting you know that I'm going to go looking for Jack. He's somewhere in the Cascades area. I've left my son with my mom just in case you don't hear from me in the next few days. I'm going to take some supplies and head in.

The last thing Lana texted me was that she had found something, or Jack had showed her. I've forwarded all those texts in the next email just to put them on record. Either way, if you read those texts, she said that Jack "made new ones."

I don't know what that means, but I'm going to find out. Wish me luck!

Sam

May 17, 2022, 10:04 a.m.

To: Douglas Eustance, douglas.eustance@cobaltmining.com
From: Flo Martinez, fmartinez@martinezfamilylaw.com
Subject: Whitley family

Hello, Mr. Eustance,

You don't know me, but I'm writing as a concerned representative and family attorney for Lana Halford, Jack Whitley's ex-spouse, and, by association, Lana's children Tracy and Aron. As you may have seen in the news coverage from the beginning of May, the Whitley children and Lana are currently hospitalized with a mysterious condition, while both Samantha Halford, Lana's sister, and Jack are presently missing somewhere in the northern Cascades wilderness.

It has been approximately one week since a missing persons report for Ms. Halford and Mr. Whitley were filed with Thunder Bay Police. Based on information supplied by myself and Ms. Samantha Halford, the police attempted a search of the 500 km^2 area but, unsurprisingly, there has been no evidence of either Mr. Whitley or Ms. Samantha Halford found. Some fibers originating from a sweater of Aron's were discovered in a small clearing with a well-used fire pit, five km north of the furthest reaching trail extension, well past the swimming area known as Pitt's Bottomless. I've indicated the site in the attached topographic map.

These circumstances have led me to reach out for your advice and possible services, as your employer, Cobalt Mining, tasked Jack and yourself with the surveying of the Cascades area starting in the spring of 2020. I am unsure if Thunder Bay Police have reached out to you or to Cobalt Mining for assistance; I came across your name in the testimonial documents attached to the divorce proceedings and given the lack of leads and your apparent familiarity with the area, decided to reach out to you.

If you would be willing to engage in a search of the Cascades area, my office is prepared to compensate you at a daily rate.

I look forward to hearing from you.

Sincerely,
Flo Martinez, B.A. (Hons.), J.D.
Martinez Family Law

Dear Kelli

Ai Jiang

Methods of reading the following:

1) Strike outs first, then plain text.

2) Together, all at once, chaotically.

***

~~08/10/2014~~
09/05/2017

Dear ~~Kelli~~ Kelly,

~~It has been three months, but I've found a way for you to return.~~

~~Perhaps you might think me deranged; perhaps you won't see this letter at all. But I have been reading about substitute ghosts, and if everything goes according to plan, you can come back in Jisui's body. Yes, I know. We don't like her. But I'm convinced that the grief she gave us was part to blame for your death. You don't have to confirm. I know. Because just before I found your body drifting, airborne, by the tree out back, I had shared similar thoughts. And perhaps, if you'd waited a day later, a similar fate.~~

~~None of them ever saw how she menaced us. They saw what they wanted to see.~~

Dear Kelli

I had to dig through the evidence bin to fish this out. Could you imagine the expression on the officers' faces to find smoothed-out sheets now crumpled, as if by magic? That the next day they had all disappeared from the bag, even though no fingerprints were found?

They tossed the empty evidence bag in the trash rather than reopen the case—too scared of what we've become to do their jobs.

According to their records, they haven't contacted you after initial questioning. For of course you were only the *estranged* ex-boyfriend of a cousin, and I was only the psycho twin who couldn't grapple with her sister's death. The transcript to that conversation was quite an interesting read. You were always the best liar in the family, after all. And apparently—the best at hiding.

You've made yourself quite difficult to find.

~~Dad already accepted, on my behalf, the offer from the nearest institution. I know we hoped we could go overseas to that university in Scotland we always dreamt about, to be far enough from Dad so he would no longer have us under his thumb. But the University of Toronto is only a half hour drive away. Not that I would be homesick anyhow.~~

~~Also, it's where Jisui has decided to attend.~~

It seems you're no longer at the university, at least, nor anywhere near the old apartment you shared with that girl.

~~I have convinced Father to allow our rabbit-teeth-dusty-haired cousin be my roommate. It didn't take much convincing because it seems that it'd had been Father's plan all along. *A good influence* was what he said she'd be. Really, he only wanted to save money. Regardless, this is what we want. He's only done us a favour. Perhaps the only favour he's ever done for us.~~

All your social media hasn't been updated since the day the trial concluded. You seem to have done a pretty good job wiping your existence. Though I suppose it wasn't too difficult as you have few ties to begin with in this world.

Then why run? What have you to live for?

At least Kelli and I have each other.

I'll write again when we make the move into the dorms. Until then, don't drift too far.

Love,
Minghe

***

~~09/07/2014~~
9/6/2017

Dear ~~Kelli~~ Kelly,

Yes, I changed my name. Well, my "preferred" name at least. I changed it to what you said you always wanted to be called, what I call *you* now. My legal name is still Minghe. Our high school career counsellors said it would be easier for me to find a job if my name wasn't so "foreign", though our last name "Pang" likely gives us away, anyway. It's not quite right for me to say they told us this, but they implied it, which I think is the same thing, really.

On the bright side, our professors never get our name wrong.

What did you change your name to now, Kelly? Don't be afraid. It'll all soon be over. I know you're too afraid to look in the mirror. I know I was. Still am.

But you know what's funny? Jisui *also* changed her name. To what? Of course, it has to be Kelly. Her reasoning? So, she could blame me for things that actually her fault because both her parents and our parents won't believe she's actually talking about herself in third person anyhow. How clever she must think she is. But don't worry. Everything is going according to plan. I'd told her I love her name, that the two of us could be twins. *Gag.* As if she could ever replace you. Though I suppose she will—or you will. We

~~will be the angel and devil on her shoulders, and I am sure soon she too will drift in the wind. Soon. Soon.~~

You know how impatient we are, Kelly. Stop running.

~~Since you started whispering all the terrible things in her ears, about how Molly is a traitor and Jordan has been spreading rumors about her hygiene, she has been avoiding me, even though I am in all of her classes. Admittedly, it wasn't hard because of the behemoth size of our courses, overflowing with over 300 students. Our voices are too alike, I suppose. I should have thought about that. You had better speed up the process, Kelli. I'm tired of taking these life science classes with her. As soon as you've convinced her that the afterlife is better than this one, we can both switch back into those English lit courses we've always dreamt about taking together.~~

We checked places you used to frequent, that Ramen bar near Bay, the bookstore on Dundas.

Alas, we never had good luck, did we?

Love,
Minghe

***

~~02/18/2015~~
09/7/2017

Dear ~~Kelli~~ Kelly,

~~Kelly told Dad I have a boyfriend. It isn't my boyfriend, it's hers, but she needed a way to talk about him without getting yelled at by Auntie. That means I'm the one being yelled at instead. Why didn't I tell Dad and Auntie the truth? To them, everything Kelly says is truth, just because she had made them believe we're a liar.~~

We asked your ex where you were, but unfortunately, she didn't know either. We were almost tempted to take her this time, but you know you're the only one we want.

That would be more fun, wouldn't it?

~~Any who, her new boyfriend Jackson doesn't impress Dad or Auntie unfortunately, and he's someone I would never think of falling in love with. Not just because of Dad's disapproval, but because of what we heard him whisper to his friend on the phone while waiting for Kelly to return to the dorm, thinking we couldn't hear, while we pressed our ear to the bathroom door, with the shower running. They called this *yellow fever*, or at least that's what you read online on Reddit: "Yeah. Women where she's from, in particular, are so fragile, docile, quiet, kind, it's great." He meant he saw Kelly as a petite little sexual thing, as moldable as clay.~~

~~When Kelly returned, Jackson gave her an easy smile, and that was that.~~

~~Why did I never tell her? Well, I'm the liar after all. They won't last the year, anyway.~~

We kind of regret not telling you. Maybe we could've become friends if we did.

Maybe none of us had to die.

Love,
Minghe

***

~~04/30/2016~~
09/08/2017

Dear ~~Kelli~~ Kelly,

~~*We* lasted the year. More than that, actually.~~

~~This is quite the interesting collection of letters you've got going here. It's interesting how even until the end, you're still blaming everything on me, insisting that *I'm* the one copying *you*, when we~~

~~both know it's the other way around. Change your name. It's weird how similar it is to mine.~~

~~A liar never stops lying. I *volunteered* to be your dorm-mate only because I felt sorry for you, wanted to watch out for you, since we're cousins. But screw this, screw you. I'm moving out. Have fun with your new roommate.~~

~~Say hi to your dad for me. I can't imagine he'll be happy now that you've driven away the only "friend" you have left.~~

It seems you did in fact remain in contact with someone after all, *Jackson*. Auntie isn't the best keeper of secrets. Once spoiled, always spoiled. It was the money trouble again, wasn't it? Lucky you didn't succeed, or else we would have never heard her complain at dinner.

Love,
~~Kelly~~ Minghe

★★★

~~06/21/2016~~
09/09/2017

Dear ~~Kelli~~ Kelly,

~~Kelly tattled to Dad like I thought she would. Dad wasn't impressed with us, even though his trust in Kelly seemed to wane just a little, with her spouting "nonsense" about ghosts and whatnot. He never was superstitious, or at least he likes to pretend he isn't. Kelly hasn't been able to block out your whispers even as she was packing up to move out it seems, but it doesn't seem to be working anymore now that she knows what we've been up to. I suppose we could find another substitute, but that might take some time. Or perhaps we could go find Kelly. She's now living with her boyfriend somewhere off campus. Dad did pass me the address.~~

It seems you've made quite the new life by yourself. Never pegged you as the customer service type. I know you hate people. Though

I suppose you had little option, even with Jackson's med degree. It is difficult to fake something like that, even for you.

But don't worry. You won't have to think about these things much longer.

Don't blink. You might not wake tomorrow.

Love,
Minghe

***

~~07/18/2016~~
09/10/2017

Dear ~~Minghe~~ Kelly,

~~I'm sorry, but this was the only way. I promise: we will get Kelly, but you know how impatient I am. I couldn't wait any longer.~~

It seems even you cannot fully escape the guilt. Listen to my voice, keep listening, and everything will be okay. You will be happier once you drift like us.

Love,
~~Kelli~~ Minghe

***

~~08/01/2016~~
09/11/2017

Dear ~~Minghe~~ Kelly,

~~I hope you're happy now.~~

~~I know you hate me, and I know my body will now be Kelli's, but please find me another.~~

~~I want to go home.~~

Hilarious to think that you believed twins would betray one another.

Love,
~~Jisui~~ Minghe and Kelli

****

~~08/25/2016~~
09/12/2017

Dear Kelly,

~~Dad and Auntie suspect nothing.~~

~~You were always a good liar, and we have you to thank for that, now.~~

Auntie was shocked to say the least about Jackson has taken a sudden reinterest in her daughter, but as *you* always said, *we* are the best liars, so I suppose we still have you to thank for that.

Love,
Minghe and Kelli

****

~~08/25/2016~~
09/12/2017

Dear ~~Minghe and Kelli~~ Jisui,

~~Funny that the two of you think you've won. Turns out Jackson was more rattled by my death than he'd let on. I'd thought his new girl might be a better substitute, but I'm not complaining.~~

~~Your *boyfriend* has returned, *Jisui*, and he misses you very *very* much—so don't keep him waiting too long.~~

Indeed, we have returned. Though we have no doubt you won't keep us waiting.

Don't worry, we will be ready.

Love,
~~Jisui~~ Minghe and Kelli

No Blood, No Bones

Zachary Rosenberg

From the writings of Harald Sigurdson,
Dated 794 A.D.

Day 1

The village was not simply empty, Svein. That should have been
our first warning.

We arrived here, three ships full of raiders strong along these
eastern shores, our holds empty, famished for plunder. How we had
laughed with Thorkell and Ragnar, after the thralls told us all we
had to know. Along the Mediterranean existed dozens of these
villages, little jutting communities of Christian and Jew without
defense. My Hebrew slave Avram told me much of them, these
lands of his birth. They were peaceful people, yet their communities
were rich with treasures contained within their temples and abbeys.

Do you remember how we spoke of our envy for our brother
Thorkell and Ragnar Knutson for setting sail first, Svein? Ah, but
you knew how to cheer me up. You reminded me we would arrive
to raucous feasting and drinking. You vowed that when you arrived
days after me, we would laugh and sacrifice to Odin for granting
us riches and victory.

But as our ships pulled closer, no fires burnt as beacons upon the
beaches, no scent of meat touched us. There was nothing but the
salt of the sea and the hiss of the wind.

Erik was first to voice his unease. "Could it be they ambushed Thorkell and Ragnar?"

I did not believe it possible. I still do not. I pulled Avram close with the other slaves and demanded he tell us if this was a village that looked battle-ready. He did not need to answer, for I saw it in his face. Mighty as he claimed his "Hashem" was, it was only one god. Ours were many, and warriors besides.

Though the outer walls of the houses in the village were scarred as though by fire and steel, as we set through the village in one single mass, we found nothing. No bodies, no blood. Not human, nor animal. Looming in the corner of the village, like some mighty wolf perched above its den, lay the abbey with its stone walls. The sun cast a curious shadow, beaming down upon us. I was the first to open a door to a house near a copse of thick trees littered with fruits.

The scent of sweet jam reached me first as I pulled the door open. Little jars lay dashed upon the floor, the clay broken and cleaned of all but little droplets of jam. Tostig murmured at my side and pointed with his ax, for the floor was covered in flour. The footprints appeared like those of chickens. Only larger, perhaps near the size of my own feet. Or Avram's, who stared at them with a mute surprise in his eyes. I thought nothing of it then, Svein. I shoved him and told the slave to tell me where the others would be. He looked back at me like he was awakening from a slumber, not even seeing me for a moment. I grew enraged. Was I not his master these last four years? Had I not taken him fairly from one of our raids? Did he have no gratitude that I spared him from the sword when we slew so many of his people?

"I do not know, master." His Danish had gotten better. "Perhaps they are in the abbey?"

"Why would they be in the abbey?" Erik growled. "It is still light out. We were only days behind Thorkell's ship!"

I looked toward the abbey. Curiously, the windows appeared boarded and sealed from this distance. "It is the strongest looking place near this village. Easy to fortify. They could have fled there from Thorkell's raiders."

Erik shrugged. "Or they might have run off into the woods. The slave might know the direction."

"There is a village several days' journey from here," Avram confirmed. "But I haven't been here in years. How would I know where they went and why?"

He was holding something back. But he was a good slave, and I knew such a return must be troubling for him. I would give him a day. Then I would be less charitable. I looked down at the room one last time, looking at the prints on the ground, the broken jars.

In the corner of the room was a pot that smelled foul. Upon closer inspection, I found a stew of meat, herbs, and plants. The wood beneath it had all the signs of a charred fireplace, but the stew had been left to go bad or burnt.

"Who would take jam and leave the meat?" Erik asked, a scoff on his lips. My men were warriors. We came here for conquest and plunder, not to ponder strange mysteries. The slaves kept themselves from our wrath, murmuring among themselves.

"Perhaps they saw the ships coming and fled into the woods with our own in pursuit," said I. "If that is the case, they'll have left signs on the trees to mark their passing." How often had we done this, Svein? Since our first raid together, so many years ago. How proud Father was that we worked so well together. "Tostig, take a small force and travel to the woods. Half a mile. Report what you find."

He did not argue, taking several warriors with him. "I'll report back soon," he said with a final salute and prayer to Tyr. They walked from us, weapons at ready, until the trees consumed them. I looked at Avram, whose gaze flitted from house to house.

I opened my mouth to say something, I have forgotten what.

The first scream tore out from the woods, as though someone had ripped it from Tostig's very soul. I have seen many men die, but even those given the blood eagle do not scream like that. But the scream was not the worst. No, worst was how abruptly it *ended*.

We waited, listening. Armed men, reeking of salt and fear. I saw it in each pair of eyes, some instinctive terror. As though we could feel the wrongness through our very innards. The scream came again, and it was Tostig's voice.

We shrank back, far from the woods. The men formed a shield wall. To calm my nerves, I am writing this missive now, a record to you when you arrive days hence. I hear something within the trees, shifting within and calling to us with Tostig's voice.

But it sounds low, muffled, as though it is forced through the lungs of a drowned man. I hear Avram approaching now, his voice hurried.

"The abbey," he babbles to me in his rough Danish. "We need to get to the abbey."

Day 2

I am writing to you from within the abbey, Svein. Though there is no comfort here.

I say without shame that I listened to the word of a Hebrew slave. When Avram offered his solution, I shouted the order to fall back. With Odin, Tyr, and Thor as my witness, I am no coward. I have faced insurmountable odds knowing that to perish will be to travel to the feasting halls with our forebears. But this time, we retreated.

We fell back as one, slave and warrior, toward the abbey. The heavy doors were unlatched, and we found our way inside. I could feel it the entire time, something watching us from the woods and behind the houses. I knew it was there, had been there from the start. Hidden eyes had pierced us from the second we set foot to these cursed shores.

We slammed the doors shut and reinforced them. But not

moments after we finished our barricade, I heard it from the other side of the door. Blades, or claws, squealing against stone.

The windows had already been boarded. It took effort to bring the men back under control. To ensure they would proceed, we ordered the slaves to walk before us. One warrior proposed a sacrifice of the slaves on the spot. Though I considered it seriously, I decided against it. Against the unknown, any man might matter, even a slave.

And I could not shake the knowing look in Avram's eye, the rapid breathing expelled from his lips. I promised myself we would speak later, and I would question him more thoroughly, perhaps beginning with a broken finger if he remained reticent.

We would have the abbey to ourselves. I brought us down the hall, to a great chamber and instructed the men that we would move only in groups. No man was to be left alone. We would go in pairs at least. No matter where.

Gunnar, you will recall his foul temper, objected. He spat on the ground and cursed me for a fool. "There are dozens of us," he protested. "Tostig and the others were caught off guard, but we are ready and armed. We should not cower behind these walls!"

"And where are Thorkell and the others? Where are the townspeople?" I returned. I fought to quell my nerves, reassuring myself with the next words I spoke. "Svein and the others will reach these shores within days. There's bound to be food in this place. Keep to groups and be careful."

"And what of Tostig and the rest?" Hissed Gunnar. "Are you giving him up for dead?" He raised his voice, roaring as though trying to be heard through the stone. "Tostig! Can you hear us?" He looked at me, glowering. As though I was the only thing holding back Tostig's return. But when Gunnar opened his mouth, it was Tostig's voice that came first.

It carried from outside, a loud cry that was unmistakably Tostig's voice. "I'll report back!" The shout, just outside the window. Like a drowned man, learning to speak again. Tostig's words, Tostig's voice. And yet, not Tostig.

I do not know what became of him and those other men within those woods. I pray to the All-Father he spares me that knowledge, for the voice was terrible enough. We remained together and secured the abbey. The windows and doors were bolted tight and shut. We remained in groups, roaming as one, though I could hear it outside the abbey walls at all times. Moving as no human should. Stealthy, but with flaws in its creeping as though by design. I thought I could hear the unearthly prowl of Fenrir, the slithering of Jormungandr. We tried to ignore it, pretend it wasn't there. We pretended it was nothing but a normal siege, responding in kind.

We combed through every nook and crevice together. The food stores remained robust, though again I noted the curious breaking of jars meant to hold jams and preserves. There was not a single drop of blood, but we found stores of meats and cheeses. I have slain enough monks to know they live lavishly.

The only hint of human conflict was a staircase in the corner of the ground floor, leading deep into the earth. Only I and three other men dared to venture down below, into the fetid blackness. I used a spare rushlight to light my way, noting the marks on the walls. Down below was the entrance to a cave. One glance within revealed a deep plunge, so far that I could not see the end.

Before the entrance was a ring of stones, each carved with symbols. Those in my party believed them runes, but I knew Avram well enough to recognize the Hebrew writings of his people. Next to them was a sword, carved with Viking runes.

I knew Thorkell's blade well. Nowhere in the abbey was there any sign of Thorkell, though. No sign that any living being had ever drawn breath here.

I left that grim abyss, retreated up those stairs with the stones and my men. We spoke little of what we had seen below, though I caught Avram staring at me apart from the other slaves.

I hated him then. Him, and his knowing gaze. Only with the greatest of efforts did I keep from offering him to the gods then and there. I needed him still, needed his knowledge. His are a weak people, suborned to their betters throughout the world. The Hebrews have been driven out time and again with their one god powerless to help them. But in spite of weakness they are an *ancient* people, whose written knowledge stretches back thousands of years.

He knows more.

I must find out what.

I Know Not the Day Anymore

It is dark now, Svein. My rushlight burns low and my sanity frays. I do not think I have much longer remaining to me. Are you close? Are you approaching? You were days behind us, were you not? Or does this foul thing possess the ability to steal the very passage of time from us?

But first I must explain if there is even the slightest chance this letter may salvage your life. We hid behind the walls and our refuge became a siege. We claimed rooms of the monks, sleeping uneasily on the beds and floors. Three men to a room, not counting slaves. We ate in the great hall from the food stores, no man was ever alone at any time. Outside, the night was still. I fetched Avram, having put off our talk too long. I told him he would willingly tell me all he knew without complaint.

"What if I do not?" He asked, challenging me. I seized him by the shirt, informing him that he would speak truth. The Hebrew's lip curled, as though in contempt and suddenly I saw that despite the years with me, he did not *fear* me.

I did not matter, for all I could offer was death and pain.

I could not respond, I could only let him stare through me. For a moment, I doubted if I even existed. But then he spoke. "We have a name for them," he murmured. I saw it in his face. Though he did not fear me, he feared what lay outside the abbey and he knew I was his best hope of survival. "We call them the Sheydim." He knew only what his mother had told him, but he spoke of creatures that predated the founding of the world, forged in the crucibles of the deep abyss. More terrible than our Draugr or Jotun, Svein.

But the Sheydim were meant to be gone. Locked away by the name of their weak Lord in the blackest arenas of the earth. I thought of the cave and the broken binding, the collection of stones that I now held. I demanded Avram tell me more. What did they want?

He answered simply: "The stories say they delight in sweetness. In jams or fruits, or in the ripest terror in the human soul."

"What do they appear as?" I demanded.

"Whatever they wish. But they cannot disguise their feet."

"What happens to those they take?"

He looked at me without words. Either he did not know, or the truth was too terrible to be placed into speech. I did not pursue the answer, for I feared it. Instead I asked how it might be stopped. We were safe, weren't we? Behind the walls of the abbey?

"They will never stop hunting," he murmured. "Across the forests, the seas. They hunt entire family lines to extinction, and they will never stop. Unless the name of God is drawn across them, to blind them."

I looked at the stones I had taken. A great anger filled me then and I struck the slave. How dare he, Svein? How dare he place his weakling god of sheep above our own warriors? Ours are the gods who bring the thunder and the flames. Odin of his gallows, Thor of storms, Freyr of the blade. It would be they who would be our shield.

In the morning, we would hunt. We would win. We would sacrifice. I slept, secure in my plan. I awoke with the dawn kissing my eyelids through the cracks in the stone. My men were with me, Avram as well. We retrieved our weapons, grumbling among ourselves how we could not wash after days at sea.

When we met the others at the hall, it did not take long to realize many of us were missing. Of the dozens I had brought along on our ships, barely enough to maintain a raiding party remained. Gunnar led his men to the rooms and opened the doors.

They were unlocked, but there remained no sign any men had ever been there.

Nothing except the firm indents on the beds. There was no blood, no bones, though I found little strands of hair that a man might leave upon his own pillow.

We fought among ourselves. Gunnar demanded we go forth. We might reach the ships, he protested. I could not explain my unease, but I knew deep in my very bones his plan was foolish. The abbey was sealed yet and our numbers now diminished, I argued. We could stay together, in one camp. We should not separate again. I stared at Avram with the other slaves and Gunnar followed my gaze.

He broke from me and walked to the slaves. He took a man who struggled bravely, though not enough. Roaring prayers to Odin, Gunnar opened his throat with a blade and bled him over the floor, headless of my demands that he cease. My authority was a vestige, its spine shattered in our terror. With the blood on his hands, Gunnar proclaimed the gods were with us. He took up his sword and led a contingent of men toward the door. "We will find it and slay it," he vowed.

He would fight his way to our ships. He would seize the day and no monster would stand in his path. The men with him thundered and beat their shields, as though they were running toward a holmgang with a mortal enemy. They unsealed the door and threw it open. As one, they charged out, to the town.

Avram seized my arm and implored me to remain. The remaining men lingered with me, frightened as I was. We closed the doors, but the screams still reached us. They reached a pitch so terrible that more than one man moaned as if dying himself in my sight. I saw pale faces and twisted lips. Then outside, came the call.

"We will find it and slay it." Gunnar's voice, a mocking metallic screech. It became a chant, repeated over and over across the village. Men clasped their hands over their ears, and I let my sword fall from my hand.

Scarcely a score of us now remained within the abbey. No fewer than five men tore away the coverings from the windows and rushed out. They tried to run for the dragon ships, but as we desperately hammered the boards back into place, I saw them run beneath the shadows in the village and never emerge. One almost made it; I knew he was in full sight of the beach and the ships. Something caught him and drew him back between the houses.

Then the barricade was replaced, and I saw no more.

We stayed together as one, but night soon fell. We stayed awake for one entire evening, then a second. The food stores were plentiful, and we would not starve, but eventually sleep claimed us. We tried to sleep in shifts, with sentries posted. Our dwindling numbers made us now only ten men, even with the slaves. I kept Avram by me. Damn my pride, I delayed asking him how to stop this madness.

When my eyes grew too heavy, I slept. I must have been out only hours, yet when I opened my eyes, several men and slaves were gone. The abbey was no haven, Svein. It was a larder.

Day passed to night again. With no further progress, my pride fled me. I sought Avram. I found him at work near stones, holding a dagger I had given him, using it to scratch runes into the rocks. "What are you doing?" I demanded of him.

"Carving the name of God into the stones," he told me. He looked at me, determination in his eyes. "It is the only thing to hold the Sheydim at bay. I can carve enough to erect a circle, like the one at the cave. It might even be enough to banish the damned thing."

"How do you know these incantations?" I asked him, striding forth.

No Blood, No Bones

"I know the names of God," Avram said with conviction. The tone in his voice, as though his weak god could be a comfort! Brother, you have killed slaves for less insolence than this. I hope you'll not think me weak for failing to cut him down.

Avram hesitated with his knife, not meeting my gaze. He waited a long moment before he spoke. "If I carve more, for you as well, you would be able to hold it back. Fight it. Or would you kill me to take the stones from me?"

I hesitated and he snorted softly. Yes, I considered it, for my survival meant more than a mere slave. "I will carve more. Plenty for all. But I have a condition, master." He positively spat the word. "My freedom. And the freedom of the others. In return for this, I will give you these stones and carve more for myself and your Dane."

I took the stones, snatching them from him. Upon them was Hebrew. I clasped them to my breast and praised Thor for knowledgeable slaves. "I will give you freedom," I told him. And I meant it. I gave him the stones from below, so he might know what to carve.

Night fell, and I kept watch over Avram still carving away to scratch his damned runes into new rocks. I lifted my eyes for but a moment when I saw one of the other men approach. You remember Ubba, Svein. A big man, strong. He approached me cautiously, hesitantly. He walked uneasily, wobbling upon his boots as though they were suddenly an ill fit.

He raised a hand as he approached, asking how Avram was proceeding. I told him to return to the others, asked why he had separated from the rest, even if it was just a hallway away. He stepped closer, his footfalls loud upon the floor. Thumping closer and closer.

I saw his smile beneath the rushlight. Wide across his face, like a pale worm beneath the shadow of his beard. "How is it proceeding?" he whispered. His breath was close enough for me to smell, and it was like plunging my head into a fresh-open grave. The fire danced in the black pupils of his eyes. Eyes that never blinked.

I told him to return, to leave me now. I fumbled with my sword and made it an order. He smiled wider, tapping his boots upon the ground as he asked just what was wrong. I demanded he stay away and not touch me. I drew my sword and he followed my eyes down to his feet. I recalled the prints in the flower, within the village.

"Do you want me to remove my boots?" He asked, without blinking still. I had my sword out, though I knew it would do no good. But Ubba stepped back, into the corridor, as Avram worked. He slid away, and the rushlight winked out.

I had only one avenue of escape. Was this what Thorkell and Ragnar had felt at the end? What had this entire village known in its final moments? Others tried to run, others vanished. The slaves remained with Avram. They huddled close together, frightened. This unholy thing was in the abbey with us.

I am a man of honor, but I am only a man. I told Avram the stones would be our salvation. We would wait in one room, the last of the Danes. I asked to see his stones. When my fingers closed about them, I knew I was safe. Avram watched me expectantly for them to be returned.

I pushed him from me. "The rest of you," I said, "will take your chances in these halls. I honor my bargain." They would be our diversion, as I arranged the stones out along the door. We would wait, let it hunt. Then we would flee to the ships with our salvation.

Avram watched me, his eyes narrowed grimly. The slaves moaned and wailed, but he did not seem shocked. Only disappointed. "All I ever expected from you," he whispered. If I did not need him to draw the creature, I would have slain him.

"I give you your freedom, slave. Count yourself fortunate." My last words to him. I closed the door and waited to hear the screams of the slaves, of Avram. Yet they did not come. My last men, just five of us now, out of an entire raiding party, paced the room uneasily. We waited.

I turned away for only a moment when the door swung open. The cavern gaped wide, a black hallway before us. But the stones were disturbed, dashed aside, as though contemptuously swept by a foot. I knelt by to see them, parsing through the runic symbols of Avram's Hebrew.

I did not see it, but I remembered the rocks on the floor of the cave, where we had found Thorkell's ax. They were different letters carved into the rock, similar enough to the ones below, but *subtly* altered enough to be different completely. And the stones I had given Avram were gone. I searched frantically through all Avram had given us, but it was then I realized.

He had kept the stones from below.

He had given us decoys. Avram, a mere slave, had fooled us. Fooled *me*.

So incensed was I that I tore from the room. I rushed out the hall, roaring Avram's name, though my soldiers called at my back. I tore down, calling the cursed Jew's name. But he did not reveal himself. He and the slaves were unquestionably hidden with their protection. I had misjudged their intelligence, and they had left me defenseless. I was a warleader, a raider, a Viking.

 Now I am nothing but bait.

For hours I must have roamed the halls, shouting and roaring. Until at last, exhaustion took me and I wandered back. It will not shock you what I found waiting for me in that room.

Nothing. My men were gone. Only a desk, with rushlights and my parchments, as though assembled for me to finish. I am writing this now upon them, my final log. I can no longer say how much time has passed.

Zachary Rosenberg

 When I am done, I will rip away the barricade at the window and attach these pages to a stone. I will fling them as far as I can upon the beach. Find it, Svein. Read it.

And go. Flee these shores, turn back at once this place with its ancient god and almost as ancient monsters. Perhaps a ship will be missing when you come, taken by Avram and his slaves. I can no longer even bring myself to despise the Hebrew. Perhaps I can take comfort that someone from this damned expedition survive with life and soul intact.

I am nearing the end of my writings, Svein. Please, brother. Do not carry this curse home to your children. Take the ships and do not let it follow to our home. Let me be the last it claims.

The night is moonless, the rushlight is almost gone. I know I will soon know the fates of the others, of Thorkell, Gunnar, Tostig, and all the rest. It is a mystery I can forestall no longer.

It must be outside. Is that the click of nails upon the stones? Is that the scrape of claw on rock? Do I hear the soft laughter just outside of these walls even now?

Goodbye, brother. I wish I could say that I would meet you in Valhalla. But no feasting hall will await me, of that I am sure. I am laughing over these final pages, finishing them. The rock is nearby, with the rope of my swordbelt. I must act now, for I hear . . .

Thorkell?

Yes, I hear him. Our brother, Svein. His voice. Has he been hiding in the seas? His voice is muffled, as though forced through clumps of seaweed. But I'd know him anywhere.

And I must answer. Hearing his voice brings me such clarity! Let this letter serve as a reminder of what almost was. Come and find us, Svein, find your brothers. For now I go with Thorkell.

And we shall find these treacherous slaves together.

No Blood, No Bones

These ancient documents, remarkably preserved, were recovered from the belongings of Dr. Thor Svenson in 1982, shortly after the doctor's disappearance.

PFC Nathaniel Hart Has Died

G. Nicholas Miranda

The following documents were mistakenly declassified, and materials scanned into the National Archives database under the FOIA (Freedom of Information Act). User Watch_Puppy81 *managed to screenshot copies of many of the items before they vanished from the National Archives website (www.archive.org). When* Watch_Puppy81 *inquired about the remaining files, they were told that no such records exist, despite the batch/collection numbers appearing on the digital scans. We here at* BeyondExtra.com *are publishing them as a means to force the government to not only release the remaining documents, but also to acknowledge the events to which they pertain that cost the lives of so many US soldiers.*

G. O. Stanley—Editor, BeyondExtra.com

BeyondExtra.com—*Everything you need to know about the stuff they don't want you to know.*

***

PFC Nathaniel Hart Has Died

Handwritten letter.

PFC Nate Hart
July 15, 1969
Somewhere in Nam

Mom,

We're packing up base. Again. Don't know where we are now, don't know where we're going. Couldn't pronounce or spell it even if I did. Hopefully somewhere nearer the coast, but I doubt it.

You'll be happy we haven't seen much action. Not like some other guys. My God. We've all heard stories, but . . . I try not to think about it. Lucky so far. Every day we hear that the war is close to over, but we still hear the crackle of gunfire at night. And each night it's a little closer.

As always: food's bad, weather's bad. Everything is bad here.

Only nine months, eighteen days left.

Love,
Nate

****

Western Union Telegram. Dated: July 17, 1969.

919A—EST. JUL17 69. BRS 175

MR AND MRS COLBERT HART, DONT PHONE DONT DELIVER BTWEEN 10PM AND 6AM. REPORT DELIVERY

6150 NORTHTON AVE DAYTON OHIO

I DEEPLY REGRET TO INFORM YOU THAT YOUR SON, PFC NATHANIEL R HART USMC HAS DIED 16 JULY 1969 IN VIETNAM FROM WOUNDS RECEIVED WHILE IN COMBAT OPERATIONS AGAINST HOSTILE FORCES.

G. Nicholas Miranda

PLEASE ACCEPT MY DEEPEST SYMPATHY. THIS WILL CONFIRM PERSONAL NOTIFICATION MADE BY REPRESENTATIVE OF THE US MARINE CORPS.

***

Stamped Unsendable/Undeliverable on July 19, 1969. Handwritten letter.

PFC Nate Hart
July ?, 1969

Mom,

In hospital. I forget a lot of things. I hurt everywhere—still have all my parts.

In a room, just me. I've heard other guys but not seen. Crying. Moaning. Sure hope they're okay.

No idea what happened. All blank for now.

But I'm fine. Should be coming home with Purple Heart.

Love,
Nate

***

Portion of audio transcript from debriefing. Dated: July 21, 1969. Typed.

[Dr. VanSchnete] What can you recall from the moments directly before the event?

[PFC Hart] I was loading munitions into crates for the Hueys to airlift to the new location.

[Dr. VanSchnete] About what time was this?

148

PFC Nathaniel Hart Has Died

[PFC Hart] I couldn't tell you. The sun was out.

[Unknown Male] The evac began shortly after 1400 hours. Helos first, then trucks with equipment and personnel.

[PFC Hart] I guess so, sir. But I don't remember leaving base.

[Dr. VanSchnete] We know the last radio call was placed approximately 1600.

[Unknown Male] Then why ask about what time he was loading?

[Dr. VanSchnete] We know something happened after 1600 hours. His memory only goes back to sometime before that. I'm setting the control for the tests.

[Unknown Male] So he's useless.

[Dr. VanSchnete] Not at all.

[Unknown Male] How so?

[Dr. VanSchnete] He's still here.

[PFC Hart] Yeah. *(grunt in discomfort)* Right here.

(four pages missing from transcript)

[Dr. VanSchnete] I'm not that kind of doctor, Private.

[PFC Hart] Oh.

[Dr. VanSchnete] I study the metaphysical correlation between our advancing technology and our perception of reality. More specifically, its implications in wartime.

(long pause)

[Dr. VanSchnete] You aren't supposed to understand it. Basically,

G. Nicholas Miranda

I'm trying to understand how grunts like you evolve the way you fight wars in regard to the future technologies.

[PFC Hart] Like ray-guns and things?

[Dr. VanSchnete] In a way. More precisely, I'm looking to see if you are a better fighter right now knowing that you might one day get to use a ray-gun. Or, perhaps your grandchildren.

[PFC Hart] Did Charlie hit us with some kind of ray? Do the Reds have that Buck Rogers stuff?

[Unknown Male] No. The convoy was not attacked by the Vietcong.

[PFC Hart] Friendly?

[Unknown Male] Definitely not.

[PFC Hart] What happened, sir? If it wasn't them and it wasn't us?

[Unknown Male] That's classified at—

[PFC Hart] (pounding on table) I almost died. For fuck's sake! Where are the rest of the guys? How many made it?

[Dr. VanSchnete] Private, please—

[PFC Hart] When—*(groans)*—when can I go home?

****

From Dr. Louis VanSchnete to his associate and partner, Dr. Jacob Kritzel. Dated: July 22, 1969. Stamped Undeliverable/ Unsendable on July 22, 1969. Typed letter.

Jacob,

I am writing to you from a place in the world I am not permitted to address. I don't know if this will even reach you.

PFC Nathaniel Hart Has Died

Something has happened.

Yesterday, I was debriefing PFC Nathaniel Hart about an—*incident*, is what I'm supposed to call it. There was some kind attack on a caravan. Nearly all were killed. But what is remarkable is that PFC Hart has died. And not just once.

He was barely alive when he was brought here, and he died at least twice during his surgery. But, then, his heart stopped on at least four other occasions during recovery—and for no less than six minutes each time! He was revived and seems perfectly fine.

I truly believe he will succeed where our first trials failed.

I will keep you informed of PFC Hart's condition. I have already begun a casebook and will send you page transcripts as often as I can.

Always.
L.

***

Report filed by unidentified person on July 23, 1969 (possibly Unknown Male on debriefing audio transcript). Original document was redacted by addressee before filing. Typed message.

From: [*redacted*]
Locale: [*redacted*], Vietnam

To: [*redacted*]
Locale: Pentagon—Washington, D.C.

RE: Project Boundary

16 July, 69. Convoy enroute to [*redacted*] was completely destroyed by unknown hostile. 15 survivors, 185 casualties.

Per Directive [*redacted*], survivors were evaluated and airlifted to predetermined facility.

PFC N. Hart was the first to awaken. He has no recollection of the attack, but, as noted in the accompanying file by Dr. Louis VanSchnete, has sustained full cardiac arrest on multiple occasions and been successfully resuscitated. Of note is the length of time PFC Hart has been in arrest. Shortest amount of time: 4.5min. Longest: 7.25min. Repeat: PFC Hart has died no less than six times and remains stable.

This confirmation by Dr. VanSchnete makes PFC N. Hart a prime candidate for Project Boundary. Consider this the official request to proceed as outlined in [*redacted*].

Per Dr. VanSchete's request, I must inform you that PFC Hart is exhibiting some side effects, of which I have been witness. At times, he becomes combative and disoriented. He had a single, life-threatening injury, which is the cause of his cardiac trauma, which has been treated and he is no longer considered in danger. His other injuries were superficial. He complains of phantom pains, however, in places where he has no injury. No concern is warranted, I believe.

***

Handwritten letter.

PFC Nate Hart
July 24, 1969
Unknown. Vietnam, still, maybe?

Mom/Dad,

They said it was nine days since the convoy was attacked. They said I was nearly dead. But, honestly, I feel great! And I'm not just saying that so you won't worry.

I feel like a million bucks.

PFC Nathaniel Hart Has Died

I keep going to speak to this Doc. He's a nice guy—studies some weird stuff, though. I laughed because they'll give anyone a PhD if they use a lot of long, garbled words to explain something no one understands anyway. But I guess that's why he gets to wear that white coat and I get fed cold oatmeal and water that tastes like the inside of a tuna can.

They tell me a few other guys made it out of the convoy, but I don't know who. Haven't seen or heard from any of them. Hope Carter made it. He owes me $10 from cards!

Still no word on when I might get outta here, but I'm sleeping easy because I know that my next stop is HOME.

Love,
Nate

✷✷✷

Typed letter.

Office of the US Marine Corps
Dayton, OH
7 August, 1969

Mrs. Delores Hart,

Again, we offer our deepest condolences regarding the loss of your son, PFC Nathaniel Hart. You have the eternalgratitude of this office, the entire USMC, and the whole of the United States.

We are greatly concerned with your telephone call and letter, however. I have rechecked our records and verified that, in fact, PFC Nathaniel Hart has died. His personal effects are currently being sent to you, but parcel post travels much slower than standard mail or telegrams. Rest assured, we will not take this matter lightly. The office commander, Maj. J. Ruttledge Grice, has launched an investigation into the letter supposedly sent from your deceased son.

G. Nicholas Miranda

During these times, it may not be unheard of for dissenters and anti-war propogandists to send forgeries as a means to stir up contention between the American people and the government. We ask for your patience in the matter while we look into it further.

Yours,
Edith H.
Secretary to Maj. J. R. Grice

***

Handwritten note addressed to unknown person [likely the Unknown Male]. Undated.

CHECK YOUR MAILROOM! SOMEONE LET DEAD MAN'S LETTER GET SENT OUT . . . THAT HE WROTE A WEEK AFTER HE DIED! OPERATION IN JEOPARDY!

***

Handwritten document. Audio notes transcribed by Dr. VanSchnete into his casebook. Transcript mailed to Dr. Kritzel on August 6, 1969.

DV: The time is 0900 on August 4th. Subject is Private First Class Nathaniel Hart, henceforth to be referred to as Subject 61. With me are nurses John Haywood and David Trembor. Also present is—

X: Don't say my name.

DV: Very well. I'll call you X.

X: You aren't actually going to do anything? Just talk into that thing?

DV: My medical training is rudimentary. Subject 61 has been made as comfortable as possible on the table. He appears apprehensive. States that he feels quite well.

154

PFC Nathaniel Hart Has Died

Haywood: Both injections are prepared.

DV: Thank you. Proceed.

Haywood is about to administer the first injection. The chemical compound is classified, but my associate, Dr. Kritzel, has made several adjustments to the formula since . . . .We have learned much in the last two years.

X: What if he doesn't survive?

DV: That's kind of the point.

X: *(audible grunt)*

DV: Haywood has finished the injection. Trembor will begin monitoring blood pressure.

Trembor: 121-over-77.

DV: Elevated, as expected. Previous experience has taught me that a sense of unawareness is likely one major key needed for the desired outcome.

Trembor: 119-over-77.

DV: Will continue to monitor until 61's heartrate begins to retard.

(audio stop/start)

DV: 61's heartrate has fallen to 45 B-P-M. Body temp is . . . ? Haywood?

Haywood: 97-point-3.

DV: 61 is approaching the threshold. Trembor will continue to provide subject data while Haywood keeps time. Uh . . . someone else will be providing instruction to 61 during this time.

(long pause)

Trembor: He's going. Full arrest! Subject 61 has died.

Haywood: Beginning timer.

DV: *(To X)* That's you're cue.

X: Private. This is your acting C-O. Your orders are as follows: note your location and remember any details. Any and all information is crucial for mission success. Repeat: any and all information is vital.

DV: Step one is complete.

Haywood: 30 seconds.

Trembor: Temp is at 97-point-oh.

DV: Temperature's falling a bit fast. We are proceeding to step two. *(To X)* If you're ready?

X: Repeat: note your location and remember all possible details.

(pause)

Haywood: 1 minute.

DV: We are allowing 61 to push past the standard time limit one might ordinarily face. The brain can survive for more than two minutes without oxygen before damage sets in. And 61 has proven he can go well past that. We don't know why yet. Perhaps a kind of fluke, or mutation.

X: Or maybe he just doesn't want to die.

DV: Indeed.

(audio stop/start)

Haywood: 3 minutes, 30 seconds.

PFC Nathaniel Hart Has Died

DV: Moving on to step three.

X: Private. You are to take any steps necessary to interact with your environment. Try and touch or move things. This is mission-critical. Repeat: note and attempt interaction with your environment.

DV: We will begin resuscitation procedure in 90 seconds. The acting C-O will continue repeating 61's orders at 20-second intervals.

(audio stop/start)

DV: Trembor? Please administer the second injection.

X: No. Wait. Not yet.

DV: We must. The formula needs time to be integrated into the bloodstream.

X: Private Hart!

DV: What are you doing? *(sounds of struggling, Trembor grunting)* We need to give him the second shot so it can work its way through his body while Trembor does the chest compressions.

Trembor: Hey!

X: Private, you are to make your way to Hanoi.

DV: Are you insane? We don't know—

X: Locate Ho Chi Minh.

DV: You bastard!

X: We need his location, Private.

DV: You can't— *(garbled)* The unknowns are beyond dangerous.

(more struggling) Get him away! Why are all you idiots all the same?! Something new comes along and the very first thing you do is—

X: I'm trying to save lives, Doctor.

(garbled; static; intense buzzing and snapping)

Haywood: Jesus!

DV: Trembor, give him the shot! Now!

X: What—*(choking)*

DV: Haywood, start chest compressions.

Haywood: But—

DV: Now! I'm stopping this.

Trembor: Okay. Go!

X: *(straining)* Help . . . me . . .

(audio stop/start)

DV: The time is 0945. 61 was revived at . . . 0912 and 24 seconds. He is currently recuperating in his room. X is also in recovery. Haywood and Trembor did a thorough examination. He has several contusions on his neck and lacerations on his face. He looks . . . beaten.

Outcome yields a few possibilities, but we will not know the extent of the damage X may have caused until 61's debrief.

***

PFC Nathaniel Hart Has Died

Stamped Undeliverable/Unsendable on August 14, 1969. Handwritten letter.

PFC Nate Hart

Mom/Dad,

I'm so tired. There are no windows. No clocks. When I sleep, I never know for how long. Sometimes they come and wake me up for more tests.

Feels like the more I sleep, the harder it is to stay asleep.

Am I in a psych ward? Did I get shell-shocked from the convoy? One minute I'm in my room, the next I'm in some building, in city, in a country . . . Are these mad dreams?

The Doc does his best. He asks, I answer. Two men, both nurses, keep me comfortable as best they can. Uncle Sam likes to make everyone miserable, so I don't hold it against them.

Still don't know where I am. And, like I said, some days I'm in a different place all together.

I feel stronger, though. Like I have an energy inside me that not only keeps me going, but also gives me more overall. Funny, right? I said I'm tired, but also have all this energy. That's the thing about this place. I'm weak, but strong; here, but somewhere far away, too.

HOME SOON.

Love,
N.

***

G. Nicholas Miranda

Stamped Undeliverable/Unsendable on August 16, 1969. Handwritten letter.

Mom/Dad,

I'm dying. Every day. At least it feels like it. Today is a good day.

I'm dreaming. Distant places. Sometimes there's people. And I remember the strangest things. Voices. Things around me. Seems like sometimes I'm wherever for a long time. Sometimes it's seconds. Many times I'm angry when I wake up. I want to come home.

LOVE,
N.

***

Hand-written note dated August 20, 1969 from Edith H. to Maj. Grice, USMC.

Sir—Mr. Hart called again, re: the attached. Demands any info on PFC N. Hart.

Threatening legal action.

EH

***

Unfiled report; began by Maj. Grice on August 13, 1969. Typed form.

Comments: Notified of letter from Mrs. Delores Hart regarding possible error in death records for PFC Nathaniel Hart. She claims to have received letter from son dated several days after his reported death.

Contacted Active Affairs office and received confirmation that PFC Nathaniel Hart has died. Replied to Mr./Mrs. Hart's letter restating unfortunate death of their son. EH advised that may be possible anti-war sympathizers.

On 12 Aug., FBI was contacted as well as Secret Service about possible mail fraud and falsifying gov't identification. Noted to both:

—handwriting is similar to PFC Hart

—correct postage and routing as would come from Vietnam

13 Aug: Agent Millan, FBI, assigned to investigation. Preliminary deduction concurs with theory of anti-war demonstrators; also, but very small chance, letter was pre-dated. Servicemen will write several letters at one time with progressing dates to mail at once if they are going to be on the move for long periods of time. This does not account for content, which references events which happened after PFC Hart left base with convoy.

14 Aug: Received call from Agent Millan. Agent is reassigned; we are to abort further inquiry into matter. Orders from within Joint Chiefs.

★★★

Casebook of Dr. VanSchnete. Handwritten entries.

8/30/69

0430: Sub 61 having seizures. Trembor monitoring vitals. Not clear of cause. 61 was responding well recently.

0700: Have scheduled interview with 61 for later. X apprehensive about proceeding. Think he's still shaken from 61's outburst.

1400: 61's mental state in serious question. X managed to come into the room this time. First time being in same location as 61 since. 61 gave no indication he recalled what happened. I believe this makes X even more fearful. But this is what he wanted!

G. Nicholas Miranda

***

Stamped Undeliverable/Unsendable September 1, 1969. Typed letter.

Jacob,

I believe our worst fears are being realized.

While Subject 61 has shown remarkable progress in Project Boundary, I do not believe he can withstand much more. His body is as good as can be, but his mind . . . he's *so young*. No one should endure what this young man is going through. Repeatedly having his heart stopped for longer and longer periods. Sending his very soul across greater and greater distances.

Mr. X has been keeping his distance lately, which I can only thank heaven for. His meddling is what has concerned me from the beginning. But on our last test, he came into the room after 61's heart had stopped. He began whispering to him, keeping his instructions secret from me.

I know 61 will suffer because of it; I feel I am failing him.

It was never supposed to be like this. Our research was meant to save lives. The government simply supplied us with the most valuable resources. Now I fear they have started seeing results and are eager to push us aside. I also know that HE is working against me . . . against us. I believe he thinks he's "learned" enough to proceed without my guidance.

As always, I shall continue to keep my notes. I do not know if the powers-that-be are letting them through, but I will rest easier knowing that I have the research.

Yours,
L.

***

PFC Nathaniel Hart Has Died

Portion of audio transcript from debriefing. Dated: September 3, 1969. Typed.

[Dr. VanSchnete] Subject Sixty-one? Do you know the date?

[61] No.

[Dr. VanSchnete] What about the year?

[61] Nineteen sixty-nine.

[Dr. VanSchnete] Very good.

[61] Feels like I'm not here.

[Unknown Male] Then where are you? Are you up for this?

[61] Yeah.

[Unknown Male] I need a report on your last assignment.

[61] Understood, sir.

[Unknown Male] Were you able to locate the target?

[61] Yes, sir.

[Unknown Male] Were you able to carry out your orders?

[61] Yes, sir. Target was in his hospital room.

[Unknown Male] Well, that should have made it pretty easy.

[61] It was.

[Unknown Male] Please elaborate.

[61] He was sick. I don't think he would have survived much longer on his own. I was able to move freely about the room, despite the

number of other people in there. I approached his bed. He was speaking to a young man who was writing something. When he started coughing, I grabbed his throat. He struggled but was too weak to fight me off. At this point, the others in the room realized something was wrong. Doctors came. I kept strangling him, even while they checked him over. Their hands passed through me. It's strange, though. As I held this old man's life in my hand I could feel . . .

[Unknown Male] Feel what?

[61] It's like I was telling you.

[Unknown Male] What's he talking about?

[Dr. VanSchnete] On more than one occasion, Sixty-one has made statements referring to a sensation he experiences when on assignment. He describes—

[Unknown Male] Why wasn't I made aware of this?

[Dr. VanSchnete] His task is your area of oversight. Everything that happens in between is mine.

[Unknown Male] What did you feel?

[61] Something else.

(*long pause*)

[Unknown Male] You're going to have to be more specific.

[61] You know how you can kind of sense someone standing behind you, reading over your shoulder? I can feel something, sir. Like it's swimming through the air around me.

[Unknown Male] What is it?

[Dr. VanSchnete] I don't know. You won't allow for adequate exploration of—

PFC Nathaniel Hart Has Died

[Unknown Male] Horseshit. It's just a hallucination or something. Finish the debrief.

[61] Yes, sir. *(clears throat)* Uh, I had the target, and I could feel this other thing. I know it sounds crazy. I could actually feel it moving around, wriggling right through me.

[Unknown Male] Unbelievable.

[61] The target was pronounced dead. There was a lot of commotion, but then I was gone.

[Unknown Male] Fine. That will be all. *(exits room)*

[Dr. VanSchnete] You have more, don't you?

[61] Yes, sir.

[Dr. VanSchnete] Go ahead.

[61] It's getting more *(pause)* insistent.

[Dr. VanSchnete] You still feel its presence after you wake up?

[61] The stretches of time between when I get the shot and when I get to the location are getting longer. And I can feel it with me. But it's stronger when I'm done, before I wake up back here. Are the others having similar experiences?

[Dr. VanSchnete] Do you think it's trying to communicate?

[61] It's kind of weird, but I think I can sort of understand it. Not words. Just feelings. Mostly anger. And *(lowers voice)* I won't say this to . . . whoever he is, but when I'm performing a task, I can feel its approval. Or, if I'm struggling with going through with the order, it's like it somehow comes into me, or into my head, and helps me.

[Dr. VanSchnete] Helps?

[61] Sort of puppets me?

(*long pause*)

[Dr. VanSchnete] I see.

***

Western Union Telegram. Dated: September 3, 1969.

To: Roger Stalt, Editor
News Daily News Desk

Ho Chi Minh dead at 79. Confirmed. N. Vietnamese officials state heart attack. No successor named at present.

—J. Harrison

***

Supplementary addendum to Maj. Grice's notes, dated September 3, 1969. Handwritten entry.

Received visit from Mr. Colbert Hart regarding his deceased son. He arrived brandishing another letter penned in his son's hand. What is going on? If this is anti-war protestors, they have devolved into demonic fervor, causing these poor people this kind of pain. Especially considering the contents. Edith to transcribe and attach.

***

Letter transcribed by Edith H on September 3, 1969. Typed letter.

From Nate

Dad. Mom. Firstly, I am okay.

The Doc has seen to me pretty good, and Haywood and Trembor are good guys. But we don't talk much. I keep asking when I'll be

PFC Nathaniel Hart Has Died

well enough to come home, but they never tell me.

I used to hear some of the other guys, crying out, hurt, or scared. It's mostly silent now. Maybe they went home. I hope they did.

It's every day now. I get the shot and die. I wake up in a . . . place. It's dark, like a huge cavern, but I can't see the walls. Then, I just get the feeling to go somewhere else; all I have to do is think about it and I'm there. I see people, places. I'm supposed to remember everything.

Floorplans. Second story, third door on the right. Small office, no window.

Conversations. Languages I don't understand. So many angry men.

I have touched a few people. I hurt them sometimes, if can. If I'm asked. Sometimes even when I'm not. It's hard to feel anything when I'm someplace else.

But don't worry.

I'll be home soon.

Love,
Me

★★★

Stamped Undeliverable/Unsendable September 8, 1969. Handwritten letter.

From Nate

Mom/Dad,

I'm not coming home. I'm sorry.

I think my body is becoming used to the chemicals, though. That's why I'm not so crazy. That's why I remember. It used to be that I would just dream or come around in a strange place, but now I am aware of the time between.

I'm in kind of a Noplace. That's when I start feeling the other thing that's there. It may live there. Or maybe it's like me, using the Noplace as a shortcut?

Dr. VanS might know. Might.

***

Typed letter.

Sept. 13, 1969

Jacob,

I am sorry for not sending anything recently, my friend. And of what I have sent, I do not know what was allowed to reach you. To ensure you receive this, I will censor myself.

First, you will be pleased that Sub. 61 is doing well. We are on a regular schedule and their recovery time is less than ever before. And in such short time. I do wish you were here, though, as having an ally would allow for us to have more control over the proceedings.

Second, I am afraid that there is something amiss with the general staff at this facility. I have overheard bitter discourse around corners or through doors I am about to enter, only to be met with silence upon entering. I believe this behavior is linked to the recent death of one of the mail clerks—the one in charge of sorting and sending communications. I do not know the particulars. I am only a researcher at the behest of Uncle Sam, and as such, am not privy to the goings on beneath Lady Liberty's skirts. All I know is that this young man was found deceased after a lengthy search of this location. God, I hope that nothing I have been part of led to this tragedy.

Finally, Jacob, I wish to thank you for the package you sent with those candied lemon sours, but as the military searches everything coming and going, the parcel arrived open, and with several of the lemon drops missing. Thank you very much, all the same.

Yours,
L.

***

Casebook of Dr. VanSchnete. Handwritten entries.

9/15/69
0900: 61 has died. Haywood begins time.

X waits in silence.

0903: X gives 61 instruction.

61 responds verbally?! A first!

Conversation is inaudible.

0905: X steps back. All quiet.

Boundary approaching.

0907: X repeats instruction.

No response from 61.

0910: Boundary eminent.

X repeats instruction.

61 responds: "I'm fucking trying!"

0912: Trembor instructed to give 2nd inj.

0913: No reaction from 61!

Haywood prepares epinephrine—admin ASAP

0915: 61 showing life signs, but no heartbeat??

Audible grunts. Weak movement.

0919: Still not fully out of it. What is happening?

0922: Trembor reports faint heartbeat.

X says he's uneasy. Feels something touching him. Left room.

0925: 61 heartbeat stronger. Coming around. Finally.

Farthest the Boundary has ever been pushed. 20 minutes!

***

Stamped Undeliverable/Unsendable September 17, 1969. Handwritten letter.

Mom,

It's in me. Maybe not right now, but when I'm between places, I no longer feel it around me. When I get to where I'm going, I know it's there. It's in me.

So strong.

It hates him. That man, the voice I hear in my head. It hates him as much as I do. I tried to kill him once, but I wasn't strong enough. Not on my own.

But it tells me there's another way to hurt him.

***

PFC Nathaniel Hart Has Died

Article from The Harrison Post. *September 15, 1969. News clipping.*

MOTHER, DAUGHTER DEATH INVESTIGATION

Police were called to a residence on E. Cantor St. sometime around 10:30 PM last evening for loud noises, crashing, and screams coming from inside.

Upon arriving, police had to force entry into the home where they discovered Mrs. Joanne Larkin (34) and her daughter, Beth (6), deceased.

Officer Vance was first on the scene, and says, "It was a mess inside. Looks like everything that could've been broken or shattered was busted up pretty good."

Det. William Hastings said, "We do not believe this to be a random attack. No signs of a break-in have been found, nor do we feel this was an attempted robbery. I can confirm that both females were physically assaulted, which led to their deaths."

No further information was provided.

Mrs. Larkin's husband is currently away in Vietnam.

***

Portion of audio transcript from debriefing. Dated September 18, 1969. Typed.

[61] Where's the other guy?

[Dr. VanSchnete] That's what I wanted to talk to you about. He received an urgent phone call the other night. Something happened stateside and he's gone.

[61] Oh?

[Dr. VanSchnete] Do you know anything about it?

[61] I don't.

[Dr. VanSchnete] You were away for a very long time during your last session. Almost as though you didn't want to come back.

[61] That so?

[Dr. VanSchnete] It seems a mother and her young daughter were attacked around ten-thirty in the evening. Both were killed.

[61] That's terrible, but I was asleep at ten-thirty.

[Dr. VanSchnete] You're from Ohio? You're aware of the thirteen-hour difference?

(*long pause*)

[61] Tell me about the others.

[Dr. VanSchnete] We've been over this. They're in recovery, same as—

[61] I don't mean the guys from the convoy.

[Dr. VanSchnete] Who, then?

[61] The ones who attacked the convoy.

[Dr. VanSchnete] They still don't know who hit your transport.

[61] Oh? Because I do.

[Dr. VanSchnete] You do?

[61] It was five men. Or what was left of them.

[Dr. VanSchnete] Come now. I don't think five men—

[61] With all due respect, Doc. There's a hell of a lot you haven't thought of.

PFC Nathaniel Hart Has Died

[Dr. VanSchnete] Then elaborate, please.

[61] You think I just die on your table, then wake up somewhere else like (*snaps fingers*)? That as my brain starts shutting down, I hear the orders in my ear and obey? Yes. All right. I do. But there's a whole eternity in between those slowing heartbeats. Between dying and waking. Every time. And I've made some good friends in those gaps.

[Dr. VanSchnete] Who?

[61] The first five who pushed the boundary. The ones you pushed a little too far.

[Dr. VanSchnete] You meet these men in some sort of limbo?

[61] Not anymore. They aren't there now.

[Dr. VanSchnete] Where did they go? *(long pause)* Sixty-one? Where did they go?

****

Marked—URGENT—Typed letter.

Sept. 18, 1969

Jacob,

I am sending you all of my notes thus far. Hopefully with the new mail clerk, more messages will go out, and less edited.

Something has happened.

Sub. 61 has given me reason to believe that our initial foray into going past the boundary was not the failure we first thought! Indeed, if his claims are to be believed, then we may very well have far surpassed either of our theories.

G. Nicholas Miranda

Read over the notes. You'll see what I mean.

If our tests succeeded the first time, then not only can we wash our consciouses, but we can also begin the final step, as we always discussed.

Yours,
L.

***

Stamped Undeliverable/Unsendable September 19, 1969. Handwritten letter.

Mom,

I know what I said was the truth, even if the Doc didn't. I saw his reaction. It was confusion. At first. But then, when he did figure it out, it was fear.

I wish I could give you their names, then, maybe, you could write their families. But they have either forgotten them, or just won't tell me. Those in between times—if you'd have asked me a few weeks ago, I would have told you that hell is a big, cave-like place with deep pits of lava and fire and freezing blackness. No, that's not hell. Hell is that eternity between one second and the next. That dead time between heartbeats . . . *thump-dead-thump.*

These men. They didn't go through what I've gone through. I know that much. For them it was a one-way trip. Sometimes I think they're mad that I'm always coming or going. But I know they hit the convoy. Somehow, they were able to pull together and do what I do. Lately I've been letting them come with me. They've been hitching a ride with me for a while, I just didn't know it was them. Or, rather, it. See, there is no form there. Just thought. So, the five thoughts can be one, and that one can be one with me. When I get to where we're going they're still with me, even when I do what I'm supposed to.

And I do bad things, Mom. I do what I'm told, but I do bad things.

174

PFC Nathaniel Hart Has Died

I killed people. They try and tell me it's the bad guys, but . . . who are the bad guys? Not those poor folks living in the small huts, who watch as we march and search and destroy. Not the women and children who are buried under a few inches of mud. I may have come here because my country demanded it of me, and I may have been one of first in line. But these people didn't ask for that.

But I can change what's happening, Mom. We can change it. It only took five to wipe out almost 200 in a matter of seconds. And I can go longer.

Nate

***

Casebook of Dr. VanSchnete. Handwritten entries.

Sept. 22, 1969

I don't know what to do anymore.

61 is going farther and farther past the boundary. Each time he is revived there is something different about him. He talked about an entity that interacts with him when he is in the Noplace. He described it as an observer at first—there, but at a distance. Then, he said it was closer. He said it was moving around him, "swimming," I believe he explained.

He began to describe it as an amalgamation of separate entities.

The first five.

I can't believe it, but it would be impossible for 61 to know anything about them otherwise.

The mail clerk gave me a letter 61 had written to his mother. If he is correct, if those five were responsible for attacking the convoy, then I can't even begin to imagine what that means.

Joseph initially theorized that the government's research into extrasensory perception, remote viewing, the paranormal in general, was not going far enough. During his time in Korea he was struck by the amount of pain and death he saw. A veteran himself, he thought there should be a better way to end conflicts. When he read my paper on fighting battles in the present using future knowledge . . . well, he knew he was in over his head, but it got him thinking.

Together we came up with Project Boundary: that soldiers fighting today would be at their best if they did not have to fear death.

Obviously, the government laughed at the notion of ghosts.

But we proved them wrong with the first five. They were able to do what could not be done by any regular soldier, any standard secret agent. The trouble was not being able to bring them back.

61 is the key! I know it. He is able to make contact with these five, merge with them. They can work as a single unit or independently.

***

Message from Unknown Male to Charles Halveston, Special Director of Projects. Undated. Handwritten letter.

Sir,

I believe that Project Boundary is ready for the next step. Our current subject, PFC Hart is the strongest he's ever been, as evidenced by our success with Ho Chi Minh.

I have been reviewing Dr. VanSchnete's notes. If he is to be believed, then I am sure that PFC Hart will not only be able to continue operating at longer and longer intervals, but also help lead entire units across the unknown stretch between life and death, then return.

My undocumented sessions with PFC Hart have shown again and again that he is more than up to the task. The missions to villages, to our own bases! This is as covert as it gets.

PFC Nathaniel Hart Has Died

At this time, please divert a small percentage of the wounded to our facility for further study.

****

Stamped Undeliverable/Unbendable September 27, 1969. Handwritten letter.

Mom,

There is no quiet anymore. I feel less and less like myself each time Doc takes me away to die.

Even after I—please forgive me!—killed the man's wife and daughter, he came back. I thought, the others thought, getting him away would end this, but it only made it worse. He is more determined. Pushes us so hard.

We try and hide in the Noplace, but his voice bullies us to where he wants us to go. To do what he wants me to do. And I do it. Just so that I don't have to hear him anymore.

But we have a plan. The next time he takes me to the lab without the Doc, we'll be ready.

****

Incident Report. Dated: October 1, 1969. Statement sworn/signed by Harold Barnes, SPC, US Army. Handwritten document.

On the evening of 30 September, I was taking inventory in the supply room when I heard shouting. I left the supply room and followed the disturbance to Dr. VanSchnete's lab.

Inside, I witnessed two individuals (Haywood and Trembor, both nurses) lying on the floor beside an operating table. There was blood on the floor. There was a body on the table.

Dr. VanSchnete was on the opposite side of the room, also on the floor. It appeared he had been pushed into a shelving unit of equipment. Lots of machinery lay around him and the shelves had collapsed on top of him. He was not moving.

When I went to assist, I heard the voice of another man. I do not know the man's name but have seen him many times around the compound. He appeared conscious, but was struggling to breathe. I made multiple attempts to check his airway, but he continuously swatted me away. No matter how hard I tried to help him. It was like he wanted to die.

There was a loud pop. He went still.

At that point, the body on the table began to stir. But when I stood to see what could be done to help, I was knocked off my feet by the force of the doors being blown open.

Upon regaining consciousness, I could hear the shouts and screams coming from within the facility. Realizing that I alone was unequipped to defend against an attack, I sought shelter in the supply room where my injuries forced me into unconsciousness again.

I was awakened by a medic and told by Staff Sgt. Mendez to complete this incident report.

***

Note discovered on the floor of PFC Hart's quarters. Undated. Handwritten letter.

Dear Mom, Mom, Momma, Mother, Dearest Mother, Mom.

PFC Nathaniel Hart has died.

We are coming home.

Love,
ALL OF US

In the Event ...

Liam Hogan

My Love,

Do not let the world know I died today. Tomorrow is soon enough. Today is just for you and for me. To *remember*. To celebrate our love, even as you steel yourself for the ordeals that follow.

Know this, and accept my deepest regret that I did not say it often enough or plainly enough: I love you. I have loved you from the moment I first set eyes on you, that enchanted day when you wandered oh-so-innocently into my life. And, despite the difficulties of the difference in our ages, I truly hope that over time, you came to love me. It is a hope that sustained me and, in a very real way, kept me young a while longer.

But such autumns are all too brief, and their days, as well as mine, were always numbered.

Such is life, and such is death.

Carry this last letter with you, my love, throughout the day, to guide you, step by step. Indulge me in this request, and I promise! by the end of it all, your worries and concerns, financial and otherwise, will be as nothing. But in your eagerness, please do not skip ahead. It is not meant to be read in a single sitting, the words and sentences tripping over one another. Doing so would surely spoil what I have carefully prepared. And even, dare I suggest, my sincere promise to you and to your future might be for naught, should you make an unfortunate or hasty misstep.

Liam Hogan

I am sorry to be such a nag, my love—but permit me one final time to dictate the pace for both of us. Restrain your youthful exuberance on such a mournful day as this.

If you were to turn to the last line of the pages you hold, (did you do that already, my love? Tut, tut! *Such* impatience!), you would find this letter incomplete. Do not fret, worrying that you must have dropped a few sheets, or rifle through the envelope looking for more. This is merely the *first* instalment. With your careful attention, other sheets will to be found along the way.

Think of it, if you like, as a treasure hunt. A not-so-idle entertainment to keep me anchored in your thoughts a while longer. A mystery to be solved, with a great reward at its close. You may not feel in the mood for games. You may even be distraught at my passing. But humour me, please. I do this for *our* sake, my dearest, yours and mine. And not merely as a distraction.

I trust you, of *course*, but curiosity is such a very strong pull, especially were the pages to seem greater in number than you might expect. How could you stop yourself from racing ahead to find what hides within? And so I must control the flow, and you must play along. It is more important than you could possibly know that you do as I ask. For both the living, and the dead.

Though I must, I suppose, offer you another option, lest you think me tyrannical. Perhaps you have already read my last will and testament? It is easily found, as it was meant to be, even if it too was previously sealed. A small disk of wax is protection no longer, now that I have passed. If you have seen it before reading this, then I hope you were not overly put out. In it, I have left you a small but well-appointed cottage, in the seaside town in which we honeymooned, along with an annual allowance that will allow you to live comfortably enough, if you are prudent. Perhaps not in the manner to which you have become so quickly accustomed, but far more than anything you tasted before our paths crossed.

This, then, is the alternative I offer you. But know now, and let it set your quivering mind at ease, that there is *another* will which supersedes the one you have cracked the seal from, the one that is not, in fact, the "last". Somewhere, in this grand, tired old house, lies another, rather more generous will, another testament. That is just one part of the grand prize of this treasure hunt of mine, and what, my love, we play the game for.

The living taking precedence over the dead. So to you goes the first move. If you wish, you may put aside this letter, read no further, and so accept the terms of the earlier will. Be happy with your chosen lot. Or, play for everything—except a bequest or two to my most loyal servants, ones who perhaps should have retired half a decade ago. It is your choice, my love, and should be made of your own free will. Decide now, whether or not to turn the page.

My dear, I'm so *very* glad you decided to read on! Were I still alive, it would make my stuttering heart race with delight in your bold courage. I had thought, I had the *temerity* to assume, that this would indeed be your choice, but it was never certain.

Well then. You have been patient, I think. We should speed things along. The very first thing to do, right now, even as you read this next sheet, sitting in my study, is to pour yourself a glass of the heady tonic I used to drink every evening, the one I would never let you taste. You'll find the key for the decanter on my key chain with which this letter was weighted down—take them all, you'll need the others, later.

Make sure the glass is full, my dear. And—go on—drink it down. Drink it all down.

Yes—a *most* distinctive taste. Not unpleasant, I hope? The wine that is its base is perhaps the least important part of it. A rich burgundy, for preference. The rest is a concoction of my own devising, a recipe of surprising antiquity, balancing both taste and efficacy. The struggles I have had over the years, when certain ingredients became no longer available! Others, that were once prohibitively expensive and previously near impossible to source, are now cheap and obtained over any pharmacist's counter. Such, my dear, is progress.

Liam Hogan

There. Do you not feel more relaxed already? Your nerves soothed, your skin buzzing from the tonic's stimulants? Do remember to replace the decanter's stopper—we shall be returning to it.

Now fortified, let us take a stroll around the gardens. And I do mean 'us', even if I am currently only with you as paper and ink. I have imagined your every step as I penned these words.

Exit by the side door, beneath the arch of wisteria. Take the gravel path that leads to the walled garden, there are some things I'd like to point out along the way. If, as I and my ghoulish physician predict, this fateful day arrives in early April—probably on a Wednesday, in time for a weekend funeral—then there will be some signs of new growth in the beds and in the sheltering trees above. Reassuring, is it not? Life *always* finds a way.

I spent a lot of time in this particular section of the garden, cultivating rare plants, and warning away those who might pick the flowers for their vases. Some of these blooms have *fangs*, my dear. A few can be found in the tonic coursing through your veins.

To your left, you will find belladonna. A renowned poison, but also a powerful medicine when prepared the correct way, when used in the correct doses. And there, monkshood, also known as wolfsbane, or aconite, though it is a few months before it will don its distinctive purple helm.

The opium poppies will also not be flowering yet, more is the pity. Such a *showy* delight, and their balm has long served to ease my aching body, to calm my sometimes feverish, crowded mind. One hopes *you* will not require such ministrations, for many a year yet to come.

You're approaching the end of the page, aren't you, my dear? Fortunately, the next sheets are not far away. The potting shed will be locked—always locked!—but you have the key, you have all the keys.

I hope you don't mind, I haven't been in here for a while, so there may be cobwebs. But I could hardly leave the pages out in the open, could I? Which might give you some hint at how long I have been planning this particular treasure hunt, though you would still err on the low side.

What you are looking for will be easy to find, if you follow my precise instructions. In the cabinet of chemicals—also locked—containing rooting powder, fungicides, and the like, you'll find a small jar, simply labelled "P5". Be careful to select the right one! Some of these chemicals are as unfriendly to us as to any garden pest. Open the jar, and, quickly now, before the scent fades, hold it close and breathe *deep*.

Does it tickle your pretty nose? Does it make you want to sneeze? If you close your eyes, and inhale once more, you may see stars— floating motes of light exploding against the dark. I like to imagine my brain firing whenever I do this, my synapses awash with giddy, borrowed energy.

Quite invigorating, though not, alas, to be over-indulged.

Close the jar once again. This powder comes from the ground up seed of one of my more exotic plants. Now, find which of the many small hessian seed sacks has the same distinctive aroma. When you identify it, open that sack up, careful not to spill the precious contents, and root within: the pages you are looking for are there, tightly folded.

Do you have them? We can go no further if you do not . . .

Ah excellent, you *do*! Blow the dust off, and on we go, my love. Leave behind those other sacks, all those *other* pages, with their wrong turns, their false trails and misleading instructions. You would be amazed—amused, possibly—at the effort I have put into this little game! All to keep you honest, all to keep you on the desired path.

Talking of which, continue on, along the gravel to the very end of the walled garden. Don't worry if you feel a little lightheaded, that is only to be expected! The faintness might even worsen, before it passes—have you reached the bench? By all means take a moment there, my love. Sit and look out over this peculiar garden of mine, that is now yours. I imagine you feel you would put it to better use. Flowers, or perhaps some herbs for the kitchens, hmm? But don't be too hasty. There is a wealth here of another kind, and it has served me well, this physic garden and its potent produce, as it may serve you, down the line.

You were, I believe, not particularly upset that I spent so much time pottering about down here. It meant you knew where I was, and knew I wouldn't call upon you for a little while. Freeing you up for other interests, for other parts of the grounds. For spending time with those closer to your own age, such as the head gardener's son.

Oh, do not think that I am, or was, jealous! Except of his youth, his vigour. Largely wasted, though attractive in its own crude fashion. If an employee of mine should lose their head and make improper demands of you . . . well, you never lost *yours*, did you? I thank you for that, for your discretion. You were not keen to risk everything, no matter how passionate your paramour.

And I could hardly satisfy all of your desires, could I? An old, infirm man like me? Oh, I did my best . . . especially in those halcyon days when first we wed, when I was not quite so decrepit. I might hope that I surprised you, my love, just as you must have believed you surprised me. Not quite so innocent as you first appeared, hmm?

If you have now caught your breath and are as impatient as ever, let us carry on to the artist's studio, at the very end of the gardens, a reminder, perhaps, of just how extensive these grounds are. Yes, it is secluded, but *you* knew that already. You might be horrified to know quite how familiar I am with this romantic spot, though I haven't set foot here for almost a decade.

And look, one of my servants has been here before us, and left out another glass of my tonic, and another sheet of this seemingly endless letter. Take a seat, take a glass, and read on, my love.

If I was asked, as perhaps those who will now try and weigh my life might wish to do, what I consider my most notable achievement, it may not be quite what anyone would expect. Yes, I have accumulated astonishing wealth, certainly more than one might expect from my humble upbringing. We have that in common, my love. But much of that wealth was inherited, as was the proud Malmaines name. Through marriage, not ancestry. Like you, my first marriage was to one much older, and richer, than I. My dear Emilia. It is as though she is with me still.

I have managed that wealth well enough. Surprisingly well, to those who knew me before I was married—almost as if I was born to it. But to claim that as my crowning *success*, well.

Rather, it has been to choose to do things on my own terms. And this includes even my end. To pick the moment of my passing, and the manner, and not to leave it in the fickle hands of fate, whose cruelties and indignities can linger unbearably.

You think you begin to understand why my physic garden was so important to me, and why some of those carefully cultivated plants would not be found in other gardens, too potent and deadly for such intimate proximity?

You still only know the half of it, my love. But read on, and you will learn more. If your glass is now empty—and it would be a tragedy to waste a drop of it—let us return to the house across the great lawn, taking our time to glance back at the splendid, bucolic vista that belies the artistry such grand designs require, a landscape full of unnatural nature.

Enter by the French windows, they will have been left open for you. Take a moment to let your eyes adjust. Do the gloomy rooms feel empty? They are not—*you* are here, my love. You can admire anew my extensive collection of paintings, my silverware, the fine statuary. Perhaps you will play that other idle game, and try and guess how much I paid for them, and how much they are now worth.

There are a few items less than there used to be. A few small but exquisite pieces have vanished, over the recent months. You might have thought no-one would notice, not among so many other riches, but I did. Often as not, the disappearance coincided with one of your increasingly common jaunts into town.

But it is no matter. Those pretty little items were largely bought to entertain *you*, my dear. So I do hope you got a good price for them. And I do hope, now that you are close to owning *all* that remains, you do not suffer from seller's remorse.

You know, my love, I may have been a little disingenuous when earlier I mentioned your innocence. Oh, you certainly *played* the part well enough. But there was always a calculating eye behind those delightful blushes, those little endearments you rewarded me with. How readily you accepted the gifts I showered upon you!

As to love . . . Whether, ultimately, you did indeed love me, my dear, as you sometimes professed to my utter delight especially when begging a favour . . . If you did not, if I failed to inspire even the sort of fondness one has for an avuncular uncle, or even a doddering grandfather, if I was only ever a means to your end . . . then I *quite* understand. You were at least not so cruel as to reveal your true feelings, your real intent.

But you loved what I gave you. Certainly loved the idea of having it all to yourself. You would never have been content with that cosy seaside cottage, would you? And yet, though I have planned every step, it is your choices that have led you here, and may lead you further still.

That I know you for who you are, that I was not anything like as blind or foolish as I appeared, does not lessen my feelings for, and about you, my dear. I am rather glad that you have such a sharp edge, as perhaps I once also had. I do not think a true innocent would set foot in this house, or agree to be my wife. I do not think a true innocent would prosper, as I hope *you* prosper, in the difficult days ahead.

We come once again to the end of this particular instalment. How quickly the pages fly by! So let us wander down the hall to my library. A suitable place to find more to read.

And—there, another glass of tonic already poured for you, and covered with a cloth against the dust, and another page of my spidery writing waiting for you. My loyal servants have made good use of the time we spent outside, my love, following my precise instructions to the letter.

I do hope you are not fatigued? This tonic will surely help—sip it, perhaps, this time. Make it last. You'd be surprised at how easy it is to acquire a taste for it, but it does not do to be too greedy. Sip it, surrounded by ancient wisdom, and you will soon be ready for the next steps in our amusing dance.

Look around you, my love. Like my physic garden, there was never very much for you in my library, was there? So full of dry, incomprehensible texts. No brash, colourful covers, not a romance nor an adventure among them!

These volumes speak to my interests, not yours, and once again, I think you were happy to see me head this way of an evening or on a cold, rainy day, knowing I'd be in the company of long-dead authors for some time. You might be surprised to know how lofty my reputation is amongst collectors of occult literature, and how often true connoisseurs of the arcane would beg to pay me a visit. These are your books now—or will be, shortly. Those frustrated collectors will want to visit *you*, once word of my passing reaches their ears, and will have few scruples in plundering my collection to bolster their own.

Right now, you probably wouldn't put up much of a fight. Hopefully, by the time the vultures descend, I will have convinced you otherwise. Assuming we successfully solve the next puzzle and find the next pages that will lead you a step closer to your prize.

Though I rather fear I must be boring you, my love? My pace, a little too languid, my boasts a little too tiresome? Time has yet to make the same demands on you that it has made on me, but it will. That is inevitable. These volumes may seem like a way of frittering away that time, but they are much more than that. They are my own personal way of cheating death. They contain a most intriguing puzzle, for me, and for those who owned them before, and perhaps, one day for you.

Liam Hogan

The solution to the puzzle lies not just in one book, oh no. I had to tease it together—pieces here, pieces there. The work, I suppose, of lifetimes, refined over and over to where we are today.

The texts tell of a way of gently shaking the soul from a body. Normally, such loosening of mortal ties only happens in death, and even then, it takes its time. The body is like a prison. The soul, left to its own devices, only leaves it towards the end of three days, and only as the walls begin to decay. There is good reason funeral practice around the world makes use of this measure of time, watching over the deceased day and night until they are laid to rest.

By the time the soul can escape, it is but a wisp of its former self, a mere shade. The waters of the Lethe have already washed away the person who once was, leaving only echoes, long before the ferryman takes his due.

But these texts reveal ways, complex ways, of severing those ties so that a soul may leave the body within hours, and then, with almost its full facilities intact.

Ah, but what *then*, I hear you ask? What is a soul, without a body? A short-lived thing, quickly fading to the same ghostly shadow of its former self.

This, then, is only one part of a greater puzzle. One part of the research to which I have invested both considerable time and large sums of money.

Let us return to *your* puzzle, my love. The next sheets are also in this room, though it would take you a lifetime to find them, without my help.

Are you ready? Is your glass once more empty? Have the demands of your body grown distant, muffled, as though floating on a bed of clouds? Then let us proceed!

In the middle of the third shelf beneath the bust of Nicolas Flamel—his appearance, as much as the story of his life and his discoveries, a modern invention!—you will find a particularly ancient volume, the gold letters worn from its spine, so that your eyes might skip over it, seeking meaning elsewhere. It is the one with the embossed cover, which would be familiar to you, perhaps, if you knew of Bellarmine witch bottles. The distinctive, bearded, scowling head, above a pentagram-starred medallion of a tree—the tree of life. Take this tome to the lectern; it is too fragile to be read on your lap, my dear!

Carefully open the volume to the twenty-sixth—the XXVI—page.

No, there is no letter there! But there *is* an incantation for you to read. Don't worry about the language, it is written out phonetically. Take a deep breath and read, loud and slow. Don't worry if the sounds snag at your brain, if it makes you think dreamlike thoughts. Don't worry even if you stumble; press on, my love, until you reach the very end.

Ah . . . did you hear a soft click, in the silence of those final vowels? No magic, I'm afraid. Merely Symons, lurking in the shadows, operating the mechanism as per my instructions. I wish I could have prepared something more elaborate, more dramatic, though in time you might appreciate *just* how remarkable that incantation is.

But for now, it is enough to know that a hidden hiding place has been revealed; a book, on another shelf, has been pushed forward and stands proud. Search for it! And open it, to find within the next pages of my letter.

My love, you have done so very well to get this far. You must be famished by now—you, who have almost forgotten what it is to hunger! But an empty stomach—other than that lingering tonic, which will fortify you a while longer—is necessary for what I must ask of you next.

You have spent time wandering the gardens and the house that was my home, that may shortly be yours, and yours alone. But you have not yet spent very much time with *me,* your sadly departed husband. It is time to correct that.

While you have been outside, and in the study, and in the library, my trusty servants have been busy, preparing my body. Cleaning it and dressing it. Let us go and see what they have wrought, what appearance of peace, of rest, they have been able to conjure.

You will find me in the storeroom next to the larder. Not an area you normally visit, my dear, deep in the bowels of the house, but it is dark and has the benefit of being cooled by an underground stream, and here I can lie on the great stone slab without being disturbed. Until tomorrow, when the undertaker will arrive to take away my empty husk, and to prepare it for internment in the family crypt.

Light the waiting candles, my love, the better to see me by. Does your hand tremble? Please, don't be frightened! Look at me, and look closely. Is it not almost laughable? What have you, so full of life, to fear from such a frail, withered thing? Nothing, my love. Nothing at all.

I must look quite the sight. Death does not suit me, I'd quip if I were there. Which I am, I suppose. And not just in letter form . . . Three days is a long way from having elapsed. So sit with me, my dear, in the chair provided. Don't mind the lingering incense. You might think it there to cover any unpleasant smells, but with the loving ministrations of my servants I am probably more fragrant than I have been for *quite* a while.

No, the incense is for you. A blend of my own devising. You might recognise elements from the thrice drunk tonic, from the seeds in the potting shed, and from the brittle pages you read the incantation from. They all work together, in concert, so much more than the sum of their parts!

Take my cold, fragile hand, my love, with your warm, tender one, and I will reveal to you the final sheet of this letter, the key to my fortune, and to my great secret.

Ah . . . here I am, hidden in the stiff, starched cuff! Cunning, yes? But don't let go of my hand just yet. Oh, I don't suppose you *can*. I apologise. My hand has been coated with tincture of aconite, very swift-acting. The paralysis is mostly localised and will wear off soon enough, freeing your hand when it does. No point in fighting it, my love! It is merely another step, one more hurdle for you to clear, and you have already come this far. Stay brave, and bold, a while longer.

If you peer closely at my lips, you will see they are stained red. Even redder than *yours*, my love. Symons will have fair drowned me in that tonic wine you've been drinking, using a silver funnel to pour a whole bottle down my lifeless gullet. Which is, I am sure you would agree, a most peculiar thing to do to a corpse. But there is method to the madness. Never doubt that. The tonic has the same effect on me, as I lie here in death, as it does on you, brimming with life.

It loosens the connection between body and soul.

You are the vessel, my love, into which I shall pour my spirit, before it fades any further. A little wastage is *necessary*, otherwise the fit will be most uncomfortable, and there would not be room for us both. I must lose a little to gain much. The same can be said for you.

You surely shudder at the thought. But did you really believe all of today was simply an act of loving memory? It is so much more.

You may think that my claims of love must surely have been false, for me to suggest such an abhorrent act. But again, you would be mistaken. I *do* love you, and I love what I will become, in you. Because what is the point in my love for you, if I am dead? It is better, surely, that I be alive, that I live for far longer than God intended any man to live. That way, I keep the flame for you, my ephemeral beauty, alive. And if that extended life comes at a cost . . . *well*. It is worth paying, I'm sure you'll agree. If not now, then in forty, or sixty years' time?

And yet, even with the end of the game nearly in sight, I must offer one final choice. It may not be a particularly palatable one, but a choice it is, nonetheless. Previously, I offered you a simple life, as an alternative to all my vast wealth. Now I up the stakes. What could be higher, you might wonder? What do I have, to further sweeten this side of the deal?

Ah, *aconite*. A powerful toxin, and while it is true the paralysis of your limb will fade, that will be because the poison has spread elsewhere. You may already feel its effects, the cold prickle down your spine, the numbing sensation even in the hand not locked with mine. These are as yet reversible—If you take the correct antidote, in time.

If not . . . well. You wouldn't be the first person to follow so swiftly in their spouse's graveyard footsteps, though there might be some eyebrows raised at one perishing so very young. Let us hope it doesn't come to that.

In a short while, control of your limbs will return. But know even then that the toxin is working its insidious way towards your heart. You won't have very long, I'm afraid, to find and take the antidote. Be grateful I have already prepared it for you.

Quick, turn the page—*the very last page*—to find out where it is, and where my last will and testament, leaving everything to you, awaits!

Ah. Was it not *obvious*? They are of course in the safe in my study! Where else would they be?

But though you have the required key, (have you already idly spun the heavy dial, wondering what treasures it contains? Treasures indeed!) you do not have the combination. Nor do any of my servants, nor the lawyer who drew up the will that sits inside that safe. Nor is it written down, here, or on any other pages. Only *I* know it.

You think me a cheat? That though I have now, as I promised I would all along, finally told you where to find both my will and your salvation, it is useless without me also telling you the one vital piece of information you need to access them?

In the Event . . .

But I do not, will not, *have* to, my love! Not if my memories mix into yours, not if my soul takes its place in your youthful body. This is the pact we must both enter into, if we are to survive. The only way that you can learn the combination, that you can save your life and inherit my wealth, is by taking one final brave step and letting *me* in.

It may not feel like I have left you much of an option. But this is the ultimate choice. Life or death. Perhaps the irrational heart that beats in your chest will baulk at the decision you must make to survive. So be it. All things, eventually, come to an end. I will merely describe what you must do to continue to live. It is up to you whether you go through with this final step. The one that will bind us forever. Or at least until your own body begins to fade, and I, we, must, once again, find our combined souls a new vessel, and once again, leave behind careful instructions to guide and prepare that vessel.

Though this game has been played by my rules, otherwise you would not be sitting where you are right now, there remains a chance that you might emerge as victor. That your personality will overrule mine. So in some ways, there is still all to play for. One more contest, then. One last challenge, one fateful duel. I have chosen an opponent, I believe, who would be quite my equal, if you had lived as many years as I. Whether your youthful strength and fiery anger will be enough to defeat my years of wisdom, only time will tell.

Perhaps it might even be considered a draw? *There's* an amusing thought.

It is a simple matter to take that last step, the last roll of the dice. Those cold, reddened lips of mine are still a gateway, of sorts. All you must do is bend forward and kiss me. A full, passionate kiss, drawing in the breath, and my soul, from the stopped lungs.

Do so, and we will share your body together. You will have access to my memories, the knowledge I have built up over the years, including, of course, the combination to my safe.

Liam Hogan

And I will live on, cheating death a while longer.

Best not wait too long, my love. The poison acts even now, and I'd prefer only a short period of convalescence, disguised as mourning. There is much to do, things I was too frail to attempt these last months. A packing case full of books to read. Travels to be made. Pleasures to be had.

A life to be lived.

I can hardly wait to live it with you.

My hand is cramped, my eyes weary, and I have crammed all I can into this final page of this final missive. Until the next instalment in our adventure together, my love, my dear . . .

Yours,

Wilfred, Emilia, Oscar, Constance, Harold, Imogen, Percival, Arabella de Malmaines.

Bury My Bones in the Bastard That Killed Me

Gordon B. White

Text message from a 917 area code

If you are reading this, than I am dead. Must avenge, etc. More to come.

Text message from someone with a 917 area code

*then

***

Letter received via USPS in an envelope with a "Spooky Silhouettes" stamp

Hey stranger,

Apologies for the brusqueness of my earlier missive. Time of the essence and so forth. Now that you've had one to three business days to digest, however, here it is:

I'm dead. And I need you to avenge me.

Specifically, I need you to bury my bones in the bastard who killed me.

The first thing you need to know is that I wrote this letter fairly far in advance. As a result, I've got a bit more breathing room to elaborate on the general situation in which you and I find ourselves without the pressure of, you know, being imminently killed. Regrettably, that distance also means a comparative lack of vengeance-related specifics. But don't worry, those are coming.

All will be revealed.

Which brings me to the second thing: Why you? Well, in a sense, it's perfect—you don't know me, and I don't *really* know you. At least, not in a way that can be traced online or through paper records. We've never met, but I can already tell some things about you.

You're the kind of person who has a deep sense of justice—although not necessarily bound by conventional social mores, aren't you? And from what I can tell, too, you're also the kind of person who can't bear to leave a task unfinished when you know someone's counting on you.

Tell me if I'm wrong, but you're a person whose curiosity, resourcefulness, and open-mindedness will see them through any challenge. Someone who is open to an adventure, even if you sometimes tell yourself that you aren't. I think you'll be the *perfect* avenger.

Even if things get a little . . . strange.

And so, we come to the third and final thing, which is that it's going to be a bit more difficult to get the next part of the instructions. By necessity they'll have been written much closer to the time of my passing, perhaps even by mere moments, so they're going to be *in* my person.

The specific location(s) will be coming soon (one of my more reliable colleagues is in charge of that). But in the meanwhile, here's a shopping list and money order that should cover the basics:

Bury My Bones in the Bastard That Killed Me

- Rubber gloves
- 3M Tyvek suit
- Hacksaw
- Really sharp knife x 2
- Bleach

Oh, and don't bother putting Vicks VapoRub under your nose like in *Silence of the Lambs*. That actually opens your airways *more*, and believe me, you're going to get enough as it is.

Yours truly
[illegible]

★★★

Text message from a 917 area code

Did you get the instructions yet? How long does it take you to ducking avenge me?

★★★

Text message from someone with a 917 area code

Ducking autocorrect

★★★

Text message from a 917 area code

Duck

★★★

Text message from a 917 area code
DUCK! FUCKING DUCK!

★★★

Gordon B. White

Message tied with catgut around an arrow, impaled in the drywall exactly where your head had been just a moment before you ducked beneath it

If you're reading this, you are not dead. Not like him. In that case, consider this a warning. Do not avenge him. Stop.

★★★

Typewritten note in an interoffice envelope with all prior names Sharpied out into oblivion and tied shut with greasy red string, slipped beneath your bedroom door in the dead of night

Hello.

I'm supposed to say that if you're reading this, either the text he set up got to you in time or else *they* haven't caught onto this whole "vengeance" thing yet. Personally, I think it's the former—he wasn't very lucky in life, but he did have a knack for timing.

Either way, the body is ready.

Go to the address on the attached business card and tell them you're there to identify the John Doe. If they ask, tell them it's "the messy one." It doesn't matter what name you give them, he doesn't have any friends or family willing to travel, so no one else is going to show up to call you a liar. Once they take you to the corpse, ask for some time alone to "grieve."

Ugh. Can I just say I'm glad he found you for this? I've got a talent for finding things out and passing along information, but dead bodies? Bones? Blood? *Vengeance?* Hands-on work is definitely not for me, but he was always saying how great it was to have you on his side.

Anyway, an x-ray is also enclosed. As you can see, the item you need is lodged in the mid-thorax. That's up and under his ribs, so I hope he left you a shopping list.

198

Bury My Bones in the Bastard That Killed Me

If, once you see the body, you think it'll take a while to get in there or that there might be some indecent noises as you do, just tell the attendants you were lovers. They've seen some *weird* stuff down there and know when to take a longer-than-usual coffee break. If by some chance that doesn't work, though, I've also enclosed a fifty-dollar bill. That should do it.

(If one of his letters says it was a hundred, that's a mistake—he changed it.)

Two final tips for free: One, soft tissue is only "soft" compared to bone. It can still be a slog to get through. And two, don't bother with Vicks.

***

Name signed in the visitors' log

Dr. N.O. Boday

***

Note written in pencil on a sheet of nearly translucent onionskin paper, folded up in a Cinnamon Altoids tin (one Altoid remaining, stale), pried out from a badly burned corpse's mid-thorax

Thanks. Really. I can't tell you how much I appreciate this.

Maybe you're doing this out of curiosity; maybe out of loyalty; maybe—no, sorry. They're going to kill me soon, but I've cracked it: I'm going to need you to take my resurrection bone and put it in the fucker who killed me.

The thing is, I'm not 100% sure yet which bone that is. For right now, just take my pelvis up to my lumbar spine. It's in there somewhere. Look up "resurrection bone" when you get home and then you can chuck the rest. Or keep it and make a stew!

I kid, I kid. For now, just move whatever's left of my insides aside and get scooping.

199

Hope you brought that second knife.

PS—I probably said "Bury my bones" plural in an earlier letter, although it turns out it's just the one. Still "bones" has a nicer ring to it, huh? Okay, really gotta go. Killing me, etc.

***

From the Wikipedia article "Luz (bone)," after falling down a rabbit hole of research that dead ends at https://en.wikipedia.org/wiki/Luz_(bone) (citations omitted)

In the Kabbalah tradition, the *Zohar* states that the luz is the bone in the spine that appears like the head of a snake, implying that is the sacrum at the bottom of the spine, because the sacrum is the only bone in the spine that looks like a snake's head. The sacrum has similar significance to the luz as a source of resurrection in Egyptian and Greek cultures contemporary to the *Zohar* and Talmud. The sacrum has a pattern of dimples and shape like those of the almond shell.

***

List of auto-completed phrases in the Google search bar

how to clean bones . . . for art
 . . . for dog
 . . . for soup stock
 . . . for revenge

how to disarticulate bones . . . for science
 . . . for taxidermy
 . . . for Halloween
 . . . for revenge

how much does an arrow . . . weigh
 . . . hurt
 . . . cost on Amazon.com

***

Bury My Bones in the Bastard That Killed Me

Note taped to your front door, aggressive handwriting in light blue marker

Hi neighbor!

Please don't mix compostables with trash! I saw you dump that load of bones in the bin, but those are technically compost, okay?

Best,
A friendly neighbor

PS: I sorted them for you this time. You're welcome!

****

Email spoofed to appear as if from your own personal account, timestamped "27:13 am"

Hey buddy,

It's me. It's time.

This is another pre-written letter, but seeing as we've reached the "when," the information you need on "who" and "where" should have been uploaded by an associate of mine to this link. Give it a click and then come back here.

Okay, so I take it there was a person and a place? Probably looks a little bit dangerous, right? Well, yeah! They did *kill* me after all, but they're just a person. Just your average, normal human. Other than being a murderer, of course.

Anyway, now it's your time to shine. You've got to do the "what" like we agreed: *bury my bones in the bastard that killed me.*

Specifically, I want you to cut the jerk open and ram my resurrection bone inside them. It doesn't matter where, although there are limited points of ingress (as you've no doubt seen), so I'm not saying you *have* to kill them first, but it might make things easier. Also, you don't have to stick around afterwards. If you think a resurrection bone going *in* is rough, just imagine what will happen when my bone takes root and I burst *out* of their body, covered in gore and basking in my vengeance. It's going to be orders of magnitude grosser.

Look, I know you might be having second thoughts, but there really isn't a choice at this point. Per my earlier texts, I'm assuming there was an arrow? Probably missed your head by an inch and had a threatening message tied around it?

Yeah, sorry about that, but that was only the first. Now that you've started down this path, a second one is inevitable. Then a third.

And for what it's worth, I really am sorry. But it's what you do between now and then that's going to control how your story ends.

See, you're providing the "how" of it all. While I've predicted the main beats, I can't see all the little details and nuance, which is why I picked you—I need your *vision*. Your imagination. Your unique creativity and resourcefulness are what's going to fill in the gaps and make a line between the points of my letters. That's how we craft the narrative of our adventure.

So yes, I'm asking to do something crazy, but I need you to make it your own, okay? I tell you what and you decide how. Even Steven. 50/50.

You and I are partners, and partners have each other's back. Always.

Faithfully yours.

PS—One bit of advice: maybe try to lure the bastard that killed me somewhere isolated? Abandoned houses, lonely forests, underpasses, etc.

PPS—Well, two bits of advice: cover your tracks too. Fire often works a treat.

Bury My Bones in the Bastard That Killed Me

★★★

Comments on a local neighborhood forum post titled: "Did anyone see all the flashing lights and sirens last night?"

Barbara N.: Did anyone see what was happening last night with all the police cars and the fire engines over towards the east side??

Stanley B.: East side of what? You have to be specific.

Elaine O.: It looked like a big fire at one of the houses.

Stanley B.: WHICH HOUSES?

Mike T.: @Elaine O.—Nooooo. A fire? With fire engines?

Barbara N.: @Stanley B. @Mike T.—Elaine was just trying to contribute.

Dave S.: It was one of the houses slated for demolition. I live down the street and saw what was left of it this morning while OMW to Cafe Fetch. You can smell the smoke from up the block.

Elaine O.: I love Cafe Fetch! Very charming.

Reggie D.: So sad—the way the neighborhood is changing. Losing all the single family homes.

Dave S.: Update: My downstairs neighbor was coming home at 2 am and said she saw the EMT coming out with a covered stretcher. So maybe some fatalities?

Elaine O.: Oh no. So sorry for any loss of life.

Simon G.: @Reggie D.—lol No. Single family homes are choking out affordable housing. Build an apartment where it was.

Julianne F.: I think we spotted Mitzy while walking over by the school this morning. Unless there's another gray Persian loose.

Julianne F.: Sorry wrong thread?

Barbara N.: What a tragedy.

Mike T.: Why? I bet they were more of these drug-addled wastes of life.

Simon G.: They're still people you NIMBY.

Reggie D.: Go burn some more houses for your upzoning, you density-loving libcuck.

Community Liaison Officer Sheryl Leung: Thank you all for the comments. The police are investigating this matter and will be making a public statement at an appropriate time. There is no link to occult practices, human sacrifice, or revenge. At this time, we ask you to please respect the process.

Dave S.: WTF? "Occult practices, human sacrifice, or revenge"?

Julianne F.: Mitzy is home!

Moderator: COMMENTS ON THIS THREAD ARE NOW CLOSED.

***

Typewritten note in an interoffice envelope, leaning against your bedroom door in the dead of night, with a foil-wrapped "enclosure" the size of snake's head and smelling of smoke

Hello.

No dice. Wrong guy.

More instructions probably forthcoming.

***

Message printed on a gift note in an Amazon box with one single arrow (new, still wrapped)

204

Bury My Bones in the Bastard That Killed Me

You got lucky. Don't be stupid. Give up the vengeance.

}:-(

***

Note taped to your front door, barely restrained letters in pale green marker the same color as the dog poop bag taped beneath which holds something more well-defined than poop

Bones are compost! I found this in the trash but I'm not sorting it for you again!

Sincerely,
A very peeved neighbor

***

Fortune from a three-lobed fortune cookie that came on top of a medium Domino's MeatZZa pizza you didn't order

Apologies, bucko. Things are going to get weird from here on out.

***

Gift note in Amazon box with new copy of An Adept's Guide to Lesser Urban Demons (Second Edition)

Check out page 83!

***

Page 83 in An Adept's Guide to Lesser Urban Demons (Second Edition)

THE TOOTMAN—Lesser Baron of the Sepulchral Web

One of the more abstract fungal aberrations and a frequent visitor to monuments of wet rot and/or dry ruin (e.g., sewers, abandoned malls, chain restaurants), the Tootman is not to be confused with the Toothman (see page 85).

The Tootman is a nebulous but malevolent presence, capable of overwhelming the minds of humans and other unintelligent animals to bend them to its will. Careful observers may notice the Tootman's human emissaries as they conduct their sinister errands in lightly urbanized areas, such as: procuring food vassals; drilling dimensional knotholes to the Sepulchral Web where the Tootman resides among the many smaller "toots" that serve it; and/or exacting violence against the Tootman's enemies (including all who refer to it as the Tootman). For unknown reasons, the Tootman is also obsessed with the human invention of "video games."

Favored abodes: The void of the Sepulchral Web; mausoleums in abandoned cities; particularly low-rated Olive Gardens.

Common forms: A bulbous homunculus wearing a rough, black robe with dozens of glowing eyes beneath the hood; a "Polybius" arcade cabinet; an infinitely-legged millipede braided around the flesh-tattered and rotting skull of an angel; a small human man with red hat, mustache, abnormally large and dense buttocks, and offensive Italian-American accent.

Known weaknesses: Flattery; Enochian relics; swords.

★★★

An email from a spoofed address to your personal account, timestamped "—:%% xm"

Hey friend,

It's me. Look, I want to come clean about something.

You see, I have a curse. I'm cursed.

I can foresee how events play out—that's why I've been able to do this with the messages. But I can't predict how you're going to

Bury My Bones in the Bastard That Killed Me

react. I mean, I have a hunch and I can write to you and set things up based on that hunch, but I can't *see* it, you know?

I have tactics and techniques—although let's call them what they are, *guesses*. And all I can do is guess and second guess and triple guess and respond to those guesses. I make little "guess-ghosts," if you will, effigies of all those predictions, and I set them off running. I hope it's been working. I hope it's been interesting too.

Because not knowing? Just guessing? That makes me vulnerable. I mean, I'm dead. I can't defend myself. It sucks being dead and I'm sorry I'm so needy, but at least I have you. Alive.

You're alive, and I really believe that *you* are the only person with the skills and the heart to get me the vengeance I so sorely deserve and—dare I dream?—maybe even bring me back from the dead. And, hey, if you're reading this? You've proven me right so far.

And since you've come this far, then I have absolute faith that I can ask you to go a little further.
I truly apologize for sending you to kill the wrong guy last time. That one—and anything you had to do to get him—that's on me. But this one? This one is *definitely* the bastard that killed me. So, I'm going to need you to do the deed and bury my bone(s) in him. Then we'll be clear.

I'll be forever in your debt.

PS—I was going to ask you if you know about Don Quixote and the Knight of Mirrors, but I forget why. It doesn't really matter.

★★★

Flyer dropped on your windowsill by a suspiciously friendly and literate-looking raven

Estate sale this weekend!

Art, furniture, swords, books, musical instruments, swords, clothes.

Gordon B. White

Prices so low it's almost grave robbing!

***

Page from an illuminated manuscript, found rolled up in a hidden compartment in the hilt of a surprisingly affordable sword

Know ye, holder of this magic Blade Sigart, that two Paths cleave before you:

First, the Path of the Lion: through a lifetime of discipline and dedication to the art of the Blade, thou shall become as one with the steel. Its magic will not be needed, as, in truth, neither shall the blade itself. A true King wins battle without violence.

Second, the Path of the Fancy Coward: merely draw Blade Sigart, hold on, and let it do its business. A shameful path filled with naught but blood—and fancy, fancy moves.

Choose wisely.

***

Handwritten note in what looks like grease on a paper placemat, taped inside the front door of that one Olive Garden that suspiciously never seems to be open

Closed for team meating

No ~~toots~~ olives today

Sorry for inconvenience!

***

Typewritten in an interoffice envelope with an "enclosure" wrapped in cobweb gauze that smells like unlimited bread sticks and the infinite void of the Sepulchral Web

Bury My Bones in the Bastard That Killed Me

Hello.

Not the Tootman either, it seems.

3x the charm?

****

Note taped to the brick and resurrection bone lying in the broken window-glass on your floor, malignant handwriting in seething purple marker

STOP PUTTING THIS IN THE TRASH!

COMPOST!

****

Messages printed on a series of gift notes in an Amazon box along with a pair of very thick sunglasses, a Camelbak water bottle, and a compass

- This is a contingency box for the unlikely event that vengeance is not completed. If it was, I probably would have been in a position to cancel the order. If not, the last guy must have been working for someone else, too.

- Unfortunately, I now know who that was. Limited space, but seven words: The Wizard of the Desert of Death. You're going to have to enter the Desert of Death to avenge me. But don't worry, this is it. The end.

- Be watching for final instructions. Oh, but if vengeance is done and I just forgot to cancel? Thanks! Congrats! Enjoy the swag or return for credit.

****

Email spoofed to appear as if from your own personal account, timestamped "-90:3 fm," with an attached JPEG

209

Gordon B. White

Hey you,

Me again. From the past, of course.

It's weird talking like this, isn't it? I mean, I'm writing this in real time—in my present—but you're reading it in my future, which is your present, and now I'm in the past.

It's like talking to a ghost, huh? Maybe if you believe that ghosts are just echoes that don't know their source is dead, then every letter is from a ghost. Maybe every letter I write becomes a ghost story the moment it leaves my pen (or when my finger pushes a key).

Maybe we're always talking to our dead selves and the dead selves of those around us?

Anyway, since you've come this far, thank you. All I can do is send these to you and hope they find you at the right point. I mean, sure, I've guessed as best I could and tried to control certain events or give you guidance, but what can I do beyond that? If you thought the whole "death of the author" thing made discussing literature difficult, it's got nothing on *literal death*.

And of course—trying to get revenge.

But that brings me to this last point, which is that the interpretation is still up to you. God, I'm so jealous! Because here you and I are: co-authors of this adventure, but you're the only one who gets to see the full picture. My part is cold and dead. *I'm* cold and dead.

But that last part might not have to be true. Not if you carry through on this final task.
Anyway, I wish I was there with you—not my ghost, not my bones. Me.

Thanks again.

Now get some sleep. The end is coming.

Bury My Bones in the Bastard That Killed Me

***

MS Paint-written notation next to a crude circle around an old building on the attached JPEG map of the local downtown area

Dessert—Basement

***

Scratchitti on a rusty metal fire door in a flooded basement

DO NOT OPEN

FUCKED UP MAGIC SHIT

BAD!!!

***

Scratchitti on a black rock in the empty sand, humming with energy, where the door back to the flooded basement should be

told you

***

A scroll from the Wizard of the Desert of Death, tied with emerald ribbon to the leg of a suspiciously familiar raven feasting on the remains of your very fancy battle against the Black Mask Bandit Horde, now merely a sea of shredded corpses at your feet

Interloper,

Perhaps it is out of ignorance that you continue on this fool's errand. Perhaps you believe that you are on some great mission. That there is honor in what you do. That there is some reward awaiting you at the end of all this.

You are mistaken.

211

Gordon B. White

Do you even know for whom you traverse the Land of the Dead? The ragged hordes you have bested on these plains are nothing compared to those that await you in the depths of the Desert of Death! There you will meet the most cursed of souls. Shambling skeletons with strips of sail-stiff flesh, blown across the sea of dunes. Sun-bleached wraiths, boiled down into mere wisps of wailing wind. And, most vicious of all, the hungry ghouls—dog-headed gluttons who crack bones with vicious teeth so they might suck the marrow.

Teeth strong enough to crack even the resurrection bone.

Yes, yes. I know all about the Plan. I know all about the resurrection bone and how you dodder like a puppet across the Domain of the Damned to place it in the one spot you think might make it spring back to life. But will you not be forever slipping and larking for this abominable tyrant who pulls your strings from beyond the veil of death? You will know no peace.

Can you tell me—or yourself, honest and true—why you don't just throw down the resurrection bone and leave? I think not.

Cruelly yours,

The Wizard of the Desert of Death

PS—I poisoned the paper, so you should be starting to feel the effects of the slow and creeping paralysis that leads to certain death . . .

PPS—Right . . .
PPPS—About . . .
PPPPS—Now.

★★★

Note tied to a suspiciously illiterate-looking dead raven's leg, about 100 yards further up the road towards the castle in the far distance

OPEN THIS ONE FIRST!

212

Bury My Bones in the Bastard That Killed Me

****

A sample of notes from the pockets of the many dead ghouls you and Blade Sigart leave behind on the road to the Castle of the Wizard of the Desert of Death

—Have a good day at work! Don't forget to stop by the mausoleum on the way home—we're running low on children. XOXO

—You can do this. You are not just a *ghoul*. You are a *star*.

—Pick up suit for next week temping at law firm

—Novel Idea: Travelogues from people stuck in haunted house?

—To Do: Change Xfinity plan; cancel streaming subs

***

Sign in front of the Castle of the Wizard of the Desert of Death

Duneview Real Estate
FOR LEASE
40,000 sq. ft.
Commercial / Residential / Scheming

***

List pried from ink-stained fingers of a dead man wearing a plastic wizard robe, cold and alone in an empty and unfurnished Castle of the Wizard of the Desert of Death

To Do List:

- Amazon:
- ~~Arrows~~
- ~~Raven food (e.g., peanuts??)~~
- ~~Paper / Regular~~
- ~~Paper / Poison~~

- ~~Wizard costume~~
- ~~Zelda: Tears of the Kingdom~~
- Rubber gloves (not available on Prime??)
- More goons?
- Take down sign BEFORE they get to the castle

***

Scraps of paper pinned to the corkboard in a modest office behind a door that says "PRIVATE: Do Not Enter for Vengeance" and "No Wizards Allowed! HENRY." in the Wizard's Castle

The first arrow has to miss.

Try to win them over?

Hero's Journey? Story Wheel? Exquisite Corpse?

Hire a more attentive "wizard"? This Henry guy stinks

Try to win! Them! Over!

TEXTURE cf. Chuck Palanuk (sp?)

How many twists is too many?

Look up how to use cf.

Something about "death of the author"?

App to automate emails? Texts? ~~Tweets?~~

REALLY FIRE HENRY BEFORE I DIE

guilt guilt guilt

***

Bury My Bones in the Bastard That Killed Me

Sign above the arched doorway in the castle's empty throne room, behind the cardboard boxes marked "Wizard Props," "Halloween," and "Throne, Etc."

This way home

★★★

Note tied to the end of an arrow sticking into your stomach a second after emerging from the doorway back into reality

The third arrow has to hit, though.

★★★

Really long text message from a 917 area code

Hey love,

It's me. Sorry about the ambush. Right after defeating the Wizard, too. That's gotta sting, huh?

Look, you're probably bleeding pretty bad (if not, spoiler alert!) and you don't have a ton of time. Before you call an ambulance, here's the thing, now that we've come this far together:

You were NEVER REALLY MEANT to avenge me.

I know you were expecting some grand ending to your quest. A final boss fight with the big bastard who killed me. A cathartic curtain-dropper and a slobber-knocker to give this all meaning and tie it up. But the fact of the matter is, it doesn't really end that way.

Hell, I bet no one even killed me. Not on purpose, anyway.

I mean, I am dead, but the truth is that there is no vengeance. No, you were here to carry me through this—a spectacle I designed just for you.

So yes, I lied. But I'm not sorry, because do you realize the lengths I've gone to for you? For YOU SPECIFICALLY?

215

You must have put together that this was never about the destination but about the journey, right? Guiding you through all of this—from getting my bones to the putting them into first guy (RIP stranger) to the Tootman to the Wizard—was the only way for us to go through this story TOGETHER. For us to not just become close, but COMPLICIT. And becoming complicit means that now we're intimate enough for what I'm really going to ask of you.

Your open wound? I want you to put my bone in that.

It's not going to regrow into me. I don't actually know what it will do. But if you do what I'm asking, at the very least there will be a part of me that you carry with you forever, which is more than anyone had of me before. I bet it's more than you've had of anyone else, too.

And hey, maybe it won't do much? Maybe it'll just slide down into your body and wait there, a hidden but undeniable reminder of the time we spent together. Maybe it'll nestle down inside you and, when you die one day, we can both rest together. My resurrection bone and yours, expanding together like pewter as we cool in the ground.

But hear me out: maybe—just maybe—it will become something different. Maybe it will transform into something both yours and mine, more beautiful than either of us can imagine now.

Wouldn't that be amazing? For both of us to live on and on and on in this way?

I have no more tricks up my sleeve. This is it, so I ask you once again, forget the lie of vengeance and embrace me with love. Place this piece of me inside you.

Forever yours(?).

****

Bury My Bones in the Bastard That Killed Me

Note taped to your front door, exuberant handwriting in a vibrant pink

Saw you put that bone in the green bin today. Congrats on learning how to compost properly!

Didn't that feel good?

Signed,
A proud neighbor

***

Text message from someone with a 917 area code

If you're reading this, than you've made a powerful enemy. I will be avenged.

***

Text message from someone with a 917 area code

*then, duck it

Tashlich

Emily Ruth Verona

Investigation Report
Case No: 459982026

On August 11, 2022, a construction crew renovating a first-floor bathroom at 9 Easton Street opened up a wall to find 168 disposable razors and 5 pages of folded notepaper behind what had previously been a medicine cabinet. The razors date back to at least 1924 but it is believed that the hand-written pages were deposited between 2012-2016 when the Lewin-Dodson family occupied the residence. These recovered pages have been labeled as Exhibits A-E.

Exhibit A [circa 2012]

We're supposed to do this at a body of water—a river or a lake—but the mailbox slot behind the medicine cabinet should work. Grandma said it's not a mailbox, it's a cutout for used razor blades. They're common in old houses/ When her parents were little, that's how men got rid of disposable razors. They'd use one up and push it through the slot and it would disappear like magic. Only, none of those razors actually disappeared. They just went into the wall. I asked Grandma if that means our walls are filled with old, rusty razors. She said "yes, but don't tell your sister; it'll give her nightmares".

Well, Mom doesn't know about the razor blade mailbox, and since the pipes that bring water to the sink are also in this wall, I figure the bathroom is practically a river, in its own way. The water is an important part of the tradition. There might be a prayer too, but I don't remember it. I just know that it has to be the first day of Rosh Hashanah (today) and that we're supposed to cast our sins into the water for the new year. It's called *Tashlich*. It means "to cast" in Hebrew.

When I was really small, I remember throwing bread into the pond across the street from our synagogue—the bread was supposed to represent our sins. Not that I had any back then. I thought we were just feeding the ducks. But I'm a woman now—my Bat Mitzvah was two weeks ago—and so I need to start taking serious things seriously. Be accountable for myself. At least, that's what Grandma says. Mom rolls her eyes at the whole idea, but Grandma knows all kinds of things Mom doesn't know. Like about the razors in the wall.

My best friend Meg started going to confession at her church when she was just seven. I don't know what sins a seven-year-old could possibly have, but she's gone every week since. She talks about confession all the time and it's got me thinking a lot about the things I've done in my life. I don't remember every single bad thing, but I know at least the big ones. Things that I knew were Wrong with a capital *W* but did anyway.

Only, bread wouldn't fit through this slot in the wall and so I'm writing my sins down the old-fashioned way. I'm making a list for the razor blade mailbox to take. Maybe the water in the pipes will whisper my sins up to God. Or the razors will shred them to bits. Either way, I'll have done what I'm supposed to do. I'm holding myself accountable.

So, here are my sins:

- Blaming Hattie for knocking over the lamp in the living room when it was me
- Sneaking cookies after dessert and eating them in bed (two sins for the price of one . . . Hattie and I aren't supposed to eat in our rooms)
- Telling Meg she's a know-it-all for getting a better grade than me on our math test

- Pretending to like soccer just to get James to notice me
- Crying in the bathroom when he picked Polly Harrow to be his science partner
- Not crying when we had to go to Daddy's funeral and say goodbye

Exhibit B [circa 2013]

It's Rosh Hashanah again. A new year for new sins. Unlucky thirteen for me. Mom says thirteen isn't unlucky, but there's something in her eyes when she says it—something wriggly and uncomfortable—that makes me pretty sure she's lying. Hattie thinks I'm being silly, but Hattie doesn't know anything. She gets to play with her dolls and draw pictures of horses and twirl in frilly dresses that make Mom and Grandma giggle. Just wait until she starts growing hair under her arms and leaking blood from her body every single month. When girls start picking on her and boys start laughing because she has boobs. Then she'll see. The older you get, the more you're poked and prodded like a science experiment. That's what they don't tell you when you're younger, because then you'd be scared out of your mind and wouldn't want to grow up.

Here I am, doomed to spend the rest of my life with hair sprouting every which way and having to remember to keep sanitary pads in my backpack and getting cramps so bad I want to cry during history class. But Rosh Hashanah isn't about complaining. It's about new beginnings. Even if what's new is also worth complaining about.

I don't remember what I wrote last time—a year is so long ago— and I'm sorry if there are any repeats on this list. On the other hand, a sin you commit twice is still a sin, isn't it? Having done it the first time doesn't make it any less of a sin the second time. If anything, it makes it worse, because by now you should have learned from your mistake. I guess I should write those down, too. It'll make me look bad—doubling up like that—but no one is going to see this anyway, except maybe God. But there have to be worse sinners out there than me.

Besides, *Tashlich* isn't about how we look. It's about washing our sins away so we can try again. And I do want to try again. That wanting has to count for something.

Here are my sins:

- Telling Meg she's a nerd when really, I'm just jealous that she doesn't have to study as much as I do to remember things
- Staying late at the soccer field to watch James's game even though I was supposed to walk Hattie home from school (this I did three times)
- Telling Mom her new boyfriend is an asshole (even though Paul *is* an asshole)
- Saying words like "asshole" and "shit" just to make Mom mad
- Hitting Hattie when she said she wants Paul to be our new dad
- Lying to Mom about hitting Hattie
- Lying to myself about why I hit her

Exhibit C [circa 2014]

Another no-good year gone. I'm still new to being a freshman in high school but I've seen enough and am ready for it to be over. Not that it matters. After freshman year there is sophomore year. Then junior. Then senior. Then college. Then you have to get a job. It never ends, does it? To make matters worse, Hattie has become such a little bitch. I can't stand it. She's my sister and I should be more forgiving, but sometimes I just want to shake her. According to Mom, there's too much of Daddy in me. How angry he was all the time. She whispers about it to Grandma when she thinks I'm not listening, but these days I'm always listening. I can't help myself. It's so easy. When you're little, adults keep an eye on you to make sure you're safe and when you're older they start talking to you like you're one of them—but in those in-between years, none of them really pay attention. I could spray paint "Hattie is a bitch" on the side of the house and it would take days for Mom to notice.

Hattie is only ten. That means I should be patient with her but the way she whines about everything. *Betbet, I can't reach the peanut butter! Betbet, can you check my homework? Betbet, you're not listening to me!* She goes on and on *and on*. And that stupid name. *Betbet*. It sounds like the stage name for a disgraced clown. She called me that at the football game last night—Mom made me bring her—and the way Polly Harrow and the other girls looked at me . . .

It's such a stupid name. Hattie made it up when she was a baby because she couldn't pronounce Bridget, but she is not a baby anymore. Mom insists she only calls me that because she loves me, but every time Hattie says it, her little eyes watch me cringe and a smile twists at the corner of her mouth. She knows I hate it. That's why she does it. Hattie likes to play the sweet little angel but she's no better than me. She can be mean when she wants. Cruel when she wants. She hasn't grown into knowing what to really do with that yet, but just wait until she does—she'll be a full-fledged bitch to everyone, not just to me, and I'll be able to say *I told you so.*

I'm sorry, I shouldn't be talking this way about my little sister. This isn't a diary. But I do want to add that Mom is wrong. I'm not like Daddy. Daddy was mean just to be mean. Because he could do it and get away with it. When I'm mean, there's always a reason. It might not be a good reason, but the reason is there. I wouldn't do it otherwise.

Here are my sins:

- Sabotaging Mom and Paul's engagement pictures by looking mad in every picture
- Caring what Polly Harrow thinks even though she's a bitch to Meg
- Not being nicer to Meg myself or standing up for her when I should
- Calling my little sister a bitch (here, and to her face)
- Calling Polly Harrow a bitch (even if she is one)
- Making bad pancakes for Paul on Father's Day

Exhibit D [circa 2015]

They're fighting again. Mom won't say why but I can tell. It's because of me. She and Daddy used to have the same fight. Hattie doesn't remember—she was too little—but if I close my eyes and focus hard enough, I can hear the screaming rattling around inside my head, loud as it ever was. Shrill enough to crack glass and bone alike. Paul thinks I'm spoiled—he thinks Hattie is too, but she's small and teachable and it hasn't ruined her yet. She can still grow out of it. But me, I'm spoiled through and through. Just ask Paul.

He says it's Mom's fault. That she felt so sorry for us after Daddy died, she let us get away with whatever we wanted. And maybe she did. Being spoiled isn't why Paul hates us, though. It's just an excuse. He hates us because we exist and there's nothing he can do about it. If our parents were divorced, at least he could ship us off to live with Daddy once in a while, but Daddy's in the ground so there's nowhere else to send us. Especially since Mom decided we're spending too much time with Grandma. She thinks Grandma has *bad habits* we shouldn't learn. Only, Grandma doesn't call them *bad* or *habits*. "Sometimes, Bridget, you have to do things no one wants done," Grandma told me once, I think it was not long after my Bat Mitzvah. "What we like and what's good for us doesn't always match up."

Mom likes Paul, but he's not good for us. Grandma and I both see that. She's the only one who ever lets me talk about it, though. The only one who understands. She says Grandpa was like that, too. Worse, even. Mom is too young to remember—she was Hattie's age when he died—but he used to call Grandma awful names and give her bruises as big as tennis balls all over her body. He was a bad man who thought Grandma spoiled Mom, just like Paul thinks Mom spoils us. Grandma blames herself for Mom choosing bad men over and over. But I don't think it's Grandma's fault. Some people just aren't built to see the bad. Mom is one of those people. That's why Grandma and I have to look out for her. See the bad when she doesn't.

Here are my sins:

- Convincing Meg to steal champagne with me at Mom and Paul's wedding
- Crying on purpose so Mom will take my side over Paul's
- Skipping Hattie's dance recital because I thought it would be boring
- Kissing James under the bleachers even though he's dating Polly Harrow
- Making bad muffins for Paul on his birthday

Exhibit E [circa 2016]

I think as we get older our sins get fewer but bigger. We don't do wrong quite so often, but the wrong we do reaches farther than when we were younger. Grandma has what she calls "hard-hitting" sins, but she also says they are few and far between. All of them were done for the right reasons, at the right times, even if they might not have seemed right all by themselves.

Hattie found the bad baking tin in my closet today. She didn't take it out or show it to Mom or anything like that, but she must've been going through my stuff because she asked about it after dinner. She wanted to know what "Cyanogas" means. I was smaller than her when Grandma gave me that tin, but I don't have the heart to tell Hattie what it is for. The bad baking Grandma taught me to do with it. Instead, I said it was an old container I used to keep pet caterpillars in. That was enough to make her drop it—the thought of fuzzy dead caterpillars inside. She didn't ask if there were any left or try to take a look for herself, so that's something.

I'm starting to think Hattie might not be like me after all. She's gotten so sensitive. Careful and even gentle with our feelings. Especially lately. Grandma says she has a "tender heart," and that Mom was the very same way growing up. Not like us. I suppose different traits skip different generations. There's no rhyme or reason to it. Some of us are meant to sin big and some of us are meant to sin small. Hattie is a small sinner. Mom, too. But not Grandma. Not me. So I've got to do the big sinning for all of us: my mother, my sister, and me. Grandma won't be around forever, and I've got to make sure we're safe. No matter what.

That's what I've promised Grandma I will do. And I keep my promises. I might not always do the right thing at the right time, but if I make a promise or decide to do something, I follow through. If I'm going to sin big, then I'm not going to regret it.

Here are my sins:

- Doing to Paul what I did to Daddy—what Grandma did to Grandpa

- Not crying at Paul's funeral even though Hattie bawled like a baby
- Baking a whole batch of bad cookies for James and his friends

Evidence Summary

Records show an obituary for Paul Dodson in The Star-Ledger dated August 14, 2016. It states that Mr. Dodson died from "complications related to heart failure" at the age of 46 and was survived by his wife, Marianne Dodson, and her two children from a previous marriage, Bridget Lewin and Hattie Lewin. No obituary could be found for Bridget and Hattie's biological father, Harry Lewin. With permission from his brother, Paul Dodson's body is scheduled to be exhumed on Thursday, September 29, 2022.

Cyanogas was the brand name of an outdoor ant poison popular in the 1940s. The primary ingredient is hydrocyanic acid, also known as cyanide. A full toxicology screening will be run on Paul Dodson's remains as soon as possible, taking into account the backlog of testing kits awaiting analysis for priority investigations.

The Behavioral Patterns of the Displaced Siberian Siren

Amanda M. Blake

Excerpts from the journal of Walter McElroy, Spring 2019, found among waterlogged clothing in an abandoned camp discovered by a rescue team Summer 2019, after supply plane transmissions were met with radio silence.

These excerpts have been woven together without ellipses for the purpose of illuminating the inexplicable. We at Miskatonic University offer no interpretation or annotation of the experiences described, but we feel it is important, in the name of science, to provide these last words of a beloved adjunct professor so students and academics alike may draw their own conclusions. The journal is still being restored by our Rare Books team but will be made available in full Spring 2020.

We knew something was wrong when Gaspar didn't return from scouting ahead. Yulia and I were struggling with the sleds in rocky mud that would have still been ice and snow in spring just ten years ago. I opined that we should have brought wheelbarrows instead, but Yulia couldn't hear me over the music she listens to under her earmuffs. I didn't expect her to. I'm just as content to talk with myself and the sea, as my wife can attest.

We found him at the edge of a low cliff over one of the smooth rocky beaches upon which walruses haul out as they head south. There were already a few early walruses resting on the rocks, but what left Gaspar so agape that he forgot to prep the camera to capture the moment were the creatures sunning among them. If we hadn't spared more than a glance, perhaps we wouldn't have distinguished them among their companions, but further inspection confirmed that these beasts were far enough from walruses that it bewildered me that I confused them at all.

Creatures. Beasts. Animals. It is hard to know what to call them. Beings? They had human faces and human form to their waists, where the transition to something approaching walrus or elephant seal or even humpback whale was seamless as manufacture, difficult to discern as part of one thing or another. I say they had human faces, half-human bodies, but it would be more appropriate to say that they were human-*like*. Outside of some forms of giantism, I have never seen humans with such large bodies, such broad faces—about three times the size of me or Yulia, and neither of us are small, myself by habit, Yulia by genetic destiny.

Like the walruses they resembled, they lolled on the rocks under a warmer sun than Siberia has seen in centuries for this time of year. Unlike the walruses, they lacked long tusks extending from their mouths, although when one male—bull?—opened his mouth in a cavernous yawn, he exposed long, sharp, conical teeth similar to those of walruses and seals, and where canines would be in a human, his teeth were longer, overlapping and interlocking without strain when he closed his mouth once more. I knew he was male because he lacked the pendulous mammaries of his female counterparts, and there was an innocuous sheath low on its body. He had the same long, coarse, algaed hair as the females, though, and became less distinct from them when he turned over against one of his mates.

There were fourteen in all—eleven cows and three bulls—not counting the two pups with their mothers. It was unclear at that moment if the bulls collected harems like the animals of their lower half or whether their mating habits equated to those of their upper half. To the last they were visibly emaciated, in spite of the still-prodigious mass of blubber upon which they lounged, thick over their midsections and chests. Their spines and shoulders were prominent when they crawled forward on flippered hands at the end of long, muscular human arms.

All fourteen and their young lingered in repose, sometimes roused by the walruses—who, with their poor eyesight outside the water, must have easily confused the creatures for others of their kind—but were mostly left alone to rest. Three women slept together in a pile and would not be disturbed, not even by the shuffling movements of their pinniped companions.

Gaspar postulated that they, like everything else, swam south for summer and, like the others, suffered from the increased distance and the severe diminishment of lingering sea ice that would allow them to safely rest and perhaps provide temporary shelter all spring and summer. It would explain why neither Gaspar, with his density of experience, nor I, with the benefit of breadth, had ever seen the like of these creatures during any of our lonely expeditions in a land no longer frozen in time.

It would have been better if Gaspar had waited for us to set up camp well away from the beach before making such postulations. Although the creatures were accustomed to the grunts and groans of their more beastly compatriots, Gaspar's dynamic voice carried down from the cliffs into the cove.

Yulia still listened to her music under earmuffs, and my ears had blown out after decades of ships and schooners and screaming rockers in my youth, on the rare occasion when I emerged in common society as something more than a square scientist. I'm not deaf, but I heavily depend upon the supplement of lip-reading. Gaspar had learned to speak louder with the two of us.

It pains me that his consideration might have killed him.

The three females who would not awaken remained undisturbed, but the other eleven turned over. Some struggled with bulk cumbersome on land, but like walruses and larger seals, these creatures maneuvered with a slow, graceless determination borne of strength beneath their stores of heat and energy. They were not by conventional standards what one might expect in a beach spread, but there was something about the movement—sultry in an Arctic spring, bacchanalian rather than bestial.

Three of the cows pushed themselves upright above their marine halves, raised their faces to the sky, long hair slithering over their shoulders and breasts, and parted their soft lips, exposing teeth not dissimilar to those of the bull. Walruses and seals will usually have nothing to do with humans as links in their food chain, although they've been known to satiate some curiosity for the flavor of camera lenses. Such teeth, while dangerous, are not intrinsically threatening. However, there was a different quality to these, perhaps because they were sharper, or because the mouths that housed them so closely resembled ours.

Rather than a bark or bellow, what wafted to our rocks sounded far more like whale song: low and plaintive, louder than one might expect, except that their broad bodies also included barrel caverns for their lungs, perhaps for deeper diving than the walruses they resembled.

I started over the rocks behind Gaspar. Yulia tackled me to the ground and covered my ears, first with her hands, then with the muffs I had discarded earlier due to unseasonal warmth. But she couldn't stop us both, and Gaspar was swift even over the sea-slippery rocks as he climbed down the face of the cliff.

The earmuffs muffled my already-poor hearing. It didn't completely block out the song, but the call of it was no longer as strong or urgent. With Yulia holding me down on the jagged rocks, trembling as I had never known her to be capable of, we could only watch as Gaspar stepped onto the beach.

He stumbled toward the creatures reaching for him with sharp nails at the end of hands larger than his head. He had already shed his coat, hat, scarf, sweater, and undone the fastenings on his pants, discarding layer after layer of protection from the cold as though he didn't need it anymore, although breath steamed around his head.

The cows tore through what he could not remove: through the second shirt, his pants, his thermals, then his underwear, until he was bared to the Siberian spring, which by any other reckoning was someone's winter. Claws cut through skin more easily than wool, but Gaspar didn't seem to notice beyond the initial wince, nor did he regard the cold. His erection was flushed nearly purple, eager as the females all rolled toward him, greedily grabbing at what scant marathon flesh they could, fighting to be the one over him. Their broad mouths were as wide as his face, but he kissed all three in turn, straining up to them even as one of the one-ton females moved to cover him with her body.

Through our earmuffs, we couldn't hear the crack of bone, but Gaspar's screams pierced through like the cries of seagulls. Even an old scientist like myself has the imagination and memory with which to fill in the silence.

As his cries continued to echo off the cliffs and blood arced in a fountain from his mouth, still he reached for the women, not pushing them away but pulling them down over him to touch and kiss and sing into his bleeding ears. The one that had succeeded in mounting him rocked in unmistakable motion, her bountiful body rocking with her, hair slithering and sliding like kelp, twisting and twining and curtaining Gaspar as she lowered herself further and further, crushing him like a steamroller until his arms went limp on the black rock and the screaming stopped.

When she rolled off of him, satiated, his arm wasn't the only part of him limp; his spending mingled with the female's lubrication on what remained of his crumpled body.

The screams had stopped, but the singing had not, worming its way through the earmuffs. Gaspar smiled in his ugly death, and I understood. My own erection—half-hearted at best these days without pharmaceutical aid—strained under my clothes with an insistence that I had long forgotten. Their song muffled, I knew such indulgence would kill me, but for an ancient mariner like myself, there are worse ways to go, with three sumptuous, sensuous women fighting to copulate with you, more to a single one than you could ever love on your own—but oh, for the chance to try. I felt desire in my toes and fingers, twisting in my gut, pangs in my chest, aching in my cheeks and tongue.

Three remained asleep, and the three for whom the primary urge had been completed sank their ripping canines into the tenderized flesh, but the other five continued trying to ensnare the two of us who remained. Both male and female sang, their voices slipping in and out of harmony and dissonance that was nevertheless melodic in its wildness.

Bless Yulia and her death metal. The girl hauled me up like the strong, silent mule that she is, and when I tried to return to the edge of the cliff, she boxed my ears like a nun. She hasn't a nurturing bone in her body, yet she has always taken care of me and Gaspar in her own way—not like a mother nor a wife but like a wolf at the mouth of a cave, even if she was supposed to be the artist among us, with her camera equipment and multitude of lenses. It was the wolf, not the artist, who dragged me from the cliff with hands strengthened by the clenching of far too many years for her age.

She dragged me and the sled on her own over the same mud and stone that had hindered our journey here before. As soon as distance added to the muffling of their singing, I grabbed the other rope and helped, panting like the fat old goat I am. I forced myself to push through the stitch in my side, the pounding of my beached heart that never should have agreed to such an expedition to begin with. But an old fisherman always returns to the sea, and this old naturalist had to return to the scene of humanity's crime, even at the risk of becoming victim by the very thing for which he lived. I hadn't believed there was anything new under a Russian sun.

What happened to Gaspar was a tragedy, no doubt. But I'm sure that even he would respect the thrill that arose inside me once desire had somewhat subsided, one nearly indistinguishable from the other until I could catch my breath.

Yulia didn't let me rest for long, indicating without speaking that we needed to continue further south. I was a wheezing, sweaty mess by the time Yulia finally collapsed on a stretch of grass. But she didn't let me take off my earmuffs until she turned off her music, waited for a minute, then removed her own earmuffs and waited another minute to make sure that the song could no longer reach us.

Nevertheless, we didn't fill the silence. We needed the air.

Not until we had built our tent and changed into dry clothes did I ask Yulia if she'd ever seen the like of these creatures before. I knew she had wandered places even I had not, remote wildernesses where so many others refused to tread. She said nothing at first, her thin lips a hard line while she inventoried our supplies and rationed out food for the evening. But later, as thin soup simmered on the burner, she finally spoke:

"There are always stories of strange creatures in barren places where no one lives, derived from poor eyesight, bad lighting, and embellished memories. My mother used to tell tales of *vila*, of *rusalka*, but they were always beautiful, dainty little things. These are not so dainty. If they are *rusalka* built for the cold, I have never heard of their like."

I hadn't heard of either term. I'm a scientist, a naturalist. Despite the avalanche of jokes about Sasquatch or, in the case of my area of expertise, yeti, I have no interest in cryptozoology. The study of animals has always been fascinating enough for me without having to invent new ones. Siberia isn't the Amazon. If there were anything new to find, it would probably be a new species of krill or mollusk. The keystone species—the apex predators, the great beasts—had already all been found, or so I'd believed. But Gaspar's conspicuous absence in the tent was all the reality I needed, and I had never before had reason to doubt my senses.

"*Rusalka*. Half woman, half fish, luring travelers to their watery grave. You know what they are," Yulia said, with her usual lack of tolerance for willful ignorance.

"They aren't half fish," I replied.

"There are other tales too. Some part shark, others part octopus, others part sea serpent. They have different names, but the names don't matter. What matters is that they are the stuff of myth and legend. And how do things like this stay myth and legend, Walter? I will tell you."

Yulia handed me my bowl of soup as though serving an inmate's last meal. She often frowned the way some people smiled, but this frown sank lower, the lines in her face carving deeper. "By killing all who come close enough to confirm they exist." She grimly passed the saltines. "And Gaspar had the sat phone."

I contemplated weeks of the kind of day that we had just endured and knew that I could not endure more, well past my pasture years. "You should go ahead without me. They were mostly females. With your music and the earmuffs, you should be safer."

She poured soup from her spoon back into the bowl, avoiding my gaze. "I am no safer than you, old man. Just warier of sweet promises."

It took longer for me to understand what she meant than served my pride.

They caught us while we slept, as Yulia had feared. Both of us wore earmuffs, but she couldn't sleep with her screaming music on, and she didn't have the benefit of my hearing loss to protect her further. My dreams that night were some of the most vivid that I remember in a long, faded life, smothered sweetly by their breasts over the cushion of my well-fed body, their broad tongues between my toes, between my legs, their weight and heat rolling me along with them like a tumble in a tent of pillows until they encased me, one after another.

I woke on the brink, the open tent flapping in frigid wind carrying siren song, my cock free and indifferent to the elements, melting with fever what the cold tried to freeze. I quickly covered myself, but when I reached to shake Yulia awake, there was no one there. Her sleeping bag was empty, her clothes left behind in a heap. I didn't know if she could serve them one way they desired, but I knew she could serve them in the other, and don't the stories say mermaids are the spirits of drowned women?

A frail hope—because legends are as substantial as air. I know animals. Creatures of flesh, blood, bone, cartilage, polyp. They all come from what came before, not from spirit or vengeance. I would not see Yulia again. I mourned her even as I searched in the dark tent for her discarded music player—an older model, but sturdy, with better battery than any phone. I shouted as I removed my earmuffs to stick the earbuds in and turn up the volume as high as I dared, so loud that my ears protested in pain, but I preferred going deaf to losing my life.

I put my earmuffs back on again, then broke down camp and took only what I needed, leaving behind the camera equipment and Yulia's and Gaspar's things.

I couldn't afford the burden on the sled.

And that is why it is just me in this wind-whipped tent in a howling tundra, overheated yet shivering under layers of insulation and yearning for a gas fire, or coal—although that's what got us into this in the first place, isn't it? The need to be cold when it's hot and hot when it's cold, to make our own miniature climates where we plant our feet in concrete.

The sirens are hungry and far from home and simply *not cold enough*.

And they know I'm here. Their songs follow me along the coast.

I will try to wait it out until the next supply run. If the plane comes, I will be on it and this account will simply be a primary source of one old man's ramblings, proof that senility set in and that frostbite finally reached my brain. The journal will remain a redacted relic to bury at the bottom of some bureaucrat's desk. What happened to Yulia and Gaspar will be remembered as a tragic accident, inadequately explained, filed next to the Dyatlov incident.

But I don't expect that I will still be here when the plane arrives, if it even notices that we are gone. It might be months before the university realizes they haven't heard from our little storage-room study and sends a search party. Yulia's music player is running out of power, and I don't know what she used to replenish it. I probably left it back with her things.

Should my wife ever get ahold of these too-honest words, I want her to know that she is here in my thoughts, that my lust in these last days means nothing against love that transcends passion or time, but I cannot deny its power. I am devoted, but sadly faithless in these waves of siren song that break ever closer.

I could not help myself. I could not help that I forgot.

Something Cool Behind the Waterfall

Nat Reiher

To: D. Bryson (dbryson@ic.fbi.gov)
From: Rachel Pettis (rachel@pettisinvestigations)
Re: "Mausoleum of Midghast" Video Game Walkthrough (1)
Date: November 16, 2022

Ms. Bryson,

Pursuant to our conversation over the phone, I've drafted an extensive memorandum outlining my experiences relevant to the Miller case. The first part acts as an introduction, addressing my experience with the action/roleplaying game *Brightguard* and subsequent discovery of the document you intend to act as a crucial exhibit in your ongoing investigation.

I wish I could offer more clarity on this matter than I have. Over the course of three decades as a private investigator, I've accumulated multiple encyclopedias' worth knowledge, both useful and not. Expertise in video gaming cannot be counted amidst that library of proficiency. To be candid, my experience with *Brightguard* began as a necessary exercise. I was diagnosed with Parkinsons's in the spring of last year, the result of actively ignoring a hand tremor for the better part of a half-decade. In an effort to quell the disease's progression, I began a regimen of dopamine pills and physical therapy. My PT recommended a more passive activity to maintain coordination in my hands on a regular basis. Of her two recommendations, video games and the flute, the former seemed less likely to negatively impact my marriage.

To be candid, Ms. Bryson, video games as they now exist are far after my time. When I was in high school, we had *Pong* and *Space Invaders*. That was the whole medium as I understood. My son, Brett, spent his teenage years parked in front of the television with those Escheresque controllers in his hand. (My mother-in-law has posited, multiple times, that Pettis Investigations is my only child, and that Brett was raised by PlayStation.) He's a grown man now, with a child of his own, but one of his older consoles remains in his childhood bedroom, gathering dust.

After navigating a series of menus and settings that introduced hypertension onto my list of health problems, I started to make my way through the library of games that Brett had left dusty under his television. I started with the shooters, but I found aiming the guns to be an act of impenetrable difficulty, and I ended up spraying most of my firepower into walls. After a few hours of terrorizing the Middle East, I switched to racing games, which were fun but repetitive.

I was considering a stab at the flute and a likely divorce when I discovered *Brightguard*, tucked near the bottom of Brett's sizable stash. The controls were simple enough and the game's setting, a frightening and mysterious riff on medieval fantasy, was infinitely more intriguing to me than the infinite loop of a racetrack. I created a character then entered the starter area, where I mostly just foraged for berries and killed wolves with a big club.

The early hours were tedious, but the game's enigmatic nature compelled me to continue exploring. The architecture of the story was scant, constructed primarily through riddles and allusions toward deeper meanings. For example, a wood elf mentions a hidden cave near the western edge of the forest, so you seek it out, and there's a hidden temple filled with puzzles and booby traps and undead woodland sprites who recite grisly poems in iambic pentameter while you hack away at them. And then you reach the end of the temple and fight a giant spider called the Hellspawn of Yakthorath, or whatever it was, and you spend a long, exhausting day plucked from your brief existence on this earth in the pursuit of *killing* the damn thing, only to discover that there are eight more of the infernal beasts scattered across the land.

"Your odyssey through this misbegotten realm has only begun!" chimes an annoying oracular fairy that appears periodically to accost you with unsolicited advice. "Journey now into the vast yonder, and seek thine awaited destiny through deeds both great and intimate."

Needless to say, I took the Oracle's advice.

And I am, apparently, one of the only ones. By all accounts other than my own, *Brightguard* is uniquely bad: it received poor reviews from critics and sold very few copies. My son got it at a garage sale for three bucks. I believe this summary of my experience with this game is a necessary inclusion in this memorandum because I feel, as an adult woman, some likely toxic need to justify the amount of time I spent engaging with this particular piece of media. I have never, in all my years, invested so much time and effort into such a meaningless thing.

It almost came to an end, dozens of hours into the game, when I came upon an area called the Labyrinth of Orphans, where the player character must navigate a seemingly endless maze of shifting walls while being relentlessly ambushed and assaulted by undead children. The walls of the labyrinth seemed to shift and change after every death, and I will admit that, at one point, my controller made an undignified flight across the room. After taking a nap and a beta blocker, I tracked down a small, well-aged online forum for players who were having difficulties with the game. Apparently most games have official "strategy guides," though no such book existed for *Brightguard*. But as luck (or, in my case, great misfortune) would have it, a user named StewieGoesCarnivore69 had posted their own self-made walkthrough of the game. I printed off all two hundred pages of it, conquered the labyrinth and its misbegotten children, and continued my journey through the game with the walkthrough sitting on the table beside me.

Something Cool Behind the Waterfall

The portion of this document that proved to be uniquely disturbing—and ultimately revelatory as applied to your investigation—occurs near the end of the walkthrough. The document describes a secret area whose entrance is inaccessible enough that I'd wager very few players have actually seen it. Following my trip to Cheshire, the guide was removed from the forum by the original poster. Over the course of this memo, it will become increasingly clear as to why. My copy, the relevant portion of which is scanned and pasted below, is the only remaining version.

SEE ATTACHMENT: "WALKTHROUGH (PART 16): MAUSOLEUM OF MIDGHAST.pdf"

- - - - - - - - - - - - -
B R I G H T G U A R D
- - - - - - - - - - - - -

PART 16: MAUSOLEUM OF MIDGHAST (! ! ! SECRET ZONE ! ! !)

16.1 FINDING THE MAUSOLEUM

*** RECOMMENDED LOADOUT ***

WEAPON: Sword of Leng (Enhanced)
ARMOR: Assassin's Coat
TALISMAN: Fthaggua's Bleeding Eye
SHIELD: Bane of Aldebaran (Enhanced)

[AUTHOR'S NOTE: This section can only be accessed after defeating QUEEN DRUSILLA in the PALACE OF EMBER. You will need the talisman you loot from her corpse.]

After clearing the PALACE OF EMBER, your ORACLE will appear one last time and advise you to head toward the endgame.

ORACLE'S GUIDANCE: "[Player Name]! Thou hast slain all Nine Hosts of Azathoth! Take now the Nine Seals and journey toward the Tower of Bedlam at the western edge of this cursed and forsaken realm. Stand upon its highest battlement and face that unimaginable final battle that will settle the fate of this petty planet."

The vast majority of players will take this advice. However, there is one last secret sleeping in this cursed and forsaken realm. Now that you have FTHAGGUA'S BLEEDING EYE, you're ready to unlock it and conquer the secret zone!

[ITEM DESCRIPTION: "Fthaggua's Bleeding Eye" is a palm-sized spheroid extracted from the fossilized remains of an ancient demon who fell from the stars. It is said that this artifact discharges a single drop of blood at midnight of every full moon, as the demon's ghost recalls its long-lost home among the dead stars. For years, the Royal Family of Ember passed it down from scion to scion before it finally landed in the possession of the cruel Drusilla. It grants its user the ability to briefly cross lava.]

Now that you've got the BLEEDING EYE, you can equip it to cross the Flaming Moat that surrounds the TOWER OF BEDLAM near the edge of the map. This is what your ORACLE wants you to do—what the game itself wants you to do—but before you set out for the final leg of your adventure, you might want to wander back to the SHAUNI DESERT area from the game's midway mark. It's probably been a long time since you visited this area: after you clear the TEMPLE OF SIGHS and defeat PYRE, SULTAN OF SORROW, there's really not much to go back for. So throw on a podcast and get to riding!

Still with me? Awesome! Ah! The SHAUNI DESERT! Remember to save using the GODDESS SHRINE situated near the desert's edge when you enter from the CANYON OF QUIET. The desert is massive—the devs didn't cheap out here!—so it's fine if you feel overwhelmed.

But fear not! The point of interest is in the southeast corner of the area. Turn right when you leave the canyon and keep going until you come upon what appears to be a giant rock half-buried in the sand. There's a massive lava river flowing around this spot, blocking your path forward.

Even using the EYE OF FTHAGGUA, you won't be able to make it straight across. The EYE only allows you to walk on lava for 10 seconds, which isn't long enough to round the corner of the rock and get to the other side. But again: fear not! For I am with thee. Just remember the old trope: always check behind the waterfall! In this case it's a lava moat, but bear with me.

Dismount your horse (obviously!) and keep walking south until you're hugging the edge of the mountain barrier. Creep forward slowly (SLOWLY!!!) until you're right up at the edge of the lava. If you're in the right spot, you should be able to make out the faintest hint of an indentation on the opposite side of the big rock.

Now that you're perfectly positioned—you're perfectly positioned, right?—we're ready to get started. Roll, don't run, forward into the lava, hugging the edge of the mountain. Spam that roll button like your life depends on it. If you time it right, your character should roll upward against the slope of the mountain and end up on an outcropping of rock overlooking the backside of the would-be boulder. From here, you can see that this isn't just any ordinary boulder, but an entrance—a gaping mouth with a big, inviting door flanked by two pauldrons of fire.

From here, just let the EYE's perk recharge and then make a straight shot across the lava. You'll wind up on the platform inside the boulder, with the secret door right in front of you.

Normally, you would find some kind of easter egg here: a signature from the devs or maybe even a chest full of nice rupees. But what Lionheart Studios included here is something special: a secret zone! More challenging than the TUNDRA OF YETIS and more mysterious than the CASTLE OF LOST KINGS. Before you can even open the door, your ORACLE will pop up one last time to warn you away from this area.

ORACLE'S GUIDANCE: "[Player Name]! Seek not the horrible truths beyond this door! This wretched place lies not upon the path of prophecy, but upon a more dangerous road. Below this place lies a tomb playing host to unfathomable horrors. Violence seeps through the cracks in its walls and the floors are paved with pain. Do not enter, brave traveler. Turn away, as others have, and seek brighter shores. Do not seek the Ghastly Madonnas!"

Something Cool Behind the Waterfall

You are free to take her advice. Obviously. Very few players will ever find this place, let alone enter it. But valiant players will ignore her, and enter. The round door will swing open, and a small, haunting sliver of a voice will beckon you inside.

Not for the last time, the Mausoleum speaks to you:

UNKNOWN VOICES: We wthier hree, we dilves trhee. We brun and beled and beg and srcaem. Bhelod our tmob, our bed of aicd. Slumreibng tiatn, haert so pacild.

Listen, if you wish, and enter the MAUSOLEUM OF MIDGHAST, this unearthly tomb of the GHASTLY MADONNAS.

16.2 TRAVERSING THE MAUSOLEUM

Beyond the door, you'll come upon a spiraling staircase. A cataract of pale liquid cascades down the middle. Every step you take, you hear a creak, a shudder. The walls pulsate as if they are alive and hungry. You might hear a telltale gurgling punctuated by gasps of air. Listen carefully, and you can hear the singing, echoing up from the bottom of this impenetrable place.

Can you hear it? Can you hear the singing?

At the bottom landing, the staircase empties out into a chamber: a large red room, walls stained red, and the floors carpeted with tattered rugs. There's a sofa pressed against the back wall. A box with a television sitting atop it, a dim glow burning through the box like a nuclear candle.

There's a CHILD in the corner, face pressed against the fold where the two walls meet. He is weeping, and you could hear his sobs if not for the beating drum of this place: lub-dub, lub-dub, lub-dub, lub-dub, lub-dub, lub-dub. Flutter. Lub-dub, lub-dub, lub-dub, lub-dub. Flutter. The sound of an anxious, palpitating heart trying so hard to slow and failing because this heart is scared, every drumbeat soaked in fear.

Approach the CHILD. Don't worry, he won't turn around. Hit the INTERACT button.

CHILD'S TESTIMONY: .dnno   n n   I   on ll'   S .dnno   n n   'n   I

Talk to him again. Tell the CHILD that he needs to turn his words right side up and repeat himself, otherwise you'll have to leave him here, forever, to suffer.

CHILD'S TESTIMONY: I can't turn around. She'll know if I turn around.

Ask him why he can't turn around.

CHILD'S TESTIMONY: She'll know.

Ask him again.

CHILD'S TESTIMONY: She'll know.

Ask him again.

CHILD'S TESTIMONY: She'll know. Please go away. If she finds you, she'll kill you.

Something Cool Behind the Waterfall

You won't get much more out of him. Leave the room, exiting through the tunnel to your right. The hallway empties out into several other rooms. Do not enter any of them. This dungeon is filled with fatal traps that will destroy any player who veers off the correct path.

Take a right into the bathroom? There is a large FIEND leaning over the sink, carving his face with a razor. Ribbons of flesh fall like leaves into the sink, bloody chunks collecting in the porcelain bowl. If you get too close to him, then he will blame you for his mistake, hold up a gored sliver of pockmarked skin and present it to you, asking you why you distracted him, why you're so close, what do you want now, what do you want, what do you want? The FIEND has many names and many forms, but he is always big, and angry, and he can kill you if he wants.

Don't veer left into the laundry room, either. There's a laboratory in there, boiling beakers and tubs of plastic vials leaking purple syrup. You're not allowed in there either, and if you touch anything, the FIEND will find you—or worse, SHE will find you.

There's a closet, too, just beyond the laundry room. Don't go in. It's small and cramped and hot inside and if you go in, the door will close behind you and you can never get back out. You will scream and cry and weep and beg but you will never be let back out.

Follow the blue carpet, the one that leads to the end of the passageway. Enter the last room. It's a simple square chamber with a small cot on the floor. No windows or decorations. Just the cot—and a very important item in the corner. Pick it up. It's PUP-PUP.

[ITEM DESCRIPTION: "Pup-Pup" is a small stuffed dog the color of cotton candy. He smells like cigarettes and his fur is stained with toothpaste and bits of spaghetti paste. He gets lots of kisses. Sometimes Pup-Pup writes poems and sings songs that create little glimmers of hope where there is none. Give Pup-Pup to the CHILD in the corner. Pup-Pup is all he has.]

With PUP-PUP in your possession, follow the blue rug back through the hallway. If you pay close attention, you'll notice that the FIEND is no longer in the bathroom.

Instead, he's in the main room where the CHILD is still in the corner. The FIEND sits on the couch. His jaw is rose-red, gory sinews of muscle dripping blood all over his heaving chest.

FIEND'S THREAT: "Oy! Runt! Who are you to enter my domain? To wander my halls and abuse my belongings! The Child belongs to me! This dungeon belongs to me! The whole of this world and all its peoples bend to my hand! Look me not in the eye, foolish traveler, or I'll peel your skin from your frame and drink the hearty marrow from your broken bones!"

Something Cool Behind the Waterfall

Be very careful navigating this chamber now. If you walk in front of the TV, the FIEND will come roaring off the couch. He'll kill you easily. You can hit him with every fire arrow and lighting spell you have, but he won't fall. He'll snap you like a toothpick.

Instead, walk behind the TV and approach the CHILD. When prompted, give him PUP-PUP.

CHILD'S TESTIMONY: "Oh, Pup-Pup! I thought I had lost you. Thank you, kind stranger. Thank you, fellow traveler. Thank you, brave soul."

When prompted, as the child if this is as deep as the Mausoleum goes. There's no use asking him any other questions. He will ignore them.

CHILD'S TESTIMONY: "There's another chamber here in the Mausoleum of Midghast, good friend. You have entered through the throat and seen the heart. Now you must face the stomach."

The CHILD's eyes will change color: from a calm blue to a bright and vengeful red, violent as murder. He smiles. He can't help it.

When you turn around, you will find the television gone, as are the couch and the FIEND. All that remains is a gaping hole in the ground, a pit where the overlapping carpets used to be. Get a running start if you like, and jump into the chasm to face the final task of the MAUSOLEUM.

16.3 THE GHASTLY MADONNAS

After taking the plunge, it will feel like you're falling forever. And when you finally do hit the ground, you might not even notice. This last chamber is soaked in darkness: no light sources anywhere, no windows or torches or rays of light peeking through cracks in the ceiling.

After taking the plunge, it will feel like you're falling forever. And when you finally do hit the ground, you might not even notice. This last chamber is soaked in shadow: no light sources anywhere, no windows or torches or rays of light peeking through cracks in the ceiling. Just a warm, fetal darkness you could drown in. Pull out a torch if you want, but all you'll get is a glimpse of yourself, knee-deep in hissing acid burping up drifting bubbles.

At first, you can only hear it if you listen closely. Shut your door. Close your window. Switch off your fan. Crank up the volume on your TV set and listen.

Can you hear the music?

Low notes at first, rumbling deep in your spine. Spaced, melancholic. A funeral march in winter.

Do you see her yet? Keep looking.

Higher notes after that, crystalline clarity like tiny droplets of rain lost in a waterfall you're afraid to check behind. Maybe this is what it sounds like on the other side of shut eyes. Maybe this is the music you hear in the black between stars.

Look up.

She's on the ceiling, upside down, her bandaged, bloodied fingers gliding across the keys of a grand piano, ancient as dirt and just as ugly. She wears a tattered black dress and earrings that dangle from the holes where her ears used to be. Her eyes are black sockets, seeing nothing. The moment your eye is on her, she'll turn her head downward toward you, to floor of acid and the trespasser who walks through it.

Right. Time for a boss fight! Or rather: three boss fights, back-to-back! Better stretch.

Lock onto her and don't look away. She's fast, faster than you think is possible. As soon as she sees you, she'll barrel down from the ceiling with the piano in front of her. The piano's lid opens wide, unhinges like a cobra, sharklike teeth glistening and ready to chomp down. You'll have to dodge this. If she catches between the lid and the cast-iron plate, you'll die: those teeth will grind you against the treble strings and tuning pins and that's the end of the road.

So dodge. Let her charge at you with her dread piano riding in front of her like a horse drawing a chariot. The music will get louder, more chaotic and distracting, but don't give in. Roll away from the attack and use your sword to strike her in the back. Repeat this three times until the piano itself bursts into flame and MADONNA PATRICIA collapses to the ground.

She sits there, stunned, the music usurped by cool silence. You'll have to unequip your sword here. MADONNA PATRICIA can't be killed with a sword. You have to use your hands.

Once it's done, MADONNA PATRICIA will scream and writhe and wail. Her body will disintegrate into the acid pooling on the floor.

As soon as MADONNA PATRICIA is gone, you'll hear another sounds echoing through the darkness. The sliver of tendrils slinking against the floor, splashing through the acid. And beneath that, deeper, you'll hear a gentle whisper: a *tsk-tsk-tsk*. Regardless of where you're facing, there's only one place she can spawn: right behind you.

So spin around and ready your shield. This is why we equipped the BANE OF ALDEBARAN—because MADONNA SARANIA will appear behind you, her frail body borne aloft by long, thorn-pocked vines creeping out of her eye sockets, and those black tendrils will swipe at you, dealing massive POISON-based damage. With any other shield equipped, you're done for.

Ready for another round? This Madonna is easier to read than the last. Keep your guard up until she gets six swipes in. Then, she'll queue up her next attack, an unblockable spin move that has the potential for a one-hit kill if your max health is low enough.

Something Cool Behind the Waterfall

Break out your arrows and aim for the head. It'll take her approximately four seconds to charge up the spinning attack, so hit her where it hurts. If you get her in the face, she'll throw her head back and wail like she's in agony. Don't fall for it. She's faking. Let the arrows fly while she's stunned and wait for her to repeat the six-attack pattern. Once that's run its course, shoot her in the head again. Repeat this process until MADONNA SARANIA lets out one last wail and the vines jutting from her eyes burst into flame. She will fall to the ground, helpless.

Like before, you have to equip a special weapon to finish her off. For MADONNA PATRICIA, it was your bare hands. For SARANIA, pull out the LARGE CLUB you found in the starting area of the game. Sometimes it's best to go back to basics.

And with MADONNA SARANIA gone, there's only one of the trifecta left to destroy.

Start listening again. Tune to the sound of scraping, the telltale screech of metal on stone. Follow the sound through the darkness until you find her standing in front of the wall. She's smaller than the others, hunched over and shivering, her scalp peeled away to reveal a brainpan glistening red. A bright blue pen bobs in the water next to her. MADONNA JUDIANA has carved a message on the wall. Don't worry about what she's written yet. Her guard won't stay lowered for long.

Break out the HAMMER OF ELD. One hit should do it.

And that's that! You've defeated the GHASTLY MADONNAS!

Keep a close eye on your right thumbstick. This next section turns heavily on how you position the camera. As you watch MADONNA JUDIANA's corpse dissipate into the acid, slowly turn your camera around to face the rest of the chamber. You'll see three children bathed in light, standing at the center of the room. A bright tunnel has opened behind them.

Walk toward the children. Keep the camera focused on them, only on them. Do not look behind you. Whatever you do, keep your eyes on the children and the light. Hit INTERACT to take their hands. You'll go together, bathed in gorgeous light, toward the end of this nightmare.

Exit the chamber as fast as you can and do not turn around. SHE will know if you do. Lead the children toward the light and keep your hand off the right thumbstick. Breach that golden barrier and you and your rescues will be bathed in sunlight.

It's over. It's done. You've saved them.

Moments later, your character will awaken, dazed, beside the GODDESS STATUE in the CANYON OF QUIET. You can return to the MAUSOLEUM of MIDGHAST whenever you wish, to defeat the GHASTLY MADONNAS once more. They always wake again, after all.

Something Cool Behind the Waterfall

I can feel them stirring. They never stay
dead for long.

- - - - - - - - - - - - -
C O N T I N U E T O P A R T 17 > > >
- - - - - - - - - - - - -

To: D. Bryson (dbryson@ic.fbi.gov)
From: Rachel Pettis (rachel@pettisinvestigations)
Re: "Mausoleum of Midghast" Video Game Walkthrough (2)
Date: November 16, 2022 (3:26 p.m.)

Ms. Bryson,

Now that you've read the document, I hope you appreciate (on some abstract level) the amount of distress I experienced upon playing this section of the game. The game's sudden shift from medieval fantasy to surrealist (and frankly, distressing) horror temporarily convinced me that I was experiencing some sort of sugar-induced fever dream. Or a stroke.

I scoured the Internet for mention of the "Mausoleum of Midghast" and was surprised to find its bizarre appearance in *Brightguard* had elicited very little commentary from the terminally online crowd. It seems that the first written documentation of the Mausoleum level is the same walkthrough I've posted attached above. Even one of the developers –a junior gameplay programmer named Stacy Windham—recently noted in a blog post that no one at Lionheart Studios was aware of the level's existence when the game was first published.

What struck me was that nowhere did I read mention of the mysterious inscription that the Madonna Sarania character carved into the wall of the boss chamber. If you attempt to read the message, Sarania will wail and attack you with a dagger. One hit will kill you. It took several attempts and the use of a camera, but I finally managed to decipher the code: it was a series of coordinates, written backwards: 48.384338097785° N— 122.514871519462° W. These coordinates denote the location of a small house in California near the city of Sacramento (home of

Lionhead Studios), just outside the corporate limits of Cheshire.

This house and the property it resides upon was purchased by Stuart Miller in 1998. It's a common enough name, so it took a lot of trial-and-error before I managed to determine that the Stuart Miller who owns the property at this address also served as Lead Level Designer for Lionheart Studios from 1996 to 2007, when he got himself fired for sexual harassment in an era when it was exceedingly difficult to do so. I couldn't dismiss this as coincidence.

In any other circumstances, this would have remained a saccharine fascination, something pondered and reflected upon, but which never engendered any real action. But the address was only a two hour drive away from my own home in western Nevada, and as my husband is always quick to point out, the first and only love of my life is a good loose end.

So I got in my car—and pulled the thread.

The house itself hunkered at the end of a brief stretch of gravel winding off a lesser-traveled highway a couple dozen miles outside of Sacramento. Its lemon color had faded, usurped by a patchwork of peeling paint clinging desperately to the wooden siding, and the roof practically sagged under its own weight, missing shingles offering glimpses of weathered rafters. Vines crept up the sides of the structure, twisted tendrils digging into the house like tartar staining a rotten tooth. A truck, likely undrivable, sat abandoned and pollen-caked in the yard.

The door was wide open, a tarnished silver key jutting from the lock with a fob dangling on the ring. It read simply: "Your Own Personal Eye of Aldebaran."

Seemed like an invitation to me.

Inside, I was greeted by an intense, almost ancient sort of stench. Before he moved away, my son Brett had a word for the mixture of outside and inside air: he called it "sour air", the smell that resulted from comingling the air-conditioned climate of the house with the humid, dry Nevadan outdoors. He always hated it when I left the door open, said I was brewing "sour air." As a result, I developed the habit of always shutting doors behind me without fully knowing why.

But as I stood in the dusty, unkempt living room of Stuart Miller, I finally experienced the "sour air" that Brett was always complaining about: it was an acerbic smell, bitter and thick. My first round of exploration yielded no significant findings: I combed the house, clearly abandoned, for anything else connecting the property to the elements present in the Mausoleum level.

My first discovery came in the form of a raggedy pink dog sitting on the bed of the master bedroom. The doll sat on the pillow, propped up against the backboard. It had a red nose and beady black eyes. I immediately recognized it as Pup-Pup, the same doll from the game the player must use to comfort the crying child in the corner.

There were, in my investigation of the residence, three more items of note. Each discovery turned a wrench in my stomach, and by the time I had uncovered the last relic of Stuart Miller's second career, my vision had gone cross and the urge to vomit was overwhelming.

As bleak, bitchy fate would have it, I discovered the items in the order that Stuart Miller most likely intended. After discovering the stuffed dog, I continued to explore the house with a fresher, more focused vision. My eyes were drawn to a rotted wooden piano in what appeared to be the guest bedroom. An attempt to play it yielded a scraping, jangling sound. I lifted the lid.

Nestled atop the hammers like giant motes of dust were exactly fourteen phalanx bones.

Your office identified them as the remains of Patty Denning, who went missing in Carmichael approximately fifteen years ago.

My second discovery—if you can really call it that, since hindsight dictates I was almost doomed to find these items—took the form of a trellis in the backyard. Yellowed vines curled up the frame. It wasn't made of wood. Your office identified the would-be planks and boards as the humeri, radiuses, ulnas, tibias, and femurs of Sarah Parker, who disappeared in Roseville approximately nine years ago.

And my final discovery: a thin stretch of parchment stretched over a desk in what appeared to be a study. Scrawled across this in pen were the words, "Do not turn around. SHE'LL know."

I would have spun around on the spot if something hadn't caught my eye: the inkwell, a polished black quill resting against the edge of the bowl. The curves of the bowl had been smoothed over to reduce its jagged nature, but the clenched teeth and the exposed sinus cavities made it obvious that this was the remains of a skull, likely one that had been crushed from above by some blunt object. Maybe a hammer. Your office identified this as the skull of Judy Noonan, who disappeared while residing in Citrus Heights approximately four years ago.

Based on the victims' social media profiles, your team determined that Patty Denning was an accomplished pianist, that Sarah Parker won awards for her prized tomatoes, that Judy Noonan had written the first draft of a novel and was speaking to a publisher. All victims were young moms in their early to mid-twenties. All of them left behind children.

While at the Miller residence, I had no way of knowing any of this. And yet that instinctual, almost primal, sense of *knowing* washed over me in that place. At the same time, another, more morbid realization took root.

Because skeletonization can take up to twenty years, depending on the environment, which almost lines up in the case of Denning but not in Parker's or Noonan's. I will not speculate as to what became of their organs, their muscles, their brains. I think of the final chamber where the player is forced to fight the Ghastly Madonnas, of the bubbling acid that soaks the floor, and bleak, disgusting suspicions brew in my haunted head.

"Now you must face the stomach," the pixelated child had said.

Something Cool Behind the Waterfall

Dennis Rader sent letters. Ravindra Kantrole left beer cans. The Beltway Snipers taunted the Police with tarot cards. Stuart Miller created a secret level in a fucking video game and then, when no one found it, got impatient and uploaded a how-to guide to speed things along. This is my interpretation of the facts, though I obviously defer to your office's judgment on this matter.

Upon the discovery of Noonan's remains, I returned to the living room to find that the door, which I recalled shutting behind me, was now open again. I ran outside to discover thin plumes of dust settling over the gravel driveway. The truck that had been parked outside was now gone. I returned to the inside of the house and locked myself in the master bedroom with my back against the wall. It was at this point that I contacted the authorities. Before the Police arrived at the scene, I had the occasion to note that the Pup-Pup doll was missing from its place on the bed.

I gave my statement to the local Barney Fife and now to you. This is where my part of this story ends. I'm prepared to attest to these matters as sworn testimony either in court or through an examination under oath. You have my contact information as well as my open invitation.

As I said before, I don't work these days. But you can always find me at home.

I'll have a flute in my shivering hands.

Sincerely,
Rachel Pettis, (Former) Private Investigator

RE: the hand (of god)

J.A.W. McCarthy

The following text and email records were obtained by Western Washington Post-Observer reporter Oliver Ruston-Jones during research for his June 18 story "The Only Living Girl in Harbor Place."

***

From: Alan B. Anderson <a.anderson@inforadvadv.net >
Sent: Wednesday, April 26, 2023 4:23:48 PM
To: Katie Hines <k.hines@inforadvadv.net >

Subject: the mess

Hi Katie,

David informs me there's a mess in the break room. Before you leave for the day, please take care of that. The cleaning staff won't be here until Friday, and David has determined that the mess can't be left unattended any longer.

Thanks,
Alan

Alan B. Anderson
Director of Operations
InfoForward Advances Advantage Corp

Please consider the environment before printing this email!

RE: the hand (of god)

From: Katie Hines <k.hines@inforadvadv.net >
Sent: Wednesday, April 26, 2023 4:29:23 PM
To: Alan B. Anderson <a.anderson@inforadvadv.net >

Subject: RE: the mess

Hi Alan,

I'm always happy to help, but I have an appointment right after work tonight and can't stay late. In fact, I was hoping to leave at 4:45, as we discussed yesterday. I'm not sure what the mess is in the break room, but I'm guessing someone's lunch exploded in the microwave (marinara's the worst!), or perhaps some extra dirty dishes. I'm sure whoever made the mess would be happy to clean it up once it's brought to their attention.

Thanks,

Katie Hines
Administrative Assistant
InfoForward Advances Advantage Corp

—

From: Alan B. Anderson <a.anderson@inforadvadv.net >
Sent: Wednesday, April 26, 2023 4:37:23 PM
To: Katie Hines <k.hines@inforadvadv.net >

Subject: RE: the mess

Katie,

I don't know what the mess is, but David assures me that it's urgent and needs your attention immediately. Also, don't forget to pick up the birthday cake for Vanessa. She wants one of those marzipan fruit ones from that place in Bellevue.

Thanks,
Alan

Alan B. Anderson
Director of Operations
InfoForward Advances Advantage Corp

Please consider the environment before printing this email!

———

From: Katie Hines <k.hines@inforadvadv.net >
Sent: Wednesday, April 26, 2023 4:43:01 PM
To: David Strickland <d.strickland@inforadvadv.net>

Subject: Fwd: RE: the mess

Hi David,

Alan has informed me that you found a mess in the break room (see below). I need to leave now for an appointment, so I'm hoping you can just take care of it. Extra paper towels are under the sink.

Thanks much,

Katie Hines
Administrative Assistant
InfoForward Advances Advantage Corp

———

From: David Strickland <d.strickland@inforadvadv.net>
Sent: Wednesday, April 26, 2023 4:43:16 PM
To: Katie Hines <k.hines@inforadvadv.net >

Subject: Auto Reply RE: Fwd: RE: the mess

I am out of the office until Monday June 27th. If you need immediate assistance, please contact Admin Assistant Katie Hines at k.hines@inforadvadv.net.

RE: the hand (of god)

David Strickland
Director, Information Systems
InfoForward Advances Advantage Corp

———

From: Alan B. Anderson <a.anderson@inforadvadv.net >
Sent: Wednesday, April 26, 2023 4:44:03 PM
To: Katie Hines <k.hines@inforadvadv.net >

Subject: RE: the mess

Katie,

Did you take care of the mess yet? Be sure to lock up when you're done. Also, Vanessa wants purple streamers. You might want to come in a half hour early tomorrow so you can decorate the break room. Marion says there's a great place to get funny birthday cards in Lynnwood.

Thanks for being a team player. We couldn't do this without you.

Alan

Alan B. Anderson
Director of Operations
InfoForward Advances Advantage Corp

Please consider the environment before printing this email!

———

From: Katie Hines <k.hines@inforadvadv.net>
Sent: Wednesday, April 26, 2023 4:46:57 PM
To: Alan B. Anderson <a.anderson@inforadvadv.net >

Subject: RE: the mess

Hi Alan,

I apologize, but I really do need to leave right now. I'll see what I can do about the mess, but it will likely have to wait until tomorrow. After I've picked up the cake, streamers, and card.

Thanks,

Katie Hines
Administrative Assistant
InfoForward Advances Advantage Corp

———

From: Alan B. Anderson <a.anderson@inforadvadv.net >
Sent: Wednesday, April 26, 2023 4:47:12 PM
To: Katie Hines <k.hines@inforadvadv.net>

Subject: Auto Reply RE: the mess

I am out of the office, returning Friday June 24th. Please refer all inquiries and concerns to my assistant Katie Hines at k.hines@inforadvadv.net. She'll be happy to provide assistance.

Thank you,
Alan

Alan B. Anderson
Director of Operations
InfoForward Advances Advantage Corp

Please consider the environment before printing this email!

★★★

Text records from Katie Hines and Jordan Rakhang:

{4:48:07 PM}

Katie: You won't believe this. I'm gonna be late for happy hour.

RE: the hand (of god)

Jordan: I believe it lol

Katie: haha seriously tho. I have to stay late to clean up the ducking break room. Everybody's out and I'm ducked as usual

Katie: argh *fucked

Jordan: No surprise there. Leave it. They can't keep taking advantage of you like this. Fuck them

Katie: I know, but Alan's acting like someone shit in there or something.

Jordan: Youre not paid enough for this shit

Katie: I know

Jordan: Seriously FUCK THEM

Jordan: Call in sick tomorrow. For the rest of the week. I'll help you look for a new job.

Katie: I know I know. I'll get there as soon as I can okay.

★★★

Text records from Katie Hines and Jordan Rakhang:

{5:01:33 PM}

Katie: Jordy Jordy duck. Fuck. It's not a mess

Katie: You won't believe this

Katie: Tell Sophie and Cale I'm gonna be late. Super late. Fuck. Just have fun without me.

Jordan: What's going on? Are you okay?

Jordan: We're waiting to order

Katie: So I went in the break room to see this mess and

Katie: It wasn't a mess

Katie: Like not dishes or spilled food or anything like that

Katie: Jordy it's a fucking HAND

Katie: A disembodied hand just sitting there on the table

Jordan: wtf. Like a toy or an actual human hand?

Katie: Human. Actual human. I poked at it! If it's fake, it's genius level fx

{photo attachment}

Katie: Fuck

{photo attachment}

Jordan: There's no photo. It's just black.

{photo attachment}

Katie: arghhh

Katie: I don't know why it won't come out.

Jordan: wtF

Jordan: Did you call the police?

Katie: No. I put it in my desk.

Katie: Of course I called. Or I tried to call. No one picked up. 911 just rang and rang.

Katie: I keep trying. Building maintenance isn't answering either.

RE: the hand (of god)

Katie: It's just a hand sitting there in the middle of the table.

Katie: There's no blood or anything. it's like sealed at the wrist where it's cut, no bones.

Katie: It smells really weird. Like old bandaids

Katie: Def not cleaning this up haha

Jordan: It's got to be a prank. David.

Katie: Yeah, he's an ass, but not that bad.

Katie: It's real afaik

Jordan: Fuck no

Jordan: You're alone?

Katie: Yeah, this is not good.

Jordan: babe

Jordan: Get the fuck out of there!!

Katie: There's probably a serial killer in the building. I'll never make it to happy hour now. Tell Sophie and Cale I love them.

Jordan: babe I will come get you.

Katie: No, I have my car. I'm on my way.

Katie: Seriously, I'm getting out now.

***

<h1 style="text-align:center">J.A.W. McCarthy</h1>

From: Katie Hines <k.hines@inforadvadv.net>
Sent: Wednesday, April 26, 2023 5:11:47 PM
To: Maintenance <maintenance@harborplpropertiesetc.com>

Subject: URGENT! Suite 300

Hi,

I work at InfoForward Advances Advantage in Suite 300 and I'm currently trapped in the building. I can get out of my suite, but the hallway doors are locked and my fob isn't working. I can't get to the stairs. The elevator won't respond. No one's answering at your office or the after-hours number.

There is also a very distressing situation in our break room. I'm afraid someone in the building may be trapped like me, and possibly badly injured. I haven't been able to get through to 911 or any of my coworkers. Please help!

Thank you,

Katie Hines
Administrative Assistant
InfoForward Advances Advantage Corp

***

Text records from Katie Hines, Alan Anderson, and Marion Whit:

{5:23:11 PM}

Katie: Sorry to bother you, but I'm locked in the building and maintenance isn't responding. Are either of you nearby? I believe you both have keys.

Marion: Your fob should do the trick.

Katie: My fob isn't working. I'm locked in here. I don't have keys.

Marion: Oh how awful! So sorry Katie. Did you call maintenance?

RE: the hand (of god)

Katie: You have keys, right? Could you pop by and help me out? I'll owe you!!

Marion: I can't. Already home. I'll text David.

Katie: He's on vacation.

Katie: Alan?

Katie: Marion, please. Maintenance is not responding. I'll owe you a huge favor.

Katie: There's a severed hand in here. I'm not kidding. I'm locked in here with it. I can't get through to 911. I think I'm the only one in the building. Please Marion.

Katie: Marion

Katie: Marion?

***

Text records from Katie Hines and Jordan Rakhang:

{5:31:01 PM}

Katie: Jordy?

Katie: Jordan?

Katie: I'm locked in the building. I can't get off my floor. Maintenance isn't responding I think they're gone for the day. Can't get Marion or Alan to come get me out. Fuck

Katie: 911 still isn't answering. Call them for me okay please. 4241 Harbor Pl W third floor

{5:34:58 PM}

Katie: Jordan????????

J.A.W. McCarthy

***

Text records from Katie Hines and Sophie Guerrero:

{5:35:09 PM}

Katie: I can't get a hold of Jordan. Are you still with him?

Katie: I need someone to call 911 for me.

Sophie: ??

Katie: Jordan told you, right? The hand. And I'm locked in the building.

Katie: Can't get out. Can't get through to 911.

Katie: Please call them for me. 4241 Harbor Pl W third floor

Sophie: ??

Katie: Seriously please I'm not joking.

Sophie: Who is this?

Katie: Please!! This is not a joke!!

Sophie: I think you have the wrong number

Katie: Sophie, please

Katie: What is going on??

Katie: Katie Hines. Your best friend since freshman year.

Sophie: Sorry, wrong number.

***

RE: the hand (of god)

Text records from Katie Hines and Seattle Emergency Dispatch:

{5:42:33 PM}

Katie: Please help. I'm trapped on the third floor of 4241 Harbor Pl W. My fob doesn't work. I can't reach anyone. I am unable to leave the building.

Katie: Someone else might also be here. They're injured.

Dispatch: No such address. Cross streets?

Katie: Between Wilbur and 42nd

Dispatch: It's a felony to make a false report to emergency services.

★★★

Text records from Katie Hines and Jordan Rakhang:

{5:57:59 PM}

Katie: Are you there??

Katie: Please

Katie: Can't get a hold of 911. Can't get out of the building.

Katie: Sophie's acting like she doesn't know me.

Katie: This isn't a joke. You know I'm not like that.

Katie: What is going on? Please call 911!!!

Katie: The hand. You won't believe this. It's BIGGER.

Katie: It's GROWING

Katie: Now it's almost as big as the table. A giant fleshy HAND.

Katie: I'm trying to stay away but it's a small office and it just fucking GREW.

Katie: I've been trying to take a pic, but it keeps coming out black.

Katie: A giant human hand sitting on the break room table. A giant's hand. And it moved! The last time I went in there, it twitched. I swear to god, the fingers TWITCHED and I ran out of there into Alan's office.

Katie: It smells so bad.

Katie: Am I hallucinating? Am I really in bed with you right now and this is all a dream?

Katie: Jordy please. I know this is crazy, but you have to believe me. Whatever this is, I'm not making it up and I'm trapped in here with it.

Katie: Jordy???

Katie: WTF is going on??

★★★

Text records from Katies Hines and Cale Walters-Wang:

{6:11:37 PM}

Katie: Are you there with Jordan and Sophie?

Katie: They're not answering. I need help!

Katie: I don't know what they told you, but this isn't a joke. I'm locked in the building at work. 911 isn't answering. Please call for me. 4241 Harbor Pl W third floor.

Katie: PLEASE

Cale: Wrong number.

RE: the hand (of god)

Katie: Please Cale.

Katie: This isn't funny.

Katie: Whatever you guys are doing

Katie: I need help.

Katie: I'm serious. Just call 911. That's it. PLEASE

Cale: Wrong number

Katie: This is Katie Hines. Sophie's friend. YOUR friend. Jordan's GF.

Cale: Don't know you. Stop bothering me and my friends.

***

Text records from Katie Hines, Jordan Rakhang, Sophie Guerrero, and Cale Walters-Wang:

{6:13:53 PM}

Katie: Guys

Katie: Jordy Sophie Cale???

Katie: THIS ISN'T FUNNY ANYMORE

***

From: Katie Hines <katie.boo.22@freestfoxmail.net>
Sent: Wednesday, April 26, 2023 6:59:08 PM
To: Jordan Rakhang; Sophie Guerrero; Cale Walters-Wang

Subject: HELP ME!!!

Please, guys. I don't know what is going on. This is real—I'm not fucking with you. I'm locked in the building at work and there is a GIANT HUMAN HAND in here with me! I need help!!!

I need someone to call 911 for me please please PLEASE.

Check your texts. Check your voicemails. Please answer me. I don't know if all your phones are malfunctioning. I don't know if you all thought this was some prank or if you thought it was funny to prank me, but it's not funny anymore.

I'm in trouble here and I'm scared and I need help.

4241 Harbor Pl W, 3rd Floor

Call 911. Or come here yourself. Or SOMETHING. I've been banging on the windows, but no one sees or hears me. The windows don't open. I can't get anyone outside to look up. I tried to break the windows, but they're shatterproof. I broke the fucking chair trying. I pulled the fire alarm in the hall and nothing happened.

I don't know what to do anymore. I can't wait till morning. I can't spend the night here because there's a GIANT HUMAN HAND in the break room and it's growing and moving . . . It's bigger than the table now. The fingers extend beyond the edge, almost touching the counter across the room. Last time I checked on it, it rolled on its knuckles onto its side and the fingers were wiggling like they were reaching towards me.

I can see it now from my desk, the thumb sticking up, waving at me through the doorway. It's real and it's alive and whatever is happening, whatever is doing this, I'm really scared.

Please, I can't be trapped in here with it all night. It keeps growing and growing and at this rate it'll be bigger than this office, than this whole floor by morning. I can't hide in the other offices on this floor because they're locked and they all have that safety glass—I already tried to break them. I tried to kick them in. The bathrooms are locked too. It doesn't matter anyway. I don't want to be cornered. I don't want it to touch me. The hand will get bigger and bigger and it will crush me.

RE: the hand (of god)

I'm so fucking scared. I don't know what to do. I have to get out of here.

****

Text records from Katie Hines and Jordan Rakhang:

{7:11:21 PM}

Katie: Jordy, please.

Katie: Why won't you answer? I don't know what's going on. I'm really scared. If you're mad at me, I'm really sorry. We can talk about it. I'll make it up to you. Please help me.

Katie: Jordy?

Katie: Jordan! PLEASE!!! I need help!!!

Katie: Jordan?

Katie: Okay, whoever this is, please, I need help. My name is Katie and I'm trapped in the building at 4241 Harbor Pl W. Please please call 911.

Jordan: Wrong number. Please stop.

{7:58:49 PM}

Katie: It's okay, Jordy. I forgive you.

****

From: Katie Hines <katie.boo.22@freestfoxmail.net>
Sent: Wednesday, April 26, 2023 9:27:57 PM
To: Jordan Rakhang; Sophie Guerrero; Cale Walters-Wang

Subject: the hand (of god)

First of all, I'm okay. I will be okay.

The hand takes up the whole break room now. The table's crushed, cracked in half. The wrist extends past the water cooler, pressing into the wall hard enough to crack the plaster. The fingers have split the ceiling. The knuckles are denting the floor.

I was watching it, waiting for the fingers to burst through the wall, through the doorframe, to reach me at my little desk and push me through all the walls on this floor until I'm pinned to the side of the building, or, worse, crushed into bone and pulp in the parking lot below. I thought I could figure out how I could get around it, past it, whatever. But where to go from there? If it can crack the walls and the ceiling and the floor, it can break down a door.

So, what's the point of hiding? Of running?

It occurred to me that the only way out of this building is to let the hand take me. Even if it uses my body to break the glass, I'll be out. I'll be free.

I'm sitting here typing away at my little computer at my little desk in a little office that I fucking hate. Something *unfathomable* is happening here and I'm spending my last moments trapped alone at my shitty job that barely pays me enough to feed myself. A job where I'm expected to get the birthday cake and decorate the break room on my own UNPAID time simply because I'm young and a woman. Where being a "team player" means fetching coffee and cleaning up other people's messes while looking pretty.

It's going to end here for me in this shitty place where no one respects me. They will literally take my life, and all I can hope is they spell my name right in the sympathy card to my parents.

Oh wait—that's MY job. I'm the one who sends the flowers and the cards.

Hahahahahahahahahahahahaaaa fjaklfjak aajfkajfksdj

The thing is, I don't really think this hand will kill me. Not a *real death* anyway, if that makes sense. I don't know why it's here. I don't know what it wants. But it doesn't want to hurt me.

In fact, I think we understand each other now.

At one point, as I stood outside the break room watching, the hand made a fist. Its fingers curled into the palm and released several times, over and over, like it wanted to make sure I was watching. Make sure I understood. The fingers wiggled towards me and squeezed.

"Katie, come here," it said. "Katie, come here and let me hold you."

I know that sounds crazy. How can a GIANT HAND speak to me, right? But I could tell by the way it moved. I realized it wasn't making a fist. It was squeezing, making a cup, a chair, a cradle. It wants to hold me. There was a sound as it moved, dry and soft at the same time, a crisp but gentle whisper, skin shifting against skin. Yes, I know—it literally was skin shifting against skin as the fingers came together, but this was different.

Jordan, it was the sound of my skin against yours.

Remember when you had all that dry, peeling skin on your shoulders, and I licked it? I licked every inch of it until my tongue went dry and you laughed and said I was a freak. Then, once it was dry, I rubbed my cheek against your parched shoulder, and it was like you were whispering to me even though you'd fallen asleep. I could hear your flesh, your blood, rising to meet mine.

I think this is the way falling in love is supposed to feel. We barely touched that, Jordan. I love you so much and we barely experienced it. I know that now because of the hand.

So I touched it. It called and I came. How could I not?

First, I touched the index finger. It was so soft, still human skin but almost plush and silky in every direction, like velveteen. No, it's better than that—it was like the soft folds of a kitten's shaved belly after they've been spayed. That's how I knew. I immediately thought of Shirley, the kitten we had when I was growing up. I loved her more than anything and she's the first thing I always think of when I think of home.

After that, it was so easy. The fingers extended, the palm flattened, and I crawled right into it. I fit so perfectly, my hips and shoulder blades and the back of my head sinking right into those creases. I closed my eyes and smelled clean sheets and donut dough like my dad used to make on Sunday mornings. The fingers curled around me, this gentle pressure like a heavy blanket. For the first time since I was a little kid, I felt *right*. In the right place. I didn't want to get up.

But I had to get up because I have some things to tell you before I go.

Sophie, remember how you pushed me to take a year off after graduation? You encouraged me to focus on my art. "You're so talented," you said. "I don't want to see you waste your life behind a desk." I was angry at the time, I remember. It was so easy for you to say. You have money. You can not work, you can pursue art or fashion or whatever you want—you can *fail* because your family will always be there to rescue you. You never understood that it's different for me.

My family doesn't have the money to help me. I have to have a job—even a stupid, soul-sucking desk job—to pay off my student debt. Yeah, I wanted to study art, but I would never be able to support myself with that. Following your heart is for people who can afford it. People like you.

So I was angry. I resented you, but I didn't say anything. I sat at this stupid desk job every day and resented you for getting to design your dresses and sell them in all those trendy little shops where I can't even afford a fancy candle.

Cale, I don't know you as well as Sophie, but I like you now. Well, until you wouldn't acknowledge me either, haha. But I guess we're all close enough that you felt you could get in on the joke too.

I'm gonna be honest with you: I didn't like you at first. When

Sophie started dating you, I saw a manipulator, with the way you always showed up with a new watch or shoes or how Sophie always paid your share. Did you love her for anything besides her money? But you were there for her, every minute, even when shit got real. Even when I couldn't be.

So, yeah, I approve, I guess. If anyone cares.

And Jordan. My Jordy. You hate that, but it's our thing and you let me call you that, so I guess you do love me. I thought one day we'd get married, you know? Is that stupid? You've been telling me to quit this job for forever, but I thought you were just being supportive in that well-meaning but empty way. You're not like Sophie—I know you understand, you grew up like me—but I don't think you understood that it's not easy for me like it is for you. When you were working for that ass Kyle and you told him to fuck himself, everyone *applauded* like you were a hero. You were so brave, so bold, and you got a new, better job right away. Everyone loves you.

But me, all anyone sees is a little mouse. Little Katie. Good girl Katie. Go *fetch*, Katie. I have to go along with it and I have to do it with a smile because otherwise, I'm a bitch. Suck it up, do what they say, maybe I'll get that promotion because I'm such a *team player*. You encouraged me to expect better, to demand better, to quit if I didn't get it and find a place that would appreciate me. But it's not that simple. You said you supported whatever I did, but there was never any discussion of how I would pay my rent. You said you'd help me find a new job, but you never said you'd actually *support* me. You know, the *real* shit. What about the in-between, when the unemployment runs out and I can't afford to feed myself and I'm about to lose my apartment? You never offered to move in together, to share expenses even though we share a life. Everything we have, I had to ask for, I had to make happen. You say you love me, but I need you now more than I've ever needed anyone—and *where are you?*

It's missed messages or our phones aren't working or whatever. It doesn't matter at this point. If you're reading this I'm gone, but that's okay.

The hand is calling and you know what? I want to answer. More than anything, I want to feel the way I did when I was held by that palm again. I was imagining how you all will feel when you realize I'm gone, all the nice things you'll say about me, maybe even the guilt when you notice how much you needed me. I got a little pleasure out of that.

But really, none of that matters. I'm stepping forward, not backwards.

Tell my parents I love them.

Katie

***

From: Katie Hines <k.hines@inforadvadv.net >
Sent: Wednesday, April 26, 2023 9:33:05 PM
To: David Strickland <d.strickland@inforadvadv.net>

Subject: Fwd: RE: the mess

Hi David,

About that mess you found: fuck you, you fucking coward. Clean it up yourself.

Thanks much,

Katie Hines
Administrative Assistant
InfoForward Advances Advantage Corp

***

From: Katie Hines <k.hines@inforadvadv.net >
Sent: Wednesday, April 26, 2023 9:37:36 PM
To: Alan B. Anderson <a.anderson@inforadvadv.net >

Subject: RE: the mess

Hi Alan,

So sorry, but, unfortunately, you're going to have to get someone else to drive all over two counties to get the cake and card for Vanessa's birthday. As of 9:37 pm tonight, I am giving my notice. I quit.

Best regards,

Katie Hines
Administrative Assistant
InfoForward Advances Advantage Corp

***

The Western Washington Post-Observer
June 18, 2023

THE ONLY LIVING GIRL IN HARBOR PLACE

by Oliver Ruston-Jones

No one gave much thought to the empty lot at 4241 Harbor Place West. Not until the messages from Katie Hines started.

In April, King County residents Alan Anderson, Marion Whit, David Strickland, Jordan Rakhang, Sophie Guerrero, and Cale Walters-Wang all received a series of emails and texts from Katie Hines. Anderson, Whit, and Strickland work at InfoForward Advances Advantage Corp, where Hines claimed to also be employed. Rakhang, Guerrero, and Walters-Wang are a group of friends with no connection to Hines. What they all have in common is that on the evening of April 26, 2023, Hines contacted each of them asking for help. She said she was trapped in the building at 4241 Harbor Place West.

"The strange thing is, it wasn't in April, not this year," says Whit. "People get locked in occasionally, yeah. Employees have fobs, but sometimes they don't work and only management has keys. When I got the text from Katie, though, it didn't make sense. There is no Katie Hines at InfoForward Advances Advantage Corp, and our office is on the next street over, on 42nd."

Alan Anderson confirms that no one by the name of Katie Hines is currently employed at their company. Though he did reply to Katie's emails to him, Anderson insists that exchange occurred several years ago, not in April of this year. InfoForward Advances Advantage Corp HR states that a Katie Hines was employed there from September 2014 through April 2015.

So how does Whit explain her responses to Katie in the text thread? Although she didn't recall Hines at first, Whit concurs with HR's records: "That's right, she was our admin assistant. She texted me once when she got locked in the building. But that was eight years ago. I don't know why the text records and all those emails show the date as this year. I haven't spoken to Katie since she left. I don't think anyone here has had contact with her either, and we certainly wouldn't be asking her to clean up the break room or get a birthday cake now."

When Katie Hines didn't receive the desired response from her former coworkers, she started texting Jordan Rakhang, Sophie Guerrero, and Cale Walters-Wang. The friends recount a series of baffling and concerning texts to each of them, where Katie stated that not only was she unable to leave the building, but she was also trapped in there with a severed human hand.

"It was weird. At first I thought she had the wrong number. She said we were friends from college or something, but I don't know a Katie Hines," says Guerrero. "So I thought it was a prank and I ignored her. But then it got completely unhinged. She was texting me and Cale and Jordan, talking about a giant hand that was in her office and how scared she was of it. Then she sent this email about how she was, I don't know, going to sleep in it or something?"

Walters-Wang agrees. "It was bizarre, you know? We're sitting there at happy hour and then this random girl is texting us all this weird (expletive). We kept telling her she's got the wrong number, but she wouldn't stop. Then we get this long email about how upset she is with us and how she's going with the giant hand now. Honestly, I felt sorry for her."

Jordan Rakhang initially responded to Katie's texts about the severed hand in the building, as shown in the records obtained by *The Western Washington Post-Observer*. The exchange is friendly and at times intimate, suggesting that the two were dating, before Jordan stops responding. Rakhang could not be reached for comment, and he has not responded to follow requests on his locked social media profiles. Guerrero and Walters-Wang state that, to their knowledge, Rakhang has never dated anyone named Katie.

A representative for Seattle Emergency Dispatch confirms a text exchange with Katie did occur on April 26 as the transcript shows, but they have no record of any calls from this number.

All of this might be a funny story about wrong numbers or one woman's dedication to a strange and elaborate prank, except for one sticking point: *there is no building* at 4241 Harbor Place West. According to city records, that address has been an empty lot for the past seventeen years.

"It's been so long, I can't even remember what used to be there," says Richard Compton, owner of Compton's Dry Cleaning next door. "When it was demolished, I thought something new was going in, but it's just been a big ol' hole in the ground for the past I don't know how long."

"It's an eyesore. I wish the city would do something," says Rhonda Essex, who runs the front desk at Rose & Charles Accountants across the street.

County records show Sound Bank & Trust as the owner of the lot at 4241 Harbor Place West. They state they have no record of a Katie Hines having leased or inhabited this location.

Is it possible that Katie Hines was telling the truth, that she was trapped in a nearby building but simply had the address wrong? Did she also, somehow, have the wrong phone numbers and email addresses for the friends she was trying to reach? In the text records, her pleas for help are compelling, even heartbreaking at times. Her fear is palpable, as is her belief that she had contacted the right people—people she believed could help her. Perhaps, in her panic, Katie transposed numbers or made some other mistake, one that seems to have cost her dearly. Sophie Guerrero feels this is certainly possible.

"I still think about her a lot," says Guerrero. "She obviously needed help. It's sad."

There are 39 people by the name of Katie, Katherine, or Katrina Hines in county records. None of them could be reached for comment.

Berkey Family Vacation 1988

Jacob Steven Mohr

On September 18, 1990, the following footage aired on Gordon OH station WTUV-1 beginning 1:15 AM and concluding 1:28 AM. Investigations into origins of the broadcast launched two days after the original airdate but the source of the footage were never discovered.

1.

Broadcast begins. 2.5 seconds gray static.

A FACE tilts into view. She's round-faced, blonde shoulder-length hair, scattered freckles. About 9. She looks into camera, the dark mouth of the lens reflected in her glasses.

[girl] Is it working?

A man's voice from off-screen:

[man] Is the red light on?

[girl] Where?

[man] Right there. You've got it, Bodie . . .

The frame jostles and settles as the girl, BODIE, sets the camera on a flat surface. She backs up, joined by two adults, a MAN and a WOMAN, seen from the shoulders down.

The woman puts her hand on Bodie's arm.

[woman] Ready?

[girl] Hold on . . .

Bodie lifts a poster made of magazine cutout letters glued to white cardboard. It reads:

BERKEY FAMILY VACATION 1988

[girl] Ready! Okay, three . . .

The adults join in:

[all] Two . . . One . . . BON VOYAGE!

The family waves into the lens. Bodie drops her poster and skips forward, scooping up the camera. Her smiling face fills frame; then cut to darkness.

2.

3 seconds gray static.

FOCUS through the window of a commercial airplane. The wing juts into frame, casting a shadow on white clouds beneath. The lens pushes closer to the glass, tapping against it.

Bodie's voice sings off-key:

[girl] Big old jet airliner, don't carry me too far away . . .

[woman] You're gonna run the battery down.

[girl] We brought extras.

The camera reverses, pointing past Bodie's head at the woman, as well as the man seated between them on the row. The woman's head is hidden behind the man's. She buries her nose in a large hardcover book, maybe a legal thriller.

[woman] Did we?

[girl] We brought extras. (resuming singing) Big old jet airliner . . .

The man joins in, leaning into frame holding an invisible microphone:

[girl and man] . . . coz it's here that I've got to stay-ay . . .

3.

4 seconds gray static.

A few QUICK CUTS:

- The man's dark-haired arm pushes open the door to a modest beach condo.
- The camera zooms through the condo, focusing on seashell art on the walls.
- The sliding door at the back opens. Sunlight bleeds in . . .
- RACK FOCUS on the breakers far below. Beachgoers dot the shoreline.

The camera follows Bodie into one bedroom, empty but for a little girl's suitcase beside the big white bed. Bodie jumps up onto the bed, lying on her back with her limbs starfished.

The man speaks from behind the camera:

[man] How d'you feel, babygirl?

Bodie grins and lolls her head to the side, playing dead.

4.

3.5 seconds gray static.

Camera jostles awkwardly, pointed down at white beach sand. Off-screen, the woman says:

[woman] Is it on? Is it on?

TILT UP to reveal: Bodie buried in sand shaped in a huge mound of sand. She grins up at the camera, wearing huge, pink-framed sunglasses. Her face is smeared with sunscreen.

[woman] Can you move?

Bodie shakes her head.

[woman] Try.

Bodie giggles and shakes her head again.

[woman] Go on, try.

Bodie wriggles a little beneath the sand. It cracks but doesn't budge.

[woman] Are you sure you're trying?

Bodie nods, struggling not to laugh.

[woman] I think you're turning into a butterfly in there.

The man's shadow falls across the mound of sand.

[man] Anybody who's NOT trapped under a ton of sand—race you to the water!

Bodie bursts up from the sand. The camera follows her and the man, sprinting towards the surf, both yelling. Bodie tries to shove ahead; the man lets her.

The woman calls out:

[woman] Try not to drown your father!

5.

2 seconds of static.

The camera finds the woman in a beach chair under an umbrella. Bikini straps down on her shoulders, tiny sunglasses perched on her nose. Sunbather's screen in her lap. Her head lolls back against the beach chair back for a long pause. Then she glances over at the camera.

[woman] What are you looking at?

[girl] You look pretty, mommy.

The woman laughs, trying to hide it.

[woman] I look pretty.

[girl] Sure.

[woman] What about your father, does he look pretty?

[girl] I don't see him.

WHIP PAN to the flashing water. Beachgoers scuttle left and right across frame; focus struggles a moment before settling past the breakers. Frame darts left and right, searching . . .

[woman] Right there.

[girl] Where?

[woman] Right there in the . . .

Camera zooms in on empty water.

[woman] Don't you . . .

Off-screen, the metal beach chair CLATTERS. In frame, the woman stumbles down the beach towards the water, hair flying.

[woman] JOSEPH! JOSEPH!

Frantic camera movement. White beach flies by. Sounds of Bodie's breathing.

Arrive at the shore. RACK FOCUS on the woman's bare legs running down the waterline. In front of her lies a dark form collapsed on the sand. Bodie's voice is distorted:

[girl] Daddy . . .

6.

1.5 seconds gray static.
CLOSEUP of Joseph's face. Red, roughed by waves and sand. Eyes open and red. He's breathing shallowly and very quickly. Saltwater runs from his nose and mouth.

Voices off screen:

[woman] Joe . . . can you hear me?

[girl] Daddy?

[woman] Bodie, honey. Turn that off.

[girl] What's wrong with him?

The woman's arm enters frame. The hand presses under Joseph's neck.

[woman] Go get my purse. It's got my phone.

[girl] Why does he look like that?

[woman] Bodie . . .

[girl] Why does he look like that?

[woman] Jesus Christ—will you point that fucking thing somewhere . . .

Joseph's mouth flies open. He lurches upright, sucking in a huge wet breath.

Bodie SCREAMS—the camera drops in the sand . . .

7.

6 seconds gray static.

In the beach house, at a wicker dining table. Camera pans between the woman and Joseph, eating pizza. The open lid of the pizza box obscures the woman's face partially.

The woman clears her throat. Then:

[woman] I'm sorry for yelling.

Off screen, Bodie answers:

[girl] It's all right.

[woman] And I'm sorry for cursing.

Sounds of breathing, chewing.

[woman] Mommy was scared. That's all.

Pan and zoom on the man's expressionless face.

[woman] Everybody gets scared sometimes. Right?

Closer on the man's face. He doesn't move or blink.

[girl] I'm gonna put my PJs on.

8.

4 seconds gray static.

Inside a beach house single bedroom. Lo-fi squirming darkness. Red glow at the edge of frame. Camera swings right slowly, showing a red digital clock readout: 11:55 PM. We look away, finding light beneath the bedroom door. Two pairs of feet walk by; we see their shadows, then the light outside clicks off. Voices WHISPER briefly outside:

[woman] She's asleep.

SOUNDS OF FOOTSTEPS. A door closes. Then SILENCE.

9.

3.5 seconds gray static.

Similar framing as before. The digital clock reads 12:45 AM.

Bodie MURMURS off-screen:

[girl] Mommy and Daddy are talking.

Long silence. Then voices bleed in:

[woman] Talk to me. Just tell me what happened.

[man] (unintelligible)

[woman] You owe me that. You scared Bodie half to death, me half to death . . .

[man] (unintelligible)

[woman] You looked like . . . Well. I'm not going to say what you looked like. You've got a mirror. You go tell me what you look like.

SILENCE.

[woman] You're not gonna talk? You're just gonna stare at me?

SILENCE. Bodie's breathing labors. A siren WAILS, far in the dark distance.

[woman] Fine. Whatever.

A long pause. Then another man's WET RASPING VOICE speaks:

[???] It's going to be all right, Chloe.

10.

4 seconds gray static.

Writhing darkness again. From this: Bodie's bedroom door swims into view. Her breathing, close to the camera, is a constant blast of static and wind.

Her little hand appears, twisting the knob, pushing the door aside.

The condo beyond is moonlit. Silver and gleaming. Shadows lope and flex at the corners of the frame. We press into that darkness, down a short hall. Bodie's hand pushes open another bedroom door; it glides open soundlessly.

On a huge king-sized bed: a lump of bedclothes and pillows. The camera moves forward with wobbling steps. Her breathing stops, held trembling. Joseph's face comes into view, lolled on the white pillow. One bare arm drapes across his forehead, concealing his eyes.

This shot holds. Bodie's breathing returns, sharp and scared.

[girl] That's not Daddy.

11.

2.5 seconds gray static.

We're outside on the condo balcony, looking across the dunes. The beach is dark. The moon hangs low on the water, making a wobbling stripe of light. The hoarse rushing sound could be Bodie's breathing or the wind. The noises are indistinguishable. Bodie WHISPERS off screen:

[girl] Do you hear that?

The camera spins, showing Bodie's tear-streaked face briefly. Focus on the glass sliding door leading back into the condo. The moon reflects off the surface, showing nothing beyond.

[girl] Can you hear them?

Faint wet footsteps through the glass. Shadows move on the other side. Sounds of scraping, like nails on tile. Unseen things rattle beyond the barrier.

[girl] They look like them.

[girl] They're trying to find me.

A dark shape presses against the glass. The door creaks.

[girl] Can you see . . . ?

Zoom on the shape on the glass. It's spade-shaped, but suddenly splits into fingers like an opening hand. Eight digits, maybe more. Each over six inches long.

[girl] Do you see . . .

The shape withdraws from the window. The camera reverses, showing the bottom half of Bodie's face. When she speaks it fogs the lens:

[girl] I think they know I'm here. They're just . . . waiting.

WHIP PAN to the water's edge again. The camera steadies, placed on a hard surface.

[girl] It's so cold out here. The wind . . .

[girl] I don't know what to do. I'm really tired.

A bubbling hoarse voice speaks off-camera:

[???] Bodie.

[???] Bodie.

[???] Let's go down to the water.

Off-screen, the sliding door opens with a long slow squeak. Bodie GASPS softly. A rustle of movement knocks the camera off its perch. It tumbles until it makes impact, cutting to:

12.

A FREEZE-FRAME of an earlier scene. Bodie, Linda, and Joseph stand in frame, holding the magazine-cutout poster. SLOW ZOOM on the grinning faces of the parents. SOUNDS OF SURF. The faces fill the frame, pixelated and distorted. Water sounds give way to HARSH BUILDING STATIC. Then smash to black.

Broadcast ends.

A Testament Of Wanderers

Kyle Toucher

Walpurgis County Historical Society
3235 Beltane Road
Ian Emerson, Curator

The Vanderbaum Archive
Collected Memoir and Correspondence

Note from Ian Emerson, curator:

The Reformation Brotherhood Wagon Train of 1844 is a tale largely forgotten, or perhaps ignored, by mainstream historians. It does not depict valor or conquest, but the slow disintegration of honest people strangled by the hand of fate. Whether vital or insignificant to the history of Walpurgis County I leave to the reader, but these excerpts from the journal of Mr. Claude Tanner shed light upon dark months of struggle, and, ultimately, the heartache of a people far from home.

***

March 11, 1844

Independence, Missouri. Small though it may be, this township thrives, the conflict between Joseph Smith and his Latter-Day Saints ended. Various sects remain, eager to be away from Jackson County. The Reformation Brotherhood, one of the last to organize an exodus, is a strange collection of souls; robust women accustomed to hard labor wed to simple men of the land, lone tradesmen seeking wives and fortune in the empty spaces, and bookish men with timid spouses who may have never so much as spent a night out of doors. None have ever raised a rifle in anger or fought Indians, and even fewer have spilled blood beyond that of a steer or antelope.

Thaddeus Bacchus, the Wagon Master, and I, the hired Trailman, advised the Brotherhood Elders to restock to the point of avarice before we committed to the Oregon Trail. The Elders, stoic men learned in a scripture unknown to me and adept at murmuring amongst themselves, were quick to agree. They trust the lean and conspicuously tall Bacchus as if one of their own.

The Brotherhood has yet to find a place suitable to their way of life. In the words of Linus Tuttle, one of the bookish men I spoke of, they were *"excommunicated from every state where we attempted settlement: Virginia, Pennsylvania, even Ohio. Our hope lies in the fertile valleys of the rocky mountains, or the fish-swollen streams of Oregon."* Everyone in this enticing, open land deserves their chance at happiness and abundance, and in a country sprawling as this, I can see no reason why they should not find a place to settle unmolested and unfettered. Mr. Tuttle has a hopeful face and sad eyes, a harried wife, and a young daughter who never asked for such coming hardship.

Many appear so road-weary that homesteading on the outskirt of Independence would be a welcome cessation of their travels. However, Independence's expulsion of Smith's Mormons has erected a barrier of prejudice and rejection, and no splinter group—Latter Day Saint or not—is welcome here. Their journey's end, and dreams of prosperity, lie one thousand hard miles west.

Rumor and its bedfellow the Tall Tale wander every road, and several pilgrims swoon with bright enthusiasm at these exaggerations, a contagion of joy that inevitably wears thin when reality arrives unannounced and sets the bed afire.

Kyle Toucher

March 13, 1844

I believe Thaddeus Bacchus sows seeds of dissent this night. The Elders are said to be long of study and well-lettered, trusted, and suited for leadership. However, Bacchus possesses a silver tongue and offers his persuasions with charm and effortless skill. I watched him worm through the crowd, nodding respectfully to the womenfolk, speaking to the men with calm confidence, then smiling at the children as if an actor in a stage play. He is like a wisp of smoke, touching everything for but an instant yet leaving an indelible mark. His conversations are short and delivered with stately posture and a firm handshake. Upon his departure, man and wife immediately huddle into tense debate, their expressions suspicious, their eyes wary. What rumor spreads here before the most perilous leg of our journey?

Within Thaddeus Bacchus is a light in one eye that reminds one of a salesman or carnival barker; in the other, something else. I have no words for it. Yet.

March 14, 1844

So many moving west. The frontier offers freedom, but that comes at a toll paid in toil and treasure, and often blood. We run parallel to the Santa Fe Trail for a few days, and for the moment, there is a camaraderie between all the wagon trains. When the east Kansas split comes and the thrill of that first step wanes, the guile or gall of these people will make itself evident.

March 18, 1844

So much had transpired since the last entry, I am at a loss to recount it in total.

For brevity's sake let me begin with this: With a speed I thought not possible, Bacchus has assumed leadership.

The response to his usurpation has been flaccid: little more than weak-bellied protests from the Elders. Although I clearly witnessed his politicking just one week ago in Independence, I am shocked at such rapid ascension. At the very least, I expected lively vocal dissent from the womenfolk, but there was none to be had, and there was little to no resistance from the bleary men eager to be west of anywhere. The serpent guile of Thaddeus Bacchus has borne fruit.

His intention to pivot southwest onto the Santa Fe Trail was immediately executed, and I see no logic behind this, no benefit to the party. Ahead is open range followed by harsh desert, poisoned watering holes and hostile Comanche. When I inquired his reasons for abandoning this long-held plan to traverse the northern route, his response was a stare over my shoulder and the words, "We will shimmer through this unscathed."

I remain bound not only by my promise to the people of the Reformation Brotherhood but my dependence on the monetary compensation I am due. However, this misappropriation of authority belongs to Bacchus and the spineless capitulation of the elders.

Late this evening, I witnessed a moment of unexpected candor. A furious Bernhard Schuller, an expert woodcarver eager to be in the forested northwest, and his son, a strapping lad near manhood, approached Bacchus as he sat in his wagon, poring over dusty books. Mr. Schuller's words, heated yet hobbled by his thick Germanic accent, repeated until his cheeks blossomed red, were firm and accusatory. *You defy the will of the people, those who placed their trust you.*

Following Bacchus' laughter at their protest, he ruffled the hair of the irate Mr. Schuller, an act clearly meant to humiliate. Mr. Schuller remains furious, but to attempt retreat rudderless and inexperienced is tantamount to suicide.

Although his argument did possess merit, I wondered if perhaps that accusation best lay at the feet of the Elders. Why would they have passively agreed to such larceny from Bacchus? Their gutless acceptance is genuinely mystifying, a detour from which they may never rebound.

There is more to Bacchus.

Kyle Toucher

March 23, 1844

Kansas. The Lenape have spotted us. That is of little astonishment as the land is griddle-flat and unremarkable; one would have to be blind to miss a train of over fifty-five wagons and dozens of oxen. A recent left-handed treaty has dispersed them to northeastern Kansas, and I suspect that wound still tender. The men, none of them fighters, ride with rifle at the ready. Their eyes are wide and nervous. Rumor and tall tale have given way to fear and speculation. The recent unrest with Bacchus is, of course, a constant tremor.

Bacchus tells me they will allow passage, but there will be a tax for which the Lenape are liable, yet will be paid by us. He did not state in what form those taxes would be paid, or how he came upon such information. "These are old lands," Bacchus said as he squinted toward their scouting party miles in the distance. "With old rules."

March 27, 1844

The children cry at night. I see worried fathers gathered by their fires as bereft wives coddle their offspring. The Elders keep to themselves, no longer offering the Morning Fellowship Services that appeared to be the glue keeping this band together.

The Lenape can also be heard in the gloom, whooping and hollering, beating drums in a pagan rhythm unknown to me. It is not the intense throb of war. This is something else.

March 29, 1844

Bernhard Schuller and his son, a young man named Deter, disappeared in the night. Bacchus and I spent the best part of the day looking for them, as far back as Long Medicine River. Most laid guilt at the feet of Indians, but in my experience, they limited their slave trade to the fairer sex, and that type of behavior is not common to the Lenape. When they make war, it is brutal and garish, and if these two had been taken by a hostile tribe as a warning, a treacherous display would have been made of them.

A Testament of Wanderers

The Elders have very little to say on the matter, content at night to smoke their long pipes and huddle around the fire. They are fully aware that Mrs. Schuller is now without family, and their dispassion is a mystery to me. Luckily other women will look out for Mrs. Ellis, as they are Godly, merciful, and faithful of heart.

By tomorrow I suspect the belongings of the Schuller men will be coveted by several in our troupe, and by week's end the memory of them will begin to fade.

Perhaps this is the tax of which Bacchus spoke.

Later, past midnight—

Bacchus sings to himself in his wagon, accompanied by a dissonant piping: mad flutes, notes breathed by some other as his vocal acrobatics offer no space for self-accompaniment.

Impossible still, his lantern casts no shadow—*none*—on the canvas. He is alone.

April 1, 1844

Against my wishes, the party took rest at Fever Bend, a horseshoe-shaped tributary where Perry Lake feeds the Kansas River. Although I have never been to Fever Bend, its reputation precedes it, and the first sight of the small wooden sign indicating its direction was enough for Bacchus to declare it our evening's destination.

Though I repeatedly cautioned not to drink form the shallow yellow pools, I was steadily ignored. Children frolicked in the cool water, lapping it up in greedy handfuls.

It is called Fever Bend for a reason, I told several of the women, but they were heedless. Instead, they encouraged the children to wade and drink heartily. Mr. Tuttle and his wife were keen to keep their daughter Millicent at bay, as were several others.

Kyle Toucher

Mr. Tuttle and I made an attempt to pull several children from the water, but their mothers, all by any other measure good, hearty women, met Mr. Tuttle with blows. Stunned, he released them and fled. I looked to the west, where Bacchus stood shirtless, framed by the setting sun. He leaned back, hands on his hips, and laughed.

But there will be sickness soon, followed by regret.

April 3, 1844

Typhoid has seized nearly every child that drank from the poisoned pools. They burn with fever, and their mothers proceed as if they were not told the water's dangers. Their denial perplexes me, but the illness does not. Typhoid is a terrible, slow killer if left untreated. Out here, separated from both physician and apothecary, their fate is almost certain.

April 4, 1844

Wind at night. An awful, steer-like lowing blasts the open land. Several campfires have blown out, and the continued weeping of sick children in miles empty moonlessness, resounds with a clarity I thought not possible: a warning to any living thing.

April 8, 1844

Moving again; we average eleven miles per day. Spirits are low. Thee of the children have perished, buried in graves as deep as we could dig in the stony earth. Mothers are heartbroken, fathers stare blankly ahead as they traverse the Santa Fe Trail. Eerie nights braying with wind and the cry of distant wolves are now the norm.

Bacchus spoke briefly to the party last night, thumbs in his vest, shirt opened, revealing a trove of necklaces adorned with talismans, feathers, and what appear to be blunt, worn teeth. Of what animal I can only speculate, but they are certainly molars. Do they belong to Mr. Schuller? I chide myself—*certainly not!* No white man is capable of such awful savagery.

"Fortune is won by sacrifice, as the Elders have taught you,"

Bacchus said with a nod toward the cadre of crooked old men in downturned hats and long, tattered coats. They raised smoldering pipes in acknowledgment. "Souls fall by the wayside, the desert takes its due. The Old Conflict never ends. Only its participants change."

There is minimal talk now about the disappearance of Mr. Schuller and his son. Though the widow's wagon becomes lighter as others grow heavier, it is the passing of innocents that haunts the camp. Mrs. Schuller wears her grief and shock openly, despite the best efforts from Mrs. Merriweather and the other robust matrons of the party—interestingly, the very ones wise enough to keep their children out of Fever Bend's wretched waters. When Bacchus comes near her, she eyes him with undisguised contempt as Bacchus reveals himself in increments, an unknown house guest who, over time, emerges as friend, foe, or fiend.

April 13, 1844

There is a change in the weather. A knife of cold air strikes my face when I face north, turning warm and heavy southward. Clouds bruised and rumbling stir like a great, slow cauldron, and in the distance there are mighty ingots of lightning. Thunder follows as only a subordinate can.

Linus Tuttle, who I have mentioned before, a soft man with large eyes and a face unused to wearing a beard, beckoned me to his side not long before we established this night's camp. He looked to the bruised warscape of clouds, his wife and daughter, and back to me.

"I saw . . . a *finger*, Mr. Tanner."

He whispered the words as if speaking aloud would somehow summon further sightings.

"A finger?" said I.

"Indeed, sir. Far away, hard to tell the miles in all this . . . this *flat nothing*. Down from the clouds it dropped, stirring up dust. Only for a few seconds, then it was gone."

I followed his eyes to a spot on the horizon. The clouds had turned almost witch-black, their underside seeping warped curtains of rain, the sun's final rays of the day blooming in the veil. I implored him to stay sharp and alert me if anything further caught his eye.

April 14, 1844

Although I knew the word *tornado*, I had only seen an artist's rendering.

An unimaginable roar woke the camp at dawn, and without warning, nearly two hundred souls became its hostage. It came at us with a speed I could not calculate, as its overwhelming scale defied my ability to measure. The clouds that bore the monstrous thing roiled heavenward, proud of the child it had spawned, raging with lighting and spewing rain at every angle.

  Perhaps the finger described by Mr. Tuttle was that of a repudiating God; his vicious whirlpool of ire, the very wrath of heaven wrought upon us, a rarely witnessed rebuke of our presence in this land.

When the outer edges of that mighty dust devil brushed across a wagon's planks, it exploded into a spiral of crackling wood and debris. God protect them; the entire Robinson family and three oxen took skyward. The whirlwind ejected Mr. Robinson, spinning in a hideous X-shape until he smashed into the Kansas plain, bouncing like a child's rag doll in ugly bonelessness. Lowing oxen and screaming women. Crying children and raw, feral fury.

Wagon harnesses, cooking implements, and all manner of things tore into the camp at furious velocity. Splinters the size of wheel spokes met with flesh, impaling many. Shrieks of unimaginable terror disappeared into the din of this devil-wind and the bright, arrogant sizzle of driving rain.

The mighty eye of the rising sun ignited the horizon as Bacchus, astonishingly unafraid, strode into my field of view. His jacket flapped like a jib in a gale, his hat long gone. His jaw fell open, oblivious to the detritus assailing his tongue and throat. Spit foamed in the corners of his mouth and matted his beard. With eyes wide and nostrils aflare, he raised his hands to the enemy.

In defiance of possibility—nay, *sanity*—that incessant mad piping rose, the idiot flutes from the night Mr. Schuller and his son vanished. Was I the only one capable of hearing such things, a sole receiver of these eldritch tones? Though death stalked us, roaring and snarling, how could the others not hear that insane music from Elsewhere?

Whether Bacchus resembled a Reverend preaching Revelation or a conjurer summoning familiars, I could not choose. However, his manner was content and authoritative amid rage and disaster. He swept his arms to the left as if opening heavy curtains. As he did so, the mad music throbbed with animal ferocity, rising far above the choir of screams and shrieking wind.

The tornado suddenly *changed direction*, its colossal fury taking deliberate aim, it seemed, on a small cadre of wagons seeking escape. The monster turned course, leaving my lungs empty and breathless as it rushed with the urgency of a loyal dog to its master. My chest ached for air, and my ears succumbed to hard, dark pain. Shelterless in the open range, I suffocated where I stood.

Escape would not be allowed. Nature's ire is a hellish engine, and the nemesis displayed that with brutality reserved only for war, slicing through their numbers like an invading army. To my horror, a horrendous geyser of dirt and debris became a sanguine stew as settlers and livestock were drawn into the tornado's ravenous, churning throat—then pulverized. Within seconds the rain became augmented with human and bovine, some parts recognizable, some not. The ground lay littered with felled wheels, burning lanterns, bloody clothes, and a bassinet stained so vile its equal is summoned only in nightmares.

Had Bacchus willed the tornado to obey his command? Had he *intentionally* set that prairie killer upon those that sought refuge? I dared not think such things, a horror beyond reason, an evil guaranteed to deliver a man unto Hell.

That feeding funnel twisted like a circus acrobat as it fled the rising sun. Done with its inflicting of terror, the tempest dropped the remainder of its slaughter in arrogant dismissal; crushed wagons fell to earth, broken bodies tumbled. It dissolved into ghost-white tendrils, a spectral snake snatched back into the clouds, taking with it that awful music—death's symphony played on crooked pipes and reeds—as the air returned, healing my burning lungs.

The destruction of the wagon train was unfathomable, strewn about the jagged path carved in the earth where the tornado had staked its claim. For several minutes, Bacchus remained in his pose of rapture, arms up, fingers splayed, head back, even as the survivors, many of them injured, offered aid to the critically wounded and dying. Face now alight with the new day's sun, with death lying all around him, Bacchus smiled.

April 16, 1844

The last two days were dedicated to burying the dead. Carrion birds, coyotes, and wolves absconded with a great measure of remains, both human and animal. The Lenape watched from a distance. They need not attack, as our suffering is evident.

The fleeing wagons were those of the Elders.

Bacchus refuses to assist with burials or answer questions.

April 24, 1844

Ten days since the tornado diminished our numbers by nearly half. A catastrophic loss, yet only thirty days outside of Independence. Even now, a retreat is entirely feasible before our remaining supplies are expended, and morale utterly fails. Everyone is deeply burdened with emotional suffering; Mr. Tuttle, who lost his wife in the tornado, cries daily and openly. His daughter watches the clouds and will only speak with her eyes closed as if opening them will remind her that her mother is gone. Childless couples walk in stunned silence, victims of typhoid or twister.

After speaking with several survivors, they have asked me to talk to Bacchus about abandoning this effort.

His mood has elevated since the tragedy—a stark contrast to the weary-eyed despair that has seized the remainder of the party. He is nearly whimsical in his attitude and musical in tone as he voices his desire to have us "beneath the gaze of the mountain." It is my assumption, as others, that he refers to the behemoths of Colorado. Despite this intent, I will attempt to use his current amiability as an open avenue for discussion.

April 25, 1844

I approached the Wagon Master's schooner after the evening meal. I find it rude that he dines alone, as it sends a message of disloyalty to the party, who still suffer night terrors wrought by that morning of terrible violence. I found him cross-legged in his wagon, a single lantern glowing behind him. Spread out were several books, all of them aged. A language I could not recognize was emblazoned onto their leather bindings, comprised of sharp angles and abrasive symbols. In the murk, the illustrations suggested a complex, even technical nature. Mathematics or Chemistry, mayhap; I am not a man learned in such things. He closed the book with quiet reverence, then looked at me with his half-carnival barker stare.

"Tanner," he said.

"Mr. Bacchus," I began, "There is a sentiment within the camp I wish to discuss."

He pretended nothing. "The desire to turn tail, yes?"

"Indeed. Their losses are unbearable, and with the Elders gone and the party hundreds of miles from their intended route, it all appears hopeless to them."

Bacchus raised a solitary eyebrow. The opposite side of his mouth turned upward, a crooked grin one would attribute to a hoodlum or looter. For a moment I had the impression he relished the memory of the Elders slain by the whirlwind.

"Several of them are without belongings. Worse, quite a number have lost spouses, even children, dear God. They want to head back."

In the faint drone of the prairie wind, those pipes began to blow again, the music of bedlam, obfuscated just enough to haunt both mind and spirit. Chills erupted beneath my shirtsleeves.

Bacchus lifted his chin. When he spoke, his voice was low and steady.

"And is that also your wish, Claude Tanner, hired hand, mouthpiece of downtrodden men?"

"The journey may not be cursed, Mr. Bacchus, but it is undoubtedly in peril."

"These are old lands, Tanner." He indicated his collection of weathered volumes. "With even *older* rules. Those that govern miracles. Those that shimmer."

As the wind pressed on the wagon, its nails and seams ached. Beneath that mournful lowing, flutes summoned night things to the dance.

"It is *their* charter, sir," I finally uttered.

For a moment, he seemed to consider this. He had gained control of the wagon train with persuasion and charm, and the opportunity to use those very things to waylay fears and offer comfort to greenhorns eager for leadership and hope was in his grasp.

Bacchus smiled; the carnival barker fully realized, eager to bow and tip his hat now that his offer had been accepted. The patron knows this promise is empty, but a tent bursting with wonders and enchantments is a powerful lure. I found myself amid that nefarious beguiling, stupidly prepared to believe whatever he told me, though my common sense warned otherwise.

A Testament of Wanderers

"I will address the camp tomorrow," Bacchus said, and waved me away like a servant.

***

Note from Ian Emerson, curator:

April 25 marks the unfortunate end of Claude Tanner's journal entries. Though his journal lay among the abandoned items of the Reformation Brotherhood Wagon Train's small band of defectors who turned east and fled the plains, it was sheer providence that Linus C. Tuttle, the reluctant, de facto leader of that retreating faction, also documented his experience. I have included several of his entries (in which some dates overlap) to draw a coherent picture of not only the fate of the Brotherhood but of Mr. Tuttle's ultimate service to our protector, Walpurgis Peak.

***

April 2, Year of Our Lord 1844

Since the usurpation of leadership, my entries have been sparse and infrequent.

I pray the Elders have decided wisely.

Mr. Tanner repeatedly admonished Fever Bend and its yellow waters, even the warning signs previous travelers had erected here. By sunrise, many will be sick. Thankfully, my dear Henrietta and Millicent are not among them. This Bacchus fellow is of a charlatan's lineage, anxious to slake a different thirst, one of power, a temptation to any man, and more so to those without God and guidance. I suspect an eagerness in him to see this party wander aimless.

April 12, Year of Our Lord, 1844

Tragedy is our constant companion. Typhoid takes our children. Wolves bray at us from the shadows. The very wind bests our fires and brings bad dreams. A German fellow, Schuller, one brave enough to challenge that baleful Mr. Bacchus, has mysteriously disappeared. Mrs. Schuller wanders, distraught and hurt, anger in her eyes.

I think him dead by nefarious means, he *and* his son.

Mr. Fremont and Mr. Jules have proposed approaching the Elders with our grievances. We are a people of laws and discipline, hardship and sacrifice. Did not our Lord Jesus sacrifice his very blood and breath? Can we not endure the shrieks of animals and the wind that carries them?

The weather is changing. I can feel it. Tomorrow I will speak to Mr. Tanner.

April 20, Year of Our Lord, 1844

My heart is broken.

Dearest Henrietta, so reluctant to embark on this final push west, has been taken by the Devil's wind, a wicked spiral that chose, in all this vast, flat land, the very spot where our wagon train stood. Millicent is speechless; she will not speak to me, there was no comforting her, nor did I receive any after I buried the mauled remains of my dear, blessed wife.

The Elders are dead.

Amid my other horrors, I suspect Thaddeus Bacchus is guilty of murder by diabolical means. I saw him steer that tornado toward the fleeing wagons.

I bear not false witness; my eyes did not deceive me.

April 27, Year of Our Lord, 1844

Claude Tanner, our righteous and good trail master, has been executed. Bacchus the predator, addressing the camp on their worries and woes, heartfelt losses and stripped of wealth and belongings, approached shirtless from his wagon. His schooner is a labyrinth of shadows, and radiator of incessant, awful music, its source impossible—yet so.

Around his neck hung several teeth, and it is only now that I suspect them to be those of Mr. Schuller and his son.

As Mr. Tanner spoke of our situation and the desire of many to turn back, pooling our resources and provisions in a limping escape from the horrors of the Santa Fe Trail, Bacchus charged Mr. Tanner with all his might, his voice a-fury with gibberish and nonsense. Before I could leave Millicent's side to offer aid, he drew his pistol and shot Mr. Tanner in the neck, killing him on the spot. The sight of deliberate, Godless murder after so much tragedy waves of terror through our numbers.

The Reformation Brotherhood is broken.

May 4, Year of Our Lord, 1844

After the women prepared Mr. Tanner's body for burial, Mr. Jules, Mr. Fremont, and I approached Bacchus's wagon. He sat inside, cross-legged and content, stained with Tanner's blood, adorned with the teeth of his previous kill. Terrible music emanated from that shadowy closet, a feeling of dread and apprehension immediate and overpowering. Ugly books lay scattered about, their contents obvious: witchery and night, blasphemy and self-defilement.

Mr. Fremont threw the first torch into the wagon, Mr. Jules the second. I confess, Dear Lord, I admit now as a sinner, I threw in the third. The fire was hungry and immediate. It devoured both wagon and benighted tomes, and last but not least, Thaddeus Bacchus, unmoving and unafraid, voiceless as the fire burned away skin, hair, and bone, freeing yellow rivers of boiling warlock fat and the greasy orbs of his eyes.

It is now, seven days hence, that I can write about these horrors, as murder's scar is indelible; the guilt and violation of my promise to the Lord God of Hosts an indelible stain.

Kyle Toucher

May 10, Year of Our Lord 1844

Our original number approached two hundred, and in those days we relished the thought of freedom and self-governance. Bacchus's usurpation of our Elders had drawn the darkness of this world into sharp relief, and on its heels, eclipsing the misery of typhoid brought by the impure waters at Fever Bend, that Hell-sent Kansas tornado which worked further raptures upon us and reduced our number to less than seventy. Weary of hardship and loss, we, deserters all, turn tail toward Missouri. Broken spirits and catastrophe leave bitter retreat our sole avenue.

Though not suited for the job, I lead this wrecked band eastward.

I am a murderer; may redemption lie in leadership.

May 22, Year of Our Lord 1844

Hunger. The men are shamed by their inability to find game. Several women, Mrs. Merriweather mainly, have taken to making stews from local grasses and salt-preserved pieces of Oxen slain in the tornado, but these sparse provisions are close to depletion. We cannot find the wheel ruts to guide us back, not so much as a glimpse of another west-bound band upon this nighted Satan Fe Trail.

Mr. Fremont's compass points North, then East. According to this device, the sun rose in the west today. At night I search for the north star, and see only strange constellations, a sky unknown to me. We are lost.

May 27, Year of Our Lord 1844

More than just savages watch us. Bacchus. From *Elsewhere*. I sense his eye, a window to sour dreams, bubbling from his face as *flames devour him . . . !*

Bacchus's music can still be heard most nights, carried on that deep, fearsome wind. Millicent, sweet Millicent, speaks of dreams of a snow-covered peak and glassy lakes, tall trees and golden sunrises. Despite her hardships and loss, I envy her hopeful innocence.

July 14, Year of Our Lord 1844

A month forged in despair and death. Perhaps it is starvation's mirage, but on certain days I see a mountain in the distance. A jagged knife, miles away, glaring at us through the haze—Millicent's vision come to haunt me? If so, then we head to this snow-capped promise of water, a calm lake Millicent sees in dreams. I see it no matter what direction I look, yet I tell no one, only that we approach that distant peak, the gnomon of a massive sundial casting shadows of unknown stars.

July 30, Year of our Lord 1844

Burned black as soot, Bacchus staggers in a copse of trees adjacent to our nomad's road.

He points one accusatory finger at me, then sweeps my gaze toward the mountain.

Closer each day, the gate at summer's end.

Loathsome music everywhere—

August 8, Year of our Lord 1844

I am perpetually in the corner of Mr. Fremont's eye, he of the haunted compass, the co-conspirator of murder by fire and this ragged crow's flight to nowhere.

August 18, Year of Our Lord 1844

More perish from punishing heat. Several have turned to divining rods to find water. Now the mountain is clear in its majesty, its dreadful kingship. The incinerated Bacchus caresses the deep crevices between the ribs of my emaciated mare. One boiling stew of an eye.

Kyle Toucher

August 23, Year of Our Lord 1844

The others finally see it!

Several stiffened at the sight of the titan, but I rejoice and run to embrace our rescuer, now just a few rolling days away.

However, Millicent can now see Bacchus.

"The man you burned is sitting in our wagon, papa."

September 1, Year of Our Lord 1844

I do not know how long the locals have been here. Cretins, surely; low intelligence but robust in strength. They dwell within a warren of hovels in the woods, but in their odd way, they welcomed us in friendship, with offerings of possum and muskrat already prepared for the fire.

"Dead Neck Lake," the eldest—a female, I believe—said. Rotten of breath and void of teeth. No hair to speak of and tired, rheumy eyes. Her following statement froze by blood. "Bacchus sent you."

October 4, Year of Our Lord 1844

A luxury—water in abundance—but it is presided over by the sky-gnawing tooth of an ogre. The slope-headed locals insist the *mountain* prefers the name Walpurgis Peak.

How could I ever of thought this granite brute our rescuer?

We suffer its mammoth countenance, a tyrant and its dominion. Within the camp there is an innate knowledge of the mountain's hostility toward interlopers, a malfeasance birthed in antiquity. An awful wind screams down its ugly hide; a riderless hearse, a messenger from Hell. Startled birds explode in flight at its passing, and trees bow like obedient serfs.

The catspaw this wind scratches upon the surface of the lake moves with purpose.

A Testament of Wanderers

Like Bacchus, it knows we are here.

October 6

Above, the nemesis.

Below, its minions.

With my wilderness desperation at an end, one look toward Walpurgis Peak immediately summons my confession: thrust by a murderer's shame, I have led us into a danger far greater than Indians and tornadoes.

My most dire notion of Dead Lake Lake is that it endlessly reflects Walpurgis Peak in the manner of a terrible mirror. Josephine Fremont and Geraldine Merriweather, two hearty women of steadfastness and guile, were the first to report that these reflections are bewitched.

I quote Mrs. Merriweather:

"Dawn broke as Mrs. Fremont and I went about our morning labors. As the sun, in all the tried and true clockwork our Lord set in motion, rose from the east, spilled golden upon crystalline water. We stood in reverence at God's handiwork, and for a brief moment, I imagined we had been delivered from the nightmare which cursed our band of pioneers. I turned from the sun's majesty toward the brooding mountain. A light gale caressed the face of the deep, etching a catspaw across its surface. Yet, in those breaths of wind, a *separate* reflection of that dangerous mountain showed *only where the wind had drawn the catspaw*. In defiance of nature, these new reflections depicted the mountain at *night,* summit strangled by clouds, the scythe of a crescent moon lighting its slopes and trees. It is unnatural. We should be on our way from here."

This woman is true of heart, incapable of false witness.

We know what—*who*—conjures such visions.

Kyle Toucher

October 7

After our evening repast, Millicent spoke of "wind and water voices, songs that Shimmer."

My hand trembles as I write this, I feel another—*another language*—stirring in my fingΣrtips, eager to escape. For now I can barely suppress its call. They BɅŁḴ at this tongue of imps and sṗiḲits, the voices that seek guide them upon these pages. Millicent, I suffer this burden for you.

October 11

Past Midnight. Music. Bacchus always present. My fingers, his unwilling *mЦꙅℯ*.

The camp sleeps uneasily. I hear the mutterings of bad dreams and the ache of creaking wagons as men toss in their slumbers. I am stirred from sleep by a sound carried across the silver surƒace of Dead Lake Lake. It is wordless, yet, as Millicent says, it *sings*. The mountaiՈ, that stone witch, could never utter such lilting endearments. A siren which tempts me with the gypsy pleasures of fortunes told in the dead of night; to disregard þome and hearth.

The wind drew its scar, parting the lake's bewitching stillness. A theatre of revelations played upon the mirror walls of that aquatic holler—the epoch before men, *before Eden*. I bore witness to Walpurgis Peak's ravenous acceptance of falling, wounded angels— speared, bleeding, mouths agape with curses while the war raged heavenward.

There is no greater blasphemy, to know and keep this secret.

OcṬober 21 !ДК

A great eye, charred and blackened, breaches the water with increasing regularity, the endlessly changing line of the surface spattering its black, wise pupil. The mighty spine of this lake denizen, Bacchus reborn as a serpent of the deep I have no doubt,

314

crested soon after, never once disturbing the aeons-old image of Щalᴘuᴦ́Gis Peaᴋ́. Reluctant water shed its glistening flesh in shimmering curtains, a lover's caress lamenting evening's end. I long to be a part of it . . . I turn away from food, preferring to listen to the gentle lapping of the waves.

Ꞇhe alluring lullaby stalks my shuttered rooms, haunts known only to me.

We watched the death of your mother by candlelight—she called not for you.

The old hurt. I hiss, glorious in the suffering.

When the tornado took Henrietta she thought of Bacchus, occupier of your marriage bed.

An imaginary misery? I *welcome* it. Am I not his muse?

Several times I watched Millicent, down on all fours, drinking like an animal. I envied her.

October 2‹ð2 Yeaᴿ̌ Ṏɲ̈e of Ẕero

Three more are missing.

Empty clothes and bloody boots found near the shallows. The locals chatter from the treeline.

Music . . . oh that ʍϒᵧUẔïᴋᴋ is everywhere, my dear Henrietta . . .

Mrs. Merriweather shuᴨs me, her eyes are urgent to !fuh−l·È'E!.

OᴋtoᏏer 2wentee 4 (ᴦ̵m̰! ˝Yʃ))

Ă choir of murmurs brings me to the water's edge. It laps at my feet, wraps my ankle in gentle ropes; beckoning me to the clear, Ц̩ŋwaveᵧІŋġ image of a mountain; a night one-thousand years past or future, I can not tell. The moon is red and deliberate, scarlet the water on which it shines.

Kyle Toucher

Tonight I saw the keeper of Bacchus's watching eye; its gelatinous, spade-shape of a head, the hooked beak as unrelenting as the meat-ripper of an eagle. A snake of a limb reaches the surface. Shimmering liquid silver cascaded into the lake, every future torment—*every future age*—portrayed in that shimmering curtain: ꙍalpurgis ᏢᴇᴀӅ born in fire; tunnels excavated below to allow gibbering blasphemeƧ access to their ugodly, throbbing machines; the mountain's ᗡᴇᶏᎢħ in 2077, listing like a tree felled, fatally wounded. Time and water . . . indivisible.

!Cease! Show me no more!

Millicent aches to be filled, it sings, but it the hucꝀster voice of Bacchus. *A symphony of pressure and burning, lungs gorged until they burst.*

A supplicant, sipping angelic purity.

Bring ĥĔř to me.

October 27? 2ʉ6?

Ì. Ꝛemêṃẞer.

The tornado was a call from this child of Poseidon, a lonely god imprisoned in a private sea with no one to love it, no one to grovel before it as it ṡe̱ṟ̃v̆ė̇ṡ only the vanity of Шalpurĝis ʽPeak, mirroring the mountain's cruel, eternity-defying visage.

It wants only to be cherished, and Bacchus is its agent. *I see that now . . .* He wanted us to БUГИ Ң†Ӎ ᴀŁİyΣ.

Millicent stirs at the scratching of my quill, and something else.

Shhhhh. Hush now, my love.

The cretins howl in the foothills, voices chilled by the wind from the mountain.

A Testament of Wanderers

Hand in hand, we stand belly-deep in Dead Neck L̦aƘe

Drink and breathe, sweetheart.

Something is coming.

ḂÂ₵₵Ƅụ𝐒

S꯭H̆a̧d̑őWḷȩ𝑆s.

Ȍctoßer 2Nein!

The cool tears of misfortune. That gnawing itch.

My God, it is *inside* me.

The crown of its head, the fortunes it whiŜpȩr̦s to me as it traverses
the lake in great, gliding strides. How my sweet silver is loathe to slide
from its back, only to řĕbûȋ̦d into the image of that unholy mountăin,
where the ḂA̧NJ̧Ş̣HɪȨÐ crashed into a world too blind Ŧō see them.

Oktobernacht! 30.0

Oh my lovely girl. Your moŢħer loꭚɘd̦ you so. And I ɭẟved her, and
I forgave the ȚʊRИa̧d̑ȏ *witch* brott uz? ˮHerꞫ.

I see clothes *abandoned!!* at the shore.

So others have fled? Mrs. Merriweather's ƎYƎ𝐒 did not lie.

Dead or swimming? Dreaming or . . . *eaten.*

It is not *Millicent* that Dead Neck L̦aƘe wants.

[ ]ktȪber −53

ȦΨ−summoned−ȩC̊Ỏ?

I am a ꓘꓘЍ̦ḭ̦ꓝꓝˮE gentlꭚ opening a murderer's guilt. In the catspaw
my monarch glares fierce—

317

Kyle Toucher

Walpurgis Peak ugly as it stood in ages past.

Gut slit, my soft meat tumbles, steam billows. BÂCÇʜᴜS rejoices in my suᶠᶠerinɢ—

Singing*Burning*Sining*Burning*

"We should be on our way from here."

The Samhain Tapes

Colin Leonard

"Folklore Commission of Ireland. Recording number 167. John Cahill talking to Shay Flaherty at his home in Coole, Co. Westmeath. Okay, Shay, that's recording there now."

"Do I have to speak into it? Which is the bit that catches our voices?"

"No, don't worry about that, just speak as you normally would, it's my job to worry about how it sounds. It'll pick us up just fine there on the table. Thanks again for agreeing to chat to me. Now Shay, you've lived here in Coole your entire life. In this very house?"

"Aye, in this very house all my life, sure. Where else would I go?"

"And I've been told that you'd be the man to talk to about old folk traditions in these parts."

"Folk traditions? What folk traditions?"

"Well, old customs. Games and activities and the like. How people used to celebrate special occasions in days gone by. I'd like to record accounts of how you and your family and friends would entertain yourselves. They told me up in the pub that you had some great old Halloween stories in particular."

"Aye, sure, there was many the night, not just Halloween, that we'd take to the roads for the bit of divilment. Around Christmas time we'd get up to mischief as well. We'd do the wren boys on the 26th. That would be one of the biggest nights for going around and playing tricks. Also Easter, and Ash Wednesday as well. April Fool's. But Halloween would be the big one all right."

"Sounds like there'd be any excuse for a bit of fun. What kind of games would people get up to in those days, Shay?"

"Well, some of the games we liked to play would have been carried out in the dark, when we would prowl the roads together, meself and the others."

"Was this as children?"

"Ah no, older than children, so we were."

"Young men and women, then?"

"Aye, that we were. Sure if you made it past the crib in those days, you were doing well. I had two brothers and a sister who died, and them barely out of me mother's belly. Hard times, and sure if you were strong enough to survive them, you deserved to have yourself a bit of fun."

"Would there be drink involved?"

"Drink would be taken, indeed, heh, heh."

"And songs? We're gathering recordings of old songs as well, if you can remember any."

"Ah, songs on occasion. Except if you'd be doing the sneaking to catch a stickman. You'd have to be quiet then. You couldn't be singing, or he'd hear you coming."

"A stickman? I haven't heard that one before, Shay. What was that?"

"The stickman would have been one of the Halloween games we played. You'd have to catch yourself a stickman for the evening.

He'd be there for the duration, tied up while you'd go about the other games, but you'd always come back throughout the night to have the craic with him?"

"A stickman? No, I haven't . . . "

"I remember there was a few years in a row we got Josey Halloran as the stickman. You'd always pick a weak one. The first couple of times we caught him outside near the big bonfire. Everyone came out to have a peek at our big bonfire. He'd be sneaking around in the darkness, trying to have a look at all the fun and hoping we wouldn't notice the weaselly little head on him. But we'd spot him, and we'd catch him. Eventually he learned to shut himself inside like a coward, keep his door locked. The last year we got him, we had to force our way into his house."

"What would you do to him, Shay?"

"Stickman stuff, of course. Have you never heard of catching a stickman for Halloween?"

"You and your friends would play this game?"

"Me and me friends all right. Eight of us, mostly. We'd have the masks on, and we'd head out catching after dark. We'd have the big bonfire burning. A pile that we'd gather over the days, bales of hay, branches, old boxes. You might have furniture taken from the stickman's house, or from a spindly finger's house."

"A spindly finger's house?"

"Sometimes we'd make someone play the spindly fingers. That's an indoors game. I'll tell ya later about that. The fire would be the centre of the celebrations. Everyone would come up there to watch. We'd keep the stickman there."

"Beside the bonfire?"

"Tied to his stick."

"You tied a man to a stick? That's a bit cruel, Shay."

"Aye, we'd tie him to a stick, all right, a long post that we'd drive into the ground near the big bonfire, so he'd be the stickman. But also because of what we'd do with the shite-sticks."

"Now, there's another thing I haven't heard of before. A shite-stick, you say? Is that particular to these parts and what exactly is it?"

"A shite-stick would be a pointy narrow stick or a branch that we'd pull off a tree. Something hard and whippish like a sally rod. You'd go into the fields and get yourself a good load of cowshite on the end of it and use it on the stickman."

"I'm afraid to ask, Shay."

"Stickman, stickman, we'd be chanting. All in our masks, the eight of us."

"Don't tell me you'd rub cowshite on the poor lad when he's tied up."

"No, we wouldn't rub it on him."

"Thank God for that."

"No, we wouldn't rub it *on* him. Where does shite go? Up the arse, that's where it goes. Shite up the hole. That's what the shite-sticks were for. Fill him up."

"Jesus Christ."

"Heh, heh, heh."

"I don't know if you're winding me up, Shay. I sincerely hope that you are."

"Oh, I like to play me games. But you'll know when I'm playing. I'll be wearing me mask."

"The masks. Tell us about the masks that people would wear back then, Shay. It's not like nowadays. You couldn't go into the shops and just buy yourself a mask. But I know the tradition of dressing up for Halloween goes way back. What kind of costumes would you be wearing?"

"Ah, the masks were a great part of it all. You'd need the masks, all right. With the costumes we weren't bothered that much what they were. Some of the lads would steal a dress and put that on over their own clothes for the laugh or they might wrap sacks or oilskins around themselves. But the masks were the important part."

"What were the masks made from?"

"Would you like to see them?"

"You still have one?"

"One? Sure, don't I have them all still. All eight of them. Wait there now, I'll go and get them."

"Do you need some help?"

"No, no. They're in me nightshirt drawer in the bedroom. I'll be back in a minute. Have a sup more tae there if you want."

SHUFFLE. SHUFFLE.

"Note to check the stickman reference against other oral histories in the collection. I have a feeling that Mr. Flaherty's memory might be conflating Halloween games with some form of corporal punishment or bullying that he either witnessed or took part in."

SHUFFLE. SHUFFLE. SHUFFLE.

"Here we are. Now, move yer stuff over and let me show you these."

"Fantastic, Shay. I can't believe you have all these. What is this? Leather?"

"Pigskin, that one."

"That's a scary one all right. I wouldn't like to be met by that on a dark night. And these ones are burlap. They're remarkably well preserved. You've taken great care of them. Have you ever seen the example that they have on display in the Museum of Country Life up in Roscommon? It's quite like this. Very plain but sinister."

"Sure, what would I be doing going there? To a museum no less? Here, see this one? This was mine. Do you like the big eyeholes? I used to rub soot around me eyes to darken them up as well, give a look of the Devil to them. The seven other lads all had their favourites too."

"Six, seven, eight, nine . . . You have a spare one here. There's no eyeholes on this one."

"That's for playing the spindly fingers."

"How old are these masks? Fifty, sixty years old? Are your other friends still around? I wouldn't mind having a chat with them too if they were willing to share some of their stories."

"Oh, they're all still about, so they are. Will you allow us to play the spindly fingers with you, do you think? Do you want to get a real feel for what it was like back in those days?"

"Em, what would that involve? I'd love to take some photos of these masks if I could. I don't think I've ever come across the likes of them apart from in old photographs and up in the Museum. Although the one in the museum is older than these would be."

"Ah, these have been around a long time now, longer than you might think. So will you play it?"

"Um . . ."

"You can take all the photos you want after that."

"Well, okay. Why not? What do you need me to do?"

The Samhain Tapes

"Just stay sitting there and you put on this mask."

"The one with no eyes?"

"That's the one."

"Whew! That whiffs a bit, Shay. This hasn't been washed in a while, I think."

"That's the fear you'd be smelling. Many's the frightened head's been stuck inside there."

"Hope I don't catch something from it. There better not be nits or anything on it."

"Spindly fingers."

"What do I do now?"

"Spindly fingers."

"Whoa, what was that?"

"Spindly fingers. Spindly fingers."

"Is that you touching my neck, Shay? Are you throwing your voice somehow?"

"Spindly fingers. Spindly fingers. Spindly fingers."

"That's amazing. How are you doing that? I can feel them on me. It feels just like fingers."

"One for ten and we'll leave the thumbs. Do you understand the rules? One of yours in return for us taking ten of ours away. If you don't ask us to take ours away, if you can suffer the spindly fingers on you, then you win. Do you like the spindly fingers?"

"Hey, that's a bit rough. You're strong for your age, I'll give you that."

"They're not my spindly fingers. Whose spindlies are they?"

Whisper, whisper, grunt.

"Shay, that's too rough, let me go."

"Let you go, is it? Take the spindlies away? Okay, then, but it's one for ten."

WHACK.

"Aaaagghhh. What the fuck? My finger, my finger!"

"You asked Sean to remove his spindly fingers from ya. One for ten is the rules. He removed his ten, so he took your one."

"Let me go. Who's with you? Who's holding me? Oh fuck. Take it off, take this hood off me."

"Who do you want to let go? Neck, or left arm, or right arm?"

"All of them. Let me go."

Grunt, whisper, whisper.

WHACK. WHACK. WHACK.

"Aaaahh. Aaaahh."

"They all let go, like you asked. Mick and John and Tommy. Neck, and both the arms. That's thirty spindly fingers that let go, so the lads took three of yours. Aren't we good at the sums?"

"P-please . . . "

"Spindly fingers. Who's that creeping round you now? Spindly fingers round your eyes. Can ya feel ten of them spindling around each eye like crawly spiders. I hope they don't drive their hard nails in through your hood."

"What are you doing? Stop it. My eyes."

"Should they take their spindly fingers away? Is that what ya want?"

"Please stop this."

"Is that a *yes*? Left eye, right eye, each to say goodbye to spindly fingers."

"Leave my eyes alone!".

WHACK. WHACK.

"Now, Patrick and Paul have their payments. One of your spindly fingers for each of them, in exchange for taking their tens away from your eyes. Are ya liking the Halloween game?"

"Nnnnn."

"Speak up there now, don't be falling asleep, lad."

"Nnnnn."

"Only me and Brendan left. Where's your spindly fingers going, Brendan? Oh, the trousers, is it? Sure, he might like that. Oh, the spindly fingers are twisting, twisting it off. Should he remove his spindly fingers, or should his spindly fingers remove yer balls?"

"Nnnn. No. Let, let go of me, you fuck."

WHACK.

"Aggggghhh!"

"Thumbs, that's a good name for you now, I'd reckon. Two big stupid thumbs might be all that's left on yer paws after this next go. There were a few thumby feckers going around in the old days, oh there was. We haven't gotten to play like this in the masks for a while, have we, lads?"

Grunt, grunt, grunt, grunt.

"Spindly fingers. Spindly fingers. Over the mouth, up the nose. Spindly fingers. Should I let you go?"

"Mmmmmmm."

"Can't really hear you through that hood. Spindly fingers. Nice and tight."

"Mmmmmmm. Mmmmmmm."

"Sure, maybe you want to keep your last one, maybe you do. That's fine with me. I'll let my spindlies do their work over your mouth, over your nose."

"Mmm."

"Are you awake, at all? Can you move? No? You won the game of spindly fingers. You won. You came out of it with one finger left to keep your two thumbs company. We might call you Pokey instead of Thumbs. If you don't start moving though, we might have to add you to the bonfire, won't we, lads?"

Grunt, grunt, grunt, whisper, whisper.

"How do you turn this thing off?"

CLICK.

★★★

In the grubby kitchen of the decrepit house in Coole in Co. Westmeath. The heavy yellow haze of stale bacon grease hanging in the air. The tape recorder on the table splattered with tea and blood dried in. Damp in the walls, dirt on the floor. Old man sat at the table. Bachelor smells, unloved sweat and coughs and spittle. But not alone, oh not on his own.

The Samhain Tapes

***

Grunt, grunt. Whisper, whisper.

"Ah, he was some craic, wasn't he, lads? It's good to reminisce, so it is, to remember the fun times we had. Do you want me to play the tape again, lads? I'll play it again, but then we may start getting the big bonfire ready."

"Folklore Commission of Ireland. Recording number 167. John Cahill talking to Shay Flaherty at his home in Coole, Co. Westmeath. Okay, Shay, that's recording there now."

"Do I have to speak into it? Which is the bit that catches our voices?"

Drawn Home

Red Lagoe

The following evidence has been submitted for addition to Apple County Sheriff's Department's CASE FILE 94-20993.

At the end of June 1994, three teenagers went missing from the town of Waterford in Apple County. Katie Wilson's bound book of correspondence addressed to her father was found in Vanderhill Quarry in the Waterford Hill area. Tiffany Vanderhill's personal journal was recovered from her home. Devon Cahill's related chat room discussions are documented. The following excerpts of chatroom conversations were highlighted by the detective on the case, journal entries were transcribed, and photographs of sketches were taken. These files account for the missing persons' experiences in the days leading up to their disappearances.

Katie Wilson, correspondence journal transcribed
JUNE 27, 1994

Hi Dad. I'm using this journal to do like you asked—to send letters and drawings. I know I'm a little late getting started, but Mom and I just got done moving to Waterford, so it's been a little hectic with the end of the school year and everything. It's going to feel weird writing every day and not mailing any of it until the end of summer. But I guess it'll save on stamps. It's gonna be a weird summer because I don't know anyone here, and Mom is working long hours.

Drawn Home

My plan is to get a job in town—maybe at the gas station or the diner or something.

I have to ride my bike to get there though. Ugh! I really need to save up for a car! Maybe when you mail me something back at the end of the summer, it can be a car. Hahaha, just kidding.

But if you do send something, make it a red convertible. I saw a really pretty one today. I don't even know what kind it was. All I know is that the person driving it was a jerk. Some blonde Barbie with an attitude.

I was on this back road called Darby Rd, coasting downhill (that bike ride back up the hill suuuucks!) I was heading toward town, and there was a long chain link fence that ran along the woods. I kind of wanted to climb the fence and explore the wilderness like we used to when I was little. Remember that? But it was so overgrown with weeds and brush, I'd need a machete to whack through. The cicadas were so loud it was like the woods was going to eat me alive. It was kind of creepy, actually, because I didn't pass any other cars. Then, toward the bottom of the hill, I saw a break in the green wall of forest. A locked gate in the fence—and just beyond it, a narrow gravel road carved into the shrubs and weeds and trees. Like a cavern made of green.

Kinda like this . . .

But it was green. I have your old ammo satchel still. I keep my pencils, pens, and charcoals in it . . . but I don't have room for colored pencils. I don't even know which box they're in.

It was so weird being there. I didn't even realize that I'd stopped my bike. My feet were on the ground. I couldn't hear any of the cicadas anymore. I really wanted nothing more than to skip job-hunting and wander down that path. It was a spooky feeling, like that feeling when someone is standing behind you, but nobody is there. But in this case, the someone or something was in front of me. I guess it wasn't really that scary . . . just intriguing. I couldn't look away.

But then out of nowhere, this girl came blasting down that dark road through the jungle cavern in a red convertible, squealing to a halt on the other side of the gate. It looked like she was being chased or something. She looked scared.

She hurried out of the car and ran to the gate, so I was ready to—I don't know—help her, I guess. But instead she scrunched up her face and screamed, "What the hell are you looking at?"

That's when I flipped her off and pedaled away.

She must've had a key for that gate because a minute later, she flew by with some obnoxious pop song blasting. It was the worst. I'd rather listen to the Doors or some Stones. Didn't you order some more Stones from Columbia House? I don't think they ever came before we moved.

Hey, feel free to mail CDs if a red convertible is not doable for an end-of-summer gift. I also wouldn't mind some band t-shirts. I used to borrow yours. Do you remember that? Must be nice having your shirts back in your drawer.

I wonder if your new girlfriend's kids will borrow them now. How old are they?

Anyway . . . to my ever-improving luck, Barbie was filling up at the gas station where I was going to ask for a job. She was flirting with the guy behind the counter. Some kid named Devon, who I guess is her neighbor. I had to listen to them flirt while I filled the application out. In that time, I learned Barbie's real name: Tiffany. And that her parents are loaded.

So, that's it for today. I really didn't know what to write about, but once I started, the day just spewed out of me onto the page. I'll shut up and draw something now. What do you want me to draw for you?? I know you can't really answer that, because you won't see any of this for a few months . . . why are we doing it this way again??

I guess, for lack of creativity, I'll just do a self-portrait. Sure, I could just send an updated picture, but you asked for art, right?

Brace yourself. I pretty much look exactly like you now, minus the face tattoo.

***

Red Lagoe

**Tiffany Vanderhill, personal journal
transcribed JUNE 27, 1994**

If Devon Cahill doesn't fall madly in love with me by the end of the summer, I will literally die.

OK, maybe that's a little dramatic, but seriously. I can only buy gas so many times to get his attention. What's his deal? I invited him to come see the new quarry Dad just blasted open, and he said no thanks. He was going hiking after work. Look, I love me an outdoorsy guy, but really?? He would rather go stomp around in the woods than go to a private swimming hole? Who says no to turquoise water and a blonde bombshell in a Victoria's Secret bikini?

Not that I don't have flaws or anything. But I mean . . . come on!

I want to lounge on that pebbled shore so badly, enjoying the summer heat, cooling off in the water. The color is almost as pretty as those beaches in the Caribbean. Where my parents decided NOT to bring their only daughter this year. Some family vacation! Sure, it burned a little, but they said I was 17 and needed to learn a little about responsibility. So I'm spending the week home alone . . . not like it's the first time. And I'm making my own fun. Dad said to stay out of the quarry, but there's literally nowhere else to lounge by the water around here without going to the public pool over in Eastman. Uh, no thanks!

Summer break just started, and it already sucks. Ever since the end of the school year, my friends have been avoiding me. Cara says she's too busy with family stuff. Isabelle has a job at the diner now. The new quarry is a cool spot and if I could just get someone else to hang out with me there, it'll be the new it-place to be this summer.

I have the key to the gate so I could totally charge admission if I wanted to, but Dad would kill me if he found out. He says it's not safe there. Some of his employees quit after they blasted the hole into Waterford Hill—some superstitious shit about angry ghosts or whatever. I will admit I got spooked today when I was there alone.

About halfway up the cliff wall on the opposite side of the water, I thought I saw someone. I swear to God. Super creepy. Then he was gone. There was something like a cave up there, or maybe just a shadowy spot between boulders? That was my cue to leave. I wasn't about to hang around that place alone and get murdered by one of dad's workers . . . and end up on Unsolved Mysteries or something.

I will go back, and I know I can get someone to come with me. But if Devon is going to keep playing hard to get, I'm going to have to find someone else.

***

God, what's wrong with me? I think I just zoned out for an hour. That was weird. It's already 7. I closed my eyes, pictured the water, and just stared at the cave. I seriously need to get new friends or I will lose my mind from boredom and loneliness!

***

Excerpt from chat room: Apple County Hikers/Explorers (ACHE)
Devon Cahill (HikerDev1977)
JUNE 27, 1994
9:45PM

OnlineHost: HikerDev1977 has entered the room

HikerDev1977: hi

TheseBootzR4Walkin: made it to the summit and back before dark

MamaEleanor: That's very nice. It is a lovely hike.

VicTheRichard69: hi HikerDev!

MamaEleanor: Welcome back Dev.

TheseBootzR4Walkin: Dev! I was just saying how sore I am from the Trip's Summit loop.

HikerDev1977: That one's fun. I explored a new place today outside of Waterford

VicTheRichard69: haven't been to Waterford in a long time

VicTheRichard69: didn't know there were trails out there . . .

TheseBootzR4Walkin: Waterford?? What trail is in Waterford?

MamaEleanor: That area has a lot of history.

VicTheRichard69: a history of being boring lol

TheseBootzR4Walkin: lmao

HikerDev1977: it's kinda on private property so . . .

MamaEleanor: What does "lmao" mean?

VicTheRichard69: now I'm lmfao!

TheseBootzR4Walkin: oooh, be careful on private property. People out in the boondocks will shoot you on sight. ;-)

HikerDev1977: it's out on Waterford Hill. Some land that Vanderhill Stone and Gravel bought.

MamaEleanor: That land's been closed off for years.

MamaEleanor: There used to be no trespassing signs and fences.

HikerDev1977: I guess Vanderhill took down some of the fencing when they bought the land.

VicTheRichard69: Vanderhills are assholes

TheseBootzR4Walkin: understatement of the year

HikerDev1977: nobody's been at the blast site in days, and the land uphill from it is just sitting there unexplored. I've been wanting to go for years, so as soon as I noticed the fence down, I went for it

MamaEleanor: Vanderhills had no business buying that land from the state.

MamaEleanor: It should've stayed protected forest.

TheseBootzR4Walkin: Good hiking though, Dev?

HikerDev1977: Yeah! Great views when you get up above the new quarry they blasted, but I didn't try to get any closer

TheseBootzR4Walkin: why not

HikerDev1977: I didn't know how stable the ground would be.

VicTheRichard69: always smart to avoid falling off cliffs.

VicTheRichard69: theres hope for the younger generation! lol

HikerDev1977: lol. lot of idiots out there. I try not to be one.

MamaEleanor: Like I said, that rocky foothill area outside of Waterford has history and nobody has any business being there.

TheseBootzR4Walkin: Calm down Eleanor. The boy just took a walk.

MamaEleanor: I don't fault Dev. I fault the city for letting history get forgotten. It's always about making money with them.

VicTheRichard69: and the local historian strikes again ;)

VicTheRichard69: these full sentences with punctuation are killing me MamaEleanor

TheseBootzR4Walkin: it's a hard habit to break for the older generation

VicTheRichard69: never too late to break old habits

HikerDev1977: There was some weird stuff out there in the woods tho

TheseBootzR4Walkin: color me intrigued

VicTheRichard69: like what?

HikerDev1977: About a hundred yards or so from the blast site, there was a big cinderblock wall in the hill

TheseBootzR4Walkin: huh?

HikerDev1977: I didn't want to get too close to the ledge, so I turned uphill and there were some big boulders and stuff. Maybe like a cave, but someone closed it off with cinderblocks.

OnlineHost: MamaEleanor has left the room

TheseBootzR4Walkin: creepy

VicTheRichard69: ever read The Cask of Amontillado? lmao

TheseBootzR4Walkin: yes! I love Poe. :o)

HikerDev1977: no. what's that?

VicTheRichard69: uh oh. I think we pissed off the historian. She left.

TheseBootzR4Walkin: lol! Sorry, Eleanor! We love you!

TheseBootzR4Walkin: did you make it to the top Dev?

HikerDev1977: I tried but got turned around. Just ended up at the blasted hole again.

VicTheRichard69: and you never thought you might be going the wrong way even though you were walking DOWNHILL?

Drawn Home

HikerDev1977: it got weird hiking there

TheseBootzR4Walkin: hiking new places can be disorienting!

HikerDev1977: that's the perfect way to describe it. Disorienting. I ended up back closer to the edge and got all tangled in vines and prickers. So I called it a day, but I would like to revisit.

Private Chat Room initiated by Victor Rosetta (VicTheRichard69) with Devon Cahill (HikerDev1977) JUNE 27, 1994 10:00PM

VicTheRichard69: hey, man.

HikerDev1977: hey

VicTheRichard69: just wanted to talk to you and see how you've been doing.

HikerDev1977: Ok

VicTheRichard69: how's your mom doing

HikerDev1977: still pretty sick. Stage 4 now.

VicTheRichard69: that's awful. I'm sorry you're going through this

VicTheRichard69: hiking helps clear the mind

HikerDev1977: yeah

VicTheRichard69: so do girls. haha

VicTheRichard69: got a girlfriend yet?

HikerDev1977: nah

VicTheRichard69: slim pickins out your way?

HikerDev1977: I guess . . . small town.

HikerDev1977: There is a girl who just applied at my work

VicTheRichard69: now we're talkin! Is she cute?

VicTheRichard69: I remember being your age. It really wasn't all that long ago

HikerDev1977: hey I gotta go. I don't feel good

VicTheRichard69: whats wrong

HikerDev1977: idk just feel off and my head hurts.

VicTheRichard69: alright. Take care buddy

***

Katie Wilson, correspondence journal transcribed JUNE 28, 1994

Hey Dad. This is weird. If I were writing a letter to you and mailing it each day, I'd say "hey dad" every time I write. But all these letters are part of one book. Do I count this as individual messages, and use a greeting every time? Or just one long letter that takes all summer to write?

Doesn't matter, I suppose.

So today I went to a swimming hole with none other than Bitchy Barbie herself, Tiffany Vanderhill. (Rich girl name, am I right?)

I rode my bike back toward town today and ended up stopping by that gate to the road through the woods. It's such a pretty tunnel of trees, I just sat there and hung out for a while. Nothing better to do around here.

But while I was sitting there, Tiffany pulled up in her convertible.

I was about to leave, and she yelled out asking if I wanted to see the quarry. I didn't know what to think—like, was she making fun of me? Nope. She actually apologized for yelling at me the other day and she figured she'd make it up to me by letting me be the first person to see the quarry.

I swear it was like the beginning of a horror movie. I kept thinking a bunch of jocks and cheerleaders would jump out, steal my clothes and abandon me or something. But nothing like that happened. It was actually kinda fun for a little while.

I put my bike in the trunk of her car, and we drove through the woods-tunnel-thing. It was a tight fit, like the forest was squeezing in, hoping to catch us like a Venus fly trap. So wild.

At the end of the gravel road, it opened up to this big rock quarry. I can't wait to go back. The water was like something from a vacation magazine. A tall rocky cliff made of massive boulders in a half-moon around the water. Trees and vines dangled from the edge, like they were holding onto the soil above for dear life.

It was like a secret garden that was never meant to be discovered. Kinda like this:

Red Lagoe

I haven't been able to stop thinking about that place. It's crazy to think that just last month, it wasn't a quarry at all. No water hole either. The side of the hill, or mountain, or whatever you want to call it, was blown away by Tiffany's dad's company, leaving a massive pit.

We swam and explored the quarry along a rocky ledge and it led to a little cave in the cliffside. Stalactites? stalagmites? Whatever. Both of them were in there. I think that means that the cave had been there for a long time. It was begging to be explored, but just before I had the chance to step inside, we heard movement above us toward the top of the cliff's ledge.

Tiffany yelled out, "Who's up there?" and then shouted something about it being private property, and I suddenly felt like maybe going into the cave without flashlights and stuff wasn't very smart. I was ready to wander inside with no gear and no fear . . . and no idea if there were drop-offs or anything. Not sure what I was thinking. Don't worry though. I'm smarter than that.

Came to my senses and I convinced Tiffany to head back down to the pebbled shore. She had some Boones. Maybe too many because she was swaying side-to-side, just staring off, talking about how sick she felt and how she just wanted to lie down. She was about to go up to the cave and take a nap, but I wouldn't let her.

I made her get in the car and I drove it back to her house. I seriously need a license—I'm obviously responsible enough. Once she was home, I pedaled back to my single-wide mansion in Waterford's Darby Park, and now here I am wondering when Tiffany Vanderhill will show up with the popular kids and dump a bucket of pig's blood on me. Verdict's still out on her.

But she's the key to a cool summer hangout spot, so maybe I'll give her a chance.

I mean—that cave!! I wanna crawl inside and peek around . . .

★★★

Drawn Home

**Tiffany Vanderhill, personal journal
transcribed JUNE 28, 1994**

Sometimes I wish my family wasn't who they are. Sometimes I wish that we didn't have all this money, and we just hung out and played Monopoly. Or instead of Caribbean vacations, maybe we could go camping. One time when I was little, we did a family group camp at a KOA with my aunt, uncle, and cousins. We sat around a campfire and made s'mores. Mom and Dad complained about everything, and I pretended to hate it too, so we never did it again.

We never do anything anymore.

***

God, I feel sick. My head has been throbbing since we went to the quarry earlier. I keep losing track of my thoughts. I wake up, write a little, and fall back to sleep. Maybe I need to just go to sleep for a little longer. I've drank more alcohol than that before and never felt this sick. Mom and Dad left the number to their hotel, so I could call them and let them know I caught some awful virus or something. But I'd hate to interrupt them and have them call me out on being irresponsible. I got this. I'm sixteen. I can totally handle taking care of myself a few more days.

***

It's already 9:30. Where'd the day go? I keep dreaming of the quarry. All I wanna do is go back. I want my toes in the water, my skin on the hot pebbles. Then I want to crawl into that cave to cool down, I want to light a little campfire inside and eat s'mores with my family. I want to go

***

Devon Cahill—HikerDev1977, chat room conversation
Apple County Hikers/Explorers (ACHE)
JUNE 28, 1994,
9:17PM

OnlineHost: HikerDev1977 has entered the room

HikerDev1977: hi

TheseBootzR4Walkin: I'd love to hike all of the Appalachian Trail but my kids are way too little

VicTheRichard69: kids are great

TheseBootzR4Walkin: Do you have any

OnlineHost: MamaEleanor has entered the room

VicTheRichard69: no way. No kids for me. I like my freedom. Hi Dev and Eleanor!

TheseBootzR4Walkin: hey hiking buddies!

MamaEleanor: Good evening everyone. I did some digging with another historian friend.

VicTheRichard69: Oh lord, here we go.

TheseBootzR4Walkin: :-)

HikerDev1977: I went back to the quarry site today and heard voices coming from below. I think it was one of the Vanderhills so I left.

MamaEleanor: I think you should stay away from that place.

HikerDev1977: I'm being very safe. I just want to go back for a little while and check out something. I think there's another cave entrance down in the quarry. I almost got a look. But that's when I heard the voices.

Drawn Home

MamaEleanor: Dev, stay away from that cave!

VicTheRichard69: Unless you have proper equipment, don't go exploring any kind of cave.

MamaEleanor: That cave is pure evil.

TheseBootzR4Walkin: pure evil? DUN DUN DUN! haha

MamaEleanor: The government fenced off that land almost two hundred years ago. And up until the last fifty years or so, the fencing was maintained. Waterford Hill has a tragic and mysterious history not to be trifled with.

TheseBootzR4Walkin: what r u talking about

VicTheRichard69: I've heard some of the stories, but it's all superstitious nonsense.

MamaEleanor: My friend Jeanie has stacks of correspondence from the locals, newspaper clippings, and other things stored away in her office.

MamaEleanor: She told me that there was man who lived in Burnham around the year 1800 who failed to save his family from a house fire. He had three kids who all burned alive.

TheseBootzR4Walkin: that's terrible!

MamaEleanor: According to the clippings and letters from residents, he lost his mind with grief and left Burnham for what is now known as Waterford Hill.

MamaEleanor: He just vanished into the woods, never to be seen again.

TheseBootzR4Walkin: Can you blame him?? I don't know what I'd do if . . . I'm not even going to say it about my kids.

MamaEleanor: But then children and teenagers from Burnham and surrounding towns started going missing.

TheseBootzR4Walkin: yikes!

MamaEleanor: She said the townspeople started combing the streets for these kids who had been going missing for the better part of a year. Dozens of them.

VicTheRichard69: what'd he do? offer them free candy from his horse and carriage?

MamaEleanor: Well, nobody assumed he was the one responsible for the missing kids. Not at first. They didn't put it together until they found the letters.

TheseBootzR4Walkin: what kind of letters

MamaEleanor: Kids in the area knew about some secret place in the woods, where they could leave a letter detailing their desires, and their wish would come true.

TheseBootzR4Walkin: I don't like where this is going

MamaEleanor: Jeanie hasn't had time to go through everything, but she remembered one letter from a mother. She said her boy heard about the man in the woods who granted wishes.

MamaEleanor: The boy wrote a letter about missing his father and he brought it to the woods. But when he got there, the man tried to lure him into a cave and the boy ran away.

VicTheRichard69: smart kid

MamaEleanor: The townsfolk hunted Waterford down with hounds that led them to a cave.

HikerDev1977: so they found the missing kids?

MamaEleanor: Unfortunately, they only found bodies. Dozens, all strung upright against the walls of the cave, burned down to nothing more than charred skeletons.

TheseBootzR4Walkin: that's so sad!

VicTheRichard69: He lost his children and tried to replace them . . .

TheseBootzR4Walkin: replace them with more dead kids???

VicTheRichard69: not just dead. burnt!

MamaEleanor: They couldn't find Russell Waterford. They searched the cave to a dead end, then torched the place and then sealed the only way out. That cement wall you found in the woods was where the township had burned and buried Russell Waterford alive to punish him.

TheseBootzR4Walkin: Wait, so they named the town after him?

VicTheRichard69: This is the appropriate time for a dun dun dun! Or more like, I wish this conversation was done done done. Lmao

HikerDev1977: that's a wild story

MamaEleanor: That area became known as Waterford's Hill. And when they established Waterford less than a century ago, they named it after the hill, not knowing why.

TheseBootzR4Walkin: that's disturbing

MamaEleanor: Now the Vanderhills went and blew up a tomb that should've stayed sealed.

HikerDev1977: But the cinderblock wall I found was still sealed off. Only a few cracks. The blast site is downhill.

TheseBootzR4Walkin: But you said you saw another entrance at the blast site.

TheseBootzR4Walkin: I wonder if there are bodies in there!

MamaEleanor: Please, Dev, don't go back. I'd hate for something to happen to you.

HikerDev1977: I'm sure Russell Waterford isn't a threat anymore MamaEleanor. :)

TheseBootzR4Walkin: yeah, but whose voice did you really hear today, Dev? Maybe it wasn't one of the Vanderhills. ;o) Or the ghost of Russell Waterford! Muahahahaha!

HikerDev1977: no it was the daughter. I recognized her voice . . .

HikerDev1977: the Vanderhills are actually my neighbors.

VicTheRichard69: my condolences

TheseBootzR4Walkin: whaaaat? No way!

Private Chat Room initiated by Victor Rosetta (VicTheRichard69) with Devon Cahill (HikerDev1977) JUNE 28, 1994 9:45PM

VicTheRichard69: Eleanor's a piece of work.

HikerDev1977: haha she's ok

VicTheRichard69: if you ever wanna explore the cave, let me know

VicTheRichard69: I'll bring my gear. Do it the right way

HikerDev1977: ok thanks

VicTheRichard69: feeling better today?

HikerDev1977: worse actually

VicTheRichard69: neighbors with the Vanderhills. That'll do it.

Drawn Home

VicTheRichard69: Dude, I think I might know where you live, then . . .

HikerDev1977: oh

VicTheRichard69: so the Vanderhill daughter . . . you hittin that?

HikerDev1977: What? No

HikerDev1977: I think I'm going to go back to the group chat

VicTheRichard69: just messing with you, man. Sorry. How's your mom doing today?

VicTheRichard69: you still there?

VicTheRichard69: doesn't say you signed off. You ok?

Hiker Dev1977: yeah . . . I saw a light come on next door. It's Tiffany. My neighbor.

VicTheRichard69: you watch her a lot from your window ;)

HikerDev1977: it's not like that. I mean, I think she likes me, but she's not my type

VicTheRichard69: whats your type

HikerDev1977: I don't know. I got enough going on at home

VicTheRichard69: friends can help. Talk to her. And if she's not your type you can talk to someone else you trust. I'm here if you ever need someone. Open invitation

HikerDev1977: There's something wrong with her.

**Devon Cahill—HikerDev1977, chat room conversation
Apple County Hikers/Explorers (ACHE)
JUNE 28, 1994,
9:48PM**

HikerDev1977: So, everyone, I was just looking out my window and noticed the Vanderhill girl just standing in the middle of her driveway

TheseBootzR4Walkin: waiting for a ride maybe

HikerDev1977: she's not moving. Not much . . . just kind of swaying there barefoot in her pjs

VicTheRichard69: drugs are bad, kids.

HikerDev1977: should I go check on her

TheseBootzR4Walkin: Dev, as much as I hate the Vanderhills, I think that's the right thing to do. Check on that girl and make sure she's ok.

HikerDev1977: brb

TheseBootzR4Walkin: welp. We're never gonna see him again. lol

VicTheRichard69: LOL

MamaEleanor: That's not funny.

TheseBootzR4Walkin: you started it, MamaEleanor. Lol jk!

★★★

**Tiffany Vanderhill, personal journal
transcribed JUNE 29, 1994**

I'm scared.

There, I admit it. I'm 100% beyond freaked.

Drawn Home

Last night, Katie dropped me off at home after the quarry and all I remember is writing a little in my diary, but my memory is not great. Devon was at his computer. I could see him from my window, and I thought about how badly I wanted to be somewhere other than my bedroom. But then I felt really tired and I guess I fell asleep?? But when I opened my eyes, I saw trees. I was in the woods and Devon was there telling me to go home. Maybe it was a dream, but I woke with scratched up fingertips, dirt under my fingernails, and quarry dust on my clothes.

My hands hurt. My head hurts even more. My feet are filthy. I do remember standing before a cement wall but what was that? Devon was a distant voice in this nightmare and he yanked on my arm, begging me to go home. I blinked and I was awake in my bedroom and Devon wasn't anywhere near me. I swear I heard him yelling. I heard him say "help" at one point. But he wasn't outside, and his light wasn't on in his bedroom. By then it was almost midnight.

***

Katie showed up at my door and talked me into going into town for food. But I don't even remember what I ate. It's like someone is taking an eraser to my head. I'm scared and I honestly have no idea what to do. I tried calling the hotel, but when the receptionist put me through to my parents' room, there was no answer.

I want to tell someone, but I'm not going to unload this on Katie. I hardly know her. I'd go knock on Devon's door, but I haven't seen him all day and his bedroom light is off again tonight.

Where the heck is he? Maybe at the hospital with his mom.

I'm so tired and just want to go

home.

***

Red Lagoe

**Apple County Hikers/Explorers (ACHE)
JUNE 29, 1994,
10:15PM**

OnlineHost: TheseBootzR4Walkin entered the room

TheseBootzR4Walkin: hey hey hey everyone!

VicTheRichard69: hi Bootz!

MamaEleanor: Hello, dear. We were just wondering if you and Devon were going to show up tonight. We're all usually signed in by this time.

TheseBootzR4Walkin: The kids wouldn't go to sleep, so I was a little late to the party. Don't know about Devon. Maybe he finally realized we're all older than him and not nearly as cool.

VicTheRichard69: speak for yourself

TheseBootzR4Walkin: Vic, you're like fifty.

VicTheRichard69: fifty is the new forty

TheseBootzR4Walkin: which is still OLD lol

MamaEleanor: I'm worried he might have gone exploring that area again. If he doesn't show up tonight, I have a good mind to call the police to check it out.

VicTheRichard69: and say what?? "I'd like to report a missing person . . . Yes, it's a random dude from the internet . . . No, officer, I don't know his real name . . . "

MamaEleanor: You don't need to be snarky. And we know that he lives next door to the Vanderhills. That's something to go on, isn't it?

TheseBootzR4Walkin: that's true

VicTheRichard69: I just don't see how the police will be interested in the fact that a teenager didn't sign into a chat room

TheseBootzR4Walkin: I'm sure everythings fine

MamaEleanor: I hope you're right because I found more information about Waterford Hill. Jeanie has more letters dated after they sealed Waterford in the cave. She remembered seeing one from the local doctor who noted an unusual number of children were "delirious" or "confused".

VicTheRichard69: here we go again . . . ;)

MamaEleanor: One father found his son clawing at the cement wall over the cave. His fingers were bloody and the father had to fight kicking and screaming to get him away from the cave.

TheseBootzR4Walkin: omg

MamaEleanor: The doctor had seen so many cases linked to these kids' proximity to the caves that he convinced the authorities to block it off.

VicTheRichard69: So you're saying the spirit of old Russel Waterford might still be luring children into his cave two hundred years post-mortem?

TheseBootzR4Walkin: that's a disturbing thought.

MamaEleanor: there's a lot of things that can't be explained

TheseBootzR4Walkin: ((shiver))

VicTheRichard69: Looks like Dev isn't coming tonight.

MamaEleanor: I'll say a prayer for him.

VicTheRichard69: He's fine, Eleanor. The boy just has a lot going on at home

TheseBootzR4Walkin: how would you know?

Online Host: VicTheRichard69 left the room

***

**Katie Wilson, correspondence journal transcribed
JUNE 29, 1994**

I just noticed there are figures in the cave drawing I did yesterday.

I don't remember drawing the little people inside.

***

I don't know if I have what it takes to be friends with someone like Tiffany. She's too much work and has way too many issues. Drunk out of her mind after two bottles of Boones yesterday. Spacing out all day at lunch, saying she didn't feel good. Well ,guess what! I don't feel good either, but do you see me making it everyone else's problem? No!

Sorry to vent, Dad . . . I know this isn't your problem either. It's mine. So I'll handle it.

***

I keep falling asleep. I lost most of the day. I think I'm really sick.

***

I wonder if Tiffany and I breathed some toxic fumes or something at that quarry . . .

Drawn Home

I'm scared, Dad. This guy's face keeps popping into my head when I black out. And now it looks like I drew him. When did I draw him??? It's not even my style of drawing—but I just know I did it because I saw his face somewhere.

It's the same person. The guy from the cave that Tiffany said she'd seen, and the figure in my quarry drawing . . . and this guy.

"Come home", he says.

I'm losing it, aren't I? My ears ring with his chant. Come home Come home.

Believe me, I know I sound crazy. And now, I'm sitting in my room wondering if I should rip these pages out or leave them. Maybe the smart thing to do would be to tell Tiffany she shouldn't go back to the quarry just in case it's making us sick somehow. But part of me doesn't want to. Part of me wants to go ~~home~~ back. To stand at the mouth of the cave and step into the cool, damp hole in the earth and never come out again.

It's not like anyone would miss me here. I don't think Mom has even said "good morning" or "good night" in over a week. She's passed out on the couch with a whole twelve-pack of empties around her, so I could leave now, and she'd never notice. To be honest, Dad, I doubt you'd ever notice either . . . at least not for a few months. Really, you couldn't be bothered with me sending a few letters this summer? Too busy with your new family? Did you think I wouldn't notice that you never gave me an address to mail this to. I'm assuming, but haven't said so, that you are trying to vanish from my life.

Well, fuck off. I'll figure life out myself.

***

**Katie Wilson, sketchbook diary
transcribed JUNE 29, 1994 7:00PM**

I'm losing entire minutes and hours. I'm at Tiffany's tonight. Maybe if I mark the time, I can make sense of it later. It seems the only time I remember is when I'm writing. All the in-between is getting lost. And Tiffany is even worse. She is completely out of her mind. I think maybe it's because she's been exposed to whatever is in the quarry longer than I have.

Maybe she's extra-poisoned. That sounds stupid.

***

Tiffany is desperate to go back to the quarry.

I tried telling her it might not be safe. That something there is messing with our heads, but she damn near scratched my eyes out to get out of the house.

So I stole her keys.

She didn't see me do it, and she spent about twenty minutes scouring the house for them before she said she'd just walk over there. I've never seen someone so strung out. Crazy thing is . . . I feel it too. I can't stop thinking about the man in my drawing. Come home, he says. But who the hell are you?? Why am I obsessed with the cave I didn't get to explore, and how welcoming it felt to stand in front of it, like a home that could swallow me up.

A home that actually wants me.

***

I found some pills in Tiffany's parent's medicine cabinet: Valium.

I gave Tiffany a couple to help her chill out.

***

Tiffany Vanderhill, personal journal transcribed.
Undated final entry, following previous journal entry.

I see a light at the end of the tunnel. Maybe that's cliché, but it's there like a little campfire in the cold darkness. A place that I can cozy up to and feel something other than loneliness. Devon is there, I know it. This is where my real family is. In the light.

***

Katie Wilson, sketchbook diary transcribed
JUNE 30, 1994

I don't know who drew this. It doesn't even look like something I'd draw but I've got charcoal and ink on my hands, so maybe I did. Is that supposed to be Tiffany?? I woke up at her house and she was gone.

I think I'll go home now. What else am I supposed to do? I tried to help her. And that's all a person can do. I can't be running around babysitting her all week. I need to take care of me too.

I'm sitting here in her living room, clutching to this stupid journal like it might save me from insanity somehow. Yeah, I think it's time to go home and get help.

***

It's 8PM. When did it turn 8PM?! Where are you when I need you? Why did you leave me? I guess none of that is important now. I need a doctor or something. Tiffany and me both. Writing this is all that's keeping me from blacking out.

***

9:20PM

I'm in Tiffany's car right now, facing the gate to the quarry. When I woke up here a few minutes ago, she was at the fence on her hands and knees. When she first turned around, I thought her face was really dirty, but it was blood pouring out of her mouth.

Drawn Home

She was trying to CHEW THROUGH THE FENCE!

She snarled at me like a wild dog, exposing a row of broken, jagged teeth. She was dead set on getting back to the quarry. She looks exactly as she did in the drawing from last night.

Is this going to happen to me too?

***

Tiffany came at me like a rabid animal, tackled me to the ground. I didn't fight. I can barely write this, but I'm afraid I'll forget it if I don't write it. I was too scared to do anything. Maybe I was in shock. She got the keys, unlocked the fence, and then she was gone.

Like the dark tunnel of trees reached out and sucked her in. She just fucking vanished! I blinked and she was gone. I'm going to stop writing for a bit and drive into town for help.

***

I woke up on the ledge of the quarry. I'm sitting here alone at the mouth of the cave and there's a figure standing just inside the shadow. I can make out the vague shape of a man's face . . .

Is it the man I drew? He's so sad.

I'm too scared to move, too scared to breathe because he might hear me.

***

A warm wind is rustling the leaves. I'm trying to take a minute and calm my nerves before I do anything else. Get my head straight. The vines and roots dangling from the edge of the cliff above look like snakes slithering in sync with the sway of the man in the cave.

He wants to show me something.

***

My watch died sometime around 10. The man from the cave is gone, and now all I see is a yellow glow somewhere deep within. Isn't it nice? It smells like Thanksgiving dinner. It smells like that time you brought home a roast chicken and stuffed it with Stovetop.

It smells like home. But not the Darby Park trailer home of disappointment. And not the home with no address that I'll never be welcome at. No drunken mother. No absent father.

***

I don't know how I know, but if I go in there, everything will be okay. Home in the warm embrace of the firelight at the end of the tunnel.

I'm coming home, Dad. See you soon.

***

July 17, 1994: CASE FILE 94-20993 is still open and ongoing.

VicTheRichard69 was identified as Victor Rosetta and charged with multiple counts of indecent exposure in the presence of a minor; however, aside from these private chat room conversations, no evidence was found linking Rosetta to Devon's disappearance. Security cameras from Rosetta's apartment complex verify that Victor was not seen leaving the premises the evening Devon was last seen.

Eleanor Newbury is cooperating with the investigation for supplying the news articles and letters discussed in the ACHE chat room. Detectives hope that they will help identify a potential copycat pattern.

Police and dogs have searched Waterford Hill and found no evidence of a sealed cave entrance, nor did they find an open cave in Vanderhill Quarry as the missing persons' accounts depict.

More evidence will be added as it becomes available.

Queen of This Carnival Creation

J. Rohr

Answering machine transcribed by Quintsville police
Ashley Myer calling Lorna Callow
5-23-90

ASHLEY: Hey, Lolo, it's Ashley. I'm guessing you're still under the weather, or you'da been here by now. Anyway, hope you feel better soon hun. I'm gonna birdwatch like usual, but it'll be no fun without ya, dontchyaknow? I think I'm gonna try that offshoot we saw last time. It's a li'l overgrown, but it'll be an adventure, right? Kisses and hugs.

***

MEMORANDUM FOR:
> Directors, Quintsville government departments
> Department Staff
> Police

FROM:
> Calvin West-Morgan
> Mayor of Quintsville

SUBJECT:
> The recent tragedy
> Rumor control

J. Rohr

By now, many of us are aware of the unfortunate death of Ashley Myer. What makes it truly awful is how her heartbreaking demise is being misrepresented in the public theater. Therefore, after careful consideration, all government employees are encouraged to strongly dismiss any grim rumors they encounter.

In addition, any government employee caught spreading salacious rumors will be subject to suspension and possible dismissal. Regarding journalists: directors and police officials are to respond to any inquiries with NO COMMENT. Any further elaboration should downplay the tragedy. Poor Ashley died because of a wild animal, nothing more.

We as a community need to come together to stop those who would turn this tragedy into a spectacle. After all, there's nothing here we can't handle ourselves.

Sincerely,
Mayor Calvin West-Morgan
Mayor of Quintsville
August 24, 1990

***

Courtney Wint
Chicago Tribune
160 N. Stetson Ave.
Chicago, IL 60601
August 27, 1990

Dear Ms. Wint,

It is the position of the Quintsville police, authorities, and the Department of Parks and Recreation, that the alleged incident has been blown out of proportion. That someone died is a tragic fact, but misconceptions due to unconnected vandalism, such as teenage graffiti marring our fine parks, have sparked a wildfire of speculation that is, to be frank, not true.

We have nothing else to add.

Respectfully,
The Honorable Mrs. Wilma B. Hodgkins
Director of Parks and Recreation

***

Quintsville Community Hospital
Department of Pathology

Autopsy Report

NAME: Ashley Myer AUTOPSY NO: 132248
AGE: 34 DATE: 6-5-1990
SEX: F TIME: 10:24 am
PROSECUTOR: George Bargamian
PHYSICIAN: Douglas Friedman
PATHOLOGIST: Debra Heinemann, M.D.
County Coroner ASSISTANT: Laura Statton

ANATOMIC FINDINGS:

1. Decomposed white female with early insect activity
2. Numerous abrasions, lacerations, and injuries consistent with animal attack

CAUSE OF DEATH:
Hemorrhagic shock caused by exsanguination

MANNER OF DEATH:
Could not be determined/Pending investigation

CIRCUMSTANTIAL SUMMARY:

Ashley Myer was a 34-year-old white female who left home at approximately 3:33 pm on 5-23-90 to walk the Tamarowa Nature Trail in Quintsville, IL for birdwatching purposes. She did not return home, and was found by searchers on 5-28-90, at approximately 11:00 p.m. The body was found in the woods on a game trail. No signs of foul play were noted at the scene. An autopsy was authorized by the Pope County Coroner's office.

IDENTIFICATION:
On 6-2-90 at 8:00 a.m., a complete postmortem examination was performed on the body of Ashley Myer who was identified by the Pope County Coroner's office. Persons present for the autopsy included Laura Statton as autopsy assistant.

CLOTHING AND VALUABLES:
The deceased is received wearing outdoor clothing including hiking boots, socks, jeans, underwear, bra, flannel shirt, and belt. All clothing is torn. Accompanying the body is a notebook and binoculars. A wedding ring is present on the left hand. No other valuables were discovered.

EXTERNAL EXAMINATION:
The body is that of a well-developed, well-nourished, white female adult appearing the stated age of 34 years. The body length is 63 inches, and the estimated body weight is 125 pounds. Scalp hair is brunette. Jaundice cannot be assessed in the skin or sclerae. The head is normocephalic. Irises are discolored by decompositional changes. Left eye is missing. The nose is normal. Teeth are present. Oral hygiene is good. The ears are pierced. The breasts are symmetrical without palpable masses. The genitalia are those of a healthy female adult. The anus is not dilated and has no evidence of injury. The extremities are roughly symmetric, though there are significant deforming injuries.

The following scars, and tattoos are present:
 1. A butterfly on the right ankle.

SIGNS OF DEATH:
Rigor mortis is absent, and postmortem lividity cannot be assessed.

ARTIFACTS:
No artifacts of medical or postmortem care are present.

Queen of This Carnival Creation

The following artifacts of putrefaction are present:
Skin slippage, green discoloration of the abdominal wall, marbling of the skin by intravascular hemolysis, purging hemolyzed fluid from the mouth and nose, malodorous gas bloating, air drying of the lips and fingers, fly eggs, and insect larvae.

INJURIES:
Bruises and cuts on wrists. Deep lacerations are present on the torso, thighs, right shoulder, and across the chest. The brachial arteries in the right arm are severed. Bite marks of an indeterminate species are present as well. Blunt trauma appears to have broken ribs causing a deep pulmonary laceration, and an intrathoracic hemorrhage.

✦✦✦

Nathaniel Quint's journal
January 5, 1768

I once heard Truth abandons whoso claims it. In this wither'd packet of Paper I intend a full confession, though I've no doubt I'll find ways to lie. Rather I'd pass out of existence a liar than confess what I know is real, at least that which concerns myself. I cannot ignore the stains on my soul yet feel little need to share them.

The Chain binding me is no single link. Amidst an unconquerable Tangle I find myself latched to a veritable anchor I'll forever love as it drags me into the deep—kissing Her as she pulls me down. I but glimps'd the Lady, and all else vanish'd. I never knew one could love Destruction so dearly.

I am Hers. She is not mine. I doubt anything, divine or D——, could own Her. I have seen the Lady paint the Symbols, and so command the stars. Yet, there is hope.

Seemingly subjugated I am not perceiv'd as a threat, so can by oblique means persuade Her to a course, the trajectory of which will mean, if not ruin, at least exile—away from humanity. My penance shall be serving as Her jailer. For I built the Black Church.

Now must I carry the sins born of my faith.

The few I could convince have come with me. Tomorrow we sail Westward to the colonies. Perhaps in some remote part of Virginia we will find peace, or at least some semblance of it.

***

Transcript of Coroner's Inquest
9-3-90

FRIEDMAN: Please state your name for the record.

WINT: Courtney Wint.

FRIEDMAN: And what is your occupation?

WINT: I'm a journalist. Currently, I write for the Chicago Tribune.

FRIEDMAN: Is that how you knew the deceased, Jeremy Rivers?

WINT: Yeah, yes. I've known Jeremy six, or seven years. He's a photographer.

FRIEDMAN: How would you categorize your relationship with Mr. Rivers?

WINT: Professional, but friendly. We spent time in Beirut together. I was covering the fighting there, and he was, well, taking pictures.

FRIEDMAN: Were you close?

WINT: Not especially.

FRIEDMAN: So you weren't intimately acquainted?

WINT: What do you mean?

FRIEDMAN: Do you drink, Ms. Wint?

WINT: A good martini makes for a great evening . . . but I'm no cliché, the alcoholic reporter.

FRIEDMAN: The night of the incident, had you been drinking?

WINT: Not when it occurred.

FRIEDMAN: But the police did find you intoxicated.

WINT: The police didn't go looking for me until hours afterward.

FRIEDMAN: Because you fled the scene.

WINT: I had to.

FRIEDMAN: Why?

WINT: Have you seen the car? If I stayed, I don't know what would've happened to me. She made a tree walk out into the road, and slam into us.

FRIEDMAN: You're saying you saw someone command a tree to attack your car?

WINT: I know how it sounds.

FRIEDMAN: And you insist you weren't drinking that night?

WINT: Not while we were driving, no. Look . . .

FRIEDMAN: Is it true you and Mr. Rivers argued earlier that day?

WINT: Yes. We got into a heated discussion at a local diner. He wanted to leave Quintsville because of what we've found.

FRIEDMAN: So, it was a professional argument.

WINT: Yes.

FRIEDMAN: Not a lover's quarrel?

WINT: I don't like what you're implying. Look, we found something in the woods . . .

FRIEDMAN: Whatever you think you found is irrelevant to these proceedings.

WINT: Not if it got Jeremy killed.

FRIEDMAN: Were you driving that night?

WINT: (no response)

FRIEDMAN: Ms. Wint. Were you driving that night?

WINT: Yes.

FRIEDMAN: And the car you were driving impacted a tree . . .

WINT: Yes, but . . .

FRIEDMAN: Ms. Wint, how did you lose control of the vehicle?

WINT: (no response)

FRIEDMAN: Did you lose control because you were too intoxicated to drive?

WINT: You people can go fuck yourselves.

FRIEDMAN: Didn't you tell the police, quote, (reads) "Oh God, oh God this is my fault. I got him killed. This is my fault."

WINT: That's out of context. I was upset because I convinced him to stay. He's dead because I couldn't let go of the story. He knew things were getting too dangerous, but I just couldn't . . .

FRIEDMAN: So you feel responsible?

WINT: You really think I'm dumb enough to answer that? I know a cover up when I see one.

Queen of This Carnival Creation

***

Transcribed audio
Psychotherapy notes for patient C.W.
Provided by Dr. K. Pendergast with patient's consent
Nov. 14, 1990

Patient, uh, C.W. returned for care this week. She's a professional journalist, whom I've seen previously. I first started seeing her in 1989 when she returned from Beirut. While there she covered the Lebanese Civil War for the Chicago Tribune. Suffice to say, her experiences left her a bit worse for wear. Six months later we made enough progress I stopped seeing her regularly.

It's unfortunate her issues have resurfaced. However, recent events mark an understandable return to her previous difficulties. A crash while investigating a story in southern Illinois seems to have resurrected her trauma. She watched a colleague die and was blamed for the death.

I have yet to get her to really open up about the incident. The way others have treated her so far has made C.W. defensive. I'm optimistic that given time we'll regain our previous rapport.

***

Excerpt from "Queen of This Carnival Creation"
by Professor Sandra Frye
Published 1987

Three years after T. S. Eliot's death, an original manuscript for *The Wasteland* was discovered. Published in 1971, this original draft revealed numerous unknown passages. Prior to the publication of the more well-known version, friend and fellow poet Ezra Pound suggested extensive edits cutting out huge sections.

Among the excised lines is a lengthy *lacrimae rerum*. Reminiscent of Thomas Gray's *Elegy Written in a Country Churchyard*, it borders on gothic surrealism. Reading it leaves the impression Eliot is attempting to relate some haunting vision:

> "Held hearts spurt rubies in spray serene,
> Paving the way to unfathom'd thrones of bone:
> So many an hour praying to Her unseen,
> And not a second wasted devoted to the crone.
> A New World village contains her galactic depths.
> Imprisoned by fools who never understood;
> Her glory a lost Milton might pen to breaths
> Whispering guiltless joy in her dark wood.?

It goes on to describe something Eliot calls "the Black Church" where worshipers pray to an entity called the "Queen of this carnival Creation." Her acolytes pay in flesh and blood, not always their own, to enter her "abyssal womb" to be born again. To say the least, it's more horrific than anything the poet would ever pen again, so it begs the question, what inspired this passage? The only hint is a letter Eliot wrote while in Lausanne, Switzerland.

Sent to his first wife, Vivienne, it reads:

"The dreams persist. Perhaps it's just this nervous condition, but lately, I can't help feeling attuned to the macabre. Yet, these visions are as eerily comforting as they are unsettling. I'll always regret hearing about Nathaniel Quint."

★★★

Transcribed audio
Psychotherapy notes for patient C.W.
Provided by Dr. K. Pendergast with patient's consent
Jan. 8, 1991

Progress with C.W. is slow. I cut a session short the other day. She smelled like vodka. Although she was more open, I can't encourage that kind of behavior. It's what led to some of her problems after Beirut. Alcohol as self-medication isn't a good option—she says pouring a second glass of wine. But I question the validity of what C.W. told me.

There's a burgeoning delusion as she tries to insulate herself from the Quintsville trauma.

Stress at work isn't helping.

Her editor asked C.W. to take a leave of absence. To hear her tell it, sounds like they're asking her to quit quietly. Although no criminal charges resulted from the accident, the paper feels she's lost credibility. She keeps pushing for a story the Tribune feels isn't up to their journalistic standards. C.W. laughed when she mentioned that. She said:

"Everyone wants the truth until the truth is too hard to handle."

***

MEMORANDUM FOR:
 Calvin West-Morgan
 Mayor of Quintsville

FROM:
 Wilma B. Hodgkins
 Director of Parks and Recreation

SUBJECT:
 Graffiti in local parks

Due to certain recent events, I've examined the *graffiti* in our local parks. It is my conclusion that several locations have deteriorated severely in the last few years. Environmental factors have removed large portions, leaving several vital pieces incomplete, and therefore ineffectual.

I believe this explains the unfortunate incidents of late. As such, I've dispatched a trusted crew to repair the damaged *graffiti*. I would take full responsibility for this, though I must say, budget cuts have made it difficult to routinely maintain the necessary pieces.

J. Rohr

Sincerely,
Mrs. Wilma B. Hodgkins
Director of Parks and Recreation
September 1, 1990

★★★

Nathaniel Quint's journal
September 3, 1768

In another life I might enjoy this land. The sweet odors of Fields, and the Forest abound. Fire-flies stream constantly at night as if the stars' children dance between our tents. Yet, for all the beauty there are reasons to worry.

Sounds from the Forest are at times unlike any ever heard. At a Creek we encounter'd a Barrier invisible. I heard Her chanting in the box, Her voice full of midnight intent.

One of the men asked, "What d'ye think 's best?"

A pistol shot brought silence. Yet, Death, though Visitor, soon retreated from Her.

Since then we avoid the Rivers.

We are days from any other sign of humanity. Once we glimpsed Natives, but they made odd signs and gestures. I suspect they knew something of the Unspeakable we carry.

I am fix'd on this course. So are the others. Penance for our days in the Black Church, though I doubt our chances of absolution. Perhaps that's why soliciting the Almighty produces nothing and offering the D—— all of me equates to the same silence. I am already damn'd.

Yet, while Heaven and Hell ignore me, I believe there must be some means of influencing Her. I have faith she is bound to Laws of being the same as anything that exists. Her rules may differ, but there are rules.

Queen of This Carnival Creation

***

Transcribed audio
Psychotherapy notes for patient C.W.
Provided by Dr. K. Pendergast with patient's consent
March 9, 1991

A witch queen continues to be the focal point of her delusion regarding events in southern Illinois. Several times we've discussed the accident that killed her coworker. She sticks adamantly to her story.

Usually, delusions can be circumvented with logic. Unfortunately, some patients are too entrenched in their beliefs. C.W. is dug in deep. Yet, I can't help feeling she wants this to not be true. She insists on some murderous evil entity in the woods that now haunts her dreams; however, even she doesn't want this to be the truth. That suggests to me she's aware of the implausibility of her defensive delusion.

Addendum:

I need to stop making notes regarding C.W. before bed. Sometimes the witch is in my dreams. I almost made the mistake of mentioning that to C.W. She's already got credence for her delusions from some book, *The Carnival Queen of Creation*? It says the witch connects to those who think about her. What a self-fulfilling prophecy.

***

Sandra Frye PhD.
Tulane University
English Department
6823 St. Charles Avenue
New Orleans, LA 70118
March 20, 1991

Dear Prof. Frye,

I heard about you from a friend who read your book, *Queen of This Carnival Creation*. I'm reaching out to you regarding a story I'm working on. Enclosed are photos of symbols I encountered in Quintsville, IL. The exact details are probably easier to share by phone. However, they match some of the art shown in your book.

I'll wait a day or two, give you some time with the photos. My current work as a freelance journalist has me constantly on the move, so I can't say where I'll be calling from. That is, what hotel. I'm currently covering a competition in Wisconsin: Amateur Radio Direction Finding.

When I heard you might be familiar with this subject, I felt so relieved. I've been in quicksand the last several months. With any luck you'll be a lifeline.

Gratefully yours,
Courtney Wint

***

Note left by Sandra Frye
March 22, 1991

She haunts my dreams. Sometimes, when I wake, She's beside the bed. Blink then gone. She is reaching for me. I must not answer.

I have seen the symbols binding her. The rain is washing them away. I will not be here when She's free.

Mommy loves you.

***

Queen of This Carnival Creation

Courtney Wint
1263 W. Pratt Blvd. #3
Chicago, IL. 60626
April 26, 1991

Courtney Wint,

My name is Thomas Frye. Recently my sister and I have been going through our mother's papers. We found your letter. I'm not sure how to inform you of this, but Mom won't be able to assist you. That's to say, she recently took her own life.

It wasn't entirely surprising, though no one can really prepare for such things. My mother, unfortunately, began declining mentally these last several years. We suspect a nervous breakdown of some sort, but I don't have any more answers for you than I have for myself.

All I know is that her last book, *Queen of This Carnival Creation*, put a strain on her. I was finishing high school when she started it. It was all she talked about. She practically glowed when she did. Having been raised by college professors, I know they live for the opportunity to explore some undiscovered academic avenue. At least, that's how Mom used to put it. Four years later, the book was finished, and she was never the same.

Friends keep saying it's good to talk about these things. I don't know.

I'm sorry. I can't help venting. Enclosed are the pictures you sent her. With any luck you'll be able to find someone else who can help you. My sister recommends Elsa Baptiste. She helped Mom with a lot of her research. Her address is also enclosed.

Sincerely,
Thomas Frye

***

J. Rohr

Transcribed audio
Psychotherapy notes for patient C.W.
Provided by Dr. K. Pendergast with patient's consent
April 28, 1991

I need to stop seeing C.W. She refuses to take steps to improve her situation. For instance, I've been forced to cancel several sessions because she won't show up sober. I just hope she finds someone who can help her, and the sad truth is I don't know if that's likely anytime soon.

C.W. recently began taking elaborate measures to prove her delusions. Using a time-lapse camera borrowed from her deceased colleague's boyfriend she photographed herself while sleeping. Several snapshots seem to show a figure standing beside her bed. It looks vaguely human though there's something tree-like about the thing in the picture.

A bat-woman, made of bark?

The point is I'm sure someone could fake it. Just because I can't see how doesn't make it real. Also, the fact C.W. is going that far is unhealthy to say the least.

Then there's my own blossoming *folie à deux*. Sometimes I almost want this entity to be real, for her sake. After seeing the photograph, I woke up suddenly that night, and swear for the briefest moment I saw the thing in the photo beside my bed.

Of course, with the lights on there was nothing to see.

C.W. refuses to accept this witch queen isn't real. Her delusions have begun seeping into my own imagination too much for my comfort. So, I'm referring her to a colleague. I wish her the best.

***

Transcribed audio cassette
Elsa Baptiste interviewed by Courtney Wint
August 14, 1991

Queen of This Carnival Creation

COURNTEY: You don't mind me recording?

ELSA: If you don't mind me smoking.

COURTNEY: Not at all. So, for the record, would you—name and profession.

ELSA: My name is Esla Rose-Marie Bapiste. I'm a professional researcher. You want my age?

COURTNEY: No, thank you.

ELSA: Alright (chuckle) I'd lie anyway (chuckle).

COURTNEY: (chuckle) And you primarily work on literature?

ELSA: That's right, though I do a bit of art history now and again. I get paid to wander through books lookin' for what others don't have time to find. Plus, I've got an eye for what some miss. Person once called me a "literary truffle pig," and I slapped him for it, even though it's true.

COURTNEY: You worked on *Queen of This Carnival Creation* for Professor Sandra Frye.

ELSA: Uh-huh. Sandy was a good friend. We went to college together, so workin' was always easy. I knew what she wanted.

COURTNEY: I've spoken with her family, as delicately as I could . . .

ELSA: Appreciate that—the delicacy. Shame what happened. Sandy used to always be the one singing out, *Laissez le bon temps rouler!* Towards the end, I don't think she knew how to smile.

COURTNEY: I'm sorry to hear that.

ELSA: It is what it is. But come on child, you got some questions.

COURTNEY: If you don't mind, could you elaborate on *Carnival Creation.* What led to it?

ELSA: Sandy had just finished this big piece on Djuna Barnes, *Another Night Among Horses.* Playin' the ol' truffle pig, I snuffle and stumble onto this diary by someone goin' to the salons thrown by Natalie Barney. Barney is this wealthy women who hosted these literary parties.

COURTNEY: In Paris, if I remember correctly. Prof. Frye mentions them in *Carnival Creation.*

ELSA: Glad to see you come prepared.

COURTNEY: Thanks, but you were saying.

ELSA: Anyway, there's an entry about Ezra Pound. Him being friends with T.S. Eliot's no secret. However, at one salon Pound talks about the new direction Eliot's poems are going in . . .

COURTNEY: This is about the Black Church?

ELSA: You really do know your stuff.

COURTNEY: I do my research. I wasn't always covering eating contests.

ELSA: Careful there. My Gran used to say, she used to say, "Elsie, a bitter tongue always tastes bitter things."

COURTNEY: Sorry. It's been a rough year.

ELSA: For us all.

COURTNEY: Do you want to take a break, or . . .

ELSA: Sandy always cared too much. She dove into things like a fan, not an academic. That's what made her books popular with the public, but not the critics. She seemed to lack objectivity. I don't understand how someone's s'pposed to spend four-five years reading and writing about something they don't have deep feelings for, but that's academia. They want to seem distant, so no one questions the findings.

COURTNEY: Prof. Frye didn't remain distant?

ELSA: She wrote about what she loved, and loving it made her dive into something deep as she could go. I think that's what got her so twisted this time.

COURTNEY: What is the Black Church exactly?

ELSA: Sounded to me like a ghoulish scary story, so I left it at that. Sandy, though, she got this feeling it might be true. I think she reached out into the dark, and . . .

COURTNEY: Something reached back?

ELSA: I hope not. I like to think Sandy just went over the edge. Otherwise (heavy sigh) something pulled her, and I'm sitting here doing nothing about it.

***

Seamus Bloom
4221 S. Wallace St.
Chicago, IL. 60609
June 10, 1931

Seamus,

I just got word about Frank O'Banion. Him getting arrested is no surprise. People saying he shot up an empty street, that's a bit odd. If true, I keep thinking maybe this has to do with Quintsville back in '29. Frank was never the same after that. Don't get me wrong. He was always brutal—hell, he introduced us to the Thompson, but whatever happened down there made him nuts.

The only reason I want to know is I mapped the Quintsville route. Fellow I know, Corn, he said there's an old road through the woods nobody knows about. He says it'd be perfect for running whiskey out of Kentucky. When the trucks with our booze disappeared, Frank went down to "sort it out". He left with ten guys and came back alone. Hell, he came back different.

All I'm saying is I don't want people blaming me for this. Whatever happened to Frank isn't my fault. Maybe if he told us what happened it wouldn't've eaten him insane. Anyhow, let me know.

I'm not looking forward to any one-way rides. If anyone's to blame, it's Corn Sutton.

Duffy

★★★

Transcribed audio cassette
Elsa Baptiste interviewed by Courtney Wint
August 15, 1991

ELSA: You feelin' alright, child?

COURTNEY: I'm okay. I didn't get much sleep last night.

ELSA: I know how that goes. Hope it isn't what we're chattin' about here. When we were workin' on *Queen of this Carnival* I used to have nightmares to scare the devil.

COURTNEY: What about, if you don't mind my asking?

ELSA: You can't read about the Black Church without gettin' a few creepy dreams. But like I said, I push all that out of mind. The less you think about it the better.

COURTNEY: It's kind of hard not to.

ELSA: Depends on who you are. I like pannin' for gold bits of truth, but I know when to leave well enough alone. My Gran used to say, she used to say, "Elsie, you poke that bear trap it's gonna snap."

(loud hand clap)

COURTNEY: I can't argue with that.

ELSA: And yet here we are—day two—dwellin' on the Black Church.

COURTNEY: As long as we're here, then, what can you tell me about these photos?

★★★

Nathaniel Quint's journal
February 11, 1769

Saint Augustine wrote in the *Confessions* that God "fashioned hell for the inquisitive." Months ago, I, perhaps, would agree. Yet all things change in Time. For though an inquisitive nature brought me to Her, thus my entrance to this Hell, that same nature will be our remedy.

I have observ'd the Symbols years enough to imitate them. Though She fills the air with Her hands, I suspect paint will produce the same result.

February 19, 1769

These unchart'd waters are treacherous. One night I compos'd Symbols which kept the coals a-glow. The next I unintentionally flay'd one of the men.

They blamed Her, so dug a hole into which we planted the Box. Even under all that Earth I can hear Her muffled cries. I would Confess if not for fear the others will insist I stop.

I must continue until She is destroyed, or at least immobiliz'ed in bondage.

★★★

J. Rohr

Wallace Welch
1205 Dunbar St.
Myrtle Beach, SC. 29577
June 30, 1991

Hey Wally,

The schedule for the book tour is in here, along with cover options for your next *best-seller*. We tried to get that lady you requested, Lisa Bauman, but she turned us down. Apparently, she's got standards. I said, "Horror is horror," but she's no go. Anyway, I think you'll like who we got.

That bitch was too subtle. This new kid is all gore.

Also, there's a phone number and a mailing address. A chick named Courtney Wint's been calling about your book *Gangsters, Ghouls, and Ghosts*. She wants to know if you'll share whatever you got about a place called Quintsville.

I checked her out. She used to be a reporter at the Chicago Tribune, won a few awards, but she was asked to quit after killing some photographer in a drunk driving accident. She seems legit though. I say help her out because whatever story she's working on, even if it's batshit crazy, there's no such thing as bad publicity.

Your pal,

Ralph Favreau

★★★

Courtney Wint
1263 W. Pratt Blvd. #3
Chicago, IL. 60626
8 July 1991

Dear Courtney,

It's always a pleasure to help a fellow wordsmith, especially one I assume is a fan. My oeuvre is so vast, full of far more salacious and delectable accounts, an awareness of a simple reference such as Quintsville speaks volumes. Though I've revisited several haunted locales over the years I've only mentioned Quintsville in passing in *Gangsters, Ghouls, and Ghosts*.

By the by, I've included a signed copy. No thanks necessary. You're more than welcome, though perhaps we might meet for a drink the next time I'm in Chicago. I'm passing through this Fall on a book tour promoting my latest macabre travelogue, *Scenic Slaughter*.

Meanwhile, my few notes and sparse sources regarding Quintsville are in this package as well. I hope photocopies suffice. Otherwise, I wish you the best of luck with your endeavor. However, I caution you. I didn't find anything interesting about that place, so don't waste too much time on it. There are far more fascinating stories to pursue.

Should we have that drink, perhaps I'll share one with you.

Tudo de bom,
Wallace Welch

****

Obituary for Alfie "Corn" Sutton
appeared in the Quanah Tribune Chief
January 24, 1983

RITES HELD FOR MR. ALFIE SUTTON

Mr. Alfie :Corn" Sutton, 74, of route 2, Quanah, died Wednesday, Jan. 19, in the Hardeman County Memorial Hospital.

Funeral services occurred Saturday, Jan. 22, at 3 p.m. in the First United Methodist Church of Quanah, officiated by Rev. Howard Mayweather. Under direction of the Knowles Funeral Home, burial took place in Quanah Memorial Park.

Mr. Sutton was born in Cocke County Tennessee on May 9, 1909. He moved to Hardeman County with his wife Jewel in 1950. Jewel passed away in 1980. Survivors include two daughters, Lola of Seattle, Washington, and Jean-Marie of Minneapolis, Minn.; a son, Robert of Green Bay, Wisc.; a brother, Lance of Parrotsville, Tenn.; and 7 grandchildren.

A notable member of the community, Mr. Sutton is remembered by many as a wild storyteller, who often claimed to have been a bootlegger during Prohibition. Of particular note are his ghost stories regarding Southern Illinois.

***

Courtney Wint
1263 W. Pratt Blvd. #3
Chicago, IL. 60626

Dear Ms. Wint,

I hope this finds you well. I'm Alice Sutton. Corn was my grandfather. I'd like to help if I can.

Inside are some pages I copied from my mother's journal. She wrote them to help with her Alzheimer's.

Corn used to tell us all kinds of stories. Some are in these pages. I hope they help.

It's nice that another writer likes his stories. My family has a signed copy of *Gangsters, Ghouls, and Ghosts*. Corn is only in a little bit, but we like it. Please send us your book when you're done. It would make us happy.

Sincerely
Alice Sutton

***

Queen of This Carnival Creation

from the journal of Lola Sutton
(no date)

Momma Jewel used to say, "Your Dad's made of stories." Lord if that isn't true. He can go on all night sometimes, and I think some folks come around just to hear him. Not everyone believes him, but not everything on TV is true and it's still entertaining.

I miss his stories. I don't want to lose them. So, I figure I'll write a few down. At least then my kids can have them.

My favorites are about him being a moonshiner during Prohibition. He sounds like a real pirate firecracker. He used to make whiskey with his brother Lance. They lived in Tennessee back then. That's how he got his nickname, Corn, because of the corn mash.

Corn said they used to load up trucks all the time. "More money than we knew what to do with." Barrels went North to Chicago following a trail through southern Illinois.

Then one day a shipment vanished.

Those Chicago gangsters were not happy. So, Corn followed the truck route, thinking if he solved the mystery there'd be a reward. In a town called Quintsville he met a man named O'Banion, a real killer, who got sent to recover the lost shipment.

O'Banion and Corn went into the woods on foot. Ten gangsters in tow. Not knowing what to expect, they all went armed to the teeth.

They found the trucks covered in blood, not a body in sight, but the moonshine was untouched. That turned out good because their flashlights stopped working. They used a bit of 'shine to make torches.

Corn volunteered to drive a truck out.

"Getting those keys is all that saved my life, I'm sure. Plus, I got no shame admitting them woods was spooky as hell. All kinds of whispery sounds, I ain't ever heard since, thank God."

J. Rohr

When he turned on the headlights, they all saw her.

"She stood eight foot tall. Arms spread out like spindly tree branches. Eyes smoldering coals, smoke actually pouring out them hateful gazers. And she was a woman, no doubt. Any fellow seen a lady naked knows a woman, and I knows a woman."

Her voice like a raspy wind, she said, "Are you my feed, or my followers?"

O'Banion didn't think twice. He just shot. His machine gun tore into her but didn't do much more than make her angry.

When she bellowed, Corn didn't think twice. He drove out of there quick.

A barrel fell out the back of the truck. It cracked open, and a dropped torch set it on fire. That caused her to scream something fierce.

Corn got the feeling she didn't much care for fire, but he wasn't about to slow down. In the side mirror, what with the firelight he could see her tearing the others apart. So, he drove straight back to Tennessee. Then he and Lance got out of the moonshine business.

"Sometimes I still dream about her," Corn says. Momma Jewel looks so pained whenever he mentions as much; reminding how my brother Bobby peed the bed until he was fifteen saying he sometimes saw her too . . .

★★★

Transcribed audio cassette
Elsa Baptiste interviewed by Courtney Wint
August 15, 1991

COURTNEY: I don't really have any more questions.

ELSA: Then if you don't mind turning off the tape there's something I'd like to say.

COURTNEY: Sure.

(pause)

COURTNEY (con'td): It's off.

ELSA: I've been thinking how to say this, but I'm old enough to know rehearsin' words isn't the same as speakin' 'em.

COURTNEY: Believe me, I know that problem.

ELSA: I won't bother much with the cliché, but did you know curiosity isn't what originally killed the cat?

COURTNEY: I didn't.

ELSA: It used to be care. Course, care, at the time, meant too much worry, sorrow, and so forth.

COURTNEY: Sorry. What's this got to do with . . .

ELSA: Sandy was curious at first. She was like that. But it's not what got her thinking about the end of a rope. Worry's what done her in, I'm sure. Worrying all the time about, well, the Queen of this carnival.

COURTNEY: I thought you don't believe in Her.

ELSA: I don't, or (pause) I'm doing my damnedest not to. That's how the infection gets in.

COURTNEY: What if you're already infected?

ELSA: I get the feeling that's what we've been dancing around these few days.

★★★

MEMORANDUM FOR:
   Directors, Quintsville government departments
   Department Staff

FROM:
   Wilma B. Hodgkins
   Director, Parks and Recreation

SUBJECT:
   Allegations of embezzlement

I am appalled by recent allegations lobbed at my office. To insinuate that any of my staff, myself in particular, are responsible for embezzlement is outrageous. The very idea I would take money meant for vital duties is hurtful to say the least.

Furthermore, the fact these false allegations have made their way into the press, damaging my standing in public, leaves me speechless. My family has been a part of this community since its founding by Nathaniel Quint in 1769. Few understand the importance of my job as Parks director as well as I do.

I demand an immediate public apology and retraction of these allegations.

Sincerely
The Honorable Wilma B. Hodgkins
Director of Parks and Recreation
July 9, 1991

***

Answering machine transcript
Courtney Wint calling David Williams
8-30-91

COURTNEY: David? Pick up, it's Courtney. I know it's late. Although they haven't done last call at the Oasis. It's only three a.m., but I know you think it's late . . . David, I'm sorry. We've talked about this a million times. You don't blame me, but really you should. I still feel guilty because sometimes I think Jeremy was lucky. It's over for him. I'm sorry, that's not right, but I think I know how to make her go away. This'll be done soon. The graffiti isn't graffiti.

She's trapped like a jail, and if it burns, she burns.

***

MEMORANDUM FOR:
    Directors, Quintsville government departments
    Department Staff
    Police

FROM:
    Calvin West-Morgan
    Mayor of Quintsville

SUBJECT:
    Termination of Wilma B. Hodgkins

Effective immediately Wilma B. Hodgkins is no longer Director of Parks and Recreation. Staff are advised not to follow any orders from her henceforth. A press release is being issued to the Quintsville Bugle to inform the public.

Due to certain threats made by Mrs. Hodgkins, personnel are advised to keep an eye out for her around the Tamarowa Nature Trail. She has insinuated a desire to interfere with *graffiti* maintenance in that area. As such police should be prepared to arrest her if she attempts to follow through with such threats. These threats are not to be made public knowledge.

Sincerely,
Calvin West-Morgan
Mayor of Quintsville
July 10, 1991

***

J. Rohr

Credit Card receipt

```
RUSTY'S TOOL SHED
620 MILLER LANE
QUINTSVILLE, IL 62938
(618) 385-7771
SEPTEMBER 4, 1991

INVOICE : 1932-8073
CARD NO. : XXXXXXXXXXXX7388
CARD TYPE : VISA

5GAL. 20L JERRY CAN 19.99
5GAL. 20L JERRY CAN 19.99
13OZ. GEL FUEL CANS (24 PACK) 8.99
SIRIUS SAFETY FLARES 6.99
RONSONOL LIGHTER FLUID 2.97
ZIPPO LIGHTER 14.09

AMOUNT: 73.02
TAX 6.25% 4.56

TOTAL: 77.58

X: (SIGNED BY COURTNEY WINT)
```

***

People of the State of Illinois)
)
vs.)
)
Courtney V. Wint)
D.O.B.: 07/13/68) Report No. 10-3296
SSN: xxxxxxxxx)
1263 W. Pratt Blvd. #3)
Chicago, IL. 60626)

Bill of Indictment

Queen of This Carnival Creation

The Grand Jury charges:

Count 1

That on or between September 4 and 5th of 1991, in Pope County, State of Illinois, Courtney V. Wint committed the offense of Arson in that said defendant, knowingly obtained means to start, and did produce a forest fire along the Tamarowa Trail in Quintsville, Illinois. This offense is based on a series of acts in furtherance of a single intention and design in violation of Chapter 720 ILCS 5/20-1
(a) A person commits arson when, by means of fire or explosive, he or she knowingly:
(1) Damages any real property, or any personal property having a value of $150 or more, of another without his or her consent.

Class 2 Felony

Count 2

That on or between September 4 and 5th of 1991, in Pope County, State of Illinois, Courtney V. Wint committed the offense of Aggravated Arson in that said defendant knowingly started a fire with intention to harm an as yet unidentified Jane Doe. This offense is based on a series of acts in furtherance of a single intention and design in violation of Chapter 720 ILCS 5/20-1.1
(a) A person commits aggravated arson when in the course of committing arson . . .
(1) . . . knows or reasonably should know that one or more persons are present therein or
(2) any person suffers great bodily harm, or permanent disability or disfigurement as a result of the fire or explosion.

Class X Felony

***

J. Rohr

Courtney Wint, IDOC #R24737
Logan Correctional Center
P.O. Box 1000
Lincoln, IL 62656

Hello Ms. Courtney,

I hope this finds you as well as anyone can be in your situation. I've been reading about you. I won't lie, I sleep a little easier at night now.

Are you sleeping better? I like to think Sandy's resting more peacefully.

I don't know what newspapers you've seen, and I don't yet know what I can send you in the mail. However, the mayor of that town, Quintsville, is still in an awkward spot. He refuses to release any details about the Jane Doe that died in the forest fire. A lot of folks find it odd. That said, right now the country's more interested in the presidential election than ghost stories about witch queens, and whatever.

Still, my Gran used to say, "when they're off balance that's when you shove."

You might already know this, but it's amazing some of the papers you'll get your hands on talking to the right people, especially a disgruntled politician. A lady named Wilma Hodgkins has been sending me documents I think you might like to read. What I've got for now I'll send along as soon as I can.

In the meanwhile, perhaps it's time for you to start composing your side of the story. Even if no one believes it I think it'll do you a world of good. Granted, the pieces don't always tell the whole story. They're just bones in need of meat. Put some meat on them bones, child.

Let me know what I can send to make things easier. I doubt they've got any decent beignet in there. I'll send whatever I can when I can.

Love and kindness,
Elsa Rose-Marie Baptiste
October 14, 1992

The Second Death

Christina Wilder

Ken Barrett @K_Barrett_92(2024, January 25). Found across multiple social media posts.

I don't know how much time I have.

The pain is a constant wave, and my hands are shaking, so I'm using speech to text. By now I'm probably completely incoherent, but I have to get this out there.

I've locked the door to the basement, and there are no windows. No way in or out. Now I'm posting this on all my accounts to reach as many people as possible. People who haven't been affected.

My name is Ken Barrett. I was a moderator on the Stemma forums, and when I heard someone uploaded the full video for "Odran," I deleted the link, but it keeps coming back. I may not have posted the full video, but I'm the one who's responsible for posting the first clip, and I also posted the transcription, so if anyone is going to hell for this, it should be me.

The video's still up on the band's site, and by now, it's almost everywhere.

Please, if anyone is reading this, lock yourselves away like I have. Don't watch anything, and don't listen to anything. I don't know how far this thing reaches.

I am so sorry.

Christina Wilder

***

Cached archived page post: <Pinned post from Moderator>

Subject: Read This First
Dated 08-07-2023
10:15 PM PST

This forum will remain up for archival and informational purposes and is in no way intended to reflect any support or sympathy for members of the band Stemma or their crimes. Any users expressing such ideas will be permanently banned.

Barrett, K. [K_Barrett_92]
[Online forum post]. Stemma official fansite.

***

News 06-05-2023—*First clip from official music video from Stemma has been released*

"Odran" will be the first Stemma song to have an official music video, and the band has released a clip on their site, which can be found here: *[link has successfully been removed]*.

The following is a transcript of the clip.

0:00—0:20

The only visual is a pale yellow void, scattered with beams of light. User <inspiredbyeverything> states there is a similarity between the site's design and the works of Anton Bell (1902-1935), a then-mostly unknown French artist.

0:21—0:54

As the song keeps playing, the picture changes to show a person kneeling on the floor with their hands clasped, bending forward. The picture is distorted, but some viewers report seeing the figure

394

shiver when the song reaches its first chorus: "Voices of the dead break through . . ."

0:55—1:21

Four dark figures approach, each of them holding something (the video quality is not sharp enough to determine what). The picture distorts into static, but there is still audio, with gasps and what sounds like pleading, followed by voices chanting and/or singing (difficult to understand with static and a growing hum in the background).

1:22—1:50

Static builds to approximately 150 decibels, then the clip ends abruptly.

***

Subject: Interview
From: Amy Richards (A9753R4789@zmail.com)
To: Ken Barrett (K_Barrett_92@zmail.com)
Date: October 9, 2023, 11:28 PM

Hello,

I hope this isn't too forward, but my brother was one of the Vorqual victims. He was a music journalist, working on a story on the Metal Monsters tour, but his article never got published.

I've attached the unfinished article, including his notes, and I'm hoping you might post it in the Stemma forum. I feel like Ethan would want people to read it. I also attached a waiver from Prodigy Magazine in case you were worried about copyright. They're e not going to use it for anything, and gave me legal permission and their blessing to pass it along.

Please let me know if more information is needed.

Thank you,
Amy

***

Subject: Re: Interview
From: Ken Barrett (K_Barrett_92@zmail.com)
To: Amy Richards (A9753R4789@zmail.com)
Date: October 9, 2023, 11:55 PM

Amy,

I'm sorry for your loss. I've posted the article—and thank you for sending it to me.

My condolences,
Ken

From: MAILER-DAEMON@ZMAIL.COM
Subject: [Re: Interview]
Date: October 9, 2023, 11:57 PM

This message did not reach the following recipient(s):

<[A9753R4789]@[Zmail.com]>:
This user does not exist.

***

Richards, Ethan. *"A Family Affair: Stemma's Biggest Tour Yet."* (To be published in Prodigy Magazine, Vol. 8, Issue 3) Article notes as of June 5, 2023 (almost finished).

"Are you getting this?" the band asked me as the camera panned over the crowd, screaming hordes of fans shoving at each other to get a better glimpse of their heroes. They asked again as girls lifted their tops when the band walked on stage, the boys smirking as Cait laughed and gestured at the girls to lower their shirts.

The same question was asked as they relaxed backstage, Joseph and Seth plucking at their guitars as the TV reported the local news (1). "Are you getting this?"

It's a fun assignment, following the band that's become the darling of critics and the heavy metal music scene. Stemma is a band unlike any of the other headliners on the Metal Monsters tour, and therein lies the charm of their set: they're a family act.

Cait Reyes, the matriarch and lead singer, grins with pride as she watches her boys huddle together to practice a song (she lovingly refers to them as her "blessings"). Her husband and the band's drummer, Keith, wraps a casual arm around her shoulders and taps his fingers to the beat.

"We've been wanting to do a documentary for a while now," Cait explains as the camera crew takes a break to go over footage and watch the news. "Everything came together this year. The tour, the album . . . it's all been incredible."

This is likely an understatement, as Stemma's latest album, *So Be It*, went platinum, and their music dominates social media in hashtags, fan-made music videos, and even memes.

What makes the success of *So Be It* so striking is that for the first time in the band's history, they will be releasing official music videos for a few select songs on the album.

Joseph notes this observation with a smirk. "We didn't find a filmmaker who understood our vision," he explains. "But that's going to change soon." (2)

The band won't name the director or give any details about the upcoming videos, but they do drop a few hints about their next project, which they will only refer to as "Vorqual" and is already in progress.

"Seth came up with the name," Keith notes with a proud grin. "He got the name from a 17th century German hymnal. In the context of the hymn, '*vor qual*' meant 'from agony.' It fits the project perfectly." From the couch, Seth looks over and nods silently. (3)

He may be a man of few words, but Seth Reyes is undoubtedly the wordsmith of the band. Not only is he responsible for the band's name (*Stemma*, from the ancient word for a scroll tracing one's family history), but he is also the source for Stemma's lyrics and album titles. *So Be It* was chosen because it was used by Catholic priests in their rituals for excommunication.

Fans will no doubt recognize their use of religious references, not unusual in the metal scene; some bands even claim to outright worship Satan. But Stemma has always gone a more intellectual route, using key changes and experimental techniques to showcase their talents. Cait recently learned *overtone singing*, giving her the ability to sing more than one note at a time.

"We've done so much with sound, and of course there's more to explore, but we're looking forward to breaking into the visual component of artistic exploration," Cait explains excitedly.

When I ask for more details, she only smiles.

——

Notes:

(1) They were watching a report on a missing teenager, last seen at a candy store called Sweets for the Sweet. Both of them were chuckling. I asked why, but they wouldn't answer.

(2) Right after Joseph mentioned the audience getting the "full intended experience"—this is where the band's demeanor changed. A mask seemed to slip; Keith looked at me with a strange, searching gaze. Cait's eyes went from brimming with exuberance to lifeless (Fear?) When I asked about this, they livened up again and said they planned to release a clip of their music video later tonight and asked if I'd be interested in contributing (??)

(3) Chalked this one up to metal bravado (because ancient hymns, references to torture, all that just seems like your typical prog metal band trying to fit the mold)

The Second Death

——

misc notes/to do:

Ask more about their collaboration with this director, try to get them to answer questions and not just give cryptic bullshit.
What happened to the film crew? Drugs? They all seemed fine the first night, now they're zoned out, hardly speaking. Lack of sleep?

★★★

Inbox—New Private Message

Message from: <user: matelle>
To: <moderator>
Subject: The article

Hey,

Is that article real? Because what happened to that guy was brutal.

This might be, you know, evidence.

Sent Messages:

Message to: <user: matelle>
From: <moderator>
Subject: Re: The article

I don't know what to think, at this point. I put it up without thinking and now I can't take the damn thing down.

I remember hearing about this reporter, and the film crew . . . I'm thinking I'll post some of the trial quotes, that might help offset things?

This forum is hard for just one person to manage, but every time I get someone that offers to help, they end up disappearing on me. I think hackers are messing with it, to be honest.

Anyway, thanks for the heads up. If I can find a way to take it down, I will.

Thanks again,
Ken

***

COURT TRANSCRIPT EXCERPT

Case No. 07 CR 965

THE STATE OF ILLINOIS,

Plaintiff.

vs.

JOSEPH REYES

Defendant.

TRANSCRIPT OF PLEAS OF GUILTY

PROCEEDINGS had before the Honorable JOAN L. MURPHY, Judge of Division 7 of the Nineteenth Judicial District of Illinois, on November 15, 2023.

The following proceedings were had, to wit:

Present and appearing for the State was Janet Sims, Assistant District Attorney

Present and appearing for the Defendant was David Greene, Attorney at Law

. . .

Q: Mr. Reyes, you are the only surviving member of your family?

The Second Death

A: You could say that.

Q: They were killed by responding police at the Chicago concert, is that correct?

A: In that sense, my family is dead, that is correct.

Q: What other sense could I mean?

A: I mean that they're on the other side. Waiting.

Q: Waiting, Mr. Reyes?

A: It won't be long now.

Q: Mr. Reyes, I am going to present to you what has already been received in evidence as People's Exhibit A. Do you recognize this, Mr. Reyes?

A: That was that reporter's journal. He took a lot of notes.

Q: You're referring to Ethan Richards.

A: That was his name, yeah.

Q: Would you say you spoke to Mr. Richards often?

A: Not really. Mom did. So did Dad. But I remember taking to the reporter the night before he died. He said the film crew looked worn out.

Q: What was your response?

A: I told him not to worry about it. He kept harping on it, so I figured I'd show him.

Q: And what did you show him, Mr. Reyes?

A: I took him to Seth's room, and we showed him the beginning of our project. Vorqual.

Q: Can you be more specific?

A: We showed him a video clip for "Odran".

Q: "Odran" being a song on your album *So Be It?*

A: Yes.

Q: Tell the court what happened next.

A: The reporter got sick all over the floor. Dad thought it was funny, but Mom was kind of grossed out. Then he started crying and scratching at his arms and neck.

Q: So Mr. Richards injured himself. Would you say these led to fatal injuries?

MS. SIMS: Objection, leading the witness.

THE COURT: Sustained.

Q: Mr. Reyes, what did Mr. Richards do after he scratched his arms and neck?

A: He kind of pinballed around the room. Started hitting his head against the wall. Mom said we had to make him stop or people might hear him. So Seth and I took care of it.

Q: Had you been taking any recreational drugs before this occurred?

A: No.

Q: Had you been drinking alcohol?

A: No. I've been keeping myself pure. I want to be ready when everything is revealed.

Q: Mental illness runs in your family, does it not? Annabel Levitts, your grandmother, Cait Reyes's mother, was a self-professed demonologist who wrote several books on the subject.

A: She did, but she wasn't mentally ill.

Q: In these books, Cait stated that she spoke to these demons and befriended them.

A: I read those books. That's what she did.

Q: So you believe your grandmother's claims?

A: I'm proof that it worked.

Q: Could you elaborate on that?

A: Mom couldn't get pregnant at first. My grandmother helped.

Q: You believe you owe your conception to conversations with demons?

A: It's simple. You could do it right now. Draw a triangle on your floor with chalk or ink, then stand inside it. Close your eyes, ask for help, and you'll see your answer. My mother did this, with Grandma's help, and now I'm here, breathing your air. For now.

Q: No further questions, Your Honor.

CROSS-EXAMINATION BY MS. SIMS:

Q: Mr. Reyes, I am going to read an excerpt from Exhibit A, the journal of Ethan Richards. "The band is getting more secretive, and they seem obsessed with local news stories of missing persons. These stories seem to follow us from city to city. A young couple went missing in Newark the day after the concert. When I mentioned it to the band, they just laughed. Then Joseph changed the subject and asked me if I knew anything about Anton Bell. When I told him I hadn't, he replied that I would soon." Do you remember this exchange, Mr. Reyes?

A: I do.

Q: And can you tell the court who Anton Bell is and why you asked Mr. Richards about him?

A: Anton Bell is a visionary. He's seen the other side. When the reporter asked about the disappearances, we showed him a little of what Bell saw, to help him understand.

Q: Can you elaborate, Mr. Reyes?

A: We showed him what everyone will see soon. It begins with the seduction of the willing, and the rest will follow. The Second Death awaits.

***

[Cached archived page from the "Information and History" section of the Stemma forum (cont.)]

(Note from <moderator>: Anton Bell's separate page has been added to this general overview of Stemma's work due to constant technical issues on his former individual page. This change will be permanent as numerous attempts to create a page for Bell consistently result in server issues.)

{{ Anton Bell, born in December of 1802 [day unknown], was a sculptor, painter, and performance artist. His birthplace is unknown, but Bell's medical and arrest records indicate he was estranged from his family. Bell lived in the Burningham, WA and avoided public interaction save for his eccentric performances, during which he'd fall onto the street in a crowded area and start screaming. After people would rush to help him, he'd get up and casually walk away, leaving well-meaning strangers baffled.

Bell was also known for his surreal sculptures, which he was known to place outside government buildings. The artist's work, as well as his antics, came to a head when he was apprehended in April 1830 after he'd smashed one of his creations, cut his arms and hands, and begun painting the front door of the courthouse with his blood. After being ruled unfit for trial, he was sent to the Fielding Psychiatric Asylum, where he remained until his death seven years later.

His time in the asylum was a fruitful one, with Bell completing an average of three paintings a day. Local legends of Bell surfaced, with townsfolk claiming that Bell was a sorcerer involved in dark magic. Art collectors who purchased original Bell asylum paintings claim that the brush strokes near the signature reveal a geometric symbol (See *Symbol of Alakor*).

Bell was placed in solitary confinement in the asylum in July of 1837 after he broke a restroom mirror and was found placing shards of glass in his chest. Medical records indicate that he told doctors that he was preparing himself for both the "hellish waters of Heaven and the blissful cold of Hell." Once in solitary, he was denied his painting supplies, but a sympathetic doctor allowed him a journal and crayon so that he could express himself creatively.

The diary was found under his bed when nurses discovered Bell's body on November 12th. He'd been dead approximately two days.

Bell's diary has been scanned and uploaded to Odran's site and can be found in the "Artifacts" section. His last entry on October 2nd, 1837, is considered by Stemma fans and some historians to be his final words: "I have spoken to the Buried Man, and he is correct— neither Heaven nor Hell are what they think it is; I will have to show them. They will scream in blessed horror at the naked terror of the holy and the damned." }}

***

Harris, James M.
The Echoes of the Damned: Stemma's Bloodied Legacy.
Retrieved January 6, 2024, from
<http://prodigymagazine.com/stemmalegacy>

. . . yet for a brief period of time on December 31st, 2023 at 11:57 PM EST, Stemma's site was once again active, and offered a link to the full video for "Odran", which had only existed before as a brief clip and an urban legend among fans. With its running time of 3 minutes and 1 second, it allowed some observers to watch the debut as the old year passed into the new one.

Those same people, however, have achieved dubious fame by becoming the first ones to report specific shared hallucinations. They have cited near-constant visions of people emerging from the dirt, screaming about the afterlife. Other hallucinations include a sharp, icy sensation in the chest ("like I'm being stabbed with a million little knives," Nora Geffer stated in an interview with *Psychotherapy Online Journal*), a feeling of being submerged under water, and sudden outbursts (usually screaming, but uncontrollable laughter has been reported as well). Numerous other fans have followed suit reporting the same symptoms, and the collection of symptoms is now popularly known as Bell's Haunting Syndrome . . .

***

[Cached archived thread from the "So Be It Album Discussions" section of the Stemma forum, titled "BHS . . . a real thing?"]

<brutus684>:
Posted 01-02-2024 1:30 AM

So, has anyone actually experienced this, or are people just getting really high and listening to the album (not a good idea)?

<bakboy>:
01-03-2024 7:00 AM

Yeah I wanna call out of work can I give this as an excuse?

<chrysalis_blue>:
01-03-2024 8:15 AM

My sister has it. She watched the video and it completely destroyed her.

<mobking99>:

The Second Death

01-03-2024 9:20 AM

Really? That sucks, dude.

<chrysalis_blue>:
01-03-2024 2:40 PM

Not a dude, but thanks.

Before any of you ask, no, I haven't seen the video yet

And I can't really ask my sister about it, she's in jail now.

<bakboy>:
01-03-2024 2:55 PM

Holy shit, seriously?

<chrysalis_blue>:
01-03-2024 3:22 PM

Yes. I probably shouldn't say too much because of lawyers and stuff but I haven't slept well in months so whatever.

She killed her neighbors. Smashed all their mirrors and carved weird shit into her stomach and face. Then she buried herself alive in their backyard . . . that's where the cops found her.

My sister was the nicest person you could ever meet. Volunteered at homeless shelters, organized fundraisers, that sort of thing.

Now she just scratches herself and talks about the second death and it's a goddamn nightmare.

<mobking99>:
01-03-2024 4:33 PM

. . . whoa. I'm really sorry to hear that . . . and she says it's because of the Odran video?

<chrysalis_blue>:
01-03-2024 5:41 PM

It's all she talks about now. It's why I'm determined to track this damn video down. I want to see what the hell is in this thing.

<remus_136>:
01-04-2024 3:00 AM

I found the full video. My friend recorded it on his phone when he watched it on New Year's Eve. He sent it to me but it went to my junk folder and I didn't see it until today.

I can email to anyone who's interested.

<spyfly_nyc>:
01-04-2024 6:00 AM

Any chance you could upload it?

Also, your friend saw it? Did he get BHS?

<remus_136>:
01-04-2024 8:48 PM

Here it is: [link has successfully been removed]

<spyfly_nyc>:
01-04-2024 9:03 PM

Cool, thanks man.

<remus_136>:
01-04-2024 11:36 PM

My friend is fine, by the way. In fact he's here now, he helped me put this thing up. Here's a picture as proof: [image has successfully been removed]

The Second Death

<mobking99>:
01-04-2024 11:57 PM

Dude. Not funny.

Take that picture down, seriously. I don't know where you found a crime scene photo, if not weeks, but that is not okay. He looks like he's been dead for days.

Also your link is a virus. Now every clip I look at is that weird ass video, so thanks for that.

Prick.

<remus_136>:
01-05-2024 1:00 AM

No, it's the real video, I swear. And I don't know what the hell you're talking about, my friend is fine. He read your post and laughed at it, so thanks for that, I guess.

<furybabe-777>:
01-05-2024 2:04 AM

What in the hell did you upload?? Now my TV only plays that video over and over, and my home assistant keeps playing the damn song too.

Shit. Everything is connected to my phone, too. Like, EVERYTHING. I'm screwed.

<spyfly_nyc>:
01-06-2024 9:03 PM

Guys. This video is everywhere.

Every channel, every broadcast, everywhere. And "Odran" is the only thing that plays for me now. Even if I listen to podcasts, it's playing in the background.

Is this it?? Do I have Bell's Haunting Syndrome?

I'm going offline for a while. If this keeps up I'm going to a hospital.

<miss_isobel>:
01-08-2024 4:00 AM

watch it long enough you start to understand

<p467q854>:
01-08-2024 5:13 AM

watch and listen

through the dark there is the light of hell

come and see

come and see

★★★

"Rush Hour with Riley," WCMJ 101.5 FM, Aired January 8, 2024, 6:48 PM

RILEY: . . . and that wraps up our sweet seventies mix! As always, I'm Riley, your hostess with the most-est, here to keep you company on this lovely evening, so don't you worry about that traffic jam, because we are about to slide into some hits from the eighties . . .

(Unintelligible noise in the background)

RILEY: Sorry folks, got a bit of a traffic jam right here in the station! That was my producer, Jake, he almost took a bit of a tumble, there. Jake, you good? That's our Jake, always has his earbuds in, listening to the scene's latest hits and getting too distracted to function . . .

RILEY: Yo, Jake, you okay?

The Second Death

(Low mumbling, almost inaudible)

RILEY: Uh oh, we might have a head injury here . . . Either Jake's been reading some seventeenth century French poetry or he's concussed. *(Softly, almost inaudible)* What the hell is he talking about? "The light of hell burning", what does that even . . .

(Sound of a door opening, another voice speaking, we hear him address Riley and Jake)

RILEY: Oh hey! Luckily my buddy Adam is here! Adam to the rescue, you all know Adam from our morning show, and . . . what? No, why the hell would I play a Stemma song? We're a workplace friendly station, the heaviest thing we play is Genesis. No, Adam, I'm serious, I am not the one playing it!

RILEY: Of *course* I hear it too, but I don't know where it's coming from, it's like it's . . .

(Shouting in the background, then screaming)

RILEY: Fuck, fuck, oh my God, no, Jake, stop, stop, OH MY GOD!

(More shouting and general commotion as other people enter the room)

RILEY: I can't! I can't turn it off, it won't stop playing! Where the fuck is Jake now? What do you mean you don't know, just follow the trail of fucking blood . . . Oh God, Adam, you're okay, you're going to be okay, where is that fucking first aid kit? Someone get a towel, just, just hold it against his face, oh shit . . . Adam, stop trying to talk, you'll be okay . . .

(The familiar low tone of the Emergency Broadcast System begins, then cuts back to . . .)

RILEY: . . . because he fucking ate half of Adam's face, and now we don't know where . . . oh shit. Jake? Jake, no, no, no, please stop, no, PLE—

(Transmission ends.)

Christina Wilder

****

Ken Barrett [@K_Barrett_92]. Social media post (cont.)

I can't escape it. Odran is everywhere. In my eyes, my brain, my blood.

Did you know that if you cut off your ears, you can still hear? It's softer, but I still hear it. I hear the voices. But I tried. It took time, and the box cutter blade was small, but I made it work.

I don't have the guts to go further. Something tells me that if I took out my eyes, I'd still see.

There's so much light. I've barricaded myself in here, so I don't hurt anyone. But I'm afraid I'll claw to the surface, with new eyes and ears.

I hear them coming closer. The four of them, holding instruments of torment.

I hear them singing. They're here to show me

to change me

from darkness we emerge I will pry my flesh open to see more of this light

I see it

I see it all

The End?

Not if you want to dive into more of Crystal Lake Publishing's Tales from the Darkest Depths!

Check out our amazing website and online store
or download our latest catalog here.
https://geni.us/CLPCatalog

We always have great new projects and content on the website to dive into, as well as a newsletter, behind the scenes options, social media platforms, our own dark fiction shared-world series and our very own webstore. Our webstore even has categories specifically for KU books, non-fiction, anthologies, and of course more novels and novellas.

About the Authors

Justin Allec is a writer based in Northwestern Ontario. He has previously had stories published by Eerie River Press and *ghost milk magazine*. In addition to his fiction, Justin contributes to *The Walleye Magazine*, covering Thunder Bay's music scene.

Patrick Barb is an author of weird, dark, and horrifying tales, currently living (and trying not to freeze to death) in Saint Paul, Minnesota. His published works include the dark fiction collection *Pre-Approved for Haunting*, the novellas *Gargantuana's Ghost* and *Turn*, as well as the novelettes *So Quiet, So White* (Split Scream Vol. 3) and *Helicopter Parenting in the Age of Drone Warfare*. His debut novel *Abducted* is coming from Dark Matter INK in late 2024. Visit him at patrickbarb.com

A mass of tentacles and rose vines masquerading as a person, **Amanda M. Blake** is the author of such horror titles as *Deep Down* and *Out of Curiosity and Hunger*, dark poetry collection *Dead Ends*, and the Thorns fairy tale mash-up series. For more, visit amandamblake.com

Gemma Files has been an award-winning horror author for almost thirty years. Probably best known for her novel *Experimental Film*, she has also published four other novels, five collections of short fiction, and three collections of speculative poetry. Her most recent collection, *In That Endlessness, Our End* (Grimscribe Press), was nominated for a 2021 Bram Stoker Award.

An author of travel books for almost a decade, **Sandra Henriques** started writing fiction in 2021. That same year she won the European EACWP Flash Fiction competition with "The Caretaker," a 100-word horror story. Since then, she's been published in the Portuguese horror anthologies *Sangue Novo* (2021) and *Sangue* (2022). In March 2022, she co-founded Fábrica do Terror, a website dedicated to Portuguese horror, where she acts as editor-in-chief. Recently, she wrote an entry on

Portuguese Horror Female Authors for *Enciclopédia do Terror Português* (September 2023). *Dead Letters: Episodes of Epistolary Horror* (2023) marks her debut in a foreign horror anthology.

Liam Hogan is an award-winning short story writer, with stories in Best of British Science Fiction and Best of British Fantasy (NewCon Press). He helps host live literary event Liars' League and volunteers at the creative writing charity Ministry of Stories. More details at happyendingnotguaranteed.blogspot.co.uk

Ai Jiang is a Chinese-Canadian writer, a Nebula-, Locus-, Ignyte Award finalist, and an immigrant from Fujian currently residing in Toronto, Ontario. She is a member of HWA and SFWA. Her work can be found in *F&SF, The Dark, Uncanny,* among others. She is the recipient of Odyssey Workshop's 2022 Fresh Voices Scholarship and the author of *Linghun* and *I AM AI*. Find her on Twitter (@AiJiang_) and online (http://aijiang.ca/).

Red Lagoe is the author of the forthcoming novella *In Excess of Dark* (DarkLit Press 2024) and the novel *Bloodstains by Gaslight* (Brigids Gate Press 2024). She has authored three horror collections, including her latest, *Impulses of a Necrotic Heart.* Red also edited the anthology *Nightmare Sky: Stories of Astronomical Horror,* she worked as a staff writer for Crystal Lake Publishing's *Still Water Bay* series, and her stories have appeared in several anthologies.

Grotesque creatures lurk in the ancient countryside of County Meath. **Colin Leonard** is one of them. He writes horror fiction mostly set in Ireland, and his short stories have appeared in a number of anthologies and online venues including *Horror Library Volumes 7 & 8, It Calls From The Veil, Eyes, The Vampiricon,* and *Fudoki Magazine. Country Roads,* his debut novel, was published in 2023 by Brigids Gate Press. You can find more details and connect with him at www.collyleonard.com or @collyleonard.

TT Madden (they/them) is a genderfluid, mixed-race horror, sci-fi, and fantasy writer who's been obsessed with the genre ever since they tried to climb their mother's bookcases to get to her Stephen King novels. They have two books coming out in 2024: *The Cosmic Color,* a genderbending mech-and-kaiju story with Neon Hemlock, and *The Familialists*, a suburban social horror with Off Limits Press. They can be found on most socials as @ttmaddenwrites

J.A.W. McCarthy is the Bram Stoker Award and Shirley Jackson Award nominated author of *Sometimes We're Cruel and Other Stories* (Cemetery Gates Media, 2021) and *Sleep Alone* (Off Limits Press, 2023). Her short fiction has appeared in numerous publications, including *Vastarien, PseudoPod, Split Scream Vol. 3, Apparition Lit, Tales to Terrify,* and *The Best Horror of the Year Vol 13* (ed. Ellen Datlow). She is Thai American and lives with her spouse and assistant cats in the Pacific Northwest. You can call her Jen on Twitter @JAWMcCarthy, and find out more at www.jawmccarthy.com

G. Nicholas Miranda survives the world in Dayton, Ohio where most of his writing is done during his lunch breaks. His published work has appeared in the *Books of Horror Community Anthology,* (Vol. 2 & 3), *Strange Aeon: 2021: Orbital Lovecraft,* and *If I Die Before I Wake: Tales of the Dark Deep.* When he isn't dreaming of Magic, he can be found afloat in the Sea of Ideas, hoping not to drown.

Jacob Steven Mohr does not believe in human consciousness; his works emerge as though from the ether, fully formed and fully ominous. Selections of these can be observed in *Cosmic Horror Monthly, Shortwave Magazine, Chthonic Matter Quarterly, Weird Horror Magazine,* and *The Best Horror of the Year Vol. 15.* He exists in Columbus OH.

Nat Reiher is an author-in-progress whose wife has finally convinced him to start submitting things. He writes under a pseudonym to keep his professional life (family law attorney) separate from his writing life (horror-obsessed degenerate). You can follow him @natreiher on Twitter to read all his bad takes.

J. Rohr is a Chicago native with a taste for history and wandering the city at odd hours. In order to deal with the more corrosive aspects of life, he writes the blog honestyisnotcontagious.com and makes music in the band Beerfinger. Currently, he writes article and movie reviews for *Film Obsessive*. His Twitter babble can be found @JackBlankHSH.

Zachary Rosenberg is a horror and SFF writer living in Florida. By night, he crafts horrifying and fantastical stories and by day he practices law which is even scarier. His work is out or forthcoming in multiple anthologies and publications such as Seize the Press, The Deadlands, and the Magazine of Fantasy & Science Fiction. Find him on Twitter at @ZachRoseWriter.

Gregg Stewart is an author, songwriter, musician, screenwriter, journalist, and film composer whose dark fiction tales have appeared in *The Sirens Call*, Crystal Lake Publishing's *Shallow Waters* series, and upcoming anthologies from Crystal Lake Publishing and Hellbound Books UK. Find him online at linktr.ee/greggstewart

Kyle Toucher (rhymes with *voucher*) is the author of the novel *Live Wire*, from Crystal Lake Publishing, and the novella *Life Returns*. His most recent release is the Black Hare Press Short Read *Southpaw*. After writing a slew of Godzilla stories in grade school, he read *The Exorcist* at fourteen, then bought a guitar when *Black Sabbath: Volume 4* changed his life.

Through his twenties, he fronted influential Nardcore crossover band Dr. Know, made records, and hit the road. Later, he moved into visual effects, earning eight Emmy nominations and two awards for *Firefly* and *Battlestar: Galactica*. Recent film credits include *Top Gun: Maverick* and *Devotion*.

He lives with a lovely woman, five cats, two dogs, and several guitars in a secure, undisclosed location. Find him online @kyletoucher or at www.kyletoucher.monster

Emily Ruth Verona is a Pinch Literary Award winner and a Bram Stoker Awards® nominee with work featured in *Under Her Skin*, *Lamplight Magazine*, *Mystery Tribune*, *The Ghastling*, *Coffin Bell*, *The Jewish Book of Horror*, and *Nightmare Magazine*. Her debut thriller, *Midnight on Beacon Street*, is expected from Harper Perennial in 2024. She lives in New Jersey with a small dog.

Gordon B. White is a Seattle-based author of horror and weird fiction, as well as a finalist for both the Shirley Jackson Award and Bram Stoker Award. A graduate of the Clarion West Writing Workshop, Gordon's stories, reviews, and interviews have appeared in dozens of venues. You can find him online at www.gordonbwhite.com or on most social media as @GordonBWhite.

Christina Wilder was born in Santiago, Chile, and grew up in New Jersey and Florida. Her writing has been featured in *Coffin Bell* and short story anthologies including #VSS365 flash fiction and *What One Wouldn't Do*. She lives in Tacoma, WA with her husband Chris and cat Bella. Besides writing, she is also an actor and has done voice acting for the Decoded Horror Channel. She can be found on Twitter @christinawilder, and on Instagram @christinamwilder.

Readers . . .

Thank you for reading *Dead Letters.* We hope you enjoyed this anthology.

If you have a moment, please review *Dead Letters* at the store where you bought it.

Help other readers by telling them why you enjoyed this book. No need to write an in-depth discussion. Even a single sentence will be greatly appreciated. Reviews go a long way to helping a book sell, and is great for an author's career. It'll also help us to continue publishing quality books.

Thank you again for taking the time to journey with Crystal Lake Publishing.

Visit our Linktree page for a list of our social media platforms. https://linktr.ee/CrystalLakePublishing

Follow Us on Amazon:

Our Mission Statement:

Since its founding in August 2012, Crystal Lake Publishing has quickly become one of the world's leading publishers of Dark Fiction and Horror books in print, eBook, and audio formats. In 2023, Crystal Lake Publishing formed a part of Crystal Lake Entertainment, joining several other divisions, including Torrid Waters, Crystal Lake Comics, Crystal Lake Kids, and many more.

While we strive to present only the highest quality fiction and entertainment, we also endeavour to support authors along their writing journey. We offer our time and experience in non-fiction projects, as well as author mentoring and services, at competitive prices.

With several Bram Stoker Award wins and many other wins and nominations (including the HWA's Specialty Press Award), Crystal Lake Publishing puts integrity, honor, and respect at the forefront of our publishing operations.

We strive for each book and outreach program we spearhead to not only entertain and touch or comment on issues that affect our readers, but also to strengthen and support the Dark Fiction field and its authors.

Not only do we find and publish authors we believe are destined for greatness, but we strive to work with men and women who endeavour to be decent human beings who care more for others than themselves, while still being hard working, driven, and passionate artists and storytellers.

Crystal Lake Publishing is and will always be a beacon of what passion and dedication, combined with overwhelming teamwork and respect, can accomplish. We endeavour to know each and every one of our readers, while building personal relationships with our authors, reviewers, bloggers, podcasters, bookstores, and libraries.

We will be as trustworthy, forthright, and transparent as any business can be, while also keeping most of the headaches away from our authors, since it's our job to solve the problems so they can stay in a creative mind. Which of course also means paying our authors.

We do not just publish books, we present to you worlds within your world, doors within your mind, from talented authors who sacrifice so much for a moment of your time.

There are some amazing small presses out there, and through collaboration and open forums we will continue to support other presses in the goal of helping authors and showing the world what quality small presses are capable of accomplishing. No one wins when a small press goes down, so we will always be there to support hardworking, legitimate presses and their authors. We don't see Crystal Lake as the best press out there, but we will always strive to be the best, strive to be the most interactive and grateful, and even blessed press around. No matter what happens over time, we will also take our mission very seriously while appreciating where we are and enjoying the journey.

What do we offer our authors that they can't do for themselves through self-publishing?

We are big supporters of self-publishing (especially hybrid publishing), if done with care, patience, and planning. However, not every author has the time or inclination to do market research, advertise, and set up book launch strategies. Although a lot of authors are successful in doing it all, strong small presses will always be there for the authors who just want to do what they do best: write.

What we offer is experience, industry knowledge, contacts and trust built up over years. And due to our strong brand and trusting fanbase, every Crystal Lake Publishing book comes with weight of respect. In time our fans begin to trust our judgment and will try a new author purely based on our support of said author.

With each launch we strive to fine-tune our approach, learn from our mistakes, and increase our reach. We continue to assure our authors that we're here for them and that we'll carry the weight of the launch and dealing with third parties while they focus on their strengths—be it writing, interviews, blogs, signings, etc.

We also offer several mentoring packages to authors that include knowledge and skills they can use in both traditional and self-publishing endeavours.

We look forward to launching many new careers.

This is what we believe in. What we stand for. This will be our legacy.

Welcome to Crystal Lake Publishing— Tales from the Darkest Depths.